TIME TWIST
LIZZY SHANNON

Dragon Moon

WWW.DRAGONMOONPRESS.COM

TIME TWIST
LIZZY SHANNON

Time Twist

Copyright © 2009 Lizzy Shannon
Cover Art © 2009 LW Perkins

All rights reserved. Reproduction or utilization of this work in any form, by any means now known or hereinafter invented, including, but not limited to, xerography, photocopying and recording, and in any known storage and retrieval system, is forbidden without permission from the copyright holder.

ISBN 13 978-1-897492-00-0

Dragon Moon Press is an Imprint of Hades Publications Inc.
P.O. Box 1714, Calgary, Alberta, T2P 2L7, Canada

Printed and bound in the United States
www.dragonmoonpress.com

This is a work of fiction. Names, characters, places, and incidents are the products of the author's imagination or are used fictitiously and are not to be construed as real. Any resemblance to actual events, locales, organizations, or persons, living or dead, is entirely coincidental.

FOR DAD,

JIM BLYTHE

AND FOR

AK

ACKNOWLEDGMENTS

This book would not have been possible without four wonderful women: Irene Radford, Margaret H. Bonham, Gwen Gades, and Leona Grieve.

Irene befriended me several years ago when I was a novice writer, and has mentored and encouraged me every step of the way.

Maggie took me under her wing and shaped my sometimes odd Northern Irish vernacular into something that Americans could understand. (Never shall cats be found barking again!)

Gwen, the still heart of the whirlwind, who took a chance on me and welcomed me into the family of Dragon Moon Press.

And Leona Grieve — friend, beta-reader, and editor extraordinaire.

Thank you also to:

Gabrielle Harbowy, DMP Editor-in-Charge: her remarkable eye for detail.

Lynn Perkins: for the stunning cover art.

My family: Dad, Ian and Carletta Blythe, their children Daniel and Fiona; Steve and Moya McCloskey-Blythe; and the ever-patient Neil Shannon.

Friends: Scott Simmons (BFF!), Bill Johnson, Rhoda Harwood, Carrie McClanaghan, Jessica Polanco, Melissa Winter, Liam Collins, Edith Duncan, Mitchell Johnson.

A big thank you to the Willamette Writers, and also to Dr. Eric Wall, friend and family doctor, who literally saved my skin more than once. (But not to hang on a Komodoan wall, he assures me!)

And of course my mother, Maureen Blythe, who died in 2003.

Lizzy Shannon
www.lizzyshannon.com

Part One

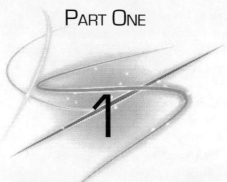

2001

CATRIONA LOGAN watched the bubbles in her cheap champagne effervesce and disperse. On the wall, a torn playbill for *Beauty and the Beast* hung crookedly, and Catriona flinched at the cacophony her companions made raising yet another toast toward it.

"One more year!"

She plastered a smile across her face and joined in. Tonight the cast celebrated the first-year anniversary of the launch of their London fringe theater musical, and had invaded the *Elephant and Castle* bar to revel in another year of paid work.

Catriona saw her name on the playbill listed under the character of Beauty and grimaced. Right now she felt far from beautiful, her thicket of red hair plastered to her head from the heavy wig she wore on stage and her pale complexion flushed from heat. Her colleagues had crammed eleven stools around the table, which should have seated only six. The décor sported a subdued brass and horse motif with a carved plaster ceiling, not much different from the Victorian era when it had been built, but cigarette smoke made everything foggy.

Catriona looked at the faces around her, all animated after tonight's performance. Her stomach twisted with guilt. She couldn't bring herself to share their enthusiasm, dreading the prospect of an infinite number of performances ahead. Her fellow actors might be happy to live like they were caught in a time warp, performing the same lines over and over, but Catriona felt trapped. Her childhood dream when growing up in Scotland was to be a professional actress in London. But she'd become disillusioned after three years of trying to make it to the West End. She suspected she'd never be good enough and would always be doomed to small productions and fringe theater.

"Any room, Cat?"

The shout close to her ear made her jump. She smiled at the slight, ginger-haired man clutching his champagne flute, and edged over, patting the barstool beside her.

"I'm going soon, Bill—squeeze in here."

He eased himself down and they leaned against each other like Siamese twins, their red hair almost matching.

Catriona peered at her wristwatch. Just another few minutes before the last train home to Brent Cross.

Bill nodded toward her untouched drink. "D'you not like it?"

"Too sweet."

"I agree." He placed his glass down on the sticky table. "Here!" he waved to the bartender, "bring us a couple of Glenfiddich shots!"

Catriona glanced at the time again. Just time for a quick one. "That sounds exactly what the doctor ordered," she grinned, her 'r's rolling. The bartender placed the shots of golden whisky before them and Catriona and Bill tapped glasses, downing the fiery liquid in one swallow.

A movement at the bar caught Catriona's eye and she glanced over. A man in a hooded raincoat stood half-obscured in the shadows, so still he looked like a mannequin. She placed her shot glass on the table and twisted round to get a better look, but he had vanished.

"What is it?" asked Bill, following her gaze.

"Nothing," she murmured and consulted her wristwatch. "Time for my train."

Getting up, she gave Bill's shoulder a squeeze and slipped on her black leather jacket. Weaving her way through the crowd, a crescendo of raucous laughter forced her to quicken her step toward the double doors, which had *Elephant and Castle* engraved on the glass. She passed through them to the quiet hallway.

The odd-looking man she'd seen stood with his back to her blocking the exit. Oblivious to Catriona, he mumbled while his fingers worked at a small black device in his palm.

Catriona tried to brush past him. Suddenly the hallway blurred and broke into a thousand jigsaw pieces. The man stood out in relief against the maelstrom, his bright blue eyes wide in shock.

Then he and the hallway dissolved into nothing.

2261

Captain T'alak's tail lashed to and fro as he waited for General B'alarg to acknowledge him. He resented his superior officer summoning him to Military Headquarters as though he were a Terran slave rather than the head of an Imperial House. B'alarg did not deserve respect—he was no more than a sycophant, the son of a common laborer who had bribed his way into the Komodoan Realm Fleet. But the war had changed Fleet hierarchy; they needed soldiers regardless of class and status.

The General ignored him and studied the holographic viewscreen on his desk. T'alak noted the image displayed a human male's profile, the skin pale and devoid of scales. His tail twitched and swished, broadcasting his impatience. Forcing it to be still, T'alak glanced round B'alarg's office. The furnishings showed standard Komodoan Fleet interior design: polished gray stone and dark metal. Water coursed down the walls, eddying in different shapes and textures. Water-sculpture flowed in every Komodoan structure, a necessity as well as an art form. Without it, a Komodoan would suffer severe dehydration. T'alak inhaled, enjoying the sulphurous green-hued condensation from the ornate sculpture. Sulphur dominated the planet Komodoa, enriching the oceans and flowing through Komodoans' veins, making their blood oxidize green.

T'alak's glance fell on an antique revolving globe of the planet Earth, which stood to the right of B'alarg's desk. He sneered when he noticed the war god *B'llumni's* destruction mantra attached to its stand. Only an upstart like B'alarg would believe in such ancient nonsense from the spirit world. Or perhaps a human, with their alien notions of devils and hells in the netherworld. T'alak suspected that was why humans feared them most; Komodoans' faces bore a decidedly saturnine look with a scaly pattern tracing the forehead.

B'alarg broke into his reverie. "Captain, sit." He pointed at one of the backless chairs in front of his desk.

T'alak dropped onto the chair, his tail twitching at B'alarg's patronizing manner. Studying the General's face, T'alak saw the coarseness of his heritage. Most Komodoans looked similar—thick dark hair, and scales on foreheads, hands, and tails. But B'alarg's hands were brutishly large; his broad tail crude and unrefined. The skin on his face looked loose, hanging in folds.

T'alak wondered if B'alarg's morph could be imminent—an unpleasant bi-yearly process for Komodoans where they shed the outer skin. His tail tightened at the memory of his own recent morph. A painful, messy, and humiliating business. General B'alarg would need to arrange his absence if it were due; he would not want T'alak to see him weak. Or worse still, if the timing meant T'alak would be forced to assist with the morph.

10 | *Time Twist*

"How can I be of service, honored General?" he inquired formally.

"The *L'umina* is needed for a sensitive mission."

T'alak's tail stiffened with interest. The *L'umina* was his ship, named in honor of the war god, *B'llumni*. "I am yours to command, honored one."

B'alarg's forked tongue flickered between his lips as he spoke, the cause of the sibilant esses in Komodoan speech. "A patriot working under cover in enemy territory is bringing back data, vital to the ascension of the Realm."

T'alak felt a surge of excitement. He had become exasperated with wasting the *L'umina* in border skirmishes. Perhaps allowing the lower classes into the Fleet wasn't a detriment after all.

"Let us transfer to tactical," hissed B'alarg, rising ponderously to his feet.

He led the way to a gleaming metal doorway between two water-sculptures. He lifted his wrist to speak into his comm bracelet, and the door slid open to reveal the hub of the Komodoan Realm military tactical center.

T'alak followed him. Here no soothing water flowed. Instead, holographic star charts of mapped space spanned the gray walls. The door slid behind them with a resounding click. Like all doors on Komodoa, it paused before closing. Faster doors had docked too many precious tails.

B'alarg moved to the far wall. "This," he pointed to a jagged run of red triangles, "is where you must rendezvous with the agent-"

"In Alliance territory?" interrupted T'alak, unable to suppress his elation. The Alliance: the allegiance between the alien races Leontor and Terran, governed by Leontor Control.

The Komodoan Realm had been at war with Leontor for almost three hundred centuries. Victory had been imminent until the Leons strengthened their army with Terran soldiers.

"The Alliance ship *Vallo* will pass through the rendezvous sector after leaving the science station on the Suzerain asteroid," hissed B'alarg. "Retrieve our agent, then with all speed, return to the Realm."

"And the *Vallo*?"

General B'alarg's heavy tail flicked. "Do not engage on any account. Your priority is to get the agent and data back here."

T'alak's tail whipped in anger. To be so close to the Alliance Armada flagship, and not confront her in battle?

"When do we launch?"

"You will be notified when we confirm the rendezvous." B'alarg touched a panel and the door slid open.

T'alak bowed, leaving the tactics chamber. His mind whirled. He had a personal debt to settle with the Alliance. Could this be it?

He paused, realizing B'alarg had remained behind. He moved to the General's globe of Earth and laid his scaled hand on top.

"Soon, you will pay," he said.

Sending the globe spinning in a cacophony of color, he swept from the office.

"Sounds like a cue for a song." Major Sam Benjamin's deep-set hazel eyes creased at the corners as he puckered up to whistle a few bars.

Colonel Grreag growled softly, regarding his human First Mate from across the desk. The man's hair color was comparable to Grreag's, but the similarity ended there. Where Grreag's tawny-gold fur grew in abundance, Benjamin's neat brown hair and clean-shaven face were regulation-standard.

Grreag imperceptibly inhaled to gauge Benjamin's mood. The human appeared calm and in good form, unlike Grreag. He shifted in his seat. His navy-blue Alliance fatigues always felt too hot and tight under the arms and across his chest and hips. It didn't help when his hackles raised or he puffed up his fur, but he had little control over that. He thought he looked ridiculous in the uniform with his fur sticking out at the neck and wrists like a Leontor bristlehog. But not wearing clothing made Terrans uncomfortable. They resented Leontor rule enough as it was, without adding any further discomfort to the equation.

Major Benjamin's whistling irritated Grreag's leonine ears and they flattened atop his head. He glared at Benjamin, noting the human's navy command fatigues fit him very well. He growled, resisting the impulse to readjust his own uniform again.

Benjamin smiled apologetically, showing a good-natured, crooked grin. "Time in a Bottle. Twentieth century popular song."

"I'm more familiar with your ricochet period of early twenty-second century."

"I find that a bit discordant."

Grreag's ears flicked in disagreement. Ricochet was so named for its lilting, cascading style. He found it as soothing as the winds across the tundra planet of Leontor. Tapping a sharp claw against his desk top he studied the chart of Earth on his office wall behind Benjamin.

12 | *Time Twist*

It displayed a pleasing blue and white rendering of what the planet looked like before the rupture scarred its surface. Grreag turned his gaze to the window to look at Earth as it was now—blistered, resembling a dull brown version of Mars. They were currently in orbit around it. Greagg kept the old picture of the planet to remind him why he spent so much time in space: to protect that spinning globe from the Komodoan Realm, their mutual enemies.

The Alliance appeared over two centuries ago when a vast spatial rift ripped into the Earth, almost destroying it. The Leontor had saved the planet, re-terraforming in return for the Terrans' aid in the war with the Komodoans. Grreag commanded the flagship *Vallo* with a senior crew of six Leontor officers, four human officers, and a crew of the best hundred and fifty humans under them. He could not complain about his humans' job performance but they showed little inclination to cooperate on a personal level. He knew most of them resented him; the rest feared him. Irritably, he smoothed the fur down on the back of his hands. At least Major Benjamin was cooperative and made a good second-in-command. For a Terran.

Seeing Benjamin giving him a curious look, he cleared his throat. "Major, I want you to see this communication from Leontor Control." Tapping a key on his desk, he brought up an older Leontor's face onto the monitor.

He growled a greeting, and then spoke in English. "Commander Grreag, here are your orders: at 0600 tomorrow proceed to Suzerain Science Station and take on board two scientists, Professor Webster and his assistant, Dr. Morrison." On screen the Leontor leaned closer. "This mission must be conducted in absolute secrecy. Professor Webster will brief you once on board. Out." The image faded and was replaced by static.

Grreag keyed it off with a sharp claw.

"Why secrecy, Sir?"

"One aspect of Professor Webster's work possibly involves temporal testing."

Benjamin raised an eyebrow. "And Leontor Control approves of that?"

"We must assess exactly what's involved once Webster's on board. Control's chief interest is weapon potential."

"But temporal? Why now, I wonder?"

"That's all I can say, Major." Grreag didn't confess that he had just told Benjamin all he knew. For Control to even consider touching temporal issues was in itself astonishing. The rupture that desecrated

Earth in the 2000's had proved to be of temporal origin. The planet Leontor only suffered minor damage, but Control had forbidden anything temporal that might cause further harm.

An alarm blared, startling them. Grreag stabbed at his desk, bringing up a holographic model of the *Vallo*.

"Actuation shows foreign matter in the chamber," he snarled.

That had been the fourth time in as many days that garbage dust from Earth's atmosphere had found its way in there.

He stood abruptly; Benjamin following suit. The Terran was taller than most humans, but Grreag towered above him.

"I'll take care of it," said Benjamin, heading for the door.

"No, I will. The control cabin's yours, Major."

Stamping out to the corridor Grreag almost ran down a couple of personnel who did not stand aside quickly enough. He intended to take his Leontor officer in charge of Actuation and threaten to put him out into space. Picking up garbage from Earth was inexcusable; there could be any number of pollutants in it.

He bent and stepped over the door's iris while it was still dilating and strode into Actuation. A young Terran female with a mane of fiery hair crouched in the center of the chamber. She gaped at him in astonishment, and Grreag stared back in disbelief.

He approached and took hold of her by the arm. Twisting, she slammed a fist at him, catching him on the nose. Amber eyes watering with pain, Grreag tightened his hold on her. He felt the bones give beneath his grip and cringed at the sickening crack.

The girl crumpled to the floor, her long flaming hair spread out like a fan over his wide-booted feet.

CAPTAIN T'ALAK stepped out of the dark stone and metal hulk of Military Headquarters into a gloomy pre-dawn Komodoan morning. This early the sulphur smelled strong, and the planet's iridescent green night-mist still shrouded the air, giving everything a hazy appearance.

T'alak's first officer and friend, Commander A'rlon, waited for him as arranged. He leaned against T'alak's star yacht, arms folded, deep in thought. As T'alak approached, he noted once again how A'rlon's tail hung limply behind him, making him difficult to read.

A'rlon looked up at his Captain's greeting. "Well?" He straightened, pushing against the yacht, which rocked gently on its cradle of air.

"This deserves to be told over some *picht*."

A'rlon raised a graceful dark brow. An expensive and highly intoxicating syrup wine, *picht* was rare on Komodoa.

They boarded the yacht and T'alak entered the departure sequence. The vessel's sleek, black form rose smoothly. It soared over the military base making the huddle of tall, spired buildings look like hatchlings' toys far below. In seconds the yacht raced toward the *L'umina* above the planet.

Settling in his seat, A'rlon glanced around the interior of the craft. T'alak followed his gaze, watching with satisfaction how A'rlon admired the smooth elegance and craftsmanship.

"Where did you procure this beauty?" asked A'rlon.

T'alak patted the compact command console. "One of the Houses owed mine a favor," he answered noncommittally. "Look at this." He caressed a blue and green panel. "It automatically converts to hyperdrive."

The yacht emitted a deep hum, rising gracefully out of Komodoa's atmosphere. The planet, stained mauve from its ninety-five percent ocean coverage, plunged rapidly away from them. The sky bled to charcoal, then ink. Threads of the Realm nebula eddied beyond the *L'umina*, the star shape of the craft silhouetted against the crimson and emerald green haze.

Both officers had been pinned to their seats during acceleration. As they left the atmosphere they could move again.

"So, whom did you have to kill to get it?" asked A'rlon dryly, leaning forward to inspect the flight console.

"Let's say I earned it for services rendered," replied T'alak. A'rlon was not Imperial born; he could not understand the particular currency between the Houses.

The *L'umina* rose before them. T'alak viewed its classical star-shaped lines with pride. He could barely contain his excitement at the thought of meeting the *Vallo* in battle. It felt akin to sexual arousal.

In his cabin, T'alak poured A'rlon a healthy goblet of *picht*. The dark maroon wine glowed richly in the metal cup, like the color of human blood when it clotted.

A'rlon lowered himself into one of the backless chairs, but T'alak couldn't sit down. When A'rlon heard T'alak's news, his scaled brow furrowed.

"If General B'alarg learns you disobeyed his order you'll be executed," he observed. "Are you certain confronting the Alliance flagship is worth the risk?"

"Do not question me!" hissed T'alak, enraged.

He pitched his goblet against the wall, the dented cup clunking to the floor. *Picht* splattered like an arc of Terran blood over the wall and floor. It had been many years ago, more than T'alak cared to admit, that the Alliance had taken everything that had ever had meaning to him.

His mate, T'alak-ra, had been traveling in a civilian convoy from the base on *S'ola*, the farthest of the two moons in the Realm. An abandoned Alliance transport collided with her ship, all hands lost. T'alak believed the Alliance had staged the collision to look like an accident.

Rage coursed through him afresh. Every Terran, every Leontor that he encountered since, he blamed for his loss. They begged for mercy, every one of them. He showed them the same compassion the Alliance had bestowed on the victims of the *S'ola* massacre. T'alak-ra would be with him now if not for the aliens' cowardice. From the moment he learned of her death he had vowed to make the Alliance pay. He had hundreds of human hides and Leontor pelts as trophies, but he had yet to capture the Alliance Armada flagship *Vallo* and her captain.

He realized Commander A'rlon watched him intently. His anger spent, T'alak got another cup and poured them both a refill. "To Komodoan dominance," he toasted.

A'rlon stood, raising his cup. "Komodoan dominance."

A'rlon went straight to his cabin after leaving Captain T'alak. His Captain's insistence on engaging the *Vallo* disturbed him. It could put their agent in jeopardy, but T'alak only thought of revenge.

A'rlon gazed round the cabin, stark and functional as all Realm fleet ships. Depending on one's mood, the lighting could be adjusted to imitate the appearance of flowing water on the walls. Real water gurgled from the fountain shrine, a luxury found only in officers' cabins. The six-foot tall shrine honored *P'jarra*, the goddess of water and peace, who offered protection and guidance.

Komodoans weren't so different from Terrans, thought A'rlon. Both had evolved from sea-living creatures, but because the equivalent of dinosaurs on Komodoa had never been wiped out, the Komodoans had kept some of that ancestry. The scaly skin on hand and face also ran down the length of the spines to envelop their versatile tails. The majority had dark eyes and obsidian hair, and all Komodoans had rich, swarthy complexions from the sulphur in their blood, which bled a vivid emerald green. Tiny gills behind their ears allowed the luxury of remaining underwater for long periods.

A'rlon tuned the lighting to reflect the ebb and flow of the Realm tide, and then back to the standard pallid green hue. He had quarters on the military base, more comfortable than the confines of his cabin, but with the uncertain timing of the pending mission, all essential crew remained on board.

He paced the cabin, his glance falling on a small rectangular box on his desk. Running his fingers over the smooth, polished Earth oak, he touched the little rusted key in the lock. His war trophy, old and fragile. The brittle wood still held a faint trace of the spicy scent it once contained. Now it held the secret to his past. Unexpectedly, regret flooded him and he slumped onto the desk stool, fingering the box. The walls of the cabin felt like they were closing in. He wanted out, to be anywhere but trapped here with his memories.

Surging to his feet, he swept the box off the desk. The lid broke loose as the box hit the floor. At the sight of it, A'rlon's face contorted. He could never leave the past behind. No matter where he ran, he would have to face it sometime. Kneeling, he reached his fingers into the box to retrieve what it held.

On the *Vallo*, Chief Engineer Uzima Khumalo acted in loco medicus when the Leontor doctor's duties took him to Earth. In Sickbay she wore the same dark green fatigues she used in Engineering, but draped an antique stethoscope around her neck to let the crew know the 'doctor was in'.

Major Benjamin arrived in time to find her bent over the unconscious girl, concentrating on setting the broken limb. Watching the process, he admired Khumalo's beautiful, coffee-colored African complexion and whorls of thick, black hair.

The newcomer's hair was a fiery-red tangle, her eyebrows a light cinnamon shade. He gently touched a strand of her hair.

"What an unusual color!" he commented.

Khumalo moved to his side, absently brushing his hand away, and Benjamin turned his attention to the redhead's jacket, which Khumalo had removed so she could operate.

"Is this leather?" he murmured, taking a sleeve between finger and thumb. "Her other clothes look like cotton but the ban on natural fibers has been around too long for them to be genuine."

"She's coming round," warned Khumalo.

The girl's eyelids fluttered and opened in blue-eyed shock. She flexed her wrist and looked in surprise at the white flexible cast on her left forearm. Khumalo laid a comforting hand on the stranger's shoulder as she helped her sit up.

"Hey, girl—go easy on that wrist for a few days. The break set cleanly, but it'll hurt for a while."

Benjamin stepped forward. "I am Major Samuel Benjamin of the Leontor and Terran Earth Alliance. How did you get on board?"

Swallowing, the redhead spoke in a strange dialect, "Toto, I don't think we're in Kansas anymore."

Benjamin was puzzled but Khumalo laughed, which relaxed the young woman. She gave a tentative smile, displaying teeth that although slightly crooked, were acceptably white and clean.

"What do you mean, aboard?" she asked. "Am I on a ship?"

"The *Vallo*."

"What country?"

Benjamin caught Khumalo's eye. "We're orbiting Earth at present."

The newcomer blinked. "Yeah, right. And you're Captain Kirk, I presume."

Khumalo chuckled. Pulling up a holographic chart of the *Vallo* she pointed to its status in relation to the planet.

The girl lifted a hand to touch it but her fingers swished through the hologram. "But which country owns it—Russia? Is this Mir?"

Benjamin hesitated. Earth hadn't had the concept of independent countries since the spatial rift. He saw something flicker in her eyes and she swallowed hard.

"That thing that attacked me, what was it?"

Khumalo's dark eyes sparkled with mirth. "Don't worry about Colonel Grreag. He's on our side and pretty friendly for a Leontor."

"You've never met a non-human," observed Benjamin curiously. "What's your name?"

"Catriona Logan; I work in the theater."

"You're a surgeon?"

Catriona sat on the crib edge. "An actress."

Benjamin exchanged glances with Khumalo, and cleared his throat.

"Where do you come from?"

"Scotland, originally."

"Your accent, is that Scotch?"

"Please," snorted Catriona, "I'm not a drink. Scottish."

"And that's where you arrived here from?"

She hesitated. "Look, all I know is one minute I was in the *Elephant and Castle* having a perfectly good shot of whisky. The next I'm facing some hairy alien beast. Now you expect me to believe I'm on a spaceship. For God's sake, pull the other one."

Benjamin's brow furrowed. He studied the young woman closely. She wore faded blue jeans with a cream-colored tank tucked in at the waist, and a pair of white shoes with laces. A snippet of history came back to him.

"Ms. Logan, what's today's date?"

"June 22nd. Why?"

"The year."

"2001." She saw their expressions. "That's not right, is it?"

Benjamin shook his head, meeting Khumalo's astounded look. "I'm afraid not."

June 22, 2001 was the date the temporal rift struck Earth.

CATRIONA LOGAN woke to find herself alone. She lay on a narrow cot in the room's center. The dim lighting and metal ceiling reminded her of morgues she'd seen on television and she sat up in trepidation. Her left forearm ached, and she flexed it within its white cast.

Several computer monitors blinked from the walls, all displaying a red and blue marquee logo. The letters 'L' and 'E' curled together, 'E' somehow cradled by the 'L'. She looked for a mouse to jiggle the screen saver but couldn't see any.

This certainly looked futuristic, but how could they expect her to believe she'd traveled through time? Chief Khumalo and Major Benjamin appeared sincere but she didn't think she could trust them. Beyond informing her she'd arrived on a spaceship two hundred and sixty years in the future, they'd been reticent about sharing anything else.

Their accents sounded odd and Catriona couldn't quite place them. They sounded like North American mixed with a dash of Australian. Yet only Americans could have those perfectly even rows of brilliant white teeth. And they both looked so healthy, taller than Catriona's five-feet-five and in great condition, with flawless complexions.

Catriona got to her feet. Running her hand along the smooth benches, she tried unsuccessfully to get something other than the marquee up on the computer monitor. She couldn't find a light switch, either, and the dim lighting made her feel claustrophobic.

"How the hell do I turn the lights on?" she demanded, just to break the silence.

Light immediately flooded the room, revealing it to be larger than Catriona thought. Several empty cots sat parallel to hers. Exploring the rest of Sickbay she found what looked like a window. It turned out to be a huge flat screen. Catriona tapped it, hoping to see something other than the marquee, but the screen stayed obstinately dark.

"Where are the bloody windows?" she said in frustration.

A jagged white line flashed onto the monitor. "Windows are in the observation cabin," replied a pleasant male voice. The white line moved in time with it, showing the voice's modulations.

Catriona took a step back. "What?"

"Windows are in the observation cabin," the voice repeated.

"I see," she snorted, "and you would be the shipboard computer, right?"

"Correct."

Catriona had said this half in jest, thinking about Eddie the shipboard computer in her favorite book, *Hitchhiker's Guide to the Galaxy* by Douglas Adams. The absurdity of talking to a computer made her feel like a character from the book. She took a deep breath.

"So, how do I get to this observation cabin, then?"

"Follow directional floor guide."

A circular door dilated to her right and yellow arrows lit up along the floor. Catriona tiptoed to the door and peered out. The dimly lit steel girder-looking corridor appeared deserted so she stepped through the doorway and crept along, following the yellow arrows. Struck by the absurd, she hummed *Follow the Yellow Brick Road*.

The lights led to a ladder, which disappeared into darkness above. Intrigued, Catriona put her hands on a rung and stepped onto it. She almost lost her grip when it moved rapidly upward. The ladder deposited her on a different level and she climbed off and followed the yellow lights to a large, circular door, patterned with Earth's star constellations. As she approached, the door dilated.

Catriona stopped in wonder. The windows stretched from floor to ceiling and outside, glittering stars studded the inkiness like diamonds sewn onto a velvet black curtain. She hurried to the window and put her hands against the pane to make certain it wasn't another monitor. Catriona could scarcely accept the truth, but here was the evidence.

The Earth spread out below, vivid against the black backdrop. She blinked and looked harder. This wasn't like the NASA photographs she'd seen. This planet looked withered, smeared with gray and brown swirls. Catriona felt like she'd run out of breath. Forcing herself to gulp in air, she leaned her forehead against the window, and stared aghast at the ruined planet.

Grreag snarled when Khumalo reported Catriona missing from Sickbay. He pulled up the ship model and located her in the observation cabin. He wondered how the infernal female had found her way there. An intruder claiming to have come from the year the spatial rift appeared shouldn't be wandering freely about the ship.

Grreag found his quarry with her face pressed against the windows. She looked smaller than he remembered. He sniffed and a cloying, oily-sweet perfume assaulted his nostrils.

"Return to Sickbay!" he ordered.

She turned to look at him. Steeling himself for the usual human reaction of fear at his proximity, he felt puzzled to see an expression he didn't recognize cross her features. She stared at him with her disconcerting alien-blue eyes. "Obey me!" he growled.

"Or what?" She crossed her arms and glared. "You'll break my other wrist?"

An embarrassed ear flicked and Grreag puffed up his fur. She was determined to keep challenging him. "It was unfortunate you got hurt."

She studied his appearance until he began to feel foolish. Then she said, "Well, you're not the Cowardly Lion, that's for sure."

Grreag wondered if he had heard her right. Cowardly? She couldn't have thought of a better way to insult a Leontor. Why didn't this human fear him?

"What happened to Earth?" she demanded.

"A spatial rupture decimated your world," he replied, then understood she hadn't known of her planet's desecration until now. Grreag felt struck at the emptiness in her eyes and regretted blurting out the words.

"Does anyone still live there?"

"Many," he said more gently. "Most cities are protected by environmental domes whilst we re-terraform. Now, come."

"I want to stay here."

Unused to having his authority questioned, he bristled. "You will return to Sickbay." Not giving her any margin for discussion, he promptly snatched her up and tossed her over his shoulders, careful not to claw her.

"Get off me!" yelled the girl, kicking ineffectually.

Khumalo looked startled when the door dilated and Grreag strode in clutching his cargo. He deposited Catriona on the nearest cot.

"Stay here!" he ordered, turned, and headed for the door.

"Yes, Sir!" shouted Catriona.

He heard vehement rustling from the cot and something thudded into the small of his back. He halted. Both human females drew in breath; then silence. He made himself breathe out to the count of five and exited without a word.

"How dare that Leontor manhandle me like that!"

Chief Khumalo moved to retrieve Catriona's hurled sneaker and handed it back to her. "Don't you mean 'Leonhandle'?"

Catriona rammed the shoe back on her foot. "I suppose you're the Wicked Witch of the West?" she snapped, embarrassed at her tantrum. "Why don't you just drop a house on my head and be done with it?"

The chief put her hands on her hips and struck an attitude. "If I'm the Witch, honey, the house should properly be dropped on my head, don't you think?"

After a second, Catriona offered a lopsided grin. "Sorry."

"No worries," smiled Khumalo. "Call me Uzi."

Catriona raised an eyebrow, "As in the gun?"

"That's what they call me." She batted her eyelashes and sat beside Catriona on the cot. "I can't imagine why."

Catriona could well imagine why; she'd be willing to bet the engineer had a short fuse with a retort as deadly as her machine gun namesake. Catriona liked her genuine, forthright manner. She thought Khumalo looked like an exotic African princess, despite the grubby appearance of her fatigues. She indicated the stethoscope around Khumalo's neck. "Are you the resident doctor?"

"Like hell. I'm actually the engineer around here. I just happen to have medic training so they rope me in when needed. The Doc's away on Ponce de Leon, right now."

"What's that?"

"Our colony planet."

Catriona blinked. "Is that where Colonel Grreag comes from?"

"No, Leontor Control gave it to us. We named it after Juan Ponce de Leon: he was the first explorer to set foot on Florida, where our main base is on Earth. But that was somewhere way back in the fourteen-hundreds." She shrugged, "It's a private joke for us Terrans; the Leons don't get it—they think we named it after them."

Catriona felt suddenly very tired. The Earth had been ruined and she was far in the future from everything familiar. How could she get back home? And if she managed to, how long before that rift destroyed everything she knew? "When did the rift happen?" she asked.

"We'll fill you in on all that over the next few days," answered Khumalo firmly.

Catriona blinked rapidly trying to stop the threatening tears. Her eyes felt gritty and sore. "Okay then. I need a long, hot bath," she told Khumalo, "with a huge glass of whisky on the side."

"We've a spritz here in Sickbay, but no bath water or booze, I'm afraid." To Catriona's questioning look she explained, "There's a no-alcohol policy on board and water's too scarce for bathing. The spritz uses liquid soap and spray toner." She slid open a panel and lifted out a sealed plastic cup filled with pre-measured drinking water.

"Better than nothing, I guess. Thank you." Catriona took the cup and peeled off the seal. The water tasted fresh and delicious but was gone too quickly.

She looked down at her rumpled jeans and tank. "I don't suppose you'd have a change of clothes? I feel like I've been wearing these for a couple hundred years."

In a way, she had.

ON THE Suzerain Alliance science station, Professor Scott Webster stood at the outer rim to stargaze. At least that's what he called these stolen moments of solitude by the windows. Smoothing his palm along the clear polyform, he still felt amazement that this monstrous structure squatted like a huge doughnut on this asteroid, light years from any civilization.

Webster had spent twenty of his fifty-two years on Suzerain. Sighing, he decided it had been a sterile life; one that did not lend itself to relationships. He smiled ruefully. What, were these regrets? A bit late for that when getting onto the *Vallo* was the opportunity he'd worked toward all his life. But he felt deeply disappointed that the Alliance only took an interest when they recognized weapon potential in the project.

Dizziness assailed him and he leaned against the windowsill. These dizzy spells worried him. He had never been sick in his life, but recently he'd been feeling pretty ill on a regular basis, and it only started after he'd begun the temporal actuate bubble tests. Steadying himself, he perched on the narrow sill to let the light-headedness pass.

He felt uneasy about the upcoming sojourn on the *Vallo*. What if Leontor Control discovered that he had already tested the temporal actuation theory and had taken a forbidden journey through time? He could lose the project and maybe his life, for Control imposed the death penalty for any tampering with the time and space continuum. Yet, he believed it was worth the risk, for if he got it right he might be able to reverse Earth's damage by putting the planet back in time before the disaster. Webster had seen Earth's past — a beautiful, lush planet unruined by the spatial rift.

He worried that his journey through time might have caused his illness. It had been physically and mentally disjointing, terrifying him. But not enough to prevent him from doing it again.

Only one other person knew what this project was capable of. Pauline.

He smiled wryly. Where would he be without his assistant? Since she joined his project a year after initial development, she had become his invaluable right hand. A shy, cautious man, it had been his policy not to become involved with a colleague. He had been successful in that until a few weeks ago. Still confused, he remembered how he woke up to discover himself lying on the laboratory floor, entwined with Pauline. Not that he hadn't imagined himself so with her many times before that. The thing is, he didn't remember how they got together.

He stirred, thinking of her firm body against his. Only now did he understand what he had sacrificed for his work. His life had been too solitary, and the very thought of Pauline made him feel young and vibrant in a way he never had before. He didn't want to consider what his life would be without her.

A step in the corridor brought him out of his daydream. As though his thoughts conjured her, Dr. Pauline Morrison stood before him, her gooseberry-green eyes shining as she smiled at him. Her sleek bob of blonde hair shone like a halo, making a beautiful frame for her lovely face. She looked better in the light-blue Suzerain jumpsuit than he did. A grin of delight spread across his face and he pulled her to him. She pressed her lips to his and kissed him with abandonment.

He surfaced, the taste of her sweet on his tongue. "Anyone could see us here!"

"Who cares?" She raised a knee to rest beside him on the ledge and lowered herself onto his lap. The silver pendant she wore on a long chain around her neck swung before his face. Webster caught it, peering closely at it.

"It's still safe, don't worry," she teased, shifting to sit alongside him on the windowsill.

Still grasping the pendant, Webster opened the round silver case to study the computer disk inside, then snapped the case closed, letting it drop back against her breasts.

Watching him through thick lashes, Morrison let her fingers play with the chain.

"You never did tell me why you insist I wear the disk like this."

Webster opened his hands, palms upward. "I wanted to give you a gift, Pauline. I felt it was the only appropriate excuse to give you jewelry. You never suspected?"

"No." She laughed. "You're so old-fashioned, but I love it. And I love you."

Webster leaned over to kiss her, but she drew back. "What's wrong?"

"Scott, I think you're overreacting about the *Vallo*."

"What do you mean?"

"When you said we should maintain a 'professional distance' on board. I don't see why."

"I just think it's best."

"Well, I don't!"

Webster blinked in surprise. At times Pauline showed a negative side and he wasn't experienced enough to deal with it.

"But you know how important this stage of the project is." He remonstrated, "I just feel that our concentration might be impaired if we're, uh..." Her expression silenced him.

She shrugged, standing. "It's your choice, Scott. Personally, I find sex beneficial to my concentration."

Webster stood also. "Please try to understand, love-"

"Oh, I understand perfectly." Turning on her heel, she stalked away.

Slumping back onto the sill, Webster listened to her retreating footsteps. Puzzled by her anger, he felt inexperienced and grossly inadequate.

The *L'umina* burst through the void of space, rushing toward enemy territory. In the middle of the ship's night cycle, an emergency call from security abruptly wakened Captain T'alak. He vaulted to his feet and into his gray, scaled tunic in seconds.

"Report."

He snapped on his comm bracelet and fastened a thick weapons belt of reptilian olive leather round his waist.

A young Komodoan officer's face filled the wall monitor, his onyx eyes tight with apprehension.

"Honored Captain, I detected an unauthorized transmission on a Terran subspace frequency."

T'alak barely contained his fury. A traitor on his ship?

"Pinpoint the exact location of the transmission and secure the area. Get me Commander A'rlon."

He slammed off the screen, bending to pull on his long, leather boots. He would flay the traitor alive and display his innards along the main ship thoroughfare for daring to betray the *L'umina*.

A'rlon stood in the bowels of engineering when T'alak's summons reached him. "You are too slow," he laconically informed the young officer on screen. "I have already apprehended the spy while you waste time. Inform the Captain." The screen went dark.

He gazed down on the lifeless body of an engineering assistant. Thick dark-green blood oozed from a chest wound. Unfortunate, he thought, reholstering his hand carbine. But one had to make sacrifices. He took a flat, silver object on a chain from his belt. Bending down, he pressed the oval-shaped metal into the dead Komodoan's hand, closing his still warm fingers around it.

T'alak arrived as A'rlon straightened. Two guards flanked the Captain and they took a stance as sentinels on each side of the door.

"So," T'alak prodded the body with his booted foot, "the traitor is no more. You should have left him alive for interrogation."

"My apologies, honored Captain." A'rlon bowed his head. "I had to prevent further transmission." It might be acceptable to kill an innocent crewman for a cause, but quite another to allow T'alak to torture him.

T'alak dropped to one knee beside the corpse. Prising the man's fingers apart he withdrew the gleaming oval object. "What's this?" he turned it over in his palm to study the circular engraving surrounding a central gray stone. "A *P'jarra* icon? Unusual for a guard to carry this." He thrust the object into A'rlon's hand. "Get it analyzed and have that filthy traitor's head displayed in the main chamber." Without a backward look, he strode out of engineering.

A'rlon ordered the guards to take the body. If a soldier carried a talisman, it would more likely be the god of sulphur and war, *B'llumni*, not *P'jarra*, the goddess of water and peace. But the feast of *O'tium* approached; the yearly Komodoan festival where both god and goddess were honored together for three days. Traditionally enemies, the joining of these deities should be a time when spiritual wounds and grudges were washed clean in *P'jarra's* holy well of forgiveness. So although unusual, a guard having this pendant was not suspicious.

A'rlon slipped it back into his belt. The lab could analyze all they wanted; it would tell T'alak nothing.

Catriona sat on the floor in Sickbay, surrounded by an alarming assortment of footwear. She lifted a monstrous thing that looked like a giant, weighted rubber galosh and dropped it on the pile. This was ridiculous. She just wanted a pair of boots like Chief Khumalo had, but couldn't get the stupid computer to understand that.

The door dilated and the chief came in. "What are you doing?"

Catriona indicated the new Alliance dark green fatigues she wore. "I need boots like yours, too."

Khumalo moved to the delivery chute. In a moment, she produced a pair of black regulation boots in Catriona's size.

"Why wouldn't the computer do that for me? I think it's doing this on purpose to annoy me. Wouldn't surprise me if these were the wrong size." She slipped her feet into the boots, fastened them, and stood up to experiment. They fit perfectly.

"You do know computers can't think like that, don't you?" asked Khumalo.

Catriona looked at her askance. "Hmph," she muttered, "I'm not so sure."

The chief shook her head and held up a silver-colored sack.

"Here are the personal effects you wore when you came on board. I removed them when fixing your wrist."

"Thanks." Catriona emptied the sack onto the cot, conscious that Khumalo studied her as she picked up an antique round, gold locket and attached the fine chain around her neck. She lifted one of the two rings—a silver cat with its tail curled around an Australian fire opal—and drew it onto the middle finger of her left hand. The other, a gold and silver Celtic band, she slipped onto the ring finger on her right hand. Sliding an ornate Wallis Simpson replica watch onto her wrist, Catriona pondered the time display. It had long since stopped, confounded by her improbable journey. Its faux stones glittered brashly in the bright Sickbay lights. She lifted a finger-sized perfume spray, which she automatically spritzed on each wrist and behind her ears before dropping it into her pocket. The rich scent of *Chanel No. 5* jolted her back to four years ago, before her parents had been killed. This had been her mother's favorite perfume. Catriona swallowed hard to contain the threatening tears and picked up the last object: her portable CD player and earphones. She fingered the machine and shoved it into a leg pocket in her fatigues, conscious of Chief Khumalo's silent observation.

"Music," she explained curtly. "A compilation of my favorites. You do still have music, I take it?"

Khumalo grinned. "Over two more centuries-worth for you to hear. I'll get you up to date on things, don't worry—a lot's happened since 2001. May I see it?" Catriona retrieved it, handing it over. Khumalo popped it open and laughed, "Look at the size of the disk! Hey, I can put this on a chip for you in no time. We have microplayers with—well, it'd be easier to show you."

"All right." Catriona handed the earphones over too. They snagged her locket chain and she fiddled for a moment to free them.

"Do you have pictures inside that?" asked Khumalo.

"My parents." She freed the earphones with a tug and relinquished them. "They died in a car crash four years ago."

Catriona realized with a shock that they'd actually been dead for

28 | *Time Twist*

over two hundred years. Her parents' deaths still lacerated her heart and she felt relief when Khumalo didn't ask any more.

"Come on," said Khumalo, "let's go to the galley for a drink."

Catriona brightened. "That's the best offer I've had all day."

✦

"So as you're from ancient Scotland, you must have tasted Haggis?" asked Khumalo. They sat at a table in the *Vallo's* octagonal-shaped galley, two glasses of golden liquid before them.

Catriona screwed up her face. "If you like internal organs boiled in a stomach, I'm sure it tastes wonderful."

Khumalo's eyes opened wide. "That's disgusting!"

"I know. Even the thought of it makes me feel like puking." She lifted her glass and took a drink. "Yuck!" She almost spat it out, but forced herself to swallow. "What the hell is this?"

"Apple juice."

"Doesn't taste like any apple juice I've ever had."

"At least the food's good," Khumalo offered. "I'll show you the berth assigned to you so you can clean up before supper. We're eating with the brass."

"Oh, not Colonel bloody Grreag!"

"He is the ranking officer; there's not much we can do about it."

Catriona swirled the juice around in her glass. "Why are aliens commanding humans?"

"We're allies in the war against the Komodoan Realm. If the Leons hadn't helped us, Earth'd be back in the Dark Ages. They put up the domes down there to keep us from extinction while they re-terraform the planet."

"I can't bear to see Earth like that — a bloody dustbowl. When I left it was beautiful."

She swallowed hard. When she'd left it she had hated it, didn't know its beauty. She'd give anything to have her world whole again. "Who are these Komodoans we're at war with, anyway?"

Khumalo gave a shudder. "Scaly, vicious creatures — they torture and kill with impunity." She took a long drink of juice. "It's said they eat human captives and use our skin for clothing."

"You can't be serious?"

Khumalo drained her glass and stood. "All right, Haggis, let's get you settled in your quarters."

Obediently, Catriona followed her from the almost empty galley.

"Not too many people using this place, are there?" she observed as the circular door closed behind them.

"Not usually. Most of us like to keep away from each other when we're off duty. Sometimes working in such close quarters can get on your nerves." She laughed. "But we get up to three months off at a time; that's when I get to do all those fun things I can't do here." Khumalo grinned as she stood back to allow Catriona to climb on the ladder first.

When the moving ladder relinquished them to a different deck, Catriona inquired, "Fun things?"

The chief laughed again. "Use your imagination, honey. I'm sure things haven't changed that much from your time!"

Catriona grinned. "I get it."

Khumalo clapped her on the back, nearly knocking her against the ladder. "Not a good idea to get involved with someone with such a small crew on board. Too intense." They moved along the corridor.

Catriona nodded. "I imagine so. Particularly if things don't go well."

Khumalo studied her with interest. "I take it you've been in a similar situation?"

"Unfortunately. I found my boyfriend screwing one of my classmates in our bed."

"Boyfriend?" Khumalo smiled. "Cute. What does that mean, your lover?"

Her voice drew the attention of a couple of passing human male crewmembers. Face burning, Catriona dropped her voice to answer. "Not necessarily."

"How can you call him a friend if you don't have sex with him?" This brought laughter from the men.

Catriona grabbed Khumalo's arm. "Chief, please. Could we finish this in private?"

Catriona's berth held a single bunk and a tiny en suite bathroom. The blank metal walls and ceiling made it look like the inside of a fridge-freezer.

Khumalo threw herself onto the bunk and leaned comfortably against the wall. Having nowhere else to sit, Catriona perched beside her.

"So, talking of lovers, why do you 'not necessarily' sleep with yours?" demanded Khumalo.

"What about STDs or getting pregnant?"

"What about them?"

"Don't you have to worry about such things?"

30 | *Time Twist*

Khumalo laughed. "STDs and immune deficiency diseases are no longer a problem, Catriona. We developed a cure last century, and the only sex is safe sex, so there's no risk of viral infection or pregnancy."

Catriona raised an eyebrow. "How does that work?"

"Sounds like our doctor had better give you a lesson on the birds and bees when he gets back. Basically, all women past puberty who request it are fitted with a membranous lining in the vagina cloned from their own skin cells. The thing is so delicate, you can't feel it's there, but it's virtually impossible to break. It's porous on one side only: allows normal bodily secretions out, but keeps other types from gettin' in, if you catch my drift."

Catriona's eyebrows shot right up under her fiery bangs. "That sounds too good to be true."

The engineer fixed her with a wicked grin. "Trust me, it's not. Well, you'll just have to get fitted and make up for all that lost time and opportunity, huh?"

"Maybe."

Catriona stifled a yawn. It felt like too much effort for her to keep talking. All she wanted to do was lie down and sleep.

Khumalo took the hint. Standing, she announced, "I'm going to clean up in time for supper. Why don't you take a nap?"

Khumalo left and Catriona stretched out on the bunk, pulling out the microplayer Khumalo had given her. Micro was right; the thing was tiny. She separated the minute earpiece from the one-inch square, wafer-thin player and adhered the piece just inside her ear. Turning the player over in her fingers in puzzlement — she couldn't see anywhere to press 'play'.

She shook it impatiently. "Play, damn you!"

At once the crystal-clear haunting voice of Karen Carpenter filled her ears. The words, *Calling occupants of interplanetary craft* sounded absurd, yet once she'd enjoyed the whimsical song. Her throat tightened and tears stung her eyes.

"Stop!" she cried and the music abruptly ended. The old seventies song upset her; once she had daydreamed of aliens landing on Earth, but a fanciful idea proved to be a far, far thing from reality. Using a fingernail to retrieve the piece from her ear she shoved both back into her pocket and stood, heading for the bathroom.

Cubicle, would describe it more accurately. She recognized the shower spritz on the wall and was bemused at the thought of using the dinky toilet in the corner. Looking into it, she saw no water. Curious, she pressed a lit panel beside the toilet and it gave an eerie huff. Tentatively, she touched her fingers inside the bowl and pressed the panel again. When the toilet huffed again her hand slipped on the surface as the bowl became frictionless. How bizarre, she thought. Yet it worked very efficiently.

Wondering how much time she had before dinner, she glanced at her stopped watch. Looking round for a timepiece in the berth, she realized how quiet and claustrophobic it was. She regretted letting Khumalo leave and longed to hear the sound of another voice. Remembering the computer, she cast around for a monitor or panel. 'His' voice would be better than nothing. She found an index card-sized monitor on the wall by her bunk and tapped it.

"What time is it?"

"Eighteen-thirty, point thirty-six hours precisely," came the male voice, accompanied by the white squiggly line on the monitor.

Riveting conversation, but then it wasn't every day one got to talk to a soulless machine. Soulless? She grinned ruefully.

"Hey, you're the Tin Woodsman, aren't you?"

"Please restate question."

"Exactly," she agreed. "Now, all we have to do is meet the Scarecrow, and find you a heart."

6

COLONEL GRREAG, Major Benjamin, and two other human officers stood as a group when the door dilated to allow Catriona and Khumalo to enter. For a moment, the redhead faltered in the doorway, daunted by the quartet of curious looks. Khumalo gave her a gentle shove and Catriona found herself face to face with Colonel Grreag.

The Leon glowered down at her. "You're recovered?"

"Yes, thank you." It looked like he expected her to say more. "I'm, em, sorry for all the inconvenience my appearance has caused."

His nostrils flared and he growled, moving away.

Major Benjamin stepped forward, his eyes creased in a friendly smile. "I trust you're feeling better now?"

Unbidden, Khumalo's advice to Catriona about being fitted for a contraceptive lining came to mind. Disjointed, she stepped back and

32 | *Time Twist*

knocked against Grreag. He glared at her and she readily returned it. She refused to let him intimidate her, but she found his alien amber-eyed stare unnerving.

The room reminded her of a theater greenroom. An informal clutter of discarded jackets lay strewn about, and a large pink plastic bottle propped up against a corner. With the officers wearing Alliance Armada fatigues of differing colors, they looked like they were in costume. And Grreag could be the Beast, waiting for his cue.

Catriona started, realizing she stared at him. Impassively, he had returned her look all the time she'd been lost in thought. Flushing, she said the first thing that came into her head. "I hope I didn't hurt your nose earlier."

He scowled. "There is nothing the matter with my nose."

"I thought that when I hit you-"

"My nose is fine!"

A startled silence shot through the room. Grreag had obviously not mentioned that she had belted him before he rendered her unconscious.

"Why would anything be the matter with the Colonel's nose, Catriona?" asked Benjamin.

Darting Grreag a look, Catriona couldn't help herself. "Oh, allergies," she shrugged. Benjamin grinned widely.

The Leon's face darkened and he stalked to the delivery chute to select his meal. Watching him, Catriona felt a pang of guilt. She had humiliated him in front of the humans.

The other officers had chosen their meals and were settling at the table. Khumalo nudged Catriona. "Let's eat, Haggis."

They joined Grreag at the food chute. The Leon had just made his selection and stood back to allow them to make their choice.

They must sup together every evening, thought Catriona, observing the relaxed and informal atmosphere. Only Colonel Grreag appeared ill at ease, not speaking unless he had to. The meals arrived down the chute in sealed packages. Khumalo grabbed both hers and Catriona's. Sitting down at the oval table, Catriona caught Grreag's eye as he sat opposite. She saw a hint of a smile around his whiskered mouth, but it looked more menacing than friendly.

Benjamin ripped the cover off his dish, quoting, *"Cry havoc! And slip loose the dogs of war!"*

Catriona followed suit, digging a fork into her spaghetti bolognese. Steam rose from it and she balked at the smell. Uzi had led her to believe the meals were good, but if someone had taken a pair of stinking socks and boiled them in valerian root, they couldn't have tasted any worse. Everyone else looked like they were enjoying theirs, except Colonel Grreag. She suddenly understood. Khumalo had given her the wrong dish!

Her stomach churned. The meat sauce on her plate looked like clotted blood over black spiders. She met Grreag's eye. A corner of his mouth lifted, exposing a single fang. Refusing to give him any chance to get the better of her she steeled herself, and shoved a forkful into her mouth.

Beside her, Khumalo inhaled loudly. "Catriona!" she yelled, making everyone jump. "Some Leon ingredients are poisonous for humans!" Catriona froze mid-chew. "But the reaction is immediate, so I guess you're all right. Go to Sickbay later if you've problems."

Grreag had not touched the spaghetti dish in front of him. To Catriona's challenging regard, he lifted up his fork and dove in. Catriona choked down her mouthful and churned her fork through the mess in front of her.

A call came through to Colonel Grreag, saving her from having to attempt a second mouthful. From the monitor on the wall came the Tin Woodsman's voice: "Personal communication from Leontor, Priority One."

"Send it to my quarters," ordered Grreag, standing.

Catriona suddenly noticed that some of her 'noodles' inched their way round the plate. She surged to her feet in disgust. Gagging, she bolted for the door.

Grreag caught up with her and marched with her to her berth. Catriona ignored him, too intent on not vomiting. Fortunately, it wasn't far. At her dilating door, she ordered, "Wait here," and left him in the corridor.

She dashed for the bathroom and just made it to the toilet in time. Heaving and gasping for breath, she looked up in mortified fury to see Grreag had followed her and witnessed the whole thing.

"I told you to wait outside!"

He bristled. "You do not give the orders on this ship."

The berth was scarcely large enough for his bulk. Catriona felt more claustrophobic than ever.

"Why did you make me eat that crap, you—*Bigfoot!*"

His ears flattened. "I will summon Chief Khumalo," he announced with exaggerated politeness.

"Don't bother!" Catriona's face flamed in mortification. Grreag reached to activate the monitor by her bunk. "I said, don't!" She slapped his hand away.

He glared at her, stark disbelief written across his furry countenance, and reached for the monitor again.

Angry beyond reason, Catriona flew at him, using her momentum to shove him back from the monitor. Grreag grabbed her, his talons cutting into her. Catriona flailed out and raked her nails across his face. Three bloody scratches appeared under the soft fur on his cheek. He roared in her face, yellow incisors large and inches from sinking into her throat. The sight shocked Catriona into gaining control. The hair on her neck stood on end, imitating the hackles that had risen on Grreag. Her gentle beast had suddenly turned into a deadly predator. Catriona looked into his furious eyes, pupils enlarged so they covered the amber iris. She realized that once enraged, like a wild animal he wouldn't back down in a confrontation. For the first time she understood how alien he was, and her heart pounded in fear.

"I'm sorry," she murmured, making her body relax as she terminated eye contact.

A shrill beep from the computer monitor made her jump and the Tin Woodsman's voice announced, "Communication pending for Colonel Grreag."

"Acknowledged," snarled Grreag and stomped from her berth.

The monitor in Grreag's quarters showed the familiar scowling face of a dark-pelted female Leontor.

"Admiral Prreaka." Grreag's ears flickered in greeting.

"I have grave news," growled Prreaka without preamble. "We received a message from an undercover operative deep in the Komodoan Realm. An agent after Webster's weapon may already be on board the *Vallo*."

Grreag resisted touching the stinging scratches on his face. "Can you be more specific?"

"That's all we know."

"You have seen my report?"

"Wait." On the monitor, the admiral reached a claw to touch a panel on her desk. "Channel now scrambled. Speak freely."

"Thank you, my friend. Did you find a human named Catriona Logan listed in the Earth archives?"

"Yes. She was presumed killed when the rupture hit in 2001."

Grreag's ears flicked in consternation. He had been so certain Logan's story was a fabrication. A ripple ran down his hackles; the timing was too convenient. She still could be the Komodoan agent.

"You will surrender her to Leontor Control?" demanded Prreaka.

"Not yet." Prreaka gave him a questioning look. "I hesitate to condemn a creature to death solely on the fact they claim to have traveled through time!" growled Grreag. His whiskers tweaked upwards, the equivalent of a human shrug. "I need more information before I decide what to do, my friend."

Prreaka's ears flickered. "Decide quickly. Go with the Great Fang, Colonel."

Grreag returned to supper. The others had finished and he'd rather have avoided it but he needed to relay the information at once.

Major Benjamin looked hard at him. "Sir, what happened to your face?"

Uncomfortable under the collective scrutiny directed at him, Grreag growled warningly, taking his seat.

Khumalo began to rise. "I'd better take a look at those."

The Leon stopped her with a glare and she sat back down.

"What happened, Colonel?" Benjamin asked again.

Irritated, Grreag suspected his Major had a very good idea of what happened, but the human apparently enjoyed putting him on the spot. "I had... an accident." Silencing any more questions with a ferocious scowl, he said, "A Komodoan operative after Professor Webster's research may be on the *Vallo*." He noted that stopped them in their tracks.

"Catriona Logan?" queried Benjamin.

Khumalo looked affronted. "Catriona's no spy!"

"We have no other suspects." Grreag kept his voice neutral. "If Logan is the operative, we don't want her to know we doubt her. This Professor Webster may well be able to verify her time travel story." He stood. "We must not, of course, rule out that someone else in the crew could be the agent. Keep vigilant. Dismissed."

7

CHIEF KHUMALO took her post at NavOps in the control cabin, waiting for Colonel Grreag to give the order to launch. The Colonel sat behind her in the center command seat. Across the cabin from Khumalo

36 | *Time Twist*

hunched a female Leontor at TactOps, Lieutenant Larrar. Khumalo had never heard her laugh or see her smile. She was young and fiercely dedicated to her job, ignoring her human colleagues unless forced to acknowledge them. Smaller than Colonel Grreag, her fur was a lighter shade, her eyes dark green.

Major Benjamin stood at Central Command, an arched console off to the right of the cabin, where he oversaw Navigation and Operations as well as Weaponry and Tactical.

Khumalo felt relief to be on duty where she couldn't hear Catriona yet again telling her how much she regretted scratching Colonel Grreag. She liked the Scottish girl just fine, but she'd go out of her mind if Catriona didn't stop bitching about the Leon. Khumalo tried to understand things from the Scot's point of view: drawing blood from the first alien you met wasn't the best start of friendly relations.

"When you're ready, Chief," Grreag's gravelly voice broke into her thoughts.

She looked up to see everyone in the control cabin watching her. Feeling self-conscious, Khumalo leaned over her console. The *Vallo* thrummed and eased out of Earth's orbit; the familiar stars quickly falling away.

A warning bleep sounded at her console and Khumalo concentrated her attention on it.

"What was that?" inquired Benjamin, turning from Central Command.

Khumalo tracked down the source. "A communication. It originated on Suzerain."

"They're under instructions for strict radio silence," rumbled Grreag.

Benjamin turned to Lieutenant Larrar. "What's our ETA if we increase velocity to maximum?"

The Leon consulted her console. "Ten-point-two minutes," she growled.

Benjamin raised an eyebrow at Colonel Grreag who nodded. Khumalo complied and the ship imperceptibly increased speed.

Minutes ticked by. The control cabin crew was tense and silent until Khumalo announced, "Coming into visual range of Suzerain."

A cragged, pockmarked cinder appeared on the screen. It grew larger at their approach until the circular structure that spanned almost half of the asteroid became visible.

A blue light pulsed on Khumalo's console, catching her attention. "We're being pinged."

"Put it on visual," ordered Grreag.

The control cabin viewer filled with the fierce features of an elderly

Leontor male, his hair yellow compared to Grreag's gold.

"Greetings, I am Rrara, Head of Suzerain. You are early, *Vallo*."

"We detected a communication from Suzerain. You're on lockdown so we increased speed to investigate," said Grreag.

Rrara scowled. "I'll look into it, Colonel. Stand by to receive the human scientists." The asteroid replaced him.

Grreag stood and gestured to Benjamin. "Major, accompany me to Actuation. Lieutenant Larrar, the control cabin's yours."

"Sir," she acknowledged gruffly as Grreag and Benjamin exited.

"I do not want Professor Webster to learn of a suspected Komodoan spy in our midst," growled Grreag as Benjamin fell into step beside him.

"I'll take care of it, Sir."

In Actuation, Benjamin slipped behind the controls. He formed an actuate bubble, which would swap instantaneously with the corresponding bubble on Suzerain.

Two figures appeared in the chamber and Grreag inhaled deeply, studying the newcomers with interest. Professor Webster simmered with energy and excitement, and his unruly mop of brown hair looked like he hadn't groomed it in days. The female beside him looked attractive for a human, with a golden-hued complexion surrounded by shining flaxen hair, her body compact and fit. Grreag detected an anxious scent about her, although she appeared untroubled and calm.

"Welcome to the *Vallo*," he boomed.

Stepping down, Webster staggered slightly. Grreag caught him.

"Thank you, Colonel." The sultry voice belonged to the blonde assistant, who had hurried to Webster's side to slip a steadying hand under his arm. "Professor Webster has been working too hard."

"Nonsense, Pauline." Webster waved her off. "I'm just over-excited at finally getting my hands on the *Vallo* engines. I'll be fine."

Grreag introduced Benjamin. "The Major will take care of your security requirements on board."

Webster looked hard at the husky Benjamin. "Splendid!"

"This evening we've arranged a reception for you, Professor," said Benjamin. "Give you both a chance to get acquainted with the crew."

"The Major will conduct you to your quarters now," growled Grreag. "Then we'll have your briefing."

Webster nodded. "That will be—"

"I'd rather we discussed security arrangements first," Dr. Morrison

38 | *Time Twist*

interrupted.

"Only if it's convenient," said Professor Webster.

"Certainly," Benjamin assured him.

Grreag led the way to his office. "I want Chief Khumalo at the briefing," he told Benjamin, who nodded.

Grreag noticed his second-in-command studying Webster's blonde assistant and growled under his breath. He hoped Benjamin would control his libido. He found the humans' obsession with mating most irritating—how any organization ran with such distractions remained a mystery to him.

Professor Webster followed Colonel Grreag into his office and watched the Leontor settle his big frame behind the desk. Webster's palms sweated now that the moment had arrived. Leons were notorious for being suspicious and abrasive. On Suzerain, Webster had had little to do with them and was apprehensive now that his project's future depended on Colonel Grreag.

Chief Khumalo and Major Benjamin filed in and stood by the door. Grreag gestured to Webster and Morrison to take the two vacant chairs right of the desk.

As they sat, Dr. Morrison looked over at Chief Khumalo. "Colonel, we have to keep this project on a strictly need-to-know basis; is Ms. Khumalo's presence necessary?"

"Chief Khumalo's presence is essential," growled Grreag. "If that is not satisfactory then you are both free to return to Suzerain."

Webster realized that although the Leon appeared calm and reasonable, his hackles had risen. "That's quite all right, Colonel," he assured him, "of course Chief Khumalo needs to know. Dr. Morrison and I are understandably rather paranoid about our work." He felt Pauline's eyes on him and avoided her gaze. "Let me fill you in on what we propose to do on the *Vallo*," he offered.

"Please." Grreag's hackles relaxed a fraction.

"First and foremost I need unlimited access to your hyperdrive engines. The work I do on board will determine my invention's feasibility."

Grreag's talon tapped rapidly on his chair arm.

"The *Vallo's* drive is new and more precise than other Armada ships," continued Webster, the Leon's impatient gesture making him nervous. "Your range is larger, and we can be more flexible with the actuate bubble size on the *Vallo*."

What he did not dare mention was that on board the *Vallo*, his time traveling experiments would be more reliable. Colonel Grreag would shut the entire project down if he knew Webster's intention. The ship engines had enough power to reconfigure the actuate bubble to travel vast distances. At such speed, the bubble would be forced further through time. Further forward or backward than he had already gone.

"If I could have time in a bottle..." Major Benjamin sang softly.

Grreag cleared his throat, interrupting him. "Exactly what is the purpose of the hyperdrive bubbles, Professor?"

"Basically to enclose an object, such as a planet, within. We can hold it in time, change the evolution, and even change the atomic structure and the way that elements respond to each other."

Webster watched Grreag carefully. He saw a flicker of something in the alien amber eyes. "The bubble can also act as an insulator, protecting whatever is within from changes outside its boundaries."

"Small comfort," remarked Benjamin, "when it could completely destroy a civilization."

"Quite," agreed Khumalo, "there's no defense against something like that."

A silence descended on the room. Webster closed his eyes, suddenly lightheaded.

Grreag growled quietly in his throat. "I need your input on a matter, but it must be treated with the same sensitivity as the hyperdrive project."

"Of course." The dizziness passing, Webster concentrated his attention on the Colonel.

"We have a human on board who claims to be from the 21st century."

Webster's eyebrows rose to his hairline. "A time traveler? From when?"

"June 22, 2001," growled Grreag. "But she appears oblivious that the spatial and temporal rupture struck Earth on that date."

"I can put together a neural scanner that could check for temporal abnormalities in her brain patterns."

Webster's mind whirled. If this woman did prove to be from the past, she could be significantly valuable for the secret project. Particularly if the temporal rupture was somehow responsible for her journey. Scanning her could tell him about the exact condition during the time travel; a blueprint that would make his temporal actuate bubbles more accurate. He'd be closer to his dream of restoring the timeline so that Earth could be changed back the way it had been.

Webster noticed Grreag's hackles had completely flattened. Scanning this person had taken the Leontor's mind off the weapon potential of the bubbles. "How long do we have before Leontor Control takes charge of her?" Webster asked.

Grreag's ears flickered. "Time enough."

"We'd best get installed in the lab, so we can commence work as soon as possible," said Webster, anxious to get started. He stood, smiling as he rubbed his hands together. "No time like the present, I always say."

8

"I CAN'T believe I lost control like that, Uzi."

Catriona put down her coffee cup and rubbed her arm. Khumalo had just removed the cast, but it felt like it was still there. They were having breakfast in the galley, Catriona trying to reconcile her temper tantrum with Colonel Grreag.

Khumalo sighed. "Catriona, of anyone, a Leontor is most likely to understand or even appreciate the physical aspect of anger."

"But that doesn't excuse it. Bloody hell, I'll have to apologize."

The engineer rolled her eyes. "Why do you care what the Colonel thinks? He probably deserved it, anyway."

"I can't even be in a room with him without both of us getting pissed off." As she spoke, the Leon came in, ordering a glass of what looked like yellow pus from the dispenser. Catriona studied him as he settled himself alone at a table. "Shit. He looks so miserable."

Khumalo glanced over her shoulder. "He always looks like that. Just let it go."

"I can't."

The engineer sighed. "Don't say I didn't warn you, girl."

Catriona got up and approached Grreag. He ignored her.

"Colonel." She was already annoyed and he hadn't even opened his mouth. "May I speak to you?"

"You already are."

They glared at each other for a moment, Catriona wishing she'd listened to Uzi. "About scratching you-"

"Do not mention it," snapped Grreag. "Is that all?"

"I don't see why you have to be so bloody rude!" The words flew out of her mouth before she could stop herself.

Growling, Grreag took a swig of the yellow pus and moved to get up. Catriona held up her hands as though to ward him off.

"Don't bother; I'll go."

Feeling humiliated and ridiculous, she turned and left the galley. Stalking blindly down the corridor she grabbed hold of the moving ladder. Why hadn't she taken Uzi's advice and left well alone? She jumped off on the deck where she'd found the observation cabin, but to her disappointment the windows had been sealed with metal screens; she couldn't see outside.

Tears of frustration welled up and she let them stream unchecked down her cheeks. She hated this ship, hated that Earth was ruined, hated Colonel Grreag and hated everything about this century. Sobbing aloud she sank to the floor and leaned her back against the covered windows. Her nose ran and she had no tissues. If there were such things in this time, she thought, angrily wiping her nose with the back of her hand.

The monitor by the door emitted a shrill beep. "Paging Catriona Logan," came the computer's voice.

Sniffling, Catriona got to her feet and moved to the monitor. She still couldn't see any buttons to operate it, so she touched her fingers to it.

"Catriona, are you there?" came Khumalo's voice.

"Yes." It came out as a croak and Catriona cleared her throat.

"Could you come down to the rec room? It's on the same deck as the galley."

"Okay."

"Are you all right?"

"I just need a bloody handkerchief!"

Catriona waited for her to ask why a *bloody* handkerchief, but Khumalo just said, "No problem, girlfriend, I'll bring something better."

Catriona tried to look at her reflection in the monitor with little success. She dabbed at her eyes with her sleeve and just hoped she didn't look too horrible.

She found the rec room without any trouble but the door didn't open for her. She knocked, grazing her knuckles on the orange-peel metal.

The door dilated. Catriona took a step inside and halted in shock. She thought she must be hallucinating, and shot a glance back into the corridor. But no, she definitely was still on the *Vallo*. The rec room held rows of maroon velvet seats facing an ornately draped stage. Dust motes swam in the intense spotlights converging from above. Catriona's

42 | *Time Twist*

pulse raced. Somehow, Khumalo had found a portal to the past!

Then Chief Khumalo and Colonel Grreag stepped into view in front of the stage, and Catriona realized a projection spanned the entire wall.

"That's the Castle Theatre in London," she said in wonder, "with the set for my show, *Beauty and the Beast*."

"I had the computer display the appearance of the theater as it looked around the date you told us you'd left London," explained Khumalo.

"How the hell did the computer know what it looked like?"

"Terran video archives."

Catriona stared at the projection, not certain how to react. For a moment, she'd thought she was home. Yet the sight of the Castle Theatre made her feel oddly empty, and she wasn't sure why. Perhaps because the dusty little theater reminded her of how disillusioned she'd been with her life in London, or maybe she instinctively knew it hadn't been real all along, just a projection.

She regarded Khumalo, then Grreag. Her stomach churned. Whatever reaction they'd hoped for, they'd gotten it. The engineer beamed ear to ear and the Leontor looked less hostile. He nodded at Khumalo, who switched off the projection. Then he turned to Catriona and offered her a solemn nod before exiting the rec room.

"What the fuck was that all about?" demanded Catriona, outrage replacing confusion.

"I'm sorry, Haggis. Colonel Grreag wanted to witness your reaction."

Catriona dug her nails into her palm to stop herself from bursting into tears again. She cleared her throat.

"I guess he liked what he saw."

"It's obvious you believed the projection was real. I'm really sorry, girlfriend." Khumalo looked distressed.

Catriona's eyes watered and her nose began running again. "Did you say you'd a haddkerchief or sobthid?" she asked, stuffy nose making it hard to enunciate.

Khumalo dug into her fatigues leg pocket and came up with what looked like a large silver bullet. "Anti-inflammatory and antihistamine inhaler. Hold it to each nostril and press the bottom."

Catriona turned away to apply the inhaler. The rec room floor was old-fashioned sprung wood with a large padded square mat in the middle. Catriona blinked at the sight of four faceless mannequins made from the same padding, standing sentinel on each corner of the mat.

Her nose cleared right up, without making the mucous membranes dry out. Her eyes felt clearer, too. "Thank you."

"I'll recycle that." Khumalo took back the inhaler.

"What are those dummies for?" asked Catriona, moving close to one to peer into its sightless face.

"They're part of Colonel Grreag's combat class. We use them when training. Look." She gestured to a rack on the wall.

Catriona saw it held half-a-dozen fencing epées, with a selection of firearms locked in a cage above.

"What kind of guns are those?" They looked sleek and streamlined compared to any weapons she'd seen before.

"Standard blasters and rifles, and a couple of Colonel Grreag's Leontor guns."

Catriona raised a fist and in slow motion took a swipe at the mannequin's nose. "I hope after seeing my reaction to the Castle Theatre projection the Colonel will be less of an asshole, now."

Khumalo chuckled and mimicked Catriona's slow motion technique and side kicked the mannequin between the legs.

"You mask your natural scent with perfume and that's his problem. Scent is part of Leontor communication and he can't read you."

"If it'll help make him a bit easier to get along with, I'll be happy to wash it off."

The rec room computer monitor beeped. "Chief Khumalo," boomed Colonel Grreag. "I need you in the lab. We've trouble with the scientists."

"On my way, Colonel," answered Khumalo, rolling her eyes at Catriona.

"You'll make alternative arrangements for your other business?" he demanded.

Catriona leaned over Khumalo's shoulder to speak into the monitor. "If you mean me, I don't think I can cause much trouble in the spritz!"

Khumalo shot her a pained look and Catriona smothered a laugh.

Pauline Morrison thought having Major Benjamin solely in charge of lab security was reasonable. The fewer people around the professor's project, the less likely security would be breached. Major Benjamin, although polite, wouldn't budge an inch.

Seeing Colonel Grreag enter the lab followed by Chief Khumalo, she realized the major had called for back up. Why couldn't they understand she only wanted the best for the project?

Chief Khumalo addressed them. "Professor, Dr. Morrison, please have a seat and tell me what the problem is." She sat on a lab stool, gesturing for the others to join her.

44 | *Time Twist*

Morrison heard a fierce grinding sound and realized the Leontor colonel gnashed his teeth.

"I need Major Benjamin to guard the laboratory personally," she told Chief Khumalo. "No one else."

"That's simply not possible," objected Benjamin. "I'm second-in-command of this vessel, not a guard."

"No one but the Major is acceptable," insisted Morrison. "The project is too important. I want Major Benjamin exclusively responsible for both its and my safety while on board."

Benjamin's eyes glinted. "Much as I would enjoy spending time with the good doctor, I just don't have the luxury."

Grreag's nostrils flared and he growled. "My presence isn't required here. Sort this out," he told Khumalo before stalking out.

Morrison felt the atmosphere lighten at Grreag's departure, but she didn't like hearing what Chief Khumalo had to say.

"Dr. Morrison, it is unreasonable to expect Major Benjamin to work with you exclusively, even if he wasn't the First Mate."

"I understand, but-"

"No, you don't. Colonel Grreag handpicked two top Terran security guards specifically for this project. They are the best the Alliance can provide."

Morrison held Khumalo's unwavering gaze. This was pointless. "All right," she acceded. "I guess we have no choice."

Professor Webster jumped to his feet and rubbed his hands together. "Come on, Pauline, let's take a break."

She knew he feared she would jeopardize the project if she insisted on being so stringent about security. Perhaps she was being overzealous, but better that than have the project threatened.

"Will you join us for a coffee, lady engineer?" Webster beamed at Chief Khumalo.

"Excellent idea," replied Khumalo.

"I have work to do," said Morrison. She watched them leave, Webster hardly giving her a backward glance. How could he be so heedless of her feelings and go off with that woman? Maintaining a professional distance with him proved harder than she believed possible. With an effort, she suppressed her resentment.

"Aren't you taking a break?" a voice intruded. She had forgotten about Major Benjamin. He grinned at her as though they'd never crossed swords.

He smiled. "Sorry, I didn't mean to startle you."

"You didn't."

"Can I do anything to help?"

She shook her head, "Thank you, no."

"You look like you need a break. How about a quick coffee?"

"Maybe later. *Some* of us need to work."

He moved closer. "Is everything all right?"

"Perfectly." She couldn't help noticing his hazel eyes shone like polished agates. "We just can't afford to take any risks with these experiments. You know how careful we have to be."

"I understand. I truly do." He grinned. "And as First Mate I give you my word you'll get the best security available."

His eyes were gentle, like Webster's. But the comparison ended there. Scott was tentative, unassuming; this man's whole demeanor spoke of taking control. She felt drawn to it and found it difficult not to be attracted when he offered her sympathy and attention, while Scott appeared indifferent to her.

"Thank you," she whispered, holding his gaze. Then abruptly she turned away. "If that's all, I need to get back to work."

Benjamin moved toward the door. "I hope we'll get a chance to talk later. You know what they say about Jill, don't you?" Morrison frowned. "All work and no play…"

"Of course." She smiled. "I'm sure I won't be working the entire time I'm on the *Vallo*."

"Good." He shot her a meaningful look as he left.

Morrison felt exhausted and drained. She sat back down and leaned her elbows on the lab bench. This was the first chance she'd had some time alone. Things were barreling out of control. She had an answer to Scott's illness and had formulated an antidote. It needed to be injected directly into his spinal column, and would be painful, so she had to work out an excuse to administer it.

Swinging round in her seat she accessed the *Vallo* computer files that Grreag had given them on Catriona Logan. Her stomach twisted as she read. The moment Grreag had told them about Catriona, Morrison suspected she knew who she was and how she'd gotten to the 23rd century. She could be none other than the girl who got caught in Scott's temporal bubble. Morrison had to decide whether to tell Scott the truth. Unfortunately, the truth would expose what she had done to protect their investment. Once it was out, Colonel Grreag may well turn them over to Leontor Control, and they'd lose the project altogether.

She felt a light fluttering in her stomach and put both her hands over it, rubbing lightly. Her breasts ached and her abdomen felt tight, stretching under her Alliance jumpsuit. She couldn't deny it any longer; she was starting to show.

Fighting tears, Morrison wondered what by the stars she was going to do. So many years she had spent celibate, she had been careless about contraception. She was pregnant.

9

CATRIONA USED the larger spritz in Sickbay to rid herself of all vestiges of *Chanel No. 5*. She found it really unsatisfying, not rinsing with water. Her hair felt heavy and unclean, although the toner did moisturize her skin.

She realized she hadn't worn any makeup since her calamitous exit from the *Elephant and Castle*. Uzi didn't wear any, not that she needed to with her lovely coloring. Catriona hadn't noticed any of the women on board using cosmetics, either, and wondered if they were even available.

She dressed in a clean set of dark green fatigues and stepped out of the spritz. A crewman worked at one of the Sickbay computers, his concentration so intense he didn't notice her. Catriona slipped past him and through the door as it dilated open.

The futuristic guns she'd seen in the rec room interested her. She made her way there and found the room free. She was amused by the thought that there must only be two types of recreation on board: fighting or watching movies. Standing on the mat, she realized how quiet the ship's engines were. She found it difficult to believe they hurtled through space so silently. She had no sensation of movement, like on a plane or fast train. And there must be some kind of false gravity—she'd have to ask Uzi how it worked.

She found the weapons cage locked, but the epées came freely from their holders. Catriona noticed two short swords that she'd mistaken for one epée, and lifted one. It felt beautifully weighted. Shifting it to her left hand, she grabbed one of the epées and swished it through the air. Taking an attack stance, she menaced one of the training mannequins.

With a pang, she remembered what fun it had been learning stage fighting at drama college. That brought her present predicament into sharp relief and tears threatened again. She hated feeling helpless and dependant. She resented being completely out of control of her own life, and if she were honest, her bravado masked her fear. Uzi told her Colonel Grreag had ordered that for now, no one except Major Benjamin and the two visiting scientists, should know exactly when she claimed to be from. Uzi said Leontor Control had a ban on time travel and any interference with the space-time continuum was swiftly met with dire consequences. Catriona's stomach lurched with foreboding. She couldn't understand why they would execute someone just because they came from another time.

She circled the mannequin and alternated thrusting the short sword and epée at it, just stopping short of touching it with either blade. A thread of thought wormed its way into her mind. If she did make it back home she would be returning to the hard, daily grind of *Beauty and the Beast*. The alternatives weren't appealing, either. The dole, or a tedious office job for regular pay, and the dread of the space rift imminent. She'd asked Uzi for the actual date when it happened but she'd stayed evasive, assuring Catriona it would be explained later on.

Frustration surged through Catriona, and she attacked the mannequin with the short sword. The blade had no safety button and the dummy's fabric ripped satisfyingly as she stabbed through it.

"What do you think you're doing?" bawled Colonel Grreag.

Sweat beading her forehead, Catriona's arms dropped to her side. "What does it look like?" she panted.

He glared down at her feet. "Take your boots off!"

Catriona dropped the sword and epée with a clatter and stepped off the mat. Grreag opened his mouth and she waited for him to shout at her, but he closed it again and moved to retrieve the discarded weapons. She saw his nostrils flare as he passed her and felt a modicum of satisfaction when his expression grew less censorious. Uzi had been right about her perfume making him hostile.

"What kind of swordplay was that?" His tone sounded almost civil.

"It's called stage fighting," she replied. "At least the epée part is."

"I have never encountered it." He put the weapons back on their holders and unlocked the weapons case.

"It's all for show."

He lifted a pistol-sized gun, huffed on it, and polished it with the back of his furry hand. "Do you know hand-to-hand combat?" he asked.

"Only the stage kind," answered Catriona warily.

He laid the gun on the case and removed his boots, tossing them off

48 | *Time Twist*

the mat. Catriona looked down at his wide, paw-like feet.

"Demonstrate," he ordered.

"It's been a while since I did this." She took a hesitant step toward him.

"Take off your boots!" he yelled.

"All right, keep your fur on!" Catriona yanked them off and joined him. His astounded expression made her want to laugh out loud.

He took a stance. "Come at me with a punch and I'll show you where you went wrong when we met."

Surprised, Catriona noted his manner was almost friendly. He was obviously in his element with combat. Swallowing hard, she took an aggressive stance and sliced a hand at his face. Easily, he parried.

"That's your first mistake." His eyes gleamed. "With a larger adversary you must disable him as quickly as possible. Striking the face is too obvious; you are unlikely to make a connection-"

"How come I hit you on the nose, then?"

The tip of a yellow fang showed. "I underestimated you," he admitted.

Catriona's jaw practically dropped. She didn't know how to take this new, civil Colonel Grreag.

"Show me what you know." He moved to the computer wall panel, and punched in a series of digits.

Catriona jumped in alarm as one of the inanimate dummies suddenly listed to life, hovering from its corner until it stood close to her.

"That's creepy," she shuddered.

"Minimum combatants," growled Grreag, his fingers working the panel again. "Let's try maximum." The other three figures moved until all four surrounded Catriona.

The hair rose on the back of her neck. Grreag folded his arms and regarded her expectantly.

"Wait a minute, you expect me to fight all four of these things?" To his nod, she gave a snort of disbelief. "One of them, maybe. All of them and I'll need a weapon."

"What weapon?"

"A Smith and Wesson?" She tried to infuse a bantering tone. The mannequins had all but hovered on top of her.

"In hand-to-hand, projectile weapons are for cowards," scoffed the Leontor.

Catriona's face burned. She had just started feeling more at ease with him and he had insulted her again. Ducking into a roll, she slipped out between two of the mannequins and tried to reach one of the short swords on the wall. Her hand fell on the weapon Grreag had left on the open case. Closing her fingers around it she dropped to one knee, pointed it at the advancing figures and squeezed what she hoped was the trigger. A white beam lasered through them, exploding them into entrails of smoldering circuits and wires, spattering a mess of components over the rec room.

Grreag wrenched the weapon from Catriona. "Have you no honor?"

"What do you mean, honor?" she spluttered. "This might be your idea of fun, but it certainly isn't mine!"

The Leontor glared at her, a myriad of emotions reflecting in his golden eyes. Finally, he turned back to the computer monitor and Catriona watched a small army of service droids hover in to clear up the mess.

Grreag pulled on his boots and locked the gun back in the case.

He turned to her. "Human, why do you not fear me?"

Catriona paused, debating whether to tell him. "This video archive of the Castle Theatre," she said. "Is the performance recorded, too?" He nodded. "Ask the computer to run it from Act One, Scene Three."

Grreag gestured that Catriona do it herself and stepped back from the computer monitor. She still didn't know how to activate it and placed herself so Grreag couldn't see her tap the monitor. The computer responded and she input the request.

As the projection of the Castle Theatre flashed onto the wall Catriona glanced at Grreag. How he would react to this, she dared not consider. Music swelled and a humanoid figure materialized, clad in Elizabethan costume of black tights with codpiece under a white silk poet-shirt.

Grreag grunted. Holding her breath, Catriona watched him glare at the image. He could have been looking at a video of a close relative.

He turned to her, "A Leontor?"

"Human. The character is a prince under a magic spell." She gave a nervous laugh. "Quite a coincidence, isn't it?"

The Beast lifted his arms in entreaty and began the song, *Drink to Me Only with Mine Eyes.*

"He is *singing*!" snorted Grreag, as though that were the worst of all possible things to be doing.

"Of course he's singing," snapped Catriona, "what the hell else would he be doing in a musical?"

Beauty entered, a striking young woman with a coronet of chestnut hair. She moved shyly toward the singing Beast.

"Wait a minute." Catriona frowned. "That's the actress I took over from when she broke her leg. Computer," she tapped the monitor, "is this the only record you have of Beauty?"

"Affirmative," answered the male voice.

"I don't understand. Who's listed as playing Beauty?"

"Actresses listed as that character include Carolyn Hunter and Catriona Logan."

"So, play the recording of Catriona Logan."

Grreag suddenly snapped into action. "Computer!" he snarled, "cancel request."

Catriona blinked. "What?"

"We have wasted enough time. Come." He strode toward the door.

"I haven't finished here."

He scowled. "You will come with me now."

"Or what?" sputtered Catriona. "You'll throw me over your shoulder again and haul me out against my will?"

"If I have to."

"Fine. First let me see my recording!"

His whiskers tweaked. "Provide the information, computer," he instructed.

"Records of Catriona Logan in the role of Beauty were lost in the spatial rupture of June 22, 2001."

Catriona felt like the air had been sucked from the room. Grreag moved to the computer monitor and ended the video.

The projection snapped off and Catriona stood in horrified silence. Tears blurred her vision and she felt lightheaded.

"Come." A gentle hand slid under her elbow, turning her round. Before she knew what she was about, she had buried her face against Grreag's ample hairy chest while she cried.

SUSPENDED ABOVE the mottled purple sphere of Komodoa, Captain T'alak finally got word to launch the *L'umina*. Within minutes the silver-hued ship broke orbit, its engines spinning at maximum through the stars.

T'alak settled into his command chair, staring sightlessly at the viewscreen. His fingers and tail flexed as though preparing for personal battle. In mere light years, the *Vallo* would be his.

He shifted his gaze to A'rlon, who stood nearby. His second-in-command appeared preoccupied and T'alak suspected he knew his thoughts.

"You are looking forward to the mission, my friend?" he inquired.

"Of course." A'rlon met his gaze, his dark eyes expressionless.

"But?" prompted T'alak.

A'rlon stepped closer. "I continue to question the wisdom of engaging the *Vallo* in battle."

T'alak's tail arched and flicked behind him. "I have waited too long for this moment, A'rlon. There may never be a better opportunity."

A'rlon nodded, turning his attention to the viewscreen. "It will be interesting to meet this agent."

T'alak's tail continued to swish. "Indeed. They've been posted behind enemy lines for many years."

"A long time to be cut off from the Realm."

"Too long. No doubt they will be grateful to return to civilization." T'alak shot A'rlon a shrewd look. "Tell me, how did *you* enjoy living among humans?"

"I don't know what you mean."

"Come, you think I don't know you were once an operative?"

"Where did you hear that?" countered A'rlon.

"Have it your own way, my friend. One day I shall learn the truth about you."

A'rlon's lips curved in a sardonic smile. "One day you shall, my friend."

T'alak dropped the banter. "What did you find out about the *P'jarra* icon we found on the spy?"

"The center stone is an Alliance transmitter encased in a meteorite chip. I have ensured it cannot be used again."

T'alak's tail curled. "Do we know how much of the transmission got through?"

"Not enough to endanger the mission. Providing that our agent is careful, even if the Alliance suspects one of us is aboard the *Vallo*, by the time they track them down, they'll be long gone."

"I know it's not the real thing, Haggis," apologized Khumalo as she handed Catriona a small leather flask, "but it's better than nothing."

Catriona put an eyeball to the flask neck. Seeing a green-colored liquid inside, she took a sip and grimaced. "What's that supposed to be?"

"Crème de Menthe. It's peppermint-flavored ethanol."

52 | *Time Twist*

"Bloody hell, are you out of your mind?" Catriona flung the flask back.

"No, but I thought *you* wanted to be." She took a swallow and shuddered. "It is kinda rough."

"I appreciate the gesture, Uzi. I just need my wits about me, right now."

Khumalo placed the flask on Catriona's bunk. "You're doing remarkably well, Haggis."

"I just can't get my head round it. I don't understand how or why I got here..." Catriona swallowed hard. "Let's get going, Uzi."

"Come on then."

They left Catriona's berth and headed for the ladder. Catriona made an effort to focus on the upcoming interview with Professor Webster.

"What are you humming?" asked Khumalo.

Catriona started in surprise. She hadn't realized she'd been doing it out loud. "*Follow The Yellow Brick Road.* 'Cause we're off to see the Wizard. Except we somehow missed the Scarecrow."

Khumalo rolled her eyes. "You don't need any alcohol, Haggis."

When they arrived at Professor Webster's lab, the long-limbed scientist unfolded himself from his computer and stood beaming at them. His bright blue eyes seemed familiar to Catriona.

"Looks like we found the Scarecrow after all," she whispered. Webster's assistant, Dr. Morrison, loomed behind him. Meeting her glacial, jade eyes, Catriona added, "and the Wicked Witch from the West."

"Shut up!" hissed Khumalo. "Professor, Dr. Morrison, this is Catriona Logan."

"At last!" Webster shook Catriona's hand. "How are you?"

"Confused, thanks."

"Be serious, Catriona." Khumalo affectionately cuffed the back of her head.

"I hope we can remedy your confusion." Webster smiled.

Catriona gazed into his warm blue eyes. A tendril of hope touched her. Maybe he really could help. He professor drew her into the lab toward a large recliner, reminiscent of a dentist's chair.

"Have you any idea how you came to be here?" he asked.

"None at all, I'm afraid."

Webster studied her closely. Catriona felt like an amoeba under a microscope. She turned her head to discover Dr. Morrison pointing an instrument at her, grimly examining the results.

"Everything normal, Professor," she reported. "The heart rate's a little fast."

"That's because I'm ahead of my time," quipped Catriona, nervousness making her feel giddy.

Meeting Khumalo's censorious gaze, Catriona fell silent and allowed Morrison to finish her examination. She noticed the doctor wore a silver pendant not unlike her own gold locket.

"Do you have photos in there?" she asked, trying to make conversation.

"No," Morrison answered.

Professor Webster attached square-shaped electropads to her temples. "She carries my data disk in there to humor me. Now, this will only take a moment."

Khumalo leaned closer to look and Webster stepped back, bumping into her.

"Excuse me, Professor." She moved out of his way.

"No problem, Chief," he winked. "It's not every day I get to rub shoulders with such a beautiful engineer."

Catriona almost laughed when she saw her new friend arch a flirtatious eyebrow at Webster. She noticed Morrison glaring at Uzi with pure hatred on her face. They must be more than lab partners, thought Catriona, filing it away to talk about later with Khumalo.

A bleep sounded from Catriona's monitor. Webster was by her side instantly.

"I *knew* it!" He pointed to the monitor where Catriona's brain patterns split into several separate traces, one of them peaking out of sight.

"Professor," said Khumalo slowly, "what exactly have you been scanning for?"

Catriona heard the concern in her voice and sat up. "What's wrong?"

"Are you doing what I think you are?" asked Khumalo.

Webster looked trapped and Dr. Morrison moved rapidly to stand by Webster. She looked like she would dispatch the engineer at the slightest provocation.

The professor spread his hands wide. "Well, I-"

"Because if it is what I think it is," interrupted Khumalo, "I *won't* report you to Leontor Control for breaking their temporal policy."

Webster blinked. "You won't?"

"If you think I would miss seeing this for myself you're wrong. Besides, you're exactly the right person to help Catriona."

Webster laughed in relief, "I knew you were a kindred spirit, Chief."

"Careful, Scott," warned Morrison in an undertone.

"Would someone please tell me what the bloody hell is going on?" complained Catriona.

54 | *Time Twist*

Webster turned his full attention on her, checking the monitor. "In all recorded instances of time travel, Catriona, there is high-frequency brain activity. Nothing official, of course, but I managed to get my hands on a couple of Leontor Control reports confirming we have had time travelers visit before." He smiled at Catriona. "But they usually *desire* to travel, unlike you."

"Did you scan them?" inquired Khumalo.

He shook his head. "Unfortunately, they, ah—were unavailable thereafter."

Before Khumalo could ask, Morrison provided the answer. "Executed as per Leontor Control policy."

"Oh, great," Catriona ripped an electropad from her temple, "It just gets better every minute."

Khumalo laid a hand on her shoulder. "That's why Colonel Grreag kept your arrival under wraps, Catriona. No one's going to be executing you anytime soon, don't worry."

"In the meantime, let's see what we can find out about your journey here." Webster gently reattached the pad. "The fact that you also display high frequency brain activity confirms my theory that we may find a pattern back to the moment of travel. If so, then we can plot exact coordinates, instead of the hit-or-miss theory I have now." Catriona's eyes shone with hope. Smiling, he continued, "If we do find such a pattern, the rest of our research with the hyperdrive bubble will be significantly enhanced. Lovely-Lady Chief, could you pull up all historical records on June 22, 2001, please?" As she did so, he turned to Morrison. "Doctor, will you prepare the neural scanner?"

Catriona heard Morrison take a sharp breath before moving away. She definitely sensed something between them; the tension felt almost tangible.

"Nothing to worry about," Webster assured Catriona, "you won't feel a thing."

"Huh, so doctors still say that, do they?"

Webster stumbled, knocking against Catriona's chair. Khumalo steadied him. "You okay?"

Morrison appeared at his side, guiding him to a lab stool. "He's been overworking, lately. Take it easy for a moment, Scott. I'll set up." Approaching the diagnostic chair, she touched a panel. Metal cuffs slid into place over Catriona's wrists and ankles.

"Is that necessary?" she demanded.

"I'm afraid so," said Webster, recovering and standing. He joined

Morrison at Catriona's side. "The straps are to protect you in case the neural scanner touches off your reflexes. Oh, just one thing. There's no chance you're pregnant, is there?"

Morrison dropped the neural scanner with a crash. It rolled between Khumalo's feet, and she bent to pick it up. Morrison's hands shook as she took it from her.

Webster frowned with concern. The blood had drained from Pauline's face and she looked suddenly fragile. "It looks like we've both been overworking, Doctor. Should we call it a day?"

Morrison shook her head. "I'm fine." She raised the scanner to Catriona's left temple and depressed a switch.

A shrillness pierced Catriona's eardrums like stiletto blades. She shrieked and struggled against the chair restraints.

Morrison pulled the scanner back. Webster stepped forward and inspected Catriona. A livid red mark spattered her temple where the scanner had touched her.

"We'll have to calibrate it lower for you, Catriona. I'm sorry; it's not supposed to hurt." Releasing her from the chair clamps, he addressed Morrison. "Rest up and we'll have it ready by tomorrow."

She gave him a long, steady look before turning and leaving the lab.

11

IN HER berth, Pauline Morrison yanked off her boots with a relieved sigh. Slumping heavily onto the berth, she massaged her feet and ankles. She would have to find a way to tell Scott the truth about Catriona Logan and his temporal experiment, before he got any worse. She thought back to when it had all begun, a few weeks ago:

She had gone to Scott's quarters to deliver some urgent data, but he wasn't there so she had looked for him in the lab. It had been late at night when most people were asleep on Suzerain. The lab was also empty but looked as though Scott had stepped out for a moment. She had a suspicion he might be testing his temporal bubble. She knew he wouldn't involve her, trying to protect her if anything went wrong.

Re-checking the lab, the outer panel now indicated a presence inside. Heart thumping, Morrison palmed the I.D. lock and found Scott huddled in the center of the lab, shivering violently. She reached his side in one bound. "What have you been doing?" She pulled at the ugly, gray coat he wore over his blue jumpsuit.

Webster's breath came in short, labored gasps. "It works, Pauline," he managed.

She took the miniature computer keypad he offered. "You've just been to the 21st century?"

"Yes, by God, it works!" Jubilant, Webster enveloped her in a hug. "The data's all on the minipad."

He released her and Morrison studied the screen. "What this tells me is that you almost didn't make it back!"

"I don't understand." He took the instrument from her. "Where's the rest of the data?"

"You should have let me assist you. It's a wonder your atoms didn't end up scattered across the continuum!" She knew her voice sounded shrill. Scott had no business testing without her assistance. He could have been trapped and unable to get back without someone monitoring the corresponding temporal bubble.

Still unsteady, Webster took the minipad to a main computer console and fed in the data. Morrison stood by, watching over his shoulder. His excitement was infectious. Scott Webster was a compelling man and many times she had wanted to initiate something more than friendship, but resisted. The project came first, always the project. She must allow nothing to endanger it.

"Look," Webster broke into her thoughts, "the mass wasn't equal on the return jump. With that extent of imbalance, it's a miracle I got back at all."

"You had nothing with you but that old coat, and that's not organic." Webster sat heavily on a lab stool. "Oh God, the girl."

"Someone saw you jump?"

"More than that," whispered Webster turning from the screen. "She collided with me as I jumped."

"And as the bubble had been formulated for only your return, her molecules got scattered."

Scott paled and looked as though he might pass out again.

"Oh God, I killed her. This is precisely the reason why Leontor Control forbade time travel experimentation. I am an egotistical bastard to think I knew better." He lifted the minipad. "I'll have to make an official report."

"Scott, you're not serious?" Morrison grabbed his arm. "They won't let us onto the Vallo-"

"I've no choice."

Morrison knew how pointless it would be to try to talk him out of it. The project would be aborted, because of a single error of judgment in all these years. They'd lose everything. Fury choked her. She *couldn't let it happen. They both had worked too hard to lose it all now. Taking a couple of breaths to calm herself, Morrison moved behind Webster's stool to massage his tension-riddled shoulders.*

"All right, Scott," she acceded, "but you can't make a report in this condition. Get some rest, and then we'll compile it together."

He stood and turned to face her. She saw the deep lines furrowing his brow and knew his devastation at the thought of losing the chance to work on the Vallo.

"Oh, Scott," she murmured and reached her hands up to lightly touch his temples.

She knew she should stop this before it began, but his raw pain coupled with her loneliness felt too intense to overcome. She slid her hands around his neck and gently drew his mouth to hers.

"Pauline…" He resisted for a moment, and then pulled her to him with a fierceness that left her breathless.

His body felt firm against her and his wiry arms held her with deceptive strength. Pauline thrust all doubts from her mind and thought only of his mouth on hers, the silky touch of his tongue on hers. Scott moved a hand and ran it through her hair and cupped the back of her head. She felt like her bones were melting and she slowly sank to her knees to the floor, drawing him with her. Sighing she strafed her fingernails across his back and held him tightly against her. At last, at last she knew what it felt like to touch him, to be touched by him.

His hand found a breast and tentatively caressed it through her jumpsuit. Pauline quivered and arched into his touch. She brought a hand from around his back and slowly unzipped the front of her suit. Scott's hand resumed its caress on her naked flesh, his thumb brushing her nipple to hardness.

She sensed his hesitation, so without breaking the kiss she reached up and began to unzip his jumpsuit. She felt him smile and they drew back from each other so that she could push the suit back over his shoulders and help peel it from his body. Pauline had never seen him undressed before and the sculpted muscles of his chest and arms surprised her. She shrugged out of her own jumpsuit, feeling exposed and vulnerable. The look of desire in Scott's eyes reassured her and with shaking hands she reached out and ran her palms down the length of his torso. He pulled her back into a kiss, and they eased to a lying position on the floor. Pauline was oblivious to the cold metal under her as Scott moved down to kiss both of her breasts in turn. His tentativeness made her wonder if she could be the first woman he'd ever been with, and a feeling of power surged through her. She gently eased him onto his back and leaned over him so she could use her tongue to caress his chest and move languidly down to the concave

58 | *Time Twist*

of his stomach. The tip of her tongue flickered around his belly button and she hesitated before moving on.

She shifted position and gently parted his legs so she could lick the insides of his thighs. As the tip of her tongue flickered over his tightening testicles, Scott groaned and strained toward her. Tantalizing him further she moved her mouth away and touched her tongue to the shaft of his penis, which brimmed with need. Grinning, she ran her tongue along its length, and when she knew he could not take any more she took him in her mouth, sucked hard and swirled her tongue around him. She rapidly got the reaction she sought. Scott's entire body shuddered and he let out a cry as he climaxed. With a grin she released him, and wiping her mouth moved up to lie beside him. He looked flushed, and a dew of sweat covered his forehead.

"I'm sorry," he said, taking her in his arms, "it's been a while."

"For me, too," she kissed him. "My turn next time."

He grinned. "What makes you think I'm capable of a next time?"

"Oh, you'd be surprised." Pauline ran lazy fingers around his nipples and up and down his torso. "See?" she chuckled a couple of minutes later.

"Your turn indeed," he smiled, rolling her onto her back. He followed her example and experimented with all the ways he could use his tongue on her without touching her where she wanted it the most.

"You're cruel," she groaned, capturing him and wrapping her legs around him to make him stop.

"I learned from the best," he murmured and kissed her.

Finally he moved and entered her with a gentleness Pauline found unbearable. She let him treat her like fine porcelain at first as he moved slowly and tenderly, then she began to rock her hips to meet his. Their movements increased in intensity until Pauline could barely think but for the pleasure scorching her body.

Afterward, lying spent on the hard lab floor, she turned her head to study the sleeping Webster. At rest, he looked years younger with the worry lines smoothed away, his face matching his body's youthfulness. She wanted to remember every detail of this first and only time with him, for he would not remember it. He had left her little choice. With reluctance she finally extricated herself, moving to her workshop adjacent to the main lab. A few moments later she returned, a syringe in her hand. She kissed him as he slept then injected a lime-colored fluid into his neck. Disposing of the syringe she lay down beside him again and nuzzled her mouth against his ear. She kissed the lobe lightly, and then began to whisper. When all was said, she relaxed beside him and slept, knowing the drug ensured her suggestions were absolute. When Scott awoke, he would have no memory of their lovemaking, his time jump, or the lost 21st century woman. And in a few weeks they would meet their destiny on the Vallo *as planned.*

But she couldn't carry it through. She wanted more time with Scott and remained with him until he awoke. Now sitting here on the *Vallo*, she realized the enormity of her mistake. She should have left Webster alone after they'd made love, but she couldn't. He'd woken to find her beside him and at first reacted in horrified shock, thinking he'd acted inappropriately. She had assuaged his fear with the warmth of her body, and they had made love again.

Convinced his present illness had affected his memory, Scott felt all the more passionately about getting onto the *Vallo* before any other debilitating symptoms appeared. Now they were on board, so close to achieving all they'd worked for, but because of her, he might die. The drug had rearranged his DNA and was mutating. If she didn't find a way to reverse or halt the mutations, they would become cancerous and kill him.

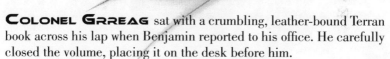

12

COLONEL GRREAG sat with a crumbling, leather-bound Terran book across his lap when Benjamin reported to his office. He carefully closed the volume, placing it on the desk before him.

Major Benjamin looked at the fading title along the spine. "The *Aeneid*, huh?"

"You have read it?"

"No, but I've heard of it." Benjamin sat opposite the Leontor. "Who hasn't been warned to 'beware of Greeks bearing Trojan horses'?"

Grreag growled softly. Not everything was as it appeared. Where would he find the wooden horse on board the *Vallo*? From where would the spy creep in the dark of night? An ear flicked toward Benjamin. "What's the status on the investigation, Major?"

"All six new crew members that we took on at our last turnover have clean records and glowing references. No hint of anti-Alliance affiliations." He crossed his legs, leaning back comfortably. "Of course, records can be altered."

"True." Grreag's claw traced the cracked leather binding on the old book. He told Benjamin about Catriona's reaction to the video test. "It may still be an act," he concluded.

"Obviously a convincing one," replied Benjamin.

Grreag nodded slowly, considering how far the Komodoans might go to steal Webster's research. When first contact had been made with the Realm, the unyielding reptoid aliens in their star-shaped warship did not give the unfortunate Leontor vessel a chance. They attacked without mercy, destroying their ship. A handful of devastated survivors were permitted to return in a cruiser as a warning. They brought horrific stories of how the lost crew had suffered torture, disembowelment, and flaying alive.

"Sir?" Benjamin's voice rang with concern.

Grreag realized he sat with his fists clenched, breathing hard. Appalled at his momentary lack of control, he swiftly pulled himself together. "Anything on Dr. Morrison?"

"Nothing significant. Born on Earth in the Naples Dome. Has a sister living, never married, no children. Sister lives in the Orly Dome, works as a botanist. No anti-Alliance connections, has never left Earth." He looked closely at Grreag. "Sir?"

Avoiding his gaze, Grreag growled, "Check out the sibling, although she doesn't sound like a candidate for espionage. What about Professor Webster? He's not a suspect?"

"Hardly, but I'm keeping an eye on him all the same."

"Interview the six new crew members without alerting suspicion," Grreag advised quietly. "Dismissed."

At Professor Webster's welcome reception, Catriona stood alone, watching the ebb and flow of guests around the professor. She didn't really feel like company but couldn't face her claustrophobic berth.

Chief Khumalo appeared beside her. "How are you doing?" She handed Catriona a flute of sparkling wine.

"Not bad for someone on death row," Catriona said, sharper than she meant to.

"Girlfriend, even if Leontor Control finds out about you, it doesn't mean they'll execute you. You may just undergo... rehabilitation."

Catriona snorted. "Exactly what does that mean?"

Khumalo shifted uncomfortably. "You'll forget your old life and remember a different past."

"Well," Catriona raised her flute, "maybe that's not such a bad thing. My past wasn't that great, anyway."

"Don't you have friends back there?"

Catriona stopped herself from snapping again; she shouldn't take out her distress on her new friend. She studied the depths of her glass, thinking about all the people who had died in 2001 while she had somehow leapt to the future.

"I left my closest friends behind years ago when I left Scotland. I've been on the move so much with one show or another, I haven't had much opportunity to make any more." She didn't say how transient friendships could be, born in theater life, and how lonely and disenchanted she'd felt in London. And with her parents gone, she had no one left in Scotland, either. Taking a sip from her flute, she wrinkled her nose. "This doesn't have much life to it, does it?"

"As per Alliance policy, it's only grape juice."

"What I wouldn't give for a decent drink."

Khumalo clinked her glass against Catriona's and moved on to continue circulating the room. Catriona decided to escape the reception. She saw little point in hanging around being miserable. As she picked her way toward the door, Colonel Grreag intercepted her.

"Where are you going?"

Catriona gritted her teeth. Having him witness her breakdown earlier had been mortifying. He had been so huge and solid; she had clung as tightly to him as though he were a life raft in a storm. Then she had soaked through his uniform and matted his fur with her tears.

His gentleness and kindness were what undid her. She thought she could have coped better with derision and scorn, but to have the big alien treat her so tenderly...

She felt near to tears again just by his proximity, and spoke sharply to cover it.

"I'm going to hijack the *Vallo* while everyone's busy. You don't mind, do you?"

Unfazed, he snorted. "You do not like social gatherings."

"Not today," she replied, surprised she hadn't riled him.

"Me neither. If we continue your stage fighting demonstration with blades, we may leave the function." To Catriona's hesitant nod, he instructed, "Wait here," and strode over to Major Benjamin.

The First Mate's face registered astonishment, and then he nodded, turning to wink at Catriona across the room. Grreag signaled for her to follow and they left the reception together.

They walked through the ship in companionable silence. Catriona

62 | *Time Twist*

listened to her own footsteps clunking on the metal floor, but Grreag made no noise at all, despite his bulk.

In the rec room, Catriona smothered a grin at the absence of the combat mannequins. Grreag removed his boots and lifted two epées from the wall. Stepping onto the mat, he faced her.

"Show me what you mean by 'illusion.'"

Catriona pulled off her boots and joined him, taking the offered epée. Grreag raised the blade up to his face and held it there, inches from his nose. Catriona realized he expected her to mirror the salute, so with a sense of dread, she did so. He whipped his blade diagonally down and Catriona emulated him. Holding blades toward each other, they took the en garde position. Grreag nodded for her to begin, so she lunged forward. She demonstrated a couple of thrusts to his chest, stopping short by a few safe inches.

"That's hardly effective," he criticized.

"That's why it's called stage fighting! We're not *supposed* to kill our fellow actors, you know. Even if some deserve it."

"I take it you know the moves, but do not touch the body?" She nodded. "Do not stop short; I will not permit the blade to touch me."

He thrust the sword at her chest and Catriona shifted her blade to parry. The force of his thrust threw her off balance and the epée flew from her grasp. She scurried to retrieve it.

"Try harder!" bellowed Grreag and lunged again.

Catriona met him, her anger fuelling a more forceful parry. She swept his sword off to the side, and quickly curved round with a backhand thrust for his kidneys. Grreag, forced to twist out of the way, looked at her with a new respect. She saw a gleam come into his eye and found herself grinning ear to ear.

"You have a natural aptitude for fencing," he announced, taking her epée and placing both weapons back on the wall.

"You didn't give me a chance to do much." Catriona wiped the sweat from her forehead.

"We'll do more in the next session."

They were to have another session? *Oh, dear God,* thought Catriona. Still, it beat the professor's reception and ghastly grape juice, anyway.

As they put their boots back on Catriona asked, "Is there anything other than juice and water to drink on this ship?"

The Leon shot her what could have been a grin, baring a yellowed fang. "A brew from Leontor called *ealu.* But it is too strong for humans."

"Maybe for this pampered lot," retorted Catriona, "but I'm willing to bet it couldn't be as strong as Scottish moonshine."

"Come." She followed him to his quarters, which turned out to be on the same corridor as her berth.

Once inside, she felt like she'd stepped into another world. Bathed in a golden glow from a huge central lamp, jagged and angular alien weaponry hung on all four walls. A blood-red tapestry rug covered most of the floor space, depicting a fierce battle. A Leon-sized bunk took up the length of one wall, and a small black table, set with a copper colored jug and two triangular cups beside it.

"That reminds me of the Japanese tea ceremony on Earth," she observed.

"Perhaps you would prefer tea to *ealu*?"

"If I wanted tea I'd go to the galley." She sat on one of two massive leather chairs facing each other over a low table, and Grreag moved the triangular cups onto the table.

Producing a liter-sized clay keg, he used a knife to unseal it. An ominous hiss sounded as steam rose from the liquid inside. Suspecting Grreag hoped for a negative reaction, Catriona prepared to keep her expression neutral as she brought the cup to her lips. Taking a sip, she looked incredulously at him. "It tastes like celery! I thought... haaaaa!"

The drink took effect. Her mouth felt as though it had come into contact with a particularly ferocious stinging nettle. As the pain subsided, she then experienced an interesting and not totally unpleasant sensation. A bit like suddenly dropping down a few feet, having left your stomach somewhere above your head.

"Whoa!" Second time around, the effect felt less painful.

Grreag sat in the chair opposite, pouring them both another cupful. Catriona curiously watched the Leon through her lashes. Sitting with his guard down, he looked so like her Beast from the show, she could almost imagine she were backstage with the cast, stealing an illicit tipple. She heard a sound and listened carefully, trying to identify it. A low rumbling vibration. She realized with a smile it came from within Grreag's chest as he purred like a giant domestic cat. *How adorable,* she thought, wondering what he'd do if she tried to pet him.

"But lions don't purr!" she blurted without thinking. The vibrations halted abruptly and she looked away, embarrassed.

"I am a *Leontor,*" he informed her. "We may look like your lions but we are assuredly not your lions, nor any of your Terran cats."

Catriona held her tongue. He looked exactly like a huge bipedal lion, except that Leontors didn't have tails.

64 | *Time Twist*

Anxious to change the subject she caught sight of a familiar-looking game across the room. "Do you play backgammon?"

He curled a lip. "Backgammon is for children. This is a strategy game for warriors."

Feeling mellow from the *ealu*, she suggested, "Would you like to show me how to play it?"

"No."

She slammed her cup onto the table. "Why are you always so rude?"

His eyes flashed and he contemplated for a moment, "You asked me if I would like to show you; I said I would not. Is that rude?"

Her brow creased. "Put like that, no."

"We have a lot to learn about our races," he rumbled, pouring them another cupful. "What is Scottish moonshine you referred to, earlier?"

"An illegally made wheat-based alcoholic spirit."

"Why illegal?"

"It's over 100% proof. If not made properly, it can blind or kill."

He grunted. "I would like to try it."

"This is much better," admitted Catriona, holding the cup to the light. It looked like a steaming Guinness. "My father used to drink nothing but Glenfiddich whisky. That's pretty good stuff, too."

"Your parents are dead, are they not?"

Catriona swooshed the *ealu* and drained the cup. Everyone she knew was dead.

"Yes," she answered curtly, hoping he wouldn't pry.

He cleared his throat. "I too, lost my parents young."

She looked at him, startled. The *ealu* had unleashed his tongue. He told her about his people's blood feud, and how an opposing clan assassinated his family. When they attacked, Grreag's mother hid him in the dark and filthy sewerage system. There the Leontor youngling had remained alone and terrified until his uncle's family found him. Grreag related the story in a cool, factual manner. Feeling empathy for him, Catriona had to admit to herself that her parents' quick death in a car accident was nothing in comparison. At least they had not suffered.

"I'm sorry," she murmured.

"I don't need your sympathy!"

"Colonel, do you ever let your guard down with anyone?"

He studied the figures on the rug at his feet. "One person. My mate." He rose, looking larger than life as his fur bristled. "A Komodoan captain killed her. But not before he had tortured her and taken her pelt."

His rage felt palpable to Catriona. She wished she had words of comfort, but she could think of nothing to say. Now at least she understood why he had such a barrier around his emotions. Grreag reached to refill their drinks. Catriona noticed he looked all blurry and wondered how much longer she should stay.

Grreag, intent on pouring the *ealu,* noticed his visitor had quietly passed out, toppling over where she sat. Amused, he lifted her legs onto the ample chair. Asleep, she looked so young and vulnerable. He would be very disappointed if she turned out to be a spy—she had been the first human who had ever made him smile.

13

WHEN GRREAG registered Major Benjamin's voice from the monitor, it took him a moment to speak. Opening his mouth, his throat felt as though he had swallowed a Terran rabbit whole. Sitting up, he cleared his throat.

"Grreag here."

"Sorry to intrude, Sir. We're waiting for you in your office."

The Leon remembered he'd called an early meeting. "On my way."

He bounded from the bunk, and discovered he was already fully dressed. His eyes darted to the chairs. Empty. Catriona must have slipped out in the night. The cover he had thrown over her lay back on his bunk. With a growl he remembered how much they had drunk in a short time. No wonder once he began to talk he couldn't stop! Hopefully the human would have been too inebriated to remember much.

He arrived at his office in minutes, joining Benjamin and Khumalo.

"Thank you for coming so promptly," he said without an apology. "Last night I received a further communication from Rrara of Suzerain, ordering us to suspend Professor Webster's experiments. No reason given."

"How did the professor react?" asked Benjamin.

"I've held off informing him."

Benjamin frowned. "Shall I call him and Dr. Morrison in for questioning, Colonel?"

"Negative. If we do that the Komodoan operative will go deeper under cover."

66 | *Time Twist*

"Professor Webster's supposed to scan Catriona today, Sir," said Khumalo.

"Permit him to do that, but keep him from the hyperdrive engines."

"With pleasure."

✦

Catriona became aware of something interrupting her slumber. She groaned and batted it away. The something grew more persistent. Opening one eye she saw Khumalo, gently shaking her from sleep.

"What?" Catriona squinted at the light.

"Sorry, Haggis, but I was worried. I thought you might need medical attention."

Catriona forced herself fully awake. "For a hangover? Don't be daft!"

"You're not injured, then?"

Catriona sat up in the bunk, her head reeling. "Do I look injured?"

"I guess not." The engineer appeared disappointed. "I thought..." She broke off, grinning.

"What?"

"You were seen leaving Grreag's quarters in a bit of a state, last night. We thought you and he might have, well... had sex."

Catriona's hangover suddenly vanished. With a shock she remembered waking up on Grreag's chair, with him snoring like a hog across the room. She couldn't remember ever having felt so ill in her entire life; not even from eating Leontor food.

"Oh, Uzi!" she groaned, "I passed out on him after only a couple of drinks of Leontor *ealu*. I had to rush to my berth to throw up!"

Khumalo laughed, perching on the edge of the bunk. "Well, that makes a lot more sense. Pity though, a lot of people are due to lose a fat lot of cash if you didn't sleep with him."

"What do you mean?"

"Uh, it wasn't my idea. Some of us bet on whether you did or didn't." She ducked as Catriona thumped her with a pillow.

"Why would I need medical attention if I had slept with him? Is he too big or something?"

Khumalo collapsed in laughter. "Barbs," she managed finally.

"Where?"

"Where do you think?"

"Oh, Lord. Ouch."

"Exactly. Anyway, you'd better get a move on. Professor Webster's waiting for you."

"I'll be right with you."

Catriona spritzed and dressed in record time, heading out with Khumalo for the lab. There were a lot more people about than usual, and they had to wait to climb on the moving ladder. Catriona maneuvered her way onto it after two crewmen jumped off, grinning openly at her.

"Why is everyone staring at me?"

"Why do you think? News travels fast on a ship this size."

Khumalo left Catriona at the lab and went on to engineering. Professor Webster hadn't arrived yet, but Dr. Morrison awaited her.

"Sorry I'm so late," said Catriona, "I overslept."

"Yes, I heard." The doctor gave her a penetrating look. She held an object in her hands that resembled a hand-held vacuum cleaner.

"Is that the recalibrated scanner?" asked Catriona.

Morrison ran her fingers over it. "Yes." Walking to the diagnostic chair, she swung it round, inviting Catriona to sit. "We may as well get started."

Resignedly, Catriona obeyed, stretching out on the chair. She flinched as Morrison slid the chair restraints in place.

"This'll just take a moment," said Morrison and she placed the scanner against Catriona's forehead and switched it on.

Catriona reared her head away and cried out. "You haven't fixed it; it still hurts!"

Morrison pushed the scanner against her temple again. "Lie still; it'll only hurt a moment."

"Hey!" Catriona twisted her head away and managed to squeeze one wrist free from the arm restraints. She levered her other arm out and manually slid back the ones round her ankles.

She scrambled to her feet. Morrison looked furious and for a moment Catriona thought she was going to physically stop her from leaving. She bolted through the dilating door and onto the ladder. Dr. Morrison had to have known the scan would hurt her. It had felt like it would crush her skull.

On the next level, Catriona heard Colonel Grreag shouting orders. She jumped off the ladder and followed the sound, ignoring the curious glances shot at her as she passed.

She found the Leon in a small office, studying a hologram of the *Vallo's* interior.

"What do you want?" he demanded, stopping his dictation and switching off the display.

Getting used to his brusqueness, Catriona didn't take offense. "Firstly, I wanted to get away from Dr. Morrison and secondly-"

"Why did you want to get away from Dr. Morrison?"

"Well, maybe it was a mistake but I felt she hurt me deliberately with that scanner."

His ears flickered. "Why would she do that?"

"I don't know."

Grreag studied her then nodded, his face darkening. "I will check it out." He waited, then prompted, "And secondly..."

"Well, I wondered how you were doing today."

"Why?" He regarded her from under his bushy eyebrows.

She tried not to grin. "I expect you've heard about the rumors going around the ship." His expression didn't change. "Oh, come on," Catriona pulled out a chair from the wall and sat. "I'm sure not much happens on this ship without your knowledge."

"Yes, I am aware of the rumors."

"It's amazing, isn't it? No matter how far one comes through time and space, human nature remains the same. Always prepared to jump to the wrong conclusions." She laughed, realizing she sounded as though she excluded herself from the human race. She noticed he studied her with an odd expression. "What?"

"You understand there is no possibility of coupling between a Leontor and a human?"

Catriona blinked. "What makes you think I would consider something like that?"

Grreag's ears flattened. "I want to ensure there are no misunderstandings."

"Typical!" shouted Catriona. "A person can't have a male friend without people getting the wrong idea. I didn't think it would extend to a damn bloody alien!" She stalked from the office.

Pauline Morrison reset the lab in preparation for Catriona's return. She would tranquilize the girl next time so she wouldn't feel any pain as Morrison extracted the data from her brain. And she'd add some of the memory drug, so that if Catriona survived the scanning, she wouldn't recall it. Angry that she had not thought of it before, she got out a vial and syringe, placing them on the bench behind the diagnostic chair.

Getting herself a measure of water she sat down at the computer and became engrossed in the hyperdrive specs.

"May I?" came a voice.

Startled, she spilled water on the desk as Sam Benjamin appeared by her side.

"Of course," she answered stiffly, and he sat on a nearby stool.

"I enjoyed the reception last night." He smiled.

Morrison hardly heard him. Her mind mulled over what she must do next. If she could get Catriona Logan back right away and scan her, she could implement the knowledge immediately, allowing the project to be completed ahead of schedule.

"We're not going to have as much time together as I thought," continued Benjamin. "How about joining me for a drink tonight?"

"Not as much time? Why?"

"The *Vallo* is almost a full day ahead of schedule, and-"

"A day?"

"Yes." He gave her a quizzical look.

By the stars, a day? That meant she had only four hours left!

"What's the matter?" Benjamin's voice interrupted.

Morrison shook her head. "Nothing."

"I see you've enough on your mind without me badgering you," he said tightly and strode from the lab.

That was stupid, she chastised herself. It was not in her best interest to alienate the First Mate of the *Vallo*. Her hand curled into a fist, nails digging into her palm. She would have to force Catriona to undergo the scanning right away.

As though on cue, the door dilated and Catriona entered. "Oh," she halted, seeing Morrison. "The Professor's not back, yet?"

Morrison rose, smiling. She had to win back the girl's trust. "Catriona, I'm very sorry the scanner hurt you, earlier. I've fixed the problem now."

Catriona hesitated. "That's okay. Sorry if I overreacted."

"Thank you. This data is very important. Can we try again?" She watched a gamut of expressions sweep Catriona's face.

"All right, then," agreed the redhead, "let's get it over with." Catriona crossed to the diagnostic chair, flopping onto it. "But no restraints, okay?"

Morrison nodded. Going to the bench she removed the syringe from its sterilized pack and drew a double dose of tranquilizer into it. Taking a smaller vial from a pocket in her jumpsuit, she added a measure of lime-colored memory drug to the mix. Excitement coursed through her as she turned from the bench, ready to inject Catriona in the neck. In

70 | *Time Twist*

a couple of minutes, she would have the temporal data.

The lab doors burst open and Professor Webster appeared. "There's something funny going on, Pauline!"

Heart beating fast, she hid the syringe down by her thigh. "What do you mean?"

"They won't let me near the hyperdrive, nor will they give me any reasonable explanation."

"Can I go, then?" asked Catriona.

"Yes, thank you, Catriona," said Webster. "We'll let you know when we're ready to proceed."

Morrison had no choice but to comply. She watched in frustration as Catriona jumped to her feet and exited the lab.

"What's going on, Scott?" Morrison demanded.

"I'm scheduled to talk to Major Benjamin about it right now. I'll be back." He strode off, leaving Morrison alone again.

She felt utterly impotent. All she needed was Catriona's brain data! Just two meager minutes to finally complete the project of ten years!

She couldn't wait any longer. Slipping the tranquilizer syringe into a leg pocket, she tucked the scanner into her belt and left the lab.

Stepping off the ladder on Catriona's deck, Morrison came face to face with Colonel Grreag. Of all people on the ship to blunder into!

"Excuse me," she mumbled, stepping aside.

"Good day, Dr. Morrison," intoned the Leon, blocking her. He pointed to the object in her belt. "What is this?"

Morrison clamped down on her temper. If only she had brought a blaster she could put an end to his meddling forever. Forcing a smile, she answered. "The scanner we'll be using on Catriona. She's been nervous about it, so I thought I'd let her see it to reassure her it's perfectly safe."

Grreag watched her, waiting for her to continue. She said nothing more and attempted to pass again. The Leon bent his craggy face close to hers.

"She does not wish to be disturbed."

Morrison took a step back. "Never mind. I'll see her later." She turned away.

To her fury, the Leon fell into step beside her. "I will escort you back to the lab."

"There's no need, thank you."

"I believe there is." His tone was final.

"If you insist." Curse the Leontor filth!

14

SAM BENJAMIN sat at a table in the galley and drummed his fingers beside an empty glass. He'd come no closer to routing out the Komodoan spy, and Catriona Logan, the obvious suspect, was most likely not the operative. Professor Webster, outraged and uncooperative because Khumalo would not let him near her engines, was also unlikely.

His thoughts drifted to Dr. Morrison. She was upset about something. If she'd only tell him what, Benjamin could help. Apart from the personal interest he had in her, as First Mate he had a right to know if something were amiss. He wondered if Morrison had an idea why Suzerain Research had prohibited further experiments. That could explain her distracted manner. He checked the time. Late, but not too late to talk to her again. Standing, he swung a leg over the chair, heading for the door.

In the corridor he bumped into Chief Khumalo, coming the other way.

"Hey," he said with a grin. "What are you doing sneaking about here?"

The engineer shifted, not meeting his eyes. "Just coming off duty." She clutched a silver attaché case close to her.

"What do you have there?" he asked. She did not look herself at all.

"Excuse me." She passed him, dilating the door to her berth.

"Hey, Uzi." What was it with everyone tonight? Benjamin followed her and stood in the dilated doorway. "What's the matter?" He reached out to touch her arm.

Pulling away, Khumalo lost her grip on the case. It clattered to the floor, bursting open. Benjamin looked in astonishment at an array of tools and explosives spilled onto the floor.

Before he knew what had happened, she'd pulled him inside the berth and he felt a stabbing pain below his left ear. Clamping his hand to his neck, he ripped a syringe out. Most of the lime-colored fluid had been discharged. Staring at the needle, his mind clouded. *What happened? Everything looked out of focus...*

"Major Benjamin," came Khumalo's voice in his ear.

"Yes?" he heard himself answer. His voice sounded disjointed as though it belonged to someone else.

"You will obey my every instruction without question," she continued. "Understand?"

72 | *Time Twist*

"Yes." Moving as though his limbs were underwater, he followed her from the room.

Catriona could not stand being cooped up in her berth one moment longer. She still felt unsettled by Dr. Morrison's behavior in the lab, and here there was nothing to take her mind off it. She wondered if Uzi were off duty yet. Slipping out into the corridor, she saw Uzi's door dilate, and the engineer herself stepped out, her back to Catriona. *Brilliant timing*, thought Catriona, about to call out. Then she watched Uzi pull someone after her.

Catriona's eyes widened at the sight of Major Benjamin stumbling into the corridor. The furtive way Uzi led him made Catriona hesitate from calling out and she ducked back into her doorway. By the time she peered out again, the two had disappeared. Something wasn't right. Catriona discreetly followed and watched them approach a chatting group of crewmembers, apparently just off duty. *Surely they'll see something's wrong*, Catriona thought. Suddenly, Khumalo and Benjamin had their arms round each other, kissing with open-mouthed abandonment.

The crewmembers fell silent. After they had turned down another passageway, Catriona could hear their speculative laughter. Hesitating, she almost turned back, but something compelled her to continue.

Scurrying after them, she found the corridor empty. She checked the doors around her but none opened. The corridor ended with a huge circular door in the wall, which dilated at her approach.

Stepping through the vast iris, she found herself in what must have been the *Vallo's* cruiser launch pad. She hadn't been permitted access to this part of the ship before. She was about ten feet above the pad — below she could see the topsides of two white arrow-shaped cruisers.

Deciding she had better call Colonel Grreag, she turned back but the door remained shut, locking her inside the launch pad. A few yards to her left stood a small control cubicle, sealed off from the pad for when it lay open to the vacuum of space. Perhaps she could contact Grreag from there. Tiptoeing forward, she held her breath as the cubicle door whispered open.

Through its window she caught sight of Uzi below in the launch pad, crouched by the outer hatch. About to knock on the glass, Catriona froze, fist aloft. By Uzi's feet lay a lifeless security guard. Around her neck swung Morrison's silver locket holding Professor Webster's disk.

Colonel Grreag entered the control cabin in time to hear of the launch pad emergency. He nodded to Lieutenant Larrar, who sat at NavOps, to take over TactOps. The young Leontor did so as a high-pitched beep sounded from the station.

"Colonel," she reported, "we can't access the launch pad, it's being blocked."

Grreag's ears flicked in frustration. He touched a computer monitor beside the command chair to link to Engineering.

"Chief Khumalo?" he boomed.

An accented male voice replied, "This is Second Engineer Lieutenant Leopold: the Chief's gone off-duty, Sir."

"Have her report to the control cabin, and find out why we can't access the launch pad. Get a team down there to slice through the door if you have to."

A few seconds later, Leopold's voice filtered back through to the control cabin. "Colonel, our traherence stream has been inverted and is blocking the launch pad."

Grreag scowled. Traherence was used to guide cruisers into the launch pad. "Can you shut it down from there?"

"I think so."

"Do it." Grreag's stomach churned. "Lock down outer launch pad door immediately," he ordered Lieutenant Larrar.

The female Leon's hands worked rapidly at her panel. "Colonel, the door won't respond."

"Keep trying!" Grreag's hackles rippled all down his spine. The spy had considered every eventuality.

15

CATRIONA STARED in disbelief as Chief Khumalo turned away from the outer hatch. Her friend looked totally unlike herself; her movements staccato, her sleek black cornrows escaping in a wild frizz. Why did Uzi have Webster's disk? Catriona knew that if the enemy got hold of it, the repercussions would be disastrous.

Catriona took a deep breath, steadying herself. She must be able

74 | *Time Twist*

to contact Colonel Grreag from here. Moving to the control panel, she peered at the complicated display. She stabbed a finger at a few keys, but the word **unauthorized** kept appearing on the monitor. Frustrated, she thumped a fist hard on the panel. A klaxon sounded shrilly in the launch pad below.

Horrified, Catriona looked back at Uzi, but she'd vanished. She heard the cubicle door slide open and in a panic, launched herself at the opposite door. Jumping through the iris to a railed observation platform above the pad, she found herself backed into a corner as Khumalo followed her.

"Uzi, what are you doing?" She hardly recognized her friend in those empty eyes. Catriona edged back as far as she could, putting her spine against the railing. "Don't come any closer."

Khumalo lunged and Catriona managed to twist aside. Instinctively she hit back, aiming for Khumalo's solar plexus. The engineer easily parried. Off balance, Catriona followed through, lashing out with her left fist. Khumalo huffed in pain as Catriona's cat ring cut into her face. A white slit appeared along her cheek, a shred of ebony skin peeling away.

Khumalo clapped a hand over the tear and made an incoherent sound through her clenched teeth. She punched Catriona right in the jaw. Catriona staggered against the railing. Another blow crunched into her, forcing her into a haphazard somersault over the rail. She grappled for a handhold but missed and hit the launch pad floor with a bone-jarring thud. Pain ripped through her left arm. Cradling the arm, she stumbled to her feet, and blinking back tears dodged around a cruiser to try and reach the main door.

Khumalo jumped down and tackled her, snapping Catriona's head back by grabbing her long hair. Catriona jabbed an elbow behind her and Khumalo sucked in sharply. Spinning around, Catriona aimed her fist to hit the engineer across the face. Blood spurted through Khumalo's fingers as she clutched her nose.

Catriona yanked the locket from Khumalo's neck, snapping the silver chain. The engineer reacted fast. Grabbing her with both hands she shoved Catriona up against the cruiser. Clutching the pendant in her right fist, Catriona stood trapped, breathing hard.

"You can hold the disk if you like," hissed Khumalo, her lips almost touching Catriona's, "for I'm taking you both to Komodoa." She toppled her into the cruiser through its open hatchway.

Catriona fell hard, banging her head on the floor. She lost her grip on the pendant and heard it skitter away somewhere close. Khumalo jumped in after her and moved to the control panel.

Intent on stopping Khumalo, Catriona tried to pull herself to a sitting position. Pain lanced through her left arm and she fell back. Rolling onto her side she began to clamber to her feet. She couldn't believe her friend would betray Colonel Grreag and everyone on the *Vallo*.

The cruiser hatch began to close. Catriona realized she'd never make it out in time. But she had to do something to stop Khumalo. Panicked, she looked around for the fallen locket containing the disk but couldn't see it. The hatch had almost closed. In desperation, she tugged the silver cat ring off her finger.

"Uzi, here's your bloody disk, you bitch!" She threw the ring in an arc toward the opening. Holding her breath she watched light glint on the metal as it neatly curved through the crack of the closing hatchway, bouncing out onto the launch pad.

Eyes blazing, Khumalo rounded on Catriona, an arm raised to strike her. Catriona shifted backwards. An explosion lit up the cruiser windows and Catriona saw the main hatch to the landing pad collapse out into space. Khumalo veered back to the control panel and took the cruiser up and out through the blown hatch.

The acceleration tossed Catriona backwards. She rolled against a black-colored sack, wrapped around what looked like a body. Something glinted near it. Her heart pounded when she recognized the silver pendant. Checking that Khumalo had returned to the panel, she reached shaking fingers to retrieve the pendant and flipped it open to reveal Webster's disk inside. Where could she hide it? Looking at it in her palm, she realized it was no bigger than an antacid tablet. Steeling herself, she shoved the disk into her mouth, forcing enough saliva to swallow it. She pushed the empty pendant out of sight under one of the seats.

In the *Vallo* control cabin, Grreag froze in alarm as a shudder went through the ship. "Report," he ordered.

Lieutenant Larrar announced, "The launch pad hatch was blown and a cruiser launched, Sir."

"Identify the pilot."

A second explosion sounded through the ship. "Incendiary device in main environmental column," reported Larrar. "Backup fully functional."

Grreag's ears flattened and the fur bristled all over his body. Thank the Fang he had insisted on the Alliance installing that backup column, and to the winds with the expense. Chief Khumalo had not reported in,

76 | *Time Twist*

which concerned him. Grreag did not like this. Not one little bit.

"Find out who's on that cruiser, Lieutenant!" he roared.

The *Vallo's* proximity alarm shrilled. On the viewer the menacing star-shape of a Komodoan Realm warship spun into range, its array of destroyers seriously outgunning the *Vallo*. Anger surged through Grreag.

"Put up armor. Is Traherence available yet?"

"Affirmative."

"Use it to haul that cruiser back!"

Lieutenant Larrar shook her head in frustration. "The Komodoan ship is blocking traherence. We don't have enough power to break the signal."

"Reroute power from other systems, but get that cruiser back here!"

Lieutenant Leopold entered the cabin, his swarthy features clouded and pinched with tension. He wore a yarmulke on the back of his head.

"Report!" snarled Grreag.

"We've contained the fire in environmental and patched the breach in the launch pad. All crew accounted for except Chief Khumalo and Major Benjamin."

Grreag hesitated fractionally. "Civilians?"

"Computer model doesn't register Catriona Logan or Dr. Morrison."

Grreag snarled. One of the females was the Komodoan operative, but which one? His head pounded as rage surged through him. Just let him get his hands on the spy, to feel the hated reptoid life choking away... He took hold of himself.

"Take NavOps," he ordered Leopold.

"I've got three life-signs on board the cruiser," reported Larrar.

On the screen, the minute white shape of the cruiser floated between the *Vallo* and the looming five-pointed hexagram of the enemy ship.

Three life signs? Grreag studied the warship. Were both Morrison and Catriona spies? He had been so intent in searching for a single agent; he had overlooked the possibility of accomplices. He obviously had intercepted and prevented a clandestine meeting between Morrison and Catriona earlier. How could Catriona have fooled him so completely? Even Professor Webster had been taken in by the deception.

A low growl escaped him. "Fire on the cruiser on my signal, Lieutenant." Grreag waited, "Now!"

Larrar slammed her palm against the TactOps panel. Two orange pellets zoomed from the *Vallo*, converging on the cruiser. A fireball lit the screen. When it evaporated, the cruiser had gone.

"The warship has us in sight," warned Larrar. A red light flickered on her console. "Incoming!"

A white streak soared through space. The control cabin lights flickered and the ship shuddered from a sharp, forceful impact. The enemy ship spun toward the *Vallo*, another volley of fire ripping into the hull.

The viewer crackled and blurred, then the Komodoan commander's image appeared. Grreag smelled fear from the humans at the sight of the scaled face, and he recognized Captain T'alak at once. Rage boiled through him. T'alak was the captain who had sent back his mate's flayed, mutilated corpse. He forced himself under control, vowing that his day for revenge would come, and focused his full attention on the viewer.

The Komodoan smirked. "How impressive you appear, Colonel Grreag. I look forward to laying your pelt on my great room floor." His dark eyes insolently eyed the Leon. "Prepare to be boarded."

"Captain," Grreag sneered, "your warship is alone in Alliance territory and the Armada is on its way. You can't hope to take all our pelts as trophies."

"No, Colonel, I just want yours."

T'alak terminated the communication and the viewer showed the vast Komodoan warship once again.

"Lieutenant Larrar," snarled Grreag, "establish contact with the nearest Komodoan base!"

"We need more power to reach that far, Colonel."

"Take it from Actuation and the traherence stream." They weren't any use while the Komodoan warship had the ability to block them.

Larrar worked at her console. "Got it," she reported.

"Transmit this message and be sure T'alak picks it up. 'From *Vallo* A-C to Leontor/Terran Alliance Headquarters. Acknowledge dispatch of Alliance Armada from sector nine-one-point-two. Targets confirmed: Komodoan Realm outer defense outposts.'"

Grreag ground his teeth and watched the Komodoan ship with its destroyers trained on the *Vallo*. Without warning the warship tilted, vanishing from view as it spun away from Alliance space.

Grreag stared at the void the ship had left. His ears stayed tense and flat.. He may have outsmarted T'alak's immediate attack, but the Komodoans could well have Professor Webster's hyperdrive weapon data.

From TactOps Larrar announced, "Incoming communication for you from Alliance Headquarters, Sir."

"On screen."

"It's stamped personal, Colonel."

"I said on screen!"

Admiral Prreaka's face filled the viewer. "Colonel Grreag, we've received a communication from the Komodoan warship *L'umina*. The operative has identified herself as Chief Uzima Khumalo."

Thunderstruck, Grreag growled, "The Fang knows my Chief is no Komodoan spy!"

Prreaka's whiskers dipped in sympathy. "I'm forwarding the communication to you." As a disheveled, hollow-eyed Khumalo replaced him.

"Forgive me," she said, "you have become like family to me, but I have a higher purpose, which I must fulfill…"

COMMANDER A'RLON waited in the *L'umina* actuate chamber to supervise Agent Y'alenon's retrieval from the *Vallo* cruiser. He wondered how Captain T'alak's long-awaited encounter with the Alliance vessel had fared. T'alak would never be satisfied, no matter how many Terran and Leontor commanders he destroyed.

As a shape materialized within the actuate bubble, A'rlon raised an eyebrow when an inert black shape appeared. He nodded to the technician who created another bubble. A few seconds later he stood face to face with a dark-skinned human, who looked half-crazed. Flesh hung in torn shreds from her face and red human blood spattered her face and clothes. Panting with exertion, she grasped an unconscious human female slumped against her. A'rlon studied them with interest. He had not been advised that humans were boarding.

The feral-looking female let the other drop to the floor and gave A'rlon a smart Realm salute; hand over heart with her eyes modestly lowered.

"Agent Y'alenon greets you, honorable Commander," she said formally.

He bent his head in acknowledgment and pointed at the black sack. "What is in that?"

"A human female; a gift for the honorable Captain."

A'rlon considered for a moment. T'alak did not much care for surprises, but an alien female might be a welcome distraction. "And this one?" He gestured to the other girl, unconscious at Y'alenon's feet.

He saw the agent had trouble answering. She made eye contact with him then quickly looked away. "You have the data?" he inquired quietly.

"No," she blurted, fighting to maintain composure.

A'rlon's tail twitched incredulously. "Why did you signal if you were not ready?"

"I had Webster's disk until this human filth got in my way. She threw the disk out of the cruiser when it was too late to retrieve it."

"You saw it fall?"

"Yes. However, the human will be of more use than any disk." A'rlon raised a skeptical eyebrow. "Professor Webster himself inadvertently brought her through time from 21st century Earth. He's convinced she holds the key to the completion of his work on the temporal weapon. He was about to use a neural scanner to extract the data from her brain patterns."

A'rlon glanced at the prostrate human. "Interesting. If we can extract this information, then you have done better than we hoped." He watched relief flood through Y'alenon and addressed the guards, "Take both humans to the Infirmary." As they obeyed he looked distastefully at the agent. "Have the Medical Officer repair your face," he ordered and strode out of the actuate chamber.

A'rlon entered the flight deck to find a furious T'alak.

"I underestimated the Leontor filth," he hissed. "But I will be back for Colonel Grreag when the Armada is not there to protect him, make no mistake."

A'rlon resisted pointing out that T'alak should not have disobeyed General B'alarg's orders in the first place. Stars above knew what consequences awaited them on Komodoa.

He murmured, "Pride goeth before a fall."

T'alak's tail curled. "Another Terran saying, my friend? But enough! We should head back to the Realm quickly."

"It would have a certain logic to do so," concurred A'rlon dryly.

He felt T'alak's eyes on him. T'alak may call him friend but A'rlon knew he was ever watchful for betrayal. Years ago in a moment of heady wine recklessness, T'alak had confessed to A'rlon he had committed treason.

T'alak's son T'alak-zan had been born with his tail paralyzed. By Komodoan law all imperfect offspring were euthanized, but T'alak had bought the services of a surgeon to remedy his baby son's affliction, and then executed the surgeon.

If the Realm learned of it, T'alak-zan would be quietly disposed of and T'alak exiled. A'rlon knew T'alak regretted the confession; their friendship had become strained thereafter. That T'alak had not killed him after telling him, let A'rlon know he probably still trusted him to a degree. But T'alak capitulated to A'rlon far more than he would if A'rlon did not carry this knowledge.

"The agent is aboard?" asked T'alak.

"I believe you'll be most interested in her briefing."

Y'alenon joined them in the Tactics Chamber wearing a new gray Realm uniform, and the last of the dark human-clone mask removed. A'rlon approved. She looked much more like the Komodoan officer she purported to be. Facial scales back in place, and her sleek, black hair and eyes restored to their natural color, Y'alenon appeared calm and competent. Although A'rlon thought she looked off-color, and off balance due to the absence of tail. The Medical Officer's talents did not run to tail grafting; the agent would have to wait until their return to the Realm.

As A'rlon expected, when T'alak learned Y'alenon hadn't brought the disk, he reacted violently.

"How could you let a mere human outwit you? What use have we for a civilian, except perhaps, for the pleasure of torture?"

A'rlon remonstrated, "Captain, hear Y'alenon out."

T'alak's tail lashed. "You have one chance to escape execution," he informed the agent.

She swallowed, lowering her eyes. A'rlon thought he understood what she must be going through. After ten Earth years masquerading as a human, she probably thought like one of them now. T'alak's ruthlessness would be a shock. She had most likely forgotten a Komodoan officer could take her life just because he felt like it. He watched her control her fear as she reported on the details of Webster's temporal hyperdrive bubble. Neither officer reacted as she spoke. A'rlon felt her nervousness increase at their silence.

"We can still create the weapon without the disk," she finished in a rush.

"What is to stop the Alliance creating it, too?" demanded T'alak.

"They couldn't do it as quickly as we can with the human female. In her we have the one essential link they needed to complete the project."

T'alak's tail swept the floor. "I want to see this essential link for myself. I hope for your hide you speak the truth."

He marched out. A'rlon followed and Y'alenon trailed behind.

On Realm warships, infirmaries were more of a courtesy than an actual area to aid the sick or injured. Technically, it was well enough equipped, but the attitude toward personnel in battle was to allow them to die with grace.

T'alak swept into the Infirmary and stopped between the two diagnostic ledges on either side of the chamber, against each respective wall. The ledges were about the usual height of a bed and the two humans occupied both. The green atmospheric mist and humidity swirled more intensely here than on any other part of the ship.

The Medical Officer bowed to T'alak, gesturing to the red-haired human. "I've cleaned up the physical injuries. Just a broken bone in the left arm, concussion, and minor surface contusions."

A'rlon stood behind T'alak, gazing on the girl's face. It was a long time since he had set eyes on a human female. Even marred by her injuries she looked stunning. Her skin was almost luminous, set off by her unusual mane of erubescent hair.

T'alak hissed an order, and Agent Y'alenon tapped the human's face, reviving her.

Catriona's eyes snapped open and focused on a figure leaning over her. She saw the scaled forehead and gasped in shock.

"Uzi?" Her voice came out like a squeak.

"I am Y'alenon."

Catriona raised herself to her elbows, wincing at a stab of pain in her arm. "Where's Uzi?"

"I wore a mask, you fool."

Catriona felt like all the air had gone from her lungs. She realized they weren't in the cruiser. She smelled an odd scent like damp catnip, and green-hued lights along the walls cast an eerie glow.

"Where am I?" she faltered, afraid of the answer.

Y'alenon stepped aside so that Catriona could see the two Komodoan officers. Catriona sat bolt upright. Appalled, she found herself naked except for an olive-colored leather brace on her left forearm and a whisper of silver cloth barely covering her body. She clutched it, gaping at the aliens' grim, saturnine features.

"Captain T'alak and Commander A'rlon of the Komodoan Realm Fleet," announced Y'alenon with a bow.

Catriona forgot to breathe. Komodoans. These were the aliens who... who ate humans. The sight of their long, scaled tails curling down to their ankles made her flesh crawl. Captain T'alak's tail undulated lithely, like a snake swaying. Terror filled Catriona and she stared in

82 | *Time Twist*

horrified fascination as A'rlon's forked tongue slithered across his lips. Swallowing heavily, she huddled under the sparse cover.

"What the hell?" came a strident female voice.

Could it really be? Catriona craned to see past the Komodoans. "Uzi?"

Chief Khumalo lay on the ledge across the room, struggling from the confines of the black sack Catriona had seen in the cruiser. Catriona felt pure joy course through her as she realized her friend was not a traitor. Outrage took over just as swiftly.

"You lied!" she shouted at Y'alenon, scrambling to get up from the ledge. "You made me think you were Uzi!"

Y'alenon ignored her. Drawing a firearm from under her tunic she marched over to Khumalo and menaced it at her.

"Catriona, don't move," warned Khumalo urgently, "don't make eye contact." Catriona halted and glanced at the two silent males, then looked away.

"What do you want with her?" demanded Khumalo, indicating Catriona. "She's a civilian."

"Don't bother to deceive us," sneered Y'alenon, "I was Pauline Morrison; I know the human's worth."

"Worth?" hissed T'alak contemptuously, "what can a civilian possibly know of importance?"

Catriona looked into his glittering, dark eyes and her blood ran cold. She saw something move in their depths, and he must have sensed her fear for a sneer twisted across his face. He studied her, poised and silent, the way a cobra might try to hypnotize its victim before striking.

"Leave her alone," Khumalo snapped, "she knows nothing."

"Be silent!" Y'alenon raised her firearm and pistol-whipped Khumalo across the head. Red blood spurted from the wound and Khumalo drooped back on her ledge.

Catriona surged to her feet shouting, "No!" Clutching her cloth tightly she tried to run to her hurt friend.

T'alak stepped in her path and backhanded her across the face. Catriona staggered back and lost her balance, the ledge breaking her fall. Her long hair swung loose, getting in her eyes. Head reeling, she fought against passing out and sat on the ledge, feet steadying her on the floor. She took a deep breath, trying to ignore the stinging across her cheekbone.

Commander A'rlon spoke. "May I suggest you remove the Alliance human? Her presence is distracting this one."

T'alak signaled to Y'alenon, who prodded Khumalo with her carbine.

Catriona watched in dismay as a Komodoan soldier entered and jostled Khumalo to her feet.

"Don't take her away!" begged Catriona.

Khumalo's head snapped up and she looked right at Catriona. "I'll be all right, Haggis—"

Y'alenon thrust her weapon hard against the engineer's ribs. Khumalo turned and kicked Y'alenon's carbine aside. Twisting she elbowed the guard and yanked the weapon from his belt. She and Y'alenon leveled the carbines at each other. Time appeared to freeze for a moment. Catriona glanced at T'alak and A'rlon but neither carried a weapon.

With his humorless smile T'alak moved to stand in front of Catriona's ledge. "What now, earthworm?" he asked Khumalo.

Catriona slid back from him but he caught her wrist.

"All right, man, all right," Khumalo raised both arms and the soldier snatched back his carbine. He and Y'alenon hauled her away.

"What's going to happen to her?" demanded Catriona.

T'alak raised his hand. She flinched but he only lifted a handful of her hair, rubbing it between his fingers.

"I have never seen human hair this color," he hissed.

Catriona forced herself not to panic. Looking T'alak in the eye had inflamed him—no wonder Uzi had told her not to make eye contact. She kept her gaze lowered and concentrated on T'alak's tail, which undulated from side to side as evenly as a slow metronome.

"The gene that causes red hair and freckling is extinct, to my knowledge of human genetics," said A'rlon.

"Proof she's from the past." T'alak tipped his hand so her hair flowed through his fingers.

Catriona felt nauseous at the sight of the scales on the back of his hand. Her thoughts flew to the *Vallo*, wondering if they knew she was here, if they'd rescue her.

Without realizing, she found herself looking straight into Captain T'alak's tenebrous eyes. He met her gaze and tore the cloth from her. She reached to cover herself but he easily plucked her hands away and restrained her. She squirmed and kicked, and he sibilated a laugh as he pushed a leg between her thighs. His tail snaked round and grasped her left ankle. Holding her wrists with one hand T'alak put his other behind Catriona's rump and pulled her against him.

Huffing with the effort Catriona tried to wrench free of his horrible touch. Her ineffectual struggling only succeeded in arousing him and he pushed her onto her back on the ledge. In panic Catriona twisted her head and bit down on his hand as hard as she could. He hissed but didn't release her. Catriona bit even harder and T'alak shifted a hand to her throat. He applied pressure on her windpipe and Catriona choked for breath, clawing at his hand.

Commander A'rlon moved into her line of sight. "We need her alive."

Then she realized her arms were free. Pulling back her right arm she jabbed her outstretched fingers at T'alak's eyes. With a sharp hiss he released her and she rolled off the ledge, jerking her leg free of his tail.

Commander A'rlon caught her and held her immobile, her back pressed against him. He bent to whisper urgently into her ear. "Be still, I won't let him hurt you."

T'alak nodded to A'rlon. "Leave us."

"Captain, she will not survive your attention. We need her alive for the information in her brain."

Catriona watched T'alak narrow a gaze at his second-in-command.

"After the scan," continued A'rlon, "you can have your fill."

T'alak looked at Catriona with an expression between lust and hunger, and then drew himself up. "You are right, my friend. And it would be a pity to ruin such an unusual hide."

Catriona gasped, understanding he meant her skin. She began to shake. Komodoans really must feast on humans, she thought, panicked anew. A'rlon laid a firm hand on her shoulder, steadying her.

"The earthworm's yours, my friend," said T'alak with a flick of his tail. "Guard her well."

He looked at Catriona one more time before stalking out.

A'RLON LET go of Catriona. She bent to retrieve the discarded cover and with shaking hands wrapped it sarong-like around her.

"Come with me," he said gently.

Catriona didn't move. He said she wouldn't be hurt, but why should she believe him? "Can I see Chief Khumalo?" her voice cracked and she coughed.

"Not yet." He touched a panel by the one of the ledges and it slid aside to reveal a drinking fountain.

Catriona's pupils widened like a cat spotting prey. Fresh running water! A'rlon stood back to let her drink her fill. She felt nervous having him stand over her, but the lure of plentiful water won over her fear.

Straightening, she watched in distaste as A'rlon used his forked tongue to drink before sliding the panel back in place. She averted her gaze. "Is Uzi all right?"

"She is safe." He reached out in a non-threatening manner to take her arm and guided her from the Infirmary.

In the corridor Catriona asked, "Where is she?"

"Be quiet, I told you she's safe."

A flash of anger surged through Catriona. She whipped her arm out of his grasp. "That's not good enough, Commander. I order you to take me to her now."

A'rlon's tail twitched and he folded his arms. "You are not in a position to give orders."

"I'm not going anywhere until I see my friend."

"Your concern is commendable, but don't try my patience." He reached for her.

"No!" Catriona shoved him as hard as she could.

He lost his footing but quickly recovered, letting out a hiss of amusement. "I'll take you to see Chief Khumalo as soon as I can."

She nodded, disarmed by his show of humor. She didn't want to alienate the one Komodoan who had shown her any kindness. Meekly she let him lead her through the maze of corridors. This ship was much bigger than the *Vallo*, and these corridors glowed with a sort of phosphorescence that gave a strange pallid hue, between gray and green.

They reached a wider passage with fewer doors along it. A'rlon approached one and laid his palm on the panel. It slid open and he steered Catriona inside. She looked around a sparse cabin, with an oval bed, desk and stool, with a smaller door leading to what must be the bathroom. A six-foot water fountain flowed in the corner. Too large for drinking from; it must be where A'rlon bathed.

He strode to the bed and keyed a wall lamp. "Come here," he instructed her. Panic fluttered through Catriona. He did expect to sleep with her. "I said, come here," he repeated sternly.

Catriona thrust herself at the door but it didn't open. She backed away and found herself at the desk. Her hand fell on a ceramic object on its surface. Closing her fingers around it she hurled it at A'rlon.

He dodged, letting it smash into the wall. "Calm down!"

Catriona felt for something else. She had to stop him touching her;

86 | *Time Twist*

she still felt the unnatural grip of T'alak's tail on her ankle. Snatching up a wooden box she flung it as hard as she could. This time it hit home, connecting solidly with A'rlon's scaled temple. It crashed to the floor, splintering into pieces. A silver pendant on a chain lay amongst the fragments, much larger than the one she had discarded in the cruiser.

"Enough!" A'rlon caught her and sat her down on the stool. Scooping up the pendant he looked closely at it before laying it gently on the desk. With a hiss he sank to one knee in front of Catriona, his tail spread out behind him. Taking her shaking hands between his, he spoke gently, "It's all right, human. I'm not going to hurt you."

He sounded so sincere. Wanting to believe him, Catriona didn't pull away. His hands felt warm, unlike T'alak's clammy touch, and the scales on his hands were not hard like she expected them to be. They felt slightly ridged but pliant.

"You told Captain T'alak he could... have his fill of me later," she stammered.

He smiled, making her blink in surprise at how it changed his whole demeanor. Gone was the terrifying, shark-eyed alien. In his place knelt a gentle man with compelling, warm eyes. She saw now that his irises were not just black as she first thought. Up close they were jeweled with flecks of color, like a starling's feather.

Realizing she stared at him, she lowered her gaze, disconcerted that he still held her hands. Sensing her discomfiture, he withdrew and rested his hands on his knee.

"I apologize if I frightened you. I needed to convince T'alak to put you in my custody so I could protect you."

She found her tongue at last. "Why do you want to do that?"

"Let's just say the less you know the better off you'll be. Now, you've had a rough time of it. The best thing for you is sleep."

She studied his face. Without those scales he would make an attractive human man. High cheekbones beneath deep-set eyes, and full lips that gave him a sensual look. He was exotic yet looked acceptably humanoid to be irresistibly appealing.

He grinned diffidently as though reading her mind. "You're safe from Captain T'alak in here." He stood once more, taking her hands in his and raising her to her feet. "We must make it look as though you fought me; he will expect it. You've enough abrasions on you, but you'd better inflict damage on me."

"Are you serious?"

"Never more so."

"I can't."

"You had no problem damaging Captain T'alak."

"That was... different." She realized they were holding hands again. Into her mind, unsought and unexpected came a sense of how it would feel to have him take her in his arms, hold her close. The spell was broken when he lifted her right hand and swiftly drew her nails across his face. Dark green liquid spurted from the gouges.

Catriona blanched at the color, and then laughed raggedly. "Who said there was no such thing as little green men?"

A'rlon raised an indulgent eyebrow. Sliding open a compartment in the desk, he produced an oval-shaped pad. "This will help you sleep."

Anxiously she scanned his face. "How can I trust you?"

"What choice do you have?" He led her to the bed.

She perched on the edge and let him press the pad to her neck. In moments, he became a blur and faded into darkness.

Colonel Grreag sat silently in his command chair and looked at his crew. Even Lieutenant Larrar appeared despondent, and he could sense the atmosphere of betrayal on board the *Vallo*.

Major Benjamin sat on an observation seat, sipping a measure of water. "I'm sorry, Sir. The last thing I remember is finding Chief Khumalo carrying a cache of explosives."

Grreag growled. Khumalo, Dr. Pauline Morrison, and Catriona Logan had vanished without trace. It looked to him that Khumalo and Logan were conspirators and had taken Dr. Morrison and Webster's data disk to the Komodoans.

The control cabin door dilated and Professor Webster and Second Engineer Lieutenant Leopold entered. Grreag noticed Leopold's yarmulke. Terrans had so many religions, he considered. Leopold's faith was one of the oldest, and had impressive rituals.

Grreag's whiskers tweaked and he made himself focus on the matter at hand. Webster sat on an observation seat to Grreag's left, and buried his head in his hands. The professor's scent was of total dejection and Grreag watched him for a moment, then flicked an ear at Leopold. The Lieutenant had been a student counselor at Alliance Cadet College before joining the Armada, and Grreag hoped he could get through to Webster.

Leopold reached out, lightly touching Webster's forearm.

"Professor?" Raising his head, Webster stared blankly. Grreag did not have to be telepathic to know what the human suffered. "You mustn't blame yourself, Professor," said Leopold, his voice musical and soothing, "you couldn't have known what would happen."

"Why didn't they take me instead of Pauline?"

"I don't think they intended to take her. She was in the wrong place at the wrong time."

Grreag forced himself to be patient, making an effort to keep his hackles down. "Professor Webster," he rumbled, "is she capable of creating the temporal weapon without you?"

Webster's head drooped. "Absolutely. And of course with the girl from the 21st century they'll have the weapon constructed long before us."

Grreag's amber eyes narrowed. "So, you're telling me Catriona Logan truly came through time?"

"Her initial brain scan confirmed it without question."

So, Catriona wasn't the spy. Grreag felt strangely exultant, but quashed his exuberance. Perhaps the brainwave patterns Webster found could have been fabricated to cover Catriona's real reason for being on the *Vallo*. But how? The answer came swiftly. Chief Khumalo, of course. The accomplice. She'd be capable of concocting any data necessary.

He drummed a claw on his chair arm, no longer in control of his hackles. "Professor, with the *Vallo* hyperdrive engines could you create a temporal bubble large enough to enclose the planet Komodoa?"

"Theoretically, yes. But it's never been tested. If the bubble collapsed, the planet would be destroyed."

Grreag stood, moving to gaze at the glimmering stars on the viewer. What choice did he have? If the Komodoan Realm created the weapon, they could and would use the technology to destroy the Terran Colonies and Leontor. The universe as they knew it would cease to exist. He had to retrieve that data, no matter the consequences. But a whole species, exterminated because of him? He came to a decision and turned to face the others.

"Lieutenant Leopold, you and Professor Webster begin work on creating a temporal bubble immediately." He addressed Larrar at NavOps. "Lieutenant, plot a course at maximum velocity to take the *Vallo* into the Komodoan Realm!"

18

CATRIONA WOKE up with the shock of nightmare pumping blood loudly in her ears. She breathed until her pulse slowed, and she looked around the dim room. She tried to sit up, but to her stupefaction the bed wallowed around her. Instead of a mattress with bedclothes, the loamy bed turned out to be a cocoon of warm, malleable jelly. Her head rested safely harnessed in a net that held it above the surface, leaving the rest of her submerged. Gingerly, she unclipped the harness and tentatively touched the gel. Despite its slimy look, the bed felt as soft as brushed cotton. Experimenting, Catriona raised one knee, then the other. The bed matched her movements, keeping her fully supported at all times. How amazing. She tried kicking her legs but found it impossible to move violently or jarringly.

Stretching her legs over the side of the bed, she stood. The cocoon obligingly withdrew with a sucking sound and the gel dried quickly on her skin, leaving a faint but pleasant mossy scent. The cover she'd used as a wrap stayed sodden, so she untied it and dropped it to the floor. The cabin felt cold. She copied A'rlon from earlier and touched the wall to activate the light. The room immediately flooded with that unearthly green glow. A glint caught her eye and she moved to the desk to look at the oval silver pendant lying there. A'rlon had touched it with an air of reverence. She made out the engraved pattern of a female form with long flowing hair, which entwined with her tail to circle round her. At the center a cinereal stone was embedded, the engraved female holding it in her crossed arms.

A sudden cramp doubled her over. Catriona dropped the pendant back on the desk and scurried to the narrow bathroom doorway. She had worried that Webster's disk might be detected in her digestive system, but it hadn't. The door slid aside, revealing a cubicle that contained a narrow pedestal with a tail rest and tiny sink. A few unpleasant minutes later, Catriona triumphantly held Professor Webster's newly washed disk in her hand.

The sink proved sufficient to make her presentable, but her body ached so much she really longed for the shower out in the cabin. Debating, she decided to risk A'rlon coming back before she'd finished. After all, he had already seen her naked, not much point in becoming coy now. She looked around for somewhere to leave the disk, then brought it out to the cabin, carefully placing it to the side of the shower. The cool, flowing

90 | *Time Twist*

water felt delicious on her abused body. As she relaxed she worried about Uzi and what kind of night she might have had.

Catriona's throat hurt where Captain T'alak had choked her. She massaged her neck and scrubbed her body vigorously, paying particular attention to her ankle where his tail had twined. Then she ran the water over her hair and used her fingers to comb out the tangles.

"What in the Realm do you think you're doing?"

Catriona jumped, her heart almost stopping. At the sight of A'rlon she ducked out of the shower, dripping water on the floor. "Isn't this where you bathe?"

"Bathe?" His expression slid from outrage to incredulous. Finally he gave a hiss of laughter. "My dear human, you have just bathed with the spirit of the Goddess *P'jarra.*"

Spirit? Incongruous thoughts of crystal clear vodka cascading over her flashed into Catriona's head. She looked properly at the tall fountain, seeing the hewn stone patterns beneath the water. Her body tingled as she realized how close A'rlon stood, his body heat tangible. Goosebumps rippled over her flesh and her nipples hardened. Catriona covered them but A'rlon had seen and abruptly took a step back.

"The scrub is in here." He turned and approached the bathroom.

Catriona twisted round and bent to retrieve the disk from the floor. Straightening, the blood ran from her head; she felt dizzy and found herself careening over. A'rlon lunged forward in time to steady her. Catriona let the dizziness pass and stepped away from him, placing herself in the bathroom doorway.

"I looked in here but could only find a sink," she babbled, terrified he'd seen her pick up the disk.

"I should have demonstrated how to initiate the wall spray." The corner of his mouth quirked. "But it looks like you solved the problem magnificently. May *P'jarra* bring you peace, human."

Relieved the disk's presence remained secret, Catriona now felt reprehensible that she had bathed in a shrine. What she had done felt tantamount to using a holy water font as a spittoon.

"I'm sorry, Commander. I wouldn't have done that if I'd known."

"No harm has been done. And while we're alone, the name is 'A'rlon'." Brushing aside any further apologies, he withdrew a bundle from his belt and handed it to her. "Here are your belongings, and something to wear."

Catriona retreated to the bathroom, the disk still safe in her palm. Unwrapping the bundle, she found her microplayer and jewelry rolled up in a robe of soft, voile-like fabric. Holding up the garment she pulled it on and fastened the wide belt around her waist. The fabric shimmered like the Aurora Borealis, greens and purples. It was akin to a Japanese kimono but very short, just reaching down to her thighs. The back flapped loosely where it had been cut generously to accommodate the Komodoan tail and her breasts strained against the flat front. He hadn't given her any underwear or footwear.

She appraised the microplayer. It appeared unharmed and she slipped it under her wide belt. Putting on her Celtic ring and watch, she opened her locket to ensure her parents' pictures were still inside. The photos had obviously been peeled out for inspection and put carelessly back. Catriona felt glad the Komodoans hadn't damaged it, although seeing her parents' images captured in black and white emphasized how utterly alone she felt, so far away from her time. She snapped closed the lid, gratified that so far she'd prevented Webster's disk from falling into Captain T'alak's hands.

A shudder rippled through her as she remembered his assault on her in the Infirmary. She was thankful that A'rlon had stopped him, but she wasn't certain how far she could trust him. She'd seen the look in his eyes when he'd her caught her from falling over. He'd tried to hide it, but she'd recognized his desire. Her stomach did a strange flip-flop and she held onto the edge of the sink for a moment. Something in her responded to the thought of him desiring her.

What could be wrong with her; how could she be attracted to an alien? And one with a tail and a forked tongue, she reminded herself with a more forceful shudder.

She took a breath and straightened. Raising her arms to put the locket over her head, she paused, struck by an idea. Sliding a fingernail under her mother's picture, she slipped the disk underneath. It fit her gold locket just like it fit Dr. Morrison's silver one. She fastened the chain securely around her neck. Composing herself, she left the privacy of the bathroom to find A'rlon at his desk.

"Feeling better?" he inquired.

She nodded, making an effort not to finger the locket. "When can I see Uzi?"

"After we're on Komodoa."

Catriona gasped audibly. "What? You said I wouldn't be hurt, but how can you guarantee that if we're going there?"

A'rlon made an impatient noise. "We haven't time to debate it, we're coming into orbit around Komodoa and T'alak will be here soon. For your own safety, I suggest you behave as docilely as possible."

"What do you mean?"

"For a start, don't look him in the eye." Catriona frowned, then glanced away from him. "You can look at me, Terran, just don't do it in public. Do not look at any Komodoan male that way."

"Why not?"

His tongue feathered his lips for a moment. "It isn't seemly."

"Does that apply to Komodoan women too?"

He nodded tersely. "There's no time to explain Realm etiquette to you, T'alak's on his way. He will expect me to have broken your spirit. The more obedient you are, the better the possibility you may stay under my protection."

"You mean like your slave?" Catriona's voice rose.

"It's the only way a human might survive on Komodoa."

His blunt answer struck her like a blow. She stared at him, trying to imagine what life as his slave would be like. The very idea was repulsive.

"You're going to be all right, Catriona," he said gently.

She started at the sound of her name on his lips. Once more it struck her how handsome he appeared except for that tail.

"What's it like, having a tail?" she blurted, then flushed.

"Uncomfortable."

That surprised her. Captain T'alak swished his about like a third arm. She looked at A'rlon's again. It barely moved at all, and certainly didn't express his mood the way T'alak's did.

Her distaste must have been evident for A'rlon hissed a sigh. "You're not repulsed by Leontor ears or whiskers, are you? I assure you that our tails are as essential and as perfectly normal as any of their differences."

Leontors! Thoughts of Colonel Grreag and his barbs came suddenly to mind. Unbidden, Catriona found herself wondering what similar differences a Komodoan might have. Appalled, she abruptly changed the subject.

"What does T'alak want with me?"

"The same as Professor Webster, but T'alak won't care how he extracts the data from you."

That didn't surprise her. "A'rlon, why are you helping me? What's in it for you?"

His face darkened. "Don't ask so many tiresome questions."

Catriona recoiled. She had just begun to feel like she could trust him. Anger fueled by fear surged through her.

"Well, if I'm that tiresome, why don't you bloody well fuck off! I'll get out of this without you."

He looked like he might laugh, which infuriated her further. "And how do you propose to escape without me?"

Catriona bit her lip. "I'll find Chief Khumalo…"

He held up a resigned hand. She looked miserably at him, his face set like granite. The scratches he'd made her put on his cheek, although a shade of olive, only reminded her painfully of her skirmish with Colonel Grreag. With a sharp pang, she realized she may never see Grreag again.

"Catriona." A'rlon stood and took a step toward her. "Trust me. I'll do everything in my power to get you home."

Where was home? she wondered, fighting the urge to cry. Two hundred and sixty years ago or back on the *Vallo*? Suddenly A'rlon looked very human, his luminous eyes filled with compassion. He had extraordinary eyes; so dark they looked permanently dilated. He took her gently by the shoulders.

Catriona wanted so much to trust him as he asked, but she couldn't. Stepping away, she turned to the desk to finger the silver pendant. "What is this engraving of?" She felt acutely aware of him close behind and fiercely fought the part of her that longed to turn and bury her face against his chest.

"The goddess *P'jarra*." She breathed easier when he lifted the pendant from the desk and moved away. "Remember, it's imperative that T'alak thinks I've broken your spirit."

"Don't worry, I know what to do." Her voice cracked. "I am… I mean, I was an actress in another life." She slumped down on the desk stool.

19

WITHOUT WARNING A'rlon's cabin door slid open and T'alak marched in. Catriona hung her head and wished she'd slipped her gold locket under her robe. It felt very large and extremely obvious. She felt his eyes on her and resisted the urge to run into the bathroom.

"I trust you have had an entertaining night, my friend," hissed T'alak.

"Most enjoyable," agreed A'rlon.

"You did leave something to scan?"

"Of course." He raised his voice to Catriona, "On your feet, earthworm."

Catriona dragged herself up, avoiding looking at either Komodoan. She didn't need to imitate fright; T'alak's proximity terrified her.

"My yacht awaits to take us to the surface," said T'alak, moving into the corridor.

A'rlon gave Catriona a shove toward the doorway. She tucked the locket out of sight and walked beside him as they followed T'alak along the corridor. Watching the Captain swagger along in front of her, she hated him with every ounce of her being. What she'd do to cure him of that swagger if she ever had the chance. His tail curved side to side as he walked and she imagined a scythe in her hand to slice it from him.

The daytime lighting on the Komodoan ship gave her the impression she walked under water, sunlight flickering beneath the green surface. Sound was muted, their footfalls quiet. That strange, almost invisible green mist soaked up the acoustics.

"Did you extract any information from her?" demanded T'alak.

"She knows less about the Alliance than we do. Her intellect is basic, but she is reasonably compliant."

T'alak glanced over his shoulder and eyed A'rlon's scratches. "Not that compliant."

He halted by a large rectangular doorway and stared at Catriona. She swiftly lowered her hate-filled gaze. He shot an arm out to grasp her face, making her give a yelp of surprise.

He forced her to look up, but she managed not to make eye contact. She tried to impose what she hoped was a look of compliance, but she really wanted to dig her nails into his arrogant, dark eyes and gouge them right out.

"Excellent, A'rlon." T'alak pulled her close, and she put out her hands, bracing herself against his chest.

"I'm glad you approve, honored Captain." A'rlon placed a proprietary hand on the back of Catriona's neck and leveled a warning gaze at T'alak.

"I trust you're not getting possessive of your human, my friend."

"You know I don't like unfinished business."

Catriona held her breath and kept her eyes averted. The two Komodoans stared at each other in silence, and then T'alak pushed her away with enough force to send her sprawling on the floor.

Catriona picked herself up, wondering what A'rlon held over his superior that T'alak should back down. Replacing his hand on her neck, A'rlon guided Catriona past T'alak to the bay where the black star-yacht waited. His fingers felt cool on her skin.

In T'alak's yacht, both Catriona and A'rlon sat behind T'alak's pilot seat. She edged away so her leg didn't touch A'rlon's and watched T'alak's tail, swaying just in front of her. The seats had been designed with a gap for their tails. Over T'alak's bulky shoulder she could see the control panel and studied it closely, fascinated at how simple the vessel appeared to be piloted. Even she could do it if she had to.

Biting down hard on her lip, she considered her situation. With each passing hour, it grew more unlikely that the *Vallo* would come to the rescue. With a lurch of fear, she knew if the Komodoans scanned her and got the information Professor Webster wanted, she could be indirectly responsible for destroying the future of her own kind. A bitter laugh escaped her.

"You find something amusing?" snarled T'alak.

Catriona cleared her throat, darting a look at A'rlon, who gave her a brief nod. "I apologize, Captain," she answered through clenched teeth.

T'alak keyed in a few digits and the computer came on-line. "Keep your human quiet, A'rlon, unless you want me to do it for you."

He guided the yacht out through the *L'umina* bay hatch. They descended smoothly into the planet's atmosphere and despite her peril, Catriona felt a thrill at the first sight of Komodoa. Imagine, a real alien world. It gave her the jitters thinking of all the people she knew back in her time, living in ignorance of this enemy planet mere light years away.

The vista of the Komodoan sky mesmerized her. Predominantly mauve, deeper hues of jade and emerald green streaked through it. The planet spread out below, a vast array of rich oceans, in varying shades of green-blue, with a mixture of golds and mauves interspersed, indicating land. The panorama of alien color began to make Catriona feel nauseous.

To take her mind off the fast approaching terrain, she returned her attention to T'alak's control panel. There were four panels like something on a PlayStation game control, which at a touch 'steered'. Another controlled speed.

Tingles shot through her as she felt a light touch on her arm. A'rlon shook his head, warning her not to let T'alak see her interest in the controls. No doubt the Komodoan captain would consider it a valid excuse to deal with her in his own way. And he would not be as considerate as A'rlon, she thought, her arm still tingling where he had touched.

As they moved around the planet, the Komodoan dawn rose. Emerald-burnished trails of the mauve morning sky reached out to greet them, as the yacht swept over a cluster of light gray buildings

96 | *Time Twist*

with tall spires and minarets atop each one. They glided onto a landing pad and came to rest. Catriona saw a Komodoan soldier in a glass booth directing the sky traffic.

T'alak brought the yacht to a smooth stop. He slid open the hatch and jumped out, causing the craft to gently rock. Catriona climbed out after A'rlon and gazed at the horizon where a mass of leaden clouds boiled over the rim of the hills. She started at the sight of lightning splitting the liver-colored belly of the sky.

As T'alak led the way off the landing pad toward a huge, rectangular metal door, the soldier in the booth studied Catriona with predatory interest. She felt very conspicuous and vulnerable, and drew closer to A'rlon.

An array of hieroglyphics had been engraved down one side of the metal door. Captain T'alak smartly hit one of them, and the door swooshed aside to reveal a large elevator. The brass-colored metal floor looked unsafe and Catriona held back.

"It's just a carrier," A'rlon said, easing her inside.

Catriona's knees almost gave way as the carrier abruptly dropped. She started to reach for A'rlon's arm to steady herself but thought better of it. Captain T'alak simmered with anger beside her and she didn't want to do anything that might set him off.

They came to a stop and the door slid open in a dim, underground passage. Catriona saw barred cell doors leading into the stygian gloom, too many to count. They looked like medieval dungeons. Why had she trusted A'rlon? Once she was locked in here there'd be no chance of escape. A'rlon put a hand to the small of her back to encourage her out of the carrier but she shrank back.

Captain T'alak grabbed her arm and dragged her out.

"A'rlon!" she cried, her heels scuffling on the corridor stone floor.

T'alak glanced sharply at his second-in-command. "You've made quite an impression, my friend." Unlocking a cell door he thrust Catriona inside.

She toppled against the wall, jarring her injured arm. The door slammed shut and through the bars she saw T'alak and A'rlon stroll away without a backward glance. She started to scramble to her feet but a strong arm steadied her and helped her up.

"I told you I'd be all right, Haggis."

"Uzi!" Catriona ignored her hurt arm and hugged her friend tightly.

"Not so hard," complained Khumalo, "I think I've a cracked rib or two."

Catriona's eyes adjusted to the darkness and she looked closely at the engineer. She had a black eye, and a copious amount of dried blood had caked on her face, neck and clothes.

"What did they do to you, Uzi?"

"You should see the other guy," joked Khumalo, and then winced. "Let's sit down." They eased to the cold flagstones and sat side by side, huddling close for warmth. "Are you all right?"

"Yes. Commander A'rlon kept me safe from Captain T'alak."

"He did?" Khumalo's tone was sharp. "At what cost?"

"What do you mean?"

Khumalo shook her head. "You probably don't know why humans are popular slaves in the Komodoan Realm." Catriona felt her friend shudder. "We have no tails."

"I don't understand."

"They can fuck us harder and deeper than any of their own."

Catriona felt the hairs rise on the back of her neck.

"Owning us is a status symbol to them. A human with your rare coloring would be highly sought after."

Catriona felt a cold tendril of doubt steal into her heart. "A'rlon's not like that."

Khumalo looked her in the eye. "Girlfriend, of course he's like that; he's a Komodoan male. Well," she made an impatient gesture, "as long as you're all right."

"I am," said Catriona distractedly. Was it possible that A'rlon had deceived her into trusting him? "Did you mean what you said when you told me Komodoans ate humans?"

Khumalo snorted, the sound startling in the oppressive darkness. "No, Haggis, no. I was trying to scare you." She didn't sound convincing.

Footsteps approached. Khumalo and Catriona looked at each other and scrambled up.

"Don't make eye contact, remember," warned Khumalo.

Captain T'alak arrived with two guards in tow. He unlocked the door and came inside to steadfastly regard the two captives. Catriona wondered where A'rlon was.

"Humans," hissed T'alak, "now that the *Vallo* is gone, it is in your best interests to cooperate."

"Gone?" demanded Khumalo.

T'alak curled a lip, his tail twitching. "Don't you think if your ship survived our assault they would have rescued you by now? However, you can ensure the *Vallo's* memory will live nobly on by telling us what you know about her defenses and weapons."

Catriona watched Khumalo's onyx eyes narrow. "I don't know anything about them," she lied smoothly.

"Our agent completed her mission successfully," continued T'alak, "so it's pointless for you to be uncooperative."

Catriona bit back a retort. She knew Y'alenon had not been successful; she had the proof in her locket! She wished she'd told Uzi before T'alak had returned, now she could say nothing. Even as it was, T'alak had caught her intake of breath and his full attention had focused on her. She kept her eyes downcast and fought to keep a poker face. She felt like prey caught in his basilisk stare.

In her peripheral vision she saw him gesture and one of the guards approached. "You may know nothing," T'alak said to Khumalo, "but she evidently does."

"All right!" Khumalo stepped between the guard and Catriona. "You win, Captain."

"But..." began Catriona, but Uzi shoved her aside.

"Shut up, human," she murmured urgently. The guard drew his carbine and motioned for Khumalo to leave the cell. Offering Catriona a half-hearted wink she walked ahead, followed by the guard.

CATRIONA STARED after them in disbelief. Uzi had called her 'human!' Then she inadvertently made eye contact with T'alak and looked away. She loathed pretending to be submissive. One day, she didn't know how, she didn't know when, but Captain T'alak would pay for her humiliation.

He watched her for a moment, then left the cell, followed by the second guard. As he locked the door he sneered, "I'll be back with the scanner," and left her alone in the darkness.

Catriona listened to the clanging footsteps receding in the corridor, then moved to the door to peer through the bars. The darkness and silence pressed in on her. Imagining all kinds of macabre things creeping up on her in the shadows, she retreated to the cell corner to hunker down. Uzi had to have been with her in the *L'umina* sickbay, for Y'alenon had been there, too. But who had been in this cell with her? Why would Uzi call her 'human'? And if it had been Y'alenon, would an expert in deception slip up like that? Catriona rubbed her aching temples. Maybe Y'alenon had been trying to let her know she wasn't Uzi, but why would she? And could Commander A'rlon truly intend to help her? She shook herself as though to cast away the confusion. She would get nowhere running round in circles like this. Thank God she hadn't told Uzi that she had the disk, or it might all have been for nothing. As for the *Vallo* being destroyed, she knew Captain T'alak most likely lied about that, but she couldn't be certain.

The temperature dropped rapidly; she could see her breath misting. Drawing the flimsy fabric of the robe as far as it would go over her thighs, she curled up tightly to try and keep warm.

She had almost fallen asleep when another set of footsteps approached. A tail-less Komodoan female appeared carrying a tray. Catriona narrowed her eyes: Y'alenon. If she'd been masked as Uzi again, had there been enough time for her to return to her Komodoan look?

"I brought you some food." The spy slid open a slot at the bottom of the door and pushed a flat tray toward Catriona.

Catriona got up and moved stiffly to the door. How could she find out if it had been Y'alenon all along? She cleared her throat. "You're very good at your job," she commented.

"What's that supposed to mean?"

"Pretending to be a friend, when you were something else entirely."

"You're delusional."

Catriona's fear and anger bubbled to the surface. "I just don't know how you can let someone trust you, let them get close to you... and then you turn out to be a complete fraud. Everything you said and did was an utter fabrication."

"That's not so," hissed Y'alenon.

"So, tell me what was true!"

The spy shook her head. "I don't have to explain myself to you."

"Yes, you do. You need to explain it to the Alliance. To Grreag and the *Vallo* crew. And to Professor Webster."

"My relationship with Professor Webster is none of your concern, human."

Catriona blinked, remembering how she'd suspected Dr. Morrison and Webster of having more than a professional relationship.

"How can you fake affection like that?" she demanded.

Y'alenon's eyes narrowed. "I didn't fake it. That was the most real thing of all." She leaned close to the bars and dropped her voice to a tense hiss. "Do not repeat what I've said or I'll have you flayed alive,

100 | *Time Twist*

whether you've been scanned or not!" She turned and marched away.

Catriona listened to her footfalls long after she was out of sight. Y'alenon hadn't said it outright, but her paranoid reaction to what *was* said convinced Catriona she'd been involved with Professor Webster. This could be used to advantage, she thought, feeling a small ray of hope.

Bending to inspect what food Y'alenon had brought, she found a bowl containing a tough, black meat. A second bowl held water. Realizing how parched and hungry she felt, Catriona drank deeply of the plentiful liquid, and chewed the tough meat with distaste. She forced herself to swallow it, knowing she needed it to survive.

A long time dragged by. Maybe four hours, maybe more… Catriona lost track of time. Fat lot of use her watch was. Raising her wrist she could barely make out the gaudy faux stones on its face. She felt bitterly cold and her teeth had started to chatter. Flexing her numb feet she crawled to a standing position and limped to the door. Nothing out in the corridor but dark shadows. She attempted to hum a tune to break the silence but her voice sounded frail and lost. Listening carefully, she thought she heard water dripping in the distance.

Down the corridor the carrier made a swoosh sound and a beam of faint light fell on the flagstones. One set of footsteps approached. Heart thumping, Catriona shrank back from the door.

Commander A'rlon appeared at the bars. So relieved not to be alone anymore Catriona couldn't even pretend to be subservient.

"Where the hell have you been?" she demanded. "When are you letting me out of this bloody zoo?"

He cocked an eyebrow. "Hardly a zoo. The humans there are free to roam in their cages."

Catriona could hardly breathe. "You really have humans in zoos?" He didn't answer. She watched him remove an instrument from his sleeve and use it to scan the surrounding area. "Captain T'alak took Uzi away, you have to do something!" she said urgently.

Satisfied they were unobserved, A'rlon nodded. "I have taken care of Chief Khumalo."

Catriona gripped the bars tightly. "What do you mean, 'taken care' of her?"

He half-smiled. "Interesting you should speak of zoological gardens. I have arranged for the chief to be transferred to one where there is a research facility. She'll be safe from rape there."

"What?" shrieked Catriona. Black spots swam before her eyes.

"It's a ruse, human. Calm yourself." He gently touched one of the hands she gripped the bars with. "Captain T'alak doesn't want her and this will keep her safe."

Catriona frowned. "Doesn't want her?"

"There are plenty of humans who look like her but you are unique. Look, I promise I will get you both safely back to the Alliance."

Catriona believed him. Stretching her fingers to slip between his she took hold of his hand. "Thank you."

"Listen to me. You're to be interviewed by General B'alarg, and then scanned soon after to extract the necessary information for the temporal weapon. Cooperate long enough to stay alive until I find a way to get you and Khumalo out."

He made to leave but Catriona held onto his hand. "I, em…"

"Yes?" He waited.

She let go. "Y'alenon was… involved with Professor Webster."

"Intimately?"

Catriona nodded. "She loves him, I think."

"That would explain her erratic behavior," he said slowly, thinking. "I'll see that Y'alenon escorts you to General B'alarg. Take advantage of it and push her about the relationship. Try to get a reaction; doesn't matter if it's positive or negative."

"Y'alenon said… I mean, she told me not to tell anyone or she'd-" Catriona couldn't bring herself to repeat the word 'flay'.

"She won't harm you. All will be well, beauty."

With that he left, slipping away so quietly Catriona half-wondered if she had imagined the entire thing. Did he really call her 'beauty'? What did he mean by it, was he using the name of the character she'd played in the theater or did he think her beautiful? The thought that she even cared mortified her.

She must have slept, for she started with surprise to hear Y'alenon calling her name as she opened the cell door. Catriona stiffly got up, wondering how long she'd been asleep.

Y'alenon stepped into the cell and took Catriona by the arm. "You will come with me."

Catriona followed without resistance. To do so would only result in a struggle. Catriona suspected Y'alenon felt less confident than she acted, judging by the shadows under her eyes.

In her cell Catriona had given much thought as to how she'd get Y'alenon riled up about Professor Webster. As they entered the carrier, she said, "It must have been fascinating working with Professor Webster. But difficult, too." Y'alenon ignored her. "When you work closely with someone for a long time like that, it's hard not to become emotionally involved."

Y'alenon turned blazing eyes on her. "Be quiet!"

Catriona took a breath. "Of course, the hardest part must have been unable to say goodbye or explain-"

"I said, be quiet!" Y'alenon put a hand to the butt of her carbine and Catriona fell silent. She watched as the spy's lower lip trembled until she got control again. The carrier sighed to a stop and Y'alenon pulled Catriona into the corridor.

They were above ground, sunlight flooding through oblong windows in two beams, like searchlights. Squinting, Catriona realized there were two suns, low on the horizon. Y'alenon jerked her way from the extraordinary sight of a double sunset and marched her through a sliding doorway.

Blinded by the suns, it took Catriona a moment to see her surroundings. It appeared to be an office with water cascading down an entire wall. She blinked, seeing a heavy-set Realm officer sitting behind an ornate desk made of stone. Catriona concentrated on not looking at him, but she got the impression of a squat toad on a lily leaf. Her eyes widened at the sight of a model of Earth by the desk.

"General B'alarg, honored one." Y'alenon bowed to B'alarg. She looked ill at ease, and shot a glance at Catriona. When the General said nothing, it appeared that Catriona was expected to speak.

"Why am I here?" she demanded.

"You know why," he answered congenially in carefully cultured English, "you will be of great use to the Realm."

An object similar to Professor Webster's scanner lay on the desk by General B'alarg's scaled hand. At the sight of it, Catriona's heart sank. It didn't look like A'rlon could get her out before being scanned, and she couldn't just submit to it without a fight. What had she to lose? Swallowing hard, she saw that Y'alenon's attention had returned to the General. Catriona stepped up behind the spy and yanked the carbine from her belt.

"This is pointless, human," hissed B'alarg, standing.

Catriona gritted her teeth and held the carbine to Y'alenon's head. "Don't try anything." Grabbing Y'alenon's arm she backed them both toward the door, keeping the spy between her and B'alarg.

The door slid open to allow T'alak and A'rlon to enter. Catriona twisted, sidestepping out of the way, but Captain T'alak stepped forward, chopping the weapon from her hand. He followed through with a punch to her stomach. Gasping, Catriona doubled over and dropped to the floor, where she saw A'rlon follow after T'alak to retrieve Y'alenon's weapon. Tears blinded her as she struggled for breath. She slowly raised herself to her hands and knees and stood upright. The locket had slipped out and Catriona resisted shoving it out of sight again. Y'alenon stood quite still, not looking at her.

"Nice try, human," applauded B'alarg, sitting back down. "I would have been disappointed if you had not attempted escape." He hissed a sneer, regarding her with blank, shark's eyes.

Catriona stared at the Earth globe, aware of T'alak and A'rlon on either side of her. Her chest heaved as she tried to breathe normally. The locket felt like a millstone round her neck, and beads of perspiration formed on her forehead.

"Captain T'alak," B'alarg lifted the scanner from his desk. "Take this to Science to be recalibrated."

T'alak took the object, his tail curling to the side. Catriona's skin crawled at the sight of it. She glanced up and almost caught General B'alarg's eye.

"Commander A'rlon, keep the human somewhere suitable until then."

A'rlon bowed to General B'alarg and led her from his office.

IN THE carrier, A'rlon looked closely at Catriona. "A foolish move for a civilian, taking Agent Y'alenon's carbine," he remarked.

"You're telling me." She clutched her midsection where T'alak had punched her.

"How do know how to handle a weapon?" A'rlon doubted that a civilian from the past could do what Catriona had tried.

"*Duke Nukem.*" He frowned, so she expanded, "A computer game from back home."

"Ah." Similar programs were available in the Realm, but used for training, not entertainment.

He took Catriona directly to his chambers on the base. He slid open the door to usher her in, and watched her look blearily about.

104 | *Time Twist*

Following her gaze, he saw his chambers through her eyes. They looked almost as anonymous as his cabin on the *L'umina*. The stone floors were bare, except for a light brown Leontor pelt in front of the small, blackened fireplace. He glanced at Catriona, but fortunately she didn't recognize it. A large leather couch with a gap in back to accommodate tails sat against the wall to the right of the fireplace; a knife and short sword adorning the wall above. Two large blue-shaded lamps softened the sparseness, bathing the chamber in a pale, cold glow. He pressed a panel to initiate the water sculpture and a sharp smell of ozone permeated the air. He felt Catriona shiver beside him when the water cascaded down the far wall.

"Isn't it damp enough?" She wrapped her arms around herself.

He'd forgotten she wasn't used to Komodoa's humidity. He turned the sculpture off, immediately missing its moistness and soothing sound. He guided her into the main chamber. Pulling the leather couch out he swung it closer to the fireplace. Catriona sat down, teeth chattering. A'rlon fetched a combustible and fuel from the utility chamber and quickly lit the fire. Soon flames crackled.

A'rlon watched in fascination as the fire had a narcotic effect on Catriona. Her body appeared to melt as she unwrapped her arms and slid to a reclining position on the couch. Her eyelids appeared too heavy to keep her eyes open.

A'rlon looked round for something to put over her, and came up with a spare uniform tunic from the bedchamber. He tentatively draped it over her legs. Her eyes opened wide, then she pulled the gray padding over her entire body, curling up underneath it.

A'rlon backed off and watched her for a moment. The flames lit her unusual hair color so it resembled the burning beauty of the spires in Komodoa's ocean of Kr'isma Maris. Her breathing became even and deep as she fell asleep—he felt tempted to smooth a tangle of long hair away from her face but hesitated. The last thing he wanted to do would be frighten her when it looked like she'd finally decided to trust him.

He knelt by the fire and coaxed more heat from it by opening side vents in the fireplace. Catriona murmured in her sleep and flung an arm out from under the tunic. How pale her skin looked. She resembled a fragile Komodoan water-spirit carved in white marble.

He remembered returning to his cabin on the *L'umina* and finding her naked as a water nymph in the *P'jarra* shrine. The sight of her lithe body aroused the Komodoan instinct in him that would have had him take her there and then, whether she objected or not. He'd crushed the thought, but he felt unnerved at how strong the instinct had been.

Now seeing her trust him enough to sleep in his presence aroused other feelings; ones he didn't know he possessed. He both wanted to protect and possess her. He wanted to always keep her safe from harm, but that meant he could never keep her with him.

He rose to his feet, hissing in frustration. He had no other option — she must be returned to her people along with Chief Khumalo, and before General B'alarg's scanner was calibrated. Casting another glance over the slumbering human, he quietly strode to the door and slipped out.

Uzima Khumalo paced up and down in her locked chamber on the base. Like the cell, the walls and floor were stone, but this was brighter and warmer, with no bars. Just the locked door. The chief studied the box high on the wall by the door. No doubt this was the lock mechanism, but how different could it be to locks on the *Vallo*? She didn't trust Commander A'rlon's word that he meant to help them escape; she'd have to find a way to do it herself. She almost growled like a Leontor with anger. That reptile, A'rlon, had no one but his own interests in mind. And poor Catriona Logan was his main interest, Khumalo did not doubt for a second. Why he pretended to be their sympathetic champion she couldn't fathom. Komodoans considered human captives their property, so why would A'rlon need to win Catriona's favor?

She stopped pacing and looked at the single piece of furniture in the chamber — an oblong ottoman made of wood with a leather seat. She bent to drag it over to the door, grimacing in pain from her earlier struggle with Y'alenon and the guard. The Komodoan physique was obviously stronger than human; she'd have to find a weapon before she could take on another one in hand-to-hand combat.

Thinking of combat sharply reminded her of Colonel Grreag. The thought of her Leontor commanding officer sped her on and she climbed onto the ottoman to investigate the lock mechanism.

She had just removed the cover when the door slid open without warning. Khumalo froze in place. Y'alenon stepped through the doorway, saw her and strode into the chamber, allowing the door to slide closed.

"Get down!" she hissed. As Khumalo did so she added, "That lock cannot be tripped so don't waste your time."

"You think I'm going to take your word on that?" said Khumalo, sitting on the ottoman and leaning back against the wall. Y'alenon looked strange, all eyes and teeth — and very much on edge. The

106 | *Time Twist*

gray-scaled military tunic made the agent appear genderless, which Khumalo guessed to be the intention.

Y'alenon jerked her chin at Khumalo. "Are you badly hurt?"

Khumalo fingered the swelling on her face and eye. "Looks worse than it is."

The Komodoan reached into her sleeve and produced a round flat pad about the size of a large thumbnail. "Press this to your neck; it'll help."

Khumalo recognized the pain patch and held out her hand. Y'alenon dropped it into her palm and watched as Khumalo placed it against her carotid artery. After a moment Khumalo felt the throbbing around her ribs lessen.

"You don't usually waste these on your captives. Why me?"

Y'alenon looked uncomfortable. "I—regret that I hurt you."

"Does Captain T'alak know you're squandering medical supplies on an earthworm?"

Y'alenon moved impatiently around the chamber. "I'm not prepared to discuss my superiors with you."

"So, why are you here, girlfriend?"

The spy stopped pacing and turned to face Khumalo, her eyes filled with despair.

"I'll be honest with you," she said frankly, "I want to talk to you, but I don't know where to begin."

Khumalo studied her, convinced the spy was putting on an act. But why? Her face looked completely human in her expression, tear-streaked and beseeching for cooperation. Khumalo decided to play along.

"What do you want to talk about?"

"Nothing in particular." Y'alenon bit her lower lip.

"Ah, so you don't want me to reveal the whereabouts of the Alliance major defense compounds?"

"I already know where they are."

Khumalo stiffened. "I presume you've passed on that information to T'alak?"

"No."

"Why not?"

Y'alenon shrugged, absentmindedly picking at a hangnail on her thumb. Curiously human, thought Khumalo. Probing further, she asked, "Do you think there's no point in telling them because the temporal weapon will give the Realm supremacy anyway?"

The spy shook her head. She looked about to burst into tears.

"Y'alenon, do you regret what you've done?" demanded Khumalo.

The Komodoan's eyes widened. "What do you mean?"

"About coming back. Leaving your humanity behind."

Y'alenon's voice hardened. "I am not human."

"I don't believe you're Komodoan either. At least not anymore."

"I'll adjust." She worried at her hangnail again.

Khumalo snorted. "You don't even look like a Komodoan. Right now you look like a human child about to be scolded-"

"What do you mean?" Y'alenon bent and grabbed Khumalo by the shoulders. "What about a human child?"

"I mean you look lost," answered Khumalo in confusion.

Y'alenon jumped back as though stung. "What do you know about it?"

Khumalo got to her feet. "What's up with you, girl?"

"Leave me alone!"

Y'alenon pushed past Khumalo and made for the door but knocked into the ottoman. Stumbling, she grabbed it and threw it against the wall with such force it broke.

Khumalo ducked to avoid being hit by a stray wooden shard. Making a keening noise, Y'alenon snatched a jagged lance of wood and plunged it savagely at her wrist. Khumalo knocked the wood aside and grabbed at the agent.

"Holy shit, Y'alenon!" Blood the color of vermilion stained Y'alenon's tunic arm and soaked into Khumalo's fatigues.

Legs buckling, Y'alenon sank to the floor, sobbing. Khumalo kneeled beside her, and reached to slide Y'alenon's sleeve up so she could see the extent of the wound. It looked superficial and had already stopped bleeding.

"What's the matter, Pauline?" she asked gently, deliberating calling her by her human name.

"Tell Scott I didn't want to do it."

"I can't tell Professor Webster anything while I'm a prisoner here."

The Komodoan stared at her, her dark eyes gradually focusing. "It's too late to save him."

"Who, Professor Webster?"

Y'alenon made an effort to pull herself together. Extricating herself, she sat back on her heels. "I thought you could help me, but I must face this alone."

"You don't have to face anything alone, Pauline. If you want to go back to Professor Webster, you can help us escape with you."

Y'alenon fiercely shook her head. "I've made my choice."

"It's not too late to put things right." Khumalo leaned forward. "You

108 | *Time Twist*

can leave with us; make a new beginning."

Y'alenon bowed her head. Hardly daring to breathe, Khumalo waited. If the spy decided to return to Professor Webster, the chances of getting out of here would be doubled.

Y'alenon abruptly got to her feet and made for the door. "I've made my choice, Terran. I'll live with it."

Khumalo stumbled to her feet and went after her. "Can you live with it?" Y'alenon halted. "Can you live with yourself?" pressed Khumalo.

The door slid open, revealing Commander A'rlon. Both women froze in place. Taking in Y'alenon's distraught face and the blood smeared over both of them, he stepped inside, allowing the door to seal behind him.

"What's going on?"

Y'alenon backed up and Khumalo tentatively put what she hoped would be a comforting hand on her shoulder. Y'alenon turned her head to look at her and didn't pull away.

A'rlon raised an eyebrow. "The scanner will take four hours to calibrate. I thought you should know."

Y'alenon stared at him and he met her gaze. Khumalo looked from one to the other. Realizing some unspoken conflict went on between them, she kept silent. Y'alenon dropped her gaze and stepped away from them both.

"Don't involve me," she hissed, moving for the door.

A'rlon stayed her with a hand. "Consider your choice carefully," he said evenly, "but betray me and you will die."

She bowed her head in acknowledgement and left.

Khumalo risked looking Commander A'rlon in the eye. She needed to see the truth if she could.

"Will she give you away?" He shook his head and did not appear angered by her close scrutiny. "And you still intend to help us?"

"Of course."

Of course, nothing, she thought. What could A'rlon's agenda be in helping them? If he were found out, and he easily could be, he'd be considered a traitor to the Komodoan Realm. They tortured traitors to death and displayed their internal organs in the Capital Spire as a deterrent to anyone else that might harbor feelings of betrayal.

"All right, what's your game, man?" she demanded.

"This is no game, I assure you."

"So tell me why you want to help us? What's in it for you?"

He sighed. "Better that I tell you nothing, Chief. I will bring Catriona to you as soon as I appropriate a space-faring craft."

"Why can't you take me to her now?"

"You are supposed to be awaiting transfer to a research facility. It is safer for me to bring her here." He turned toward the door. "Take no action until my return."

Khumalo put her hands on her hips. "I'll give you an hour, Commander, no more. If you haven't brought her by then I shall come looking for you."

"That would be foolish."

"Maybe so, but I don't trust you."

He smiled, surprising her by its warmth. "All right, Chief. If I'm not back with Catriona in an hour make your way to the communication chamber, six levels up. We'll rendezvous there."

Sensing a possible trap, Khumalo frowned. "Why there?"

"Because," answered the Komodoan in even tones, "it's comparatively simple to get to from here, and is in direct carrier route to the landing pad where we docked. Satisfied?"

"No, but it'll have to do." She watched A'rlon turn and wait for the door to slide open. He strode outside, keeping his tail close as the door shut, sealing Khumalo inside alone. She bent to retrieve the wood Y'alenon had used to cut herself and held it up to inspect the sharp edge.

22

CATRIONA STRETCHED luxuriously under the fluffy quilt, careful not to dislodge the ornate wig, necessary for the upcoming scene. It always felt too hot in the Castle Theatre, and wearing a heavy brocade gown while she pretended to be asleep on stage was stifling. She loved the gown, though — a golden shade of ivory with hundreds of shimmering pearls and peach-colored roses sewn into it. The draconian stays held her curves firmly in place, accentuating bust and hips true to the fashion when *Beauty and the Beast* had been set... sometime around Marie Antoinette's time, Catriona thought. An age of fops and excess, but she loved her elaborate costumes, even the skimpy rags she wore at the beginning of the musical.

She lay still waiting for the orchestra to begin the opening to the second act. Her nose got a sudden itch and she used a forefinger to rub gently, careful not to smudge her makeup.

110 | *Time Twist*

"Where is your master?" asked a young man who played one of the pages.

Catriona frowned. The show hadn't started yet; why was he spouting his one and only line now? She listened intently and tried to peer through the enveloping darkness of the stage.

"Where is your master?" he asked again harshly.

Consciousness skewered through Catriona's brain and she sat up, unable to breathe. She'd been dreaming and the voice did not belong to the page; Captain T'alak stood by the couch.

"Where is Commander A'rlon?" he shouted, his tail pendulating behind him.

"I don't know." Catriona tried not to look at him but found it impossible not to. He dominated the chamber and the emotion emanating from him felt almost tangible. Holding his gaze she slowly slid from under A'rlon's tunic and eased to her feet. He stood between her and the entrance. She edged toward the wall that displayed the two weapons.

"Kneel in position, slave," ordered T'alak, unfastening his tunic.

Catriona warily backed up, seeing the knife in her peripheral vision to her right. His face contorted into a sneer.

"Has A'rlon taught you nothing? I have just broken fast; kneel in the position!"

Heart thumping in her chest, Catriona guessed exactly why he wanted her to kneel, but she'd see him in hell first. She carefully turned to face the wall, trying to inconspicuously ease her left hand toward the knife.

A swishing sound made her jerk her head round. T'alak had his belt in one hand and held it up like a whip.

"On your knees!" he hissed.

She twisted her face away in time before the leather sliced across her back. Crimson blooms of pain lanced through her and she collapsed in a huddle on the floor. She could scarcely take a breath, the stinging felt so intense.

Rough hands grabbed her and pulled at her robe. She cried out and arched her flayed back away from the floor. The hands withdrew and she found herself flipped onto her stomach. T'alak knelt behind her and grasped her hips to pull her back against him. She felt his rigid hardness seeking entrance and kicked out like a woman possessed. His grip loosened. She hurled herself forward, ignoring the searing pain across her back. The momentum carried her onto the couch and she grabbed the short sword from the wall. She leapt down to the floor to face Captain T'alak, the sword held ready.

With a sibilant laugh the Komodoan rose to his feet, the open tunic displaying his bare chest. Catriona noted with disgust that the smooth torso had no nipples or evidence of an umbilical cord.

"What do you hope to do with that?" he sneered.

"Castration," spat Catriona.

She lunged, using both hands to whip the blade through the air at him. T'alak easily sidestepped, but his heavy tail lagged behind. Catriona's weapon cut into it, causing tributaries of green blood to cascade down its length. With a sharp gasp, T'alak reached out and plucked the sword from her hand, blade first. Tossing it aside he skittered his tail round to snatch Catriona's ankle from under her. She lost her balance. He pushed her hard to the floor, pinning her down with his heavy weight.

Catriona fought for breath and tried to free her arms. Pain shot across her back as T'alak pressed himself between her thighs. Forcing her legs apart he ground his erection against her pelvis and scrabbled to find the hem of her robe that blocked him. With horror Catriona realized that there was nothing she could do to stop him. Tears of humiliation and pain flowed down her face and she shut her eyes, willing herself into unconsciousness. T'alak slapped her hard across the face and her eyes opened wide in shock. He leered down at her, triumph flushing his face.

"Now you are going to learn the true meaning of the word 'pain,'" he hissed.

He shifted as he readied to force himself inside her and Catriona tensed for the assault. Then she saw a flurry of movement and his weight suddenly lifted from her. She took a sobbing breath and rolled onto her side, pain tearing across her back. Above her A'rlon and T'alak faced each other, expressions contorted with anger.

"Commander," hissed T'alak in barely-controlled rage, "you have taught this human nothing, she is still feral."

"My friend," said A'rlon evenly, "why do you suppose I brought her here? I intended to instruct her tonight how to please you, assuming the scanning does not render her useless." He offered a slight bow and continued, "I understand you have just broken fast; I apologize for your disappointment."

From where she lay Catriona held her breath as a long, heavy silence stretched between the two Komodoans. At last T'alak spoke, his voice thick.

"There will be no more disappointments, A'rlon. I am posting my personal guards outside until the scanner is ready." He lifted his belt from the floor and marched out, the door closing behind him.

A'rlon dropped to one knee by Catriona and gently inspected the gash T'alak's belt had wielded.

"Don't move." He disappeared into one of the chambers and returned with a medikit. Catriona watched him snap open the briefcase-sized container and remove two round patches, one yellow, the other red. He deftly applied both to her neck.

"To ease pain and prevent infection," he explained. He took what looked like a tube of coral-colored gel toothpaste from the kit and feathered the wound on her back with it.

Catriona stiffened at the feel of the gel, and immediately experienced a sort of sparking across her back like an electrical current. The pain vanished, extinguished like a bonfire in a torrential downpour. She moved in relief and let A'rlon help her sit up. A streak of her blood stained the rug and she wiped at it. A'rlon eased the torn cloth of her robe away from the gash, smoothing more gel over her. Glancing down Catriona saw that her robe had ripped, revealing her left shoulder and most of her breast. She gasped when she realized the locket no longer hung from her neck, and looked frantically around to see where it had fallen. It glinted on the floor by the fireplace, out of reach.

Catriona didn't want to bring A'rlon's attention to it so she busied herself by lifting the tube of gel to read the label. The letters were indecipherable.

"That's amazing stuff," she murmured.

"Nothing more than marsh-peony extract," said A'rlon, "keep it. The effect will wear off in a few hours."

He took out a small sponge, shut the case and reached to pick up the discarded short sword from the floor. He used the sponge to wipe the blade clean of T'alak's olive-dried blood smear.

"I had no idea he would come here or I wouldn't have left you."

He got to his feet and replaced the sword on the wall above the couch. He made to throw the sponge on the fire, then tore it in two and handed the clean part to Catriona, indicating she use it to dry her tears. She did so, feeling self-conscious. She knew her face must be blotched and puffy from crying.

"Thank you." She handed back the sponge.

"Are you hurt anywhere else?"

She thought of how close T'alak had been to penetrating her and shuddered. It wasn't just that, although it felt appalling enough. It was also how helpless she had been, and how the bastard could have done anything to her that he wanted if A'rlon hadn't returned in time to stop him.

Seeing A'rlon's concerned expression she said, "I'm okay. At least I got to hurt his tail." She laughed shakily. "I've been wanting to do that since I met him."

He threw both pieces of sponge into the fire. "Are you hungry?"

Catriona shook her head, and then frowned. "Captain T'alak said he'd just broken fast. What has that got to do with him coming here?"

For once A'rlon didn't meet her eyes. He looked almost bashful, which was engaging in a being so normally sure of himself. "We dine once every three days," he said shortly, "after that we need to… mate."

Catriona's mouth opened in an 'o' of surprise. "What, all of you?"

"Just the males, Catriona." He met her astonished gaze and offered a sardonic smile, showing even, white teeth.

Embarrassed, Catriona concentrated on the rug beside her and ruffled the fur. A'rlon stood with his arms folded, still smiling. Her fingers twisted and worked through the rug.

"And you haven't dined?" she asked carefully.

"No," he agreed, looking highly amused at her discomfiture.

She stroked the fur down on the rug where she had ruffled it. Then she recognized what it was and surged to her feet.

"What the fuck?" She backed away in horror. "That's… that's a…"

A'rlon quickly rolled up the rug and plucked it from the floor. "A Leontor pelt. I'm sorry." He moved to one of the chambers and tossed the rug out of sight.

"How… could you?" Catriona had trouble finding her voice.

"It was a gift from T'alak."

"That's beside the point!" She could barely see for fear and anger. "What if he'd given you a human pelt?" Her gaze flew to the leather couch and she felt faint. "What's that made of?"

He followed her gaze. "The couch is covered with *sk'ndo* boar. A domestic pig on Komodoa."

"What kind of people are you?" shouted Catriona. "That rug… it could have been Grreag…" She buried her face in her hands and sank back down to the bare stone floor.

"The Leontor commander of the *Vallo*?"

"He's my friend," said Catriona from behind her hands.

A'rlon moved suddenly and crouched to pick up Catriona's locket from the floor. She tried to snatch it from him, and he took her hand and gently tipped the broken chain and locket into her palm.

114 | *Time Twist*

She clutched it and waited, expecting him to ask to see inside it, but he said, "Come," and easily scooped her from the floor and set her on the couch. "This will all soon be behind you and you'll be back with your people."

He perched beside her on the edge of the seat, his tail drooping behind him. Catriona saw he looked genuinely distressed. With his guard down he looked exposed, his beautiful, concerned eyes nebulous. He seemed vulnerable and very... human.

"You're not like the others, A'rlon," she whispered. "Who are you?" She saw the merest flicker of something register within him and leaned toward him. Whatever tenuous contact they had she needed to seize it; he was her only hope on this malevolent planet.

"Who are you?" she repeated softly. Her face was close to his and she watched his full lips part as he took breath to speak. She leaned closer and gently put her mouth to his and kissed him. He responded, the tips of their tongues touching softly, then his arms caught her and crushed her against him as their kiss grew deep and carnal. Catriona felt the locket slip from her grasp and stiffened.

He thrust her away. "I can't take advantage," he murmured, eyes ablaze with desire.

Catriona placed her hands on either side of his head and pulled him back into the kiss. "You're not," she whispered, not able to explain with words her need for him, the need to obliterate the memory of T'alak's assault, combined with the visceral, feral human instinct to conjugate life when violent death appeared imminent.

A'rlon began to ease her onto her back on the couch. Catriona tensed, remembering T'alak's weight pinning her to the floor. She gently resisted, pressing A'rlon backward until he sat upright on the couch. She moved with him and raised herself so she straddled him. He murmured in his throat and shifted so he could adjust his tail, caught sideways on the seat. He tugged it back so it hung comfortably through the gap in the lumbar area of the couch.

Catriona thrust all thought of his tail from her and captured his lips with hers. She slipped the tip of her tongue into his mouth and braced to fully explore his forked tongue. She feared it might make her gag but to her relief found no discernable difference to kissing a human. She ran her hands down the front of his tunic, trying to unfasten it. He moved quickly to help and she slid her hands inside. The broad bands of muscle stretched and tensed as he drew in breath and she was instantly aware of his need, as urgent as hers. She pulled his tunic aside, surprised to see that his leather boots reached him mid-thigh, and he wore no leggings or trousers. She realized that T'alak had been the same. Fearful of finding A'rlon too alien, she glanced down but saw that his genitalia looked no different to a human male, except he had no pubic hair. He looked large but not too large. She ached desperately to feel him inside her and murmured, moving her hips against him.

A'rlon caught her left breast with his lips and gently circled her erect nipple with the tip of his tongue. He looked startled when she pulled her torso and breast away from him, and swiftly moved her hips so that she captured him beneath her. Their eyes met and she looked steadily into his dilated pupils, then tightened her muscles around him. He strained his hips to meet her and they thrust together with an intensity that almost bordered on violence.

Catriona dug her nails into his shoulders and heard him gasp as she drew blood. He moved more urgently and his body strained as he crushed her against him. Then he uttered a long sighing hiss as all tension flowed from him like the steam escaping from a volcanic fissure.

His arms tightened around her and Catriona held him close, feeling his hot semen fill her. Although her own need had not been met, she felt satisfied at the intensity of his release. Her thighs began to cramp so she braced her hands on A'rlon's shoulders to lift herself away from him. The urgency gone, he put a hand behind her head and pulled her to him to share a slow, sensual kiss, then eased Catriona gently back onto the couch. This time she submitted gladly as he stretched over her. He leaned on an elbow and lowered his mouth to her breast as he moved his hand down the length of her torso. His fingers played in the red hair between her legs and then tenderly stroked the sensitive area between her thighs. Already swollen and aroused, her hips moved against him. He pressed a knuckle against her clitoris, causing sparks of sensation to wash through her. He startled her with his adroit knowledge of her body, and as the gentle pressure increased she gave in to the rhythmic pulse at her most sensitive spot. She felt consumed by the male smell of him, the hardness of his muscular body beneath her hands, the possessive yet protective feel of the strong arm encircling her. She submitted to the overwhelming swell of sensations and emotions rising to engulf her.

Then his hand withdrew and he rose up on his elbows, shifting down so she felt his warm breath on her shrinking stomach. His mouth touched her, assaulting her private flesh with surges of sensation like an electric current through water. She didn't know this man, but he

116 | *Time Twist*

knew her body and for that moment in time she loved him.

Finally he moved upward and skillfully glided himself back into her. She almost sobbed at the relief of his incursion as he moved sensually within her. He was gentle at first, then thrust harder as her excitement mounted. A wave thrilled through her and crashed and ebbed, and she heard herself cry out. Embarrassed by her abandonment Catriona held him close, astounded at the intensity of her orgasm. His ragged breathing subsided and he shifted so he lay beside her, holding onto her as though she were a lifeline.

23

AGENT Y'ALENON knew she should terminate her pregnancy, but couldn't bring herself to do it. Before long, her secret would be out, and the fetus would either be aborted or kept viable for experimentation once the military learned it to be half-human.

It had never occurred to her she could be inseminated. But the DNA masking drug she had been taking to allow her to remain undetected on Suzerain had so altered her gene structure, she had apparently become compatible with humans. She would be an outcast if it became known she had mated with a human male. She'd be considered a pariah and would live out her life slaving in the *Uk'n* mines. T'alak and the like were not disgraced when they raped humans and kept them as slaves. That was considered acceptable because it could be included in the guise of torture. But for her to have given herself willingly would be condemned as treason.

After she ran from Commander A'rlon, she took an air-skiff out of the base to seek solitude to think. A few lurid streaks of the dying suns broke the blackness of the skies. She soared toward the *Kr'isma Maris*, searching the inky horizon for the flash of lava spurting up like a volcanic flare to light her way.

As she approached the simmering water, a flame curled up a twisted lava spire, billowing into the night sky before vanishing with a hiss. The place was the perfect complement to her state of mind; a sea dotted with tall, vicious lava spires reaching above the surface like charred fingers of drowned giants. At this hour the parched beach looked deserted. Y'alenon skidded the skiff to a halt and climbed out. She walked as close as she could to the boiling waves. The heat engulfed her at once, hot to her lungs. Crouching on the ashen beach, she stared into the glowering, green and orange depths of the sea.

Before she had gone undercover in the Alliance, this had been her most favorite place on Komodoa. Now it looked twisted and ugly, and she felt disoriented. How could life back here feel more alien than when she had lived as a human on Suzerain? And now this entity, this child grew within her. A half-human who would be deemed a freak from birth. A pain struck her as though she'd been hit. Her eyes stung and tears welled up, spilling down her cheeks. She captured a tear on her fingertip, watching it sparkle in the glow from the sea.

It was true what Khumalo had said. She was more human than Komodoan. Khumalo's question haunted her: Can you live with yourself?

Y'alenon realized her decision had been made all along. No, she could not live with herself. Not if it meant murdering her unborn child—this miraculous blend of herself and the human—the only man she'd ever loved. She bent her head as though praying, listening to the hiss of the water. The sound might be the whisper of her ancestors. At last, she stood. The **Kr'isma Maris** boasted being the most breathtaking sight on the planet, but Y'alenon was oblivious to its dreadful beauty as she strode back to the air skiff.

In the locked chamber, Uzima Khumalo waited as patiently as her nature would allow. Time crept slowly by with no sign of A'rlon or Catriona. It began to look like her distrust of Commander A'rlon had been fully warranted. According to her calculations, it was long past the hour that he said he'd bring Catriona to her. She decided she couldn't wait any longer. Propping the broken ottoman against the door she balanced on it and continued to work at disconnecting the lock with Y'alenon's makeshift lance.

After a few irritating failures, the door slid open to reveal a single guard outside. She jumped down into the open doorway and tackled him. With a swift and exact punch to the back of his neck, she knocked him out cold. Satisfied to actually be doing something instead of waiting, Khumalo grinned with satisfaction as she let him drop unconscious to the floor, and dragged him into the room.

Expecting more resistance, she was surprised to find only one guard. The Komodoans did not expect their laboratory rat to stage an audacious escape from within the heart of the military base. Fingering the fallen guard's tunic, Khumalo decided it would be better protection against weaponry than her fatigues. She stripped him and donned the Komodoan's bulky uniform tunic. Taking his carbine and slipping it into her belt, Khumalo stepped back into the corridor.

Finding it empty and silent, she headed for the nearest floor carrier. As she approached, the door slid open and an elderly Komodoan male in sapphire blue civilian dress came out, almost colliding with her. His dark eyes widened at the sight of her.

"Hey, man," murmured Khumalo, smartly swinging a right hook. She caught the Komodoan as he fell. Spotting some seating in a recess to the left, she dragged the inert male there, propping him up on a bench, and draped his tail in a natural manner down behind him. Wiping her hands free of its touch she slipped back to the carrier and studied the hieroglyphics on the wall to discern which would take her to the communications chamber.

In A'rlon's chambers, Catriona and he stretched on their sides against each other. Catriona's robe lay askew, exposing her naked body to the air. She shivered and A'rlon pulled her closer against him. He still wore his tunic, and she nestled into his warm, quilted embrace. She had never known anything quite like the love-making she had just experienced. She felt satiated and liberated, despite the fact she remained a prisoner on Komodoa. A'rlon's arm holding her felt safe and strong, and the heat of his body radiating against her back made her stomach flutter at the memory of him inside her. If she kept her eyes closed maybe time would stay still and she'd never have to face being scanned...

She became aware of A'rlon's watchful stillness. She sensed him to be wide awake, their intimacy at an end. She knew she had to face the reality of her situation. Unless A'rlon could prevent it, Captain T'alak would scan her brain with the probably lethal instrument. And even if she survived that, how would A'rlon keep T'alak from torturing and killing her in his own, particular manner? Dread filled her, and she shifted uneasily.

"A'rlon, how are you going to get me away before Captain T'alak uses the scanner?"

He spoke softly into her hair. "I'll find a way; he won't get his hands on you, don't worry."

Catriona twisted round onto her back to look into his eyes. "Are you an agent, like Y'alenon?"

"Don't start that again, Catriona. It's better you don't know anything about me. If you're interrogated then you can't incriminate yourself. Or me." In one fluid move he released her and got to his feet.

Catriona swallowed hard at the sight of his tail. In the heat of their lovemaking it had been easy to forget he wasn't human. Catriona felt revulsion sweep through her. What had possessed her to be intimate with an alien?

But then she looked into his dark eyes and her feelings flip-flopped into desire again. She smothered her confusion and sat up, hugging her knees to her chest. A thread of pain ran across her back and she retrieved the marsh-peony gel from the floor. The locket had dropped near it and she picked it up.

A'rlon took the gel from her and moved behind so he could dab a new layer onto her healing lash. His touch felt impersonal, all hint of the passionate lover gone. He handed her the tube and began to straighten his uniform. Catriona adjusted her robe so it covered her and slipped the marsh-peony gel, the locket, and the microplayer safely under the wide belt. She so wished for a proper bath but knew she hadn't time.

A'rlon was all business, fastening his belt and smoothing down his cap of black hair. She wanted to speak but couldn't find the words. He moved to the fireplace and extinguished the fire. Catriona mutely watched, feeling the air cool as soon as he doused the flames.

He caught her watching him and reached into his belt to withdraw the *P'jarra* pendant. Turning to her he slipped the chain over her head, letting the pendant fall against her chest.

"To keep you safe."

He gently cupped her face and looked into her eyes. She thought she saw sadness in their dark alien depths, then the moment passed and they became hard as flints. He dropped his hands and strode to the door to open it. Two guards blocked their exit.

"Good day," A'rlon greeted them perfunctorily.

"Honored Commander," said the elder guard. "I have orders-" He didn't get any further.

"You dare to question me?" hissed A'rlon.

"Honored one, no one is to leave until-"

"Until the scanner is ready. Why do you think I leave now?"

The guard stepped aside. "I apologize, honored one."

"You're relieved."

A'rlon led Catriona down the corridor. Over her shoulder she saw the guards' tails lashing. Slanting through the corridor windows, the

120 | *Time Twist*

lavender dawn began to insinuate itself into the horizon. Two quarter moons were still visible.

They took the floor carrier, which transported them upward for a few tense and silent moments. They emerged into an empty corridor, where A'rlon moved to a door that slid open to reveal an unconscious Komodoan guard lying swaddled in his underclothes.

Despite the danger, Catriona stifled a laugh.

"Is that what you wear under your uniforms? You and Captain T'alak don't wear those."

Unheeding, A'rlon gripped her arm, pulling her toward the carrier.

"I'll never be able to take Komodoan soldiers seriously again," giggled Catriona, her amusement verging on hysteria.

"Catriona, shut up!" A'rlon hissed. "Chief Khumalo has already gone ahead to the rendezvous. If she's caught and gives away the plan..."

"I know."

Catriona's mirth plummeted and her heart felt leaden. She'd suspected all along that if her scan couldn't be prevented, A'rlon might be forced to kill her. Blithely she'd kept faith it wouldn't come to that, believing his promise to get her away in time. After the depth of his tenderness in making love with her, it felt impossible that those gentle hands could take her life. She felt oddly detached and distant, still not believing it could happen.

The carrier transported them upward and they stepped out into a vast labyrinth of computer screens and consoles. A Komodoan soldier was bent intently over one of the consoles, and A'rlon motioned for Catriona to stay put as he edged toward him.

Catriona held her breath and strained to watch A'rlon's stealthy progress. She felt the microplayer shift under her belt and snatched hold of it before it fell. The sound alerted the guard who spun round, aiming a carbine at Catriona. Except the guard had kinky black hair and most definitely did not resemble a Komodoan male.

"Uzi!" shouted Catriona, about to run to her, but hesitated. "Or are you Agent Y'alenon?"

"What does it look like, Haggis?" Khumalo grinned, lowering her weapon. Catriona ran up to her and snagged her cheek between finger and thumb. The flesh felt real.

"Give me a break, girl. It's really me." Khumalo pushed Catriona away and shoved the carbine in her belt.

"Impressive work, Chief," observed A'rlon. "Status?"

"I had almost gained access when you interrupted."

"They'll be onto you in seconds if you don't show the computer the right DNA." He held his palm against the computer monitor and an array of green and blue panels lit up.

He turned to Catriona and took hold of the silver pendant. Prying out the center stone he handed it to Khumalo.

"Try this, Chief. Deep space Alliance transmitter chip. The only problem is that anything, whether coded or not, will be intercepted by the Military and may not make it to Alliance space."

"Unless we sent something that wouldn't immediately be recognized as a message," said Khumalo.

"How about this?" asked Catriona. She pulled the microplayer from her belt and handed it to him. "It plays music. 21st century music, to be precise."

"And who else but Catriona could have sent it?" nodded Khumalo.

They turned their attention to the console. In a few moments they sent Catriona's music out, hopefully finding an Alliance target beyond Komodoan space.

"Let's get out of here," said A'rlon.

He grabbed Catriona's hand and all three ran for the carrier. Catriona saw Uzi peering closely at her and at the state of her torn robe. She must wonder what had transpired between them. Catriona tried to smile reassuringly, but the corners of her mouth quivered.

"Get to T'alak's star-yacht when I give the word," ordered A'rlon. "Then get the hell out of here."

"What about you?" asked Catriona.

"Never mind about me."

Catriona felt a hollow panic. "But-"

A'rlon held her close to him for a moment, silencing her. The carrier came to a stop.

They stepped out... and found themselves looking down the muzzle of a carbine.

Agent Y'alenon streaked the air-skiff back to the military base, heading straight for Headquarters' personnel landing pad. T'alak's yacht was docked there along with a selection of personal and military craft. She landed, jumping out. With grim determination she approached the guard on duty in the booth.

"You are unauthorized to land here," he informed her, leering openly at her lack of tail.

122 | *Time Twist*

Aiming her carbine, she pumped a blast at full power into him. He vanished before he knew what hit him. Y'alenon's face betrayed none of her tension as she turned toward the carrier and waited for it to come to her summons. With a metallic clink, the door slid open.

Y'alenon found her weapon kicked from her grasp before she could aim it. Commander A'rlon stood before her flanked by the two human captives.

"I'm on your side," she hissed.

"Since when?" said Khumalo as A'rlon retrieved the fallen carbine.

"I've already dispensed with the guard."

Catriona looked at the empty booth. "What guard?"

"Exactly."

A'rlon gave a half-smile and twisted the carbine in his hands. Handing it back to Y'alenon, he said, "I'm glad you came to your senses."

Khumalo gave her a wink. "You'll be all right, girl."

Catriona noticed that Y'alenon looked A'rlon right in the eye, and rather than annoyed by this breach of Komodoan etiquette, he appeared to approve, quirking a good-humored eyebrow.

A shrill alarm squawked over the landing pad, making Catriona's heart rate accelerate.

"Agent, take the humans and pilot Captain T'alak's yacht," ordered A'rlon, "plot a course for the Alliance border."

Y'alenon nodded to Khumalo and started for the black yacht. Catriona hesitated, searching A'rlon's face. "What about you?"

Chaos ensued as military personnel spilled out of the carrier and flooded the landing pad. Deadly carbine fire slashed around their ears.

"Go now!" A'rlon pushed Catriona hard.

She ran, tripping over her feet and feeling sick to her stomach. Khumalo crouched at the yacht's open hatch.

"Hurry up!" she yelled and followed Catriona's headlong dash into the hatchway.

Catriona peered out searching for a glimpse of A'rlon but she lost him in the surging mass of military.

"Get back!" warned Khumalo as a white streak of carbine fire narrowly missed her. She shoved Catriona further into the yacht.

Y'alenon put the computer on-line and the black vessel hummed and shifted. She looked up and spotted the *P'jarra* pendant around Catriona's neck.

"What are you doing with that?" She snatched it and ripped it off.

"Hey!" objected Catriona. A bone-shaking jolt shook through the yacht, knocking her off balance.

"They've put a traherence stream on us," muttered Y'alenon. "Chief, take over." She grabbed her carbine and leapt out the hatchway toward the control booth, dodging fire.

Blasts sizzled and pinged off the yacht, terrifying Catriona with their shuddering force.

"Catriona, take the helm." Khumalo moved to the hatchway with her drawn carbine.

"*Me*?"

"Coordinates to Alliance space are already programmed, you just need to get us out of here." She leaned out through the hatch and fired off a few rounds. "Catriona, take the fucking helm!"

Catriona lumbered to the console, keeping her precarious balance in the turbulent craft. Remembering how simple it had looked when T'alak flew her to the planet, she took a deep breath. Over her shoulder she saw Uzi poke her head out of the hatchway, aiming her carbine at the traherence stream console in front of the booth. Another swarm of guards converged on the yacht.

Gritting her teeth, Khumalo aimed through the volley of return-fire. Sparks flew from the hull as a shot narrowly missed her. Khumalo fired into the guards, and then kept trying to penetrate the traherence hold.

T'alak's yacht shuddered as it strained against the stream, whining in protest. Out on the pad, Catriona's heart jumped to see A'rlon leaping into the booth, ousting the guard. Khumalo leaned way out and fired a final volley into the traherence stream. With a jolt, they were free. The yacht emitted a deeper hum in preparation for take off.

Khumalo screamed as a carbine blast sliced into her. She keeled over out of the hatchway.

"Uzi!" Catriona stumbled after her, slipping on the fresh blood spilled on the floor.

Khumalo lay face down on the metal flooring of the landing pad.

"Cease fire!" commanded a voice, and Captain T'alak strode to the hatchway. "Take him." T'alak pointed with his chin and Catriona gasped in horror to see A'rlon in the custody of armed Komodoan guards.

T'alak kicked Khumalo's inert body aside before climbing into his yacht. Catriona backed up and shrank against the console.

A voice came from the hatchway. "Hey, man, kick a person when they're down, would you?"

Catriona's fear evaporated to see Khumalo grab T'alak's tail and yank down hard. Confounded, he staggered. Seizing the advantage Catriona ran at him and shoved. Khumalo ducked as the Komodoan

124 | *Time Twist*

captain fell through the open hatchway.

"Go, Catriona, go!" she yelled, crawling in and slamming the hatch closed.

Catriona stumbled to the controls and threw herself into the pilot seat. Carbine fire hummed and shrilled over the yacht as she hit the navigation panel. The craft shrieked backwards into the booth and soldiers scattered like tenpins in a bowling alley.

"Forward, you ass!" Khumalo wedged herself on the floor against the passenger seat.

Catriona hit the panel again. With an agonized whine, the yacht zoomed forward, ascending from the planet.

24

AS THE *Vallo* surged through space into the Komodoan Realm, Colonel Grreag sought Professor Webster. He found the human scientist hunched over a computer console in Engineering. When Grreag approached, the intense scent of Webster's utter despondency struck him.

"How close are you to completion?" he queried, keeping the impatience from his voice.

"The temporal bubble's as ready as it'll ever be," sighed Webster, sitting up and stretching, "but there's no guarantee it's going to succeed. If it collapses, we could lose the contents."

"Understood." Grreag had little choice — if he didn't try the temporal bubble the Komodoans would create the weapon, and the Realm would control the galaxy in any timeline. Destroying the Komodoans' world was worth any risk, thought Grreag.

He left the professor to his work and walked through the *Vallo*, engrossed in his thoughts. Did he have the right to condemn the entire Komodoan species to extinction? But weren't they doing the same to the Alliance? His thoughts turned to Chief Uzima Khumalo. It was incomprehensible to Grreag that she had turned out to be the spy. It was only her confession to Alliance Headquarters that convinced him.

If Grreag were to follow regulations, he'd pull back and await orders from Headquarters. But, he thought with a growl, there were times in an officer's career when the regulations didn't apply. This was one of them.

He entered the control cabin where Major Benjamin, Lieutenants

Larrar and Leopold monitored the long-range scanners. Acknowledging them with a nod, Grreag strode directly to his office. The Terrans' anxious scent made his fur bristle, but they were not to blame. He needed to reserve his anger for the one human who was. Catriona Logan had been the first alien he had liked and opened up to, and he did not know for certain if she were a Komodoan agent or not. He felt betrayed and foolish for allowing himself to lower his guard.

Growling, he sat at his desk and poured himself a shot of Leon *ealu* from a bottle secreted there.

A call startled him. "Colonel, incoming message from the Komodoan Realm on an emergency Terran channel."

"Send it through."

To his bewilderment the same phrase of a song played over again: *Calling occupants of interplanetary craft…*

Bounding to his feet Grreag strode into the control cabin. "Identify."

After a few moments Sam Benjamin looked up with a disbelieving grin, his scent suddenly lightened to joyful.

"It's one of the songs Catriona brought with her…" He stopped short.

Grreag met his look. Was Catriona Logan attempting to contact them? Could she be innocent, after all? Suppressing the excitement rippling through his fur Grreag commanded, "Set a course for the source of that transmission."

Catriona held her breath as the mauve surface of Komodoa rapidly dropped away to the ebony of space. Until the yacht broke the atmosphere she was pinned to her seat. Then the craft changed speed as Y'alenon's programming took over, taking the most direct course to Alliance space. Once the artificial gravity kicked in Catriona jumped up to examine Khumalo's injured shoulder.

"Oh God, Uzi." Blood was everywhere.

The engineer roused herself. "Bind it," she managed.

Catriona pulled open every compartment on the yacht but came up empty. In desperation she tore the lining from Khumalo's Komodoan tunic. Twisting and winding it about Uzi's arm and shoulder, she stemmed the bleeding. The gore made Catriona gag and she swallowed hard to stop herself from being ill. If Uzi had not been wearing the bulky tunic, she would have lost her arm altogether. The shoulder had been partly ripped from its socket and Catriona could see the white of bone.

"Nice bedside manner you got there, Haggis," observed Khumalo.

The mention of haggis caused Catriona to lose control and spew up the entire contents of her stomach onto the cabin floor. As she recovered the yacht lurched and streams of light pinged off the hull.

"Fuck," rasped Khumalo. "Engage... hyperdrive."

Catriona staggered to the helm. Another blast threw her across the pilot seat. "What do I do?"

The engineer lifted her good arm and pointed. Catriona saw a green and blue panel above the front viewer and hit it. It looked as though nothing happened and she whirled to study the console. But the pursuing vessels no longer fired. In fact, they became mere pinpoints on the scanner as T'alak's yacht hurtled into hyperdrive.

"At least Captain T'alak's good for something," she said, but Khumalo didn't reply. She had passed out. Catriona took the marshpeony gel from her belt and gently smoothed it over her friend's injuries, then put another layer on her own healing back. Averting her eyes from Uzi's bloody shoulder, she used part of the tunic lining to make a rudimentary sling and strapped Uzi's arm firmly to her side.

Tearing another strip she mopped up the vomit, the stench making her heave. Catriona felt chilled with fear but perspired in the claustrophobic cabin. Again she wished she could bathe. She felt filthy and smelled overpoweringly of vomit, fear and... sex.

She collapsed into the pilot seat to watch the stars skimming by. She remembered with sadness how beautiful A'rlon's eyes were, and how he had looked at her so tenderly after making love to her. She reached to clasp the *P'jarra* pendant and felt a physical pain when she remembered it had gone.

Y'alenon had been running toward the traherence stream on the Komodoan landing pad when Chief Khumalo succeeded in taking it out. She saw Commander A'rlon overpowered in the booth and captured.

Swerving she crouched with a unit of soldiers as they fired on T'alak's yacht. When the Captain moved forward and ordered a ceasefire, she realized with dismay that the humans' escape plan had been foiled. There was no hope for her or the baby. Catriona's scan would go ahead as planned unless Y'alenon took action to prevent it. The only way she saw to stop it would be to kill Catriona before it happened. And then she'd have to take her own life to prevent her unborn child from being used for experimentation. No one would win.

She pulled out the *P'jarra* icon and said a quick prayer over it. She regretted her impulse at taking it from Catriona, but the sight of it had reminded her of Scott Webster's disk, and how Catriona stole it.

Movement at the yacht caught her eye. She slipped the pendant out of sight and rose to her feet to see. Captain T'alak fell heavily onto the landing pad. His yacht skittered backward and then shot forward and away from the base. Y'alenon's heart lifted. They'd done it! The humans were on their way to Alliance space, and there was hope yet.

She knew Captain T'alak would order pursuit so she holstered her weapon and ran toward him. He pulled himself erect with as much dignity as he could muster. Fury contorted his face and Y'alenon did not meet the seething gaze he turned on her. She stared instead at the fresh scar on his tail, wondering how he got it.

T'alak lifted his wrist to speak into his comm unit and beckoned Y'alenon. Within seconds an actuate bubble formed around them and they materialized on the *L'umina* flight deck, orbiting above Komodoa.

Hissing orders, T'alak took his command chair and Y'alenon moved to tactics to see if the *L'umina* had picked up the yacht's signal.

Captain T'alak's powerful tail swept back and forth as he sat, clutching the arms of his command chair. Fear gripped Y'alenon's heart. If he had any idea what she planned... She felt a fluttering in her abdomen and laid a protective hand there. It steadied her resolve and she felt calmer. Eyeing T'alak to ensure his attention was focused elsewhere, she accessed the computer and located A'rlon's position on board. The Infirmary. He must be wounded, not dead.

The *L'umina* shot out of orbit and followed the stolen yacht's flight path toward Alliance territory. If Catriona were to succeed in reaching the Alliance, Y'alenon would work out a way to find Professor Webster. It would be the only chance her child had for survival. Would Scott forgive her? But even that didn't matter as long as her child would live free from tests and laboratories.

Taking a deep breath, she approached T'alak, keeping her gaze lowered.

"Honored Captain, Professor Webster will still be aboard the *Vallo*. As I failed you in bringing the disk the first time, I humbly beg a second chance."

T'alak's tail twitched as he studied her. "You said we do not need the disk if we retake the human female."

Y'alenon bowed low. "Forgive my impertinence, but the disk is more important, honored one. The human is an excellent substitution, but if we have the chance to implement all the data from Webster's disk, we can do so much more."

128 | *Time Twist*

"Explain."

She straightened. "That data will show us how to seal off entire planets as well as travel through time."

His tail lashed. "You led us to believe the female to be a better prize than the disk."

Y'alenon felt a stillness from the flight deck crew as they eavesdropped. "She is, Sir. But if we have both we can create the weapon before the Alliance can. Then our victory is guaranteed." She forced herself to stay silent while he considered her words.

"Very well," he hissed at last, "create an actuate bubble that will put you on board the *Vallo* when we reach them. Be certain you succeed this time." Y'alenon bowed and made to leave but he stood, hissing, "First, you will accompany me to the Infirmary."

Y'alenon faltered, feeling the blood rush from her head. Did he know of her condition? Was he going to order the fetus to be forcibly ripped from her body?

He strode from the flight deck and she trailed behind, trying to gain control of her fright. He couldn't know; no one did. She'd stopped herself from telling Chief Khumalo, but maybe the human had guessed. And perhaps she'd shared it with Commander A'rlon, who in turn had informed Captain T'alak. She let her fingers touch the carbine in her belt and followed T'alak into the carrier. She wasn't certain why A'rlon had helped the humans to escape but she had a suspicion. It couldn't be just because Catriona Logan had taken his fancy.

The carrier deposited them at the Infirmary. The two guards at the door saluted T'alak, and Y'alenon felt their speculative eyes on her as she shadowed the Captain past them. It occurred to her that she might possibly become of intense interest to the males when they broke their fast. She had no tail, and although usually that would make her untouchable, it was well known who she was and that her tail awaited her in cryogenic storage. She'd need to make sure she was far away from any Komodoans by then.

Inside the Infirmary two more guards stood in attendance, one bare-chested. The metallic tang of fresh blood heightened by the humidity assaulted Y'alenon, and she steeled herself.

Commander A'rlon hung by his wrists from a thick chain in the ceiling, his tail and feet inches from the floor. He raised his head and looked hard at T'alak, his face bloody and bruised. His wrists were sodden green with blood where they had cuffed him.

"So, I find out the truth about you at last, my friend," said T'alak.

A'rlon raised an eyebrow over a half-closed swollen eye. "Indeed."

"The *L'umina* will soon run down your flame-haired human, A'rlon, so your efforts have been wasted." A'rlon did not reply but he didn't break eye contact. "I wonder why my trusted second-in-command would risk everything to aid an alien's escape?" T'alak slowly circled A'rlon, his tail stiff and held to the side. His movements appeared careful and restrained, but his corked fury was evident to Y'alenon. "And not just any alien," he continued, "one who held the key to dominion over the Alliance."

He came to stand right in front of A'rlon, looking up into his former friend's battered face. Y'alenon stood very still, hardly daring to breathe. A'rlon might have given away her part in the escape plan, but she didn't think so. But during torture, that might come later.

"Nothing to say in your defense, Commander?" asked T'alak. He watched A'rlon's face for a moment then turned to nod to the guards. They stepped up behind A'rlon; one held him steady while the bare-chested one grasped the back of A'rlon's uniform tunic and tore it, exposing his naked back. T'alak raised a hand palm up and the guard holding A'rlon let go of him so he swung like a trussed *volator* bird. The guard pulled a long reed-like object from his belt and put it in T'alak's waiting hand. With a smile T'alak held it up so A'rlon could clearly see it.

Y'alenon inwardly flinched when she recognized the whip T'alak held. She had witnessed punishments and interrogations where the whip proved a most effective way to extract information from reluctant mouths.

"Agent Y'alenon," hissed T'alak. She stood to attention. "Watch how we deal with traitors, lest you have forgotten."

He stepped a few paces behind A'rlon. She was surprised he intended to wield the punishment himself. Such menial work was beneath his position, both as captain and the head of his Imperial House. Then she understood when he eagerly drew back the whip to strike, and a glint of anticipatory pleasure flickered in his eyes. He considered this sport.

A swift crack sounded and livid green welts opened across A'rlon's back on either side of his spinal scales. His body jerked but he didn't cry out. The sight of fresh blood appeared to excite Captain T'alak. He whipped A'rlon with a savage enjoyment that left A'rlon spasming with pain and hissing between his clenched teeth.

T'alak's ferocity made Y'alenon cringe, and she couldn't stop her body from twitching involuntarily as though to try and stop him. She didn't think A'rlon could survive much more. The whip had sliced vicious welts, his back a criss-cross of livid green weals and torn flesh.

A bleep from T'alak's wristcomm unit arrested him mid-stroke. Breathing heavily he stepped to a computer console to answer the hail. A'rlon's body sagged and Y'alenon took a breath in relief.

"Honored one, your yacht is within range," came the flight deck report. T'alak spun the whip in a circle and handed it back to the guard.

"All hands," he said to the console, then pointed at Y'alenon, ordering her to follow him. His eyes looked feverish and he appeared highly stimulated from the beating he'd dispensed.

Y'alenon complied, and with a quick glance at A'rlon's slumped form, hurried from the Infirmary. She could do nothing to help him, and said a fervent prayer of thanks to *P'jarra* that it was not she who hung on that chain.

But T'alak forcing her to witness the beating was his implicit promise of what would befall her if she again failed to bring the disk to him.

25

GRREAG SAT rigidly in his command chair on the *Vallo*. Lieutenant Larrar monitored TactOps, Major Benjamin and Lieutenant Leopold both silently studied the computer screen at NavOps. The air smelled tense and no one spoke as they sped through space. For once Grreag would have welcomed chatter as a distraction. He noted this appeared to be the first time the humans had obeyed him without question. That compelling human, Catriona Logan, had succeeded where he had failed in bonding everyone together.

He shifted uneasily and resisted the desire to puff up his fur. He wanted so much to believe she was innocent in all this, and that he headed to liberate her from the Komodoan Realm. What if this were a trap? And he, commander of the vessel, should display only good leadership to the crew. What if his judgment had continued to be impaired, just because one human had broken through his emotional barriers?

"Colonel!" announced Lieutenant Larrar, "I'm picking up a small vessel ahead."

"Ping them," ordered Grreag.

Larrar bent over her console. "The frequency's open but no reply."

A familiar Scottish burr rang loud and clear through the control cabin: "Damn this bloody thing, how do I stop it?"

Grreag's ears eagerly flicked forward. "Catriona, this is the *Vallo*. What's your status?"

"I know it's bloody you," she snapped, "I can't stop!"

Grreag noticed the three control cabin crew eyeing him. His sense of smell couldn't tell whether they were amused or nervous.

"On screen!" he growled. A streamlined star-yacht with Komodoan markings appeared on the *Vallo* viewer.

"Good God!" said Benjamin as the craft lurched and kangarooed erratically, shuddering in protest under Catriona's ministrations.

"Colonel," advised Larrar, "several craft are in pursuit of the yacht. They're catching up."

Grreag felt like purring. If Catriona were being pursued this was not a trap.

"Actuate her out of there," he snarled, masking the feeling of sheer joy that flooded him.

Larrar shook her head. "We can't focus a bubble if the human continues piloting like that."

"Traherence stream on the entire yacht?" offered Benjamin.

"We're not lined up. By the time we are the other vessels will be on us," growled Larrar.

"By the winds, Catriona!" Grreag rose to his feet, his hackles fully raised.

On screen, five Komodoan craft spun out of hyperdrive and surrounded Catriona's yacht.

"Get us in range," ordered Grreag. They'd pull Catriona out of there the old-fashioned way if they had to. "Calibrate weapons." Sam Benjamin was already doing so, he noted with approval.

"One human life sign showing, Colonel," reported Larrar.

"Try an extended actuate bubble and see if that works."

The young Leon's talons sped over the controls and an elongated bubble began to materialize in the control cabin. Instead of Catriona, Chief Khumalo appeared, her dark eyes blinking in confusion. Leopold ran to her, a medikit in hand.

"Scan for a second human life sign!" commanded Grreag.

Larrar consulted her screen. "Nothing, sir. We're in line to attempt traherence now."

"Bring the entire craft into the cargo bay."

"Colonel, traherence can't differentiate between the human's vessel and the others," said Larrar.

Benjamin helped Khumalo to sit up. She blinked, taking a moment

132 | *Time Twist*

to get her bearings. "I don't know why you can't read Catriona's life signs." She moved stiffly to Larrar's side to examine the console.

"Colonel," reported Larrar, her voice thin with tension. "A Komodoan Realm warship is approaching. It's the *L'umina*."

"Sir, I'll form another bubble and go back for Catriona," said Khumalo.

Grreag's ears flattened, "We cannot lower armor, Chief. You know that."

"I can create a window, Sir."

Grreag hesitated. He could not risk everything with an enemy ship bearing down on them. He had to assume the Komodoans wanted Catriona alive, so she wasn't in immediate danger.

"No. Take us in close and ready weapons." He saw the angry look the Chief leveled at him, but ignored it. The dark human turned to a console and rapidly worked at the keypad with her one good arm.

Grreag had no inkling of what she planned until an actuate bubble began to form around her.

"Chief!" he roared, too late. With a distorted hissing sound, the bubble containing her vanished.

✦

Y'alenon scanned the *Vallo*, searching for a weakness in her armor. She had changed out of the padded Komodoan Realm tunic and back into the green fatigues she wore when masquerading as Chief Khumalo. The screen flickered and she studied the data, spying a window in the armor on the *Vallo's* underbelly, close to the galley. She input the coordinates and stepped into the bubble. In seconds she materialized on the *Vallo*. She had gambled on the corridor being deserted.

Keeping her head down she moved through the ship toward engineering. No one paid her any notice; she blended in as long as she kept her facial scales covered by her hair. She could scarcely breathe, she felt so nervous. How would the Alliance react to her carrying a half-human baby? But she couldn't turn back now.

She found Scott in the engine room, working feverishly dissecting code at a computer console. He looked even thinner if that were possible. She approached, jolted at his moribund appearance. "Scott!" He looked up and stared blankly at her. "It's me, Pauline."

His blue eyes widened as he took in her dark hair and eyes, and finally the arc of scales on her forehead. Recognizing her at last he gave a startled cry and surged to his feet, then stopped short. "What do you want?"

The fear and distrust in his eyes cut her deeply.

"I'm sorry, Scott. I've made a horrible, horrible mistake. I want to put it right if I can."

"The only way this can be put right is if you didn't give my disk to your people," Webster said angrily. He glanced toward the door, gauging the distance.

Y'alenon held out her hands, palms up. "I'm not here for the disk, Scott. I'm here because…" she choked but continued, "because I love you. I don't belong on Komodoa; I belong with you."

"But you're a Komodoan," he said bluntly.

"I'm not, not anymore. I'm changed but I didn't know it until I went back there. Please believe me, if I could… if I could turn back time I would and make this all go away."

A sudden wry smile flashed across Webster's face. "If you have my disk we can turn back time."

"But I don't and neither do the Komodoans. It wasn't found in the launch pad?" He shook his head. Y'alenon knew she hadn't much time before her presence on board would be detected. "I need to tell you something, Scott. Why I came back." She took a deep breath. "I'm… pregnant."

Emotions made their way across Webster's gaunt features, ending with an expression of disbelief. Y'alenon said nothing more. His reaction would dictate her next move. Webster fumbled in the pockets of his blue jumpsuit and came up with the scanner he'd intended to use on Catriona. Y'alenon tensed; if it hadn't been recalibrated properly it would harm her baby. She couldn't allow that.

Webster concentrated on the scanner, his fingers working at the controls. After a moment he moved toward her. "I've adjusted it so it can safely ascertain if you really are pregnant." His voice sounded cold and analytical. The voice of a scientist with an interesting specimen to study.

She endured the scanner as he ran it over her abdomen. He lifted the result screen and peered at the readout. "My God, you are pregnant," he breathed. "And you're human. I can't detect any cellular or genetic anomalies in you. The fetus, however…"

Fear stabbed through Y'alenon. "What's wrong with it?"

"Nothing. There are definite and distinctive human and alien signatures. The human DNA…" he paused and looked right into her eyes. "It's mine," he said in wonder.

"Ours," she corrected. They gazed at each other as he absorbed the fact he fathered this unborn child.

"What happens now?" asked Y'alenon, afraid of his answer.

A shadow fell over his face. "Leontor Control will never allow this

134 | *Time Twist*

baby to be born."

"You can't tell them."

He shook his head. "It's not up to me. You must know that you'll be arrested as soon as they find out you're here."

"But I couldn't stay on Komodoa; our baby won't survive there either."

A klaxon sounded. Shouting and the thump of running feet could be heard from main engineering.

"They've found out I'm here."

Webster's face went white and he staggered. Y'alenon steadied him and helped him sit down.

"The dizzy spells are getting worse," he said.

Y'alenon unzipped a pocket on her fatigues and pulled out a vial containing a clear liquid. The *P'jarra* pendant dropped to the floor and she bent to retrieve it. "Your illness is due to a chemical compound that suppresses the hippocampus. Your body has had a bad reaction to it, but this will put it right." She fumbled in her pockets and withdrew a sealed syringe.

The door monitor dinged but the iris didn't dilate. A voice intruded through the monitor: "Professor Webster, this is Security. Open up!"

"There's no time," said Webster.

A whining metallic sound started as Security began to cut their way into the engine room.

Professor Webster looked keenly at Y'alenon. "Do you really want us to be together, Pauline?"

Tears flowed freely down her cheeks. "With our baby, yes."

He turned to the computer he'd been working at, his fingers rattling over the keypad. "Do you trust me?" he asked.

"Implicitly."

Security had almost broken through. Webster drew Y'alenon close and hit a final key. The room wavered and faded from sight to be replaced with a swirling kaleidoscope of jeweled colors. With a shock Y'alenon understood what Scott had done. Enveloped in a temporal actuate bubble, he had removed them from this dimension.

Her last thought was of the *Kr'isma Maris*, a tongue of incandescent flame rising free above the spires of the broiling ocean.

26

CATRIONA WATCHED in panic as the Realm vessels surrounded the yacht, cutting her off from the *Vallo*. Who had sent the bubble for Uzi? The air in the cabin changed as another bubble began to form. Catriona backed away and frantically searched for something to use as a weapon. She fumbled at the metal wall compartments and managed to haul out an empty drawer, about the size of a large encyclopedia.

The bubble formed and a figure shimmered into existence. Catriona took her only advantage. As a Komodoan guard appeared, she moved quickly behind him and smacked the makeshift weapon on the alien's head as hard as she could. He buckled and Catriona dropped the drawer to snatch his weapon from him. Immediately a second bubble began to form. Catriona gritted her teeth and held the Komodoan carbine ready.

"Uzi!" she cried when the engineer appeared before her.

Arm still in sling Khumalo winked and stepped over to the console to put the yacht at a dead stop, "Hey, Haggis, you didn't think I'd leave you to face the music alone, did you?"

The air pressure indicated another actuate bubble materializing. Khumalo grabbed Catriona's weapon and shoved her aside. A Komodoan guard appeared. With her good arm Khumalo aimed the carbine and fired, but the Komodoans had changed tactic when they lost the first soldier. Uzi's target disappeared and gave way to another bubble that formed so close it knocked her sideways, the carbine tumbling to the floor. She hit her head hard on a console and collapsed in a heap. The guard reached for Catriona.

"Get off!" She snatched up Uzi's discarded carbine and aimed. The weapon fizzled, apparently without power. Catriona jumped back and used the carbine as a baseball bat on the soldier's head. He staggered but kept coming. Catriona felt the carbine hum against her hands as power surged back into it. She aimed and fired, this time the white light cut into the Komodoan, who registered surprise before he dropped to the floor.

Two new actuate bubbles brought two more soldiers. One grabbed Catriona from behind and she dropped the carbine. The other soldier hissed a laugh and moved close to her, licking a runnel of sweat from her face with his forked tongue.

"Captain T'alak ordered her intact," warned the soldier holding her.

A sudden rush of air tossed Catriona against her captor. She tipped back her head and bit hard into his throat. His blood tasted sulphurous and sour. He howled and thrust her from him.

The other soldier careened across the cabin and smashed into the wall. Catriona turned to see Colonel Grreag wiping his big hands. His fur bristled, making him appear very huge and threatening.

Holding a hand to his green-bleeding neck the Komodoan snatched hold of Catriona again. To her panic she felt an actuate bubble forming around them.

"Grreag!" she cried.

The Leon stepped forward, smartly pulled Catriona from the bubble and punched the Komodoan out.

Catriona threw her arms around Grreag and fiercely hugged him. He recoiled, his nostrils flaring. Flattening his ears, he studied her intently before bending to inspect Chief Khumalo.

A massive force blasted into the yacht, knocking both Grreag and Catriona off their feet as air rushed from the cabin. Grreag broke Catriona's fall. Both gasping in the vacuum, Grreag rolled from under her and snatched up Chief Khumalo in one arm and Catriona in the other.

The bubble deposited them in the *Vallo* control cabin. Medics quickly bore Khumalo away while Grreag and Catriona gratefully gulped in air. Grreag recovered quickly and strode to his command chair.

"Get to Sickbay," he ordered Catriona. "And get cleaned up!" He turned his attention to Major Benjamin, "What hit us?"

Dizzy and disoriented, Catriona staggered obediently toward the door. She saw her robe had been torn further during the fracas on the yacht and barely covered her breasts. Then she spotted the viewer and stopped in shock at the image of the *L'umina*.

"A temporal implosion took out our armor, Sir," reported Benjamin.

"From the *L'umina*?"

"No, Colonel. It took down their armor, too."

"Find out the origin," growled Grreag, taking his chair. "And get us back on line." He spied Catriona and she stared anxiously back. He opened his mouth to re-order her out of the control cabin but changed his mind. "Get strapped in," he advised.

Catriona gratefully sank to the nearest observation seat and buckled herself in. Her head felt like it had been in a vice. She couldn't believe Captain T'alak had pursued her all the way to the *Vallo*. She wondered if A'rlon was on the *L'umina* with him.

Benjamin looked up from Central Command. "The implosion was caused by a temporal actuate bubble, Colonel. It originated from the *Vallo* Engineering, but no corresponding bubble was created, so this one imploded when activated."

Grreag's brows furrowed deeply and his ears flickered. "Professor Webster?"

"No trace of him, Sir. He must have tried to actuate himself away."

"Where was the bubble supposed to arrive?"

"More like 'when'."

Catriona could see Grreag barely controlled his patience. "Did he make it?" he roared.

"It's unlikely."

Lights flickered on throughout the control cabin. "We're on line," reported Leopold.

On the screen the *L'umina* lit up like a holiday ornament as her power also was restored.

"Get us out of here before they charge up their weapons," ordered Grreag. "Head for the nearest outpost at maximum velocity. We must prepare as best we can now that the Realm can build the temporal weapon from Professor Webster's disk."

Catriona slipped her fingers into her belt to locate her locket. "No, they can't," she announced triumphantly. She flipped out the disk from behind her mother's picture, and stood to hand it to Grreag. She felt light-headed and clung to the arm of his command chair.

Grreag held up the disk between a clawed finger and thumb. "How did you manage that?" he demanded.

"Sir," said Khumalo, holding a scanner toward the disk, "it's coated with some kind of quantum-shielding; that's why we couldn't read Catriona's life sign on the yacht."

The *Vallo* flipped a full 180° at high speed and Catriona caught sight of the spinning on the viewer. Dizziness swamped her and the floor slammed upward to hit her in the face.

*

"You asked for me?"

At the sound of Grreag's gravelly voice, Catriona opened her eyes and looked up from her cot in Sickbay.

"I don't have much time," he added. "The *L'umina* is still in pursuit. You are feeling better?"

"Much, thanks." Her bruises and cuts had been cleaned and she had

138 | *Time Twist*

had a thorough wash in the spritz. Filmy, white pajamas replaced her torn and filthy robe and she felt more human again—less like the bedraggled and helpless alien slave she'd been forced to be on Komodoa.

"What do you want?" asked Grreag with his customary abruptness. Catriona struggled to find the right words, so he continued, "Is this about the Komodoan officer?"

"How did you know?"

"I smelled him all over you in the yacht."

Catriona flushed. "So you know... em..."

"That you mated with him, yes."

"Jesus!" Catriona cringed with mortification.

"Did he force you?"

Catriona laughed shortly. "No, I think I forced him."

"What is the problem then?" Grreag looked anxious to be away.

Catriona regretted asking for him but she'd needed to talk about A'rlon and find out if Grreag knew anything about what had happened to him. From the shelf beside her cot she lifted the tube of marsh-peony gel A'rlon had given her.

"Because he helped me escape he's probably dead."

The Leon's ears flicked forward. "You cannot blame yourself. He obviously knew what was at stake."

Catriona turned the tube over and over in her hands. "I can't bear to think I caused his death."

"You didn't; it was his choice." He watched her for a moment. "Do not be uncomfortable about your encounter with this officer. Hostages often respond in this way to their captors; I believe it is referred to as the Stockholm syndrome on Earth."

She looked away in confusion and slipped the gel into her pajamas pocket. Could that be all it had been? She'd never felt such a compelling pull to anyone like she had with A'rlon. Needing the comfort of a friend's touch she reached for Grreag's furry paw.

He drew back, rethought it and patted her hand awkwardly. "I suggest you discuss this with Chief Khumalo; she is your friend." His fur rippled and she knew his mind was on the Komodoan warship dogging them toward Alliance space.

"Go on back to the control cabin, Grreag; I'll head to my berth."

"I'll escort you," he offered, steadying her as she rose from the cot.

As they walked, she asked, "What if Captain T'alak catches up with the *Vallo*?"

"Do not concern yourself; he will do you no more harm."

"But what if he shoots us down?"

He made a gargling noise that Catriona recognized as a laugh. "He will be the only one shot down, I assure you."

She nodded, somewhat reassured.

"When do you want to return to your time?" he asked, startling her at the suddenness of the question.

She blinked. "Can I go back to it?"

"Now that we have Professor Webster's data, we can engineer a way to put you back early enough so you can go to a place on Earth that won't be devastated by the temporal rupture."

Catriona didn't know what to say. She should have been overjoyed to know she could go home if she wanted to, but she felt numb.

"It will take time before we discover how to accurately send you back," rumbled Grreag. "Until then there is no need to fear discovery by Leontor Control. I will ensure they will not find out you came through time."

"How can you do that?"

"I shall make arrangements to provide you with a new identity while you wait."

"And do what?"

His amber eyes gleamed. "I would recommend you consider applying for the Alliance Cadet College."

She gave a half-hearted laugh. "Would that mean I could work on the *Vallo* with you?"

"It could be arranged. But only if you learn discipline."

She realized he meant it, and felt a surge of warmth for him. Impulsively, she reached her arms around his neck and hugged him. He gingerly returned it, then firmly put her from him.

The alarm klaxon blazed, making both of them jump. Grreag hit the nearest computer monitor along the wall.

"Colonel Grreag," came Benjamin's voice, "the *L'umina* has gained on us."

"**STAY HERE,**" Grreag commanded Catriona and took off at a run.

140 | *Time Twist*

Heart pounding, Catriona trailed him to the control cabin. No way would she be alone if they were under attack. Belatedly she realized she still had no footwear and wore pajamas, but decided not to go back and change.

She arrived on Grreag's heels to see the *L'umina* filling the viewer, the massive hexagram looming against the stars. Lieutenants Leopold and Larrar sat at NavOps and TactOps, Major Benjamin at Command Central control, and Chief Khumalo crouched on the floor by him, working beneath the console. Her sling had been replaced by a mobile cast.

"Report," ordered Grreag taking his command chair.

"We've got armor working again but only at thirty-five percent efficiency," replied Benjamin.

"How goes repairs?"

Khumalo poked her head out from under the console. "Weapons are on-line, but I can't guarantee accuracy."

Grreag pondered, then addressed Lieutenant Larrar, "Ping the *L'umina.*"

The image of Captain T'alak, larger than life filled the screen. Catriona sucked in her breath, shrinking back against the wall. The sight of his cold eyes made her feel weak at the knees, and she remembered with fear the light of excitement in them when he'd pinned her to the floor during his attempted rape.

"Colonel Grreag," T'alak said smoothly, his sibilant voice causing Catriona to shudder. "My apologies for the intrusion into Alliance space but I have come to take back what is mine."

"And what is that, Captain?" inquired Grreag, keeping his voice even.

"You have our agent on board."

Grreag's ears flattened. "Stand by." He made a motion to Larrar, who ended the transmission. The ominous star-shape filled the viewer once more. Grreag stared at Catriona. "What does he mean?"

She felt all eyes on her and her fear increased. They couldn't think that T'alak meant her! She looked to Uzi for support and saw a familiar silver glint on the surface of the Weapons console.

"The *P'jarra* necklace!" she cried, running across the cabin to pick it up. "This is mine, how did it get here?"

"Security found it in Engineering," Khumalo told Grreag, scrambling from under the console and standing. "They didn't find an intruder, but Professor Webster had disappeared and that was on his computer keypad."

"Y'alenon took it from me," explained Catriona, "before I escaped from the planet." She looked closer at the engraving, "But the center stone had gone, there's something else in there now."

Khumalo took it and studied it. "An Alliance memory chip."

She popped it out and scanned it through the computer. Professor Webster's voice rang through the control cabin, tersely explaining that Y'alenon had accompanied him in the temporal actuate bubble.

"Wait back there," Grreag ordered Catriona to the side of the cabin where her image would not be seen on T'alak's viewscreen. She took the pendant with her. Using her finger and thumb she squeezed the broken link on the chain closed and slipped the pendant around her neck. The weight of it gave her a little courage.

Grreag gestured to Larrar, and Captain T'alak once more filled the screen.

"I'm afraid your agent and Professor Webster were killed in the implosion that knocked our ships off line," Grreag told him.

Catriona watched T'alak's eyes darken. "You expect me to believe that, you Leontor filth?"

"Believe what you like. Your agent is not on this ship."

T'alak's face became a forbidding mask. "I will accept your explanation with no repercussions if you return the 21st century human to me in exchange."

Catriona gripped the *P'jarra* pendant so hard her fingers cramped. "I am not at liberty to do so."

"It is our right, Leontor! She is not part of the Alliance and therefore not under your jurisdiction."

Colonel Grreag swiveled his head to look at Catriona. "Come here."

Catriona's stomach lurched. She put one foot in front of the other, the distance to Grreag feeling like miles. Surely he couldn't be considering handing her back to Captain T'alak?

"If she is not under my jurisdiction and as we are no longer in Komodoan space, then she has the freedom of choice." He turned to her, "Human, do you wish to return to Captain T'alak?"

"No," she stated emphatically, "I most certainly do not."

"And neither do I," came a voice from behind her.

T'alak's image registered shock and everyone in the control cabin stared. Commander A'rlon stood in the open iris of the *Vallo* control cabin door. Larrar and Leopold made to rise from their stations but Colonel Grreag stayed them.

Catriona gaped at A'rlon, hardly able to take a breath. His face looked badly bruised with livid-green abrasions, and his uniform tunic

142 | *Time Twist*

hung in tatters, sodden with bottle-green blood.

"A'rlon!" hissed T'alak, "I should have known."

"If I were you, my friend," A'rlon advised, "I would turn around and get back to the Realm as fast as my spinner could take me, before the entire Alliance Armada arrives to blast you out of the heavens."

T'alak's face contorted in rage, his complexion mottled olive.

"Prepare to die, traitor!" he spat and his image vanished from the screen. The Komodoan warship replaced him, turning toward the *Vallo*.

"Battle stations!" snapped Grreag. "Commander A'rlon, explanations can wait; take a seat. You," he addressed Catriona, "get out of here!"

Catriona ignored him and stared dumbstruck at A'rlon, not believing him to actually be alive and here. He looked more dark and alien than she remembered. She watched him carefully sit on an observation seat, shifting sideways so his tail could droop comfortably. He caught Catriona's gaze and his dark eyes sparkled a smile at her. It made her stomach flutter in a distracting way.

"Incoming," warned Benjamin.

On the viewer the Realm ship suddenly swooped, spilling phosphorent, white fire. The *Vallo* lurched, unbalancing Catriona. She scrambled to the nearest observation seat and pulled herself upright.

"Return fire," ordered Grreag, "try and dampen their carbines."

The *Vallo* spat a volley of orange torpedoes at the spinning Komodoan ship. The *L'umina* glittered with an explosion to her underside and the *Vallo* control cabin lit golden, reflecting the sputtering fire.

Another onslaught of phosphorent lightning rocked the *Vallo*, and Catriona threw herself into the chair and held on. The blasts were like a tsunami hitting a huge cruise ship. Something she thought should be very solid and safe suddenly wasn't, as it pitched and rolled uncontrollably from the wave's impact. She felt certain the *Vallo* would rend apart and cast them all out into space.

She saw Major Benjamin hanging on grimly to his computer console, legs braced against the floor. Trying to finish repairs underneath the console, Khumalo kept being tossed against him.

"Armor down another ten percent!" shouted Uzi. Catriona saw sweat glistening on her dark skin.

Another bone-jarring blast from the *L'umina* slammed into them, causing the *Vallo* to rock so violently Catriona's head bumped painfully against the back of her chair. The cabin lit up as sparks flew from the Weapons console.

"Shit, man!" yelled Khumalo from below. "How many times can I rewire this piece of crap?"

Catriona rubbed the back of her head and looked across at A'rlon. He sat upright and tense, watching Colonel Grreag, his scaly hands showing the bones of his knuckles. Another blast pounded into them and Catriona bit her lip, tasting blood. It looked like T'alak intended to blow them all to kingdom come.

She wished she weren't so helpless: she felt useless and in the way. If they did get through this, she vowed she would go to the ACC as Grreag suggested. She'd never be useless or helpless again.

Larrar's console at TactOps bleeped loudly. "Two more Komodoan Realm warships entering the sector," she announced, her voice thin.

T'alak obviously expected the ships; the *L'umina* came to a full stop, waiting.

Grreag beat a rhythm on his chair arm with a talon. Catriona swallowed down her rising panic. With these odds the *Vallo* couldn't survive. Bile rose in her throat and she looked around at her friends. Even if they survived the barrage of fire, if taken captive they'd all be subjected to T'alak's sadism. She knew he'd draw out their torture before releasing them into death.

Seeing A'rlon's damaged face and bloodied tunic she knew T'alak would make him suffer the most. And Grreag... she remembered with horror the Leontor rug on A'rlon's floor.

Catriona took a deep breath and stood. She had to go back to T'alak; it would be the only way that any of these people might survive.

"Colonel, let me-"

"Don't even think about it."

"I have to go, Grreag, don't be stupid!" she shouted.

The control cabin crew gaped at her with a mixture of shock and disbelief. Even with a clear threat to their lives from the *L'umina*, Catriona saw they were horrified at how she addressed their Leontor commander. Grreag slowly turned his head to look at her and closed one amber eye in a deliberate wink.

"Chief," he said. "Is there enough power in the drive for an actuate bubble?"

"Just about, Colonel."

All eyes moved away from Catriona and fixed on Grreag. She made herself breathe evenly as she watched the Leontor.

"Chief," he continued, "now that you have Webster's disk, is it feasible to set up a temporal bubble large enough to enclose the *L'umina* for a short period?"

144 | *Time Twist*

Chief Khumalo grinned at Grreag. "I'll give it a try." Beaming, she disappeared under the console again.

A'rlon stood. "Colonel, I can provide the Chief with exact *L'umina* dimensions. Without them we might get caught in the temporal flux."

Grreag's ears flicked back and forth. "If you please, Commander."

A'rlon stood and made his way toward Weapons. As he passed Catriona he gently touched the *P'jarra* pendant and smiled.

Lieutenant Larrar's console bleeped a warning. On the viewer two spinning stars came into focus, arriving on either side of the *L'umina.*

"We're out of time, Chief!" shouted Grreag.

"Not quite." Khumalo crawled from under Weapons and clustered with A'rlon and Benjamin at the console.

Catriona watched the viewer as the three warships began to spin as one toward the *Vallo.* They appeared to take their time, moving leisurely in for the kill. Grreag sat still like an alien Abraham Lincoln statue in his command chair.

Too afraid to be on her own, Catriona went to stand beside him. She gently reached out and touched the fur protruding over his fatigues collar.

"Just another few seconds, Colonel," promised Khumalo, her fingers working frantically at the console.

A'rlon's work done, he moved out of her way.

"Commander," growled Grreag urgently, "can you predict Captain T'alak's attack pattern?" A'rlon nodded. "Take over TactOps."

Lieutenant Larrar leapt up and relinquished her position. Catriona realized she clutched a clump of Grreag's fur in her hand, twisting it between her fingers.

"Stop that," he growled and grabbed her hand. She felt grateful when he held onto it. Her hand looked small and safe, cradled in his huge golden palm.

The ships spun inexorably closer, the *L'umina* taking the lead. Catriona saw flashes of white light running along the star points as the *L'umina* prepared to fire. A bolt seared out of one point and slashed at the *Vallo.*

A'rlon neatly slipped them aside and the shot impotently fired into space. The warship wheeled around, coming head on again. A'rlon steadied the *Vallo* and turned her to face the *L'umina.*

"The armor can't hold if they hit us," warned Major Benjamin.

"Chief?" inquired Grreag tightly.

"Just a second!"

A'rlon deftly evaded another blast from the *L'umina.* Pulsing white light flashed on the viewer as the other two warships prepared to fire.

"Implementing temporal bubble — now!" shouted Khumalo.

Catriona watched in amazement as the *L'umina* wavered, fading out of sight.

"It worked!" cheered Khumalo, giving Benjamin a high five. The other two ships halted, then flipped sideways and spun away at full speed.

"That put the willies up them!" laughed Benjamin. "Couldn't get away fast enough."

"How long will the *L'umina* be held?" Grreag demanded of Khumalo.

"Approximately fifteen minutes."

Grreag let Catriona's hand go. "Lieutenant Larrar, can you monitor the other Realm ships' communications?"

"Already am, Sir. They're reporting that..." her golden eyes grew wide. "They're reporting that the Alliance has used the 'weapon' on them." She shot Grreag an inquiring look.

"Colonel," said A'rlon. "I sent the ships a message. The Realm now believes that the Leontor-Terran Alliance has perfected the temporal weapon."

After a startled pause Khumalo and Benjamin gave each other another high five and laughed. "No wonder they're running with their tails between their legs!" crowed Benjamin.

Grreag scowled but he didn't fool Catriona. She saw the gleam in his eye.

"I would have preferred you consult me first, Commander A'rlon." He bared a fang. "But now that it is done, I approve. Send another message: tell them the Alliance will be dispatching the Armada to discuss negotiations for peace."

28

ONCE THE *Vallo* was safely soaring toward the closest Alliance outpost, Grreag turned a steely gaze on A'rlon.

"Commander, join me in my office, if you please. And you," he glowered at Catriona, "get out of my control cabin, and I mean it this time!"

"Actually Colonel, I'd like to request that Catriona be present," said A'rlon.

146 | *Time Twist*

One of Grreag's ears flickered and he curtly nodded. Catriona shot a look of trepidation at Chief Khumalo, and followed the two aliens into Grreag's office. Close up, A'rlon's back looked raw and infected. Catriona could only imagine how painful it must be. T'alak had only given her one lash, and the pain from that had been unbearable. God knew how many lashes had laid A'rlon's back open.

"Shouldn't he go to Sickbay first?" she asked.

Grreag growled and lowered himself into his chair. He gestured for A'rlon to take a seat opposite.

"Later, Catriona," A'rlon assured her.

"At least let me put this on him." Catriona pulled out the tube of marsh-peony gel from her pocket. Without waiting for permission she squirted some onto her fingers and carefully smoothed it over A'rlon's injured back and around the scales down the center. He tensed, but as it took effect she felt his taut muscles relax under her fingers. She let her hands rest on his feverish skin for a moment. It scarcely was feasible that a mere few hours earlier she'd lain in a passionate embrace with him.

"Thank you." He turned to smile at her.

Catriona grabbed a chair from the wall and started to drag it over to the desk.

"Sit back there," instructed Grreag, "and if you open your mouth again I'll put you in the brig."

Catriona uttered a 'tsk' noise of impatience and sat down, crossing her legs and folding her arms across her chest. A'rlon eased himself carefully onto the human-friendly seat, sitting sideways to accommodate his tail.

Grreag and A'rlon stared at each other across the desk. Catriona grew worried as the silence stretched for several seconds. Then Grreag burst into loud purring and A'rlon hissed in laughter.

"What's so funny?" demanded Catriona, wondering if they'd gone mad.

Grreag produced his bottle of Leontor *ealu* and two cups, and poured out two generous shots.

"Some refreshment, Lieutenant Colonel?"

"Thank you."

A'rlon raised his glass in salute and downed it. The two aliens turned to grin boyishly at Catriona, who stood with indignation.

"Just what the bloody hell is going on?"

"Catriona," said Grreag, "please meet Lieutenant Colonel Jack Haven of Alliance Intelligence. He's been undercover in the Realm for some time."

She stared at A'rlon, multiple emotions clashing within her. "You're human?"

"Half-human. I'm sorry I couldn't tell you."

Catriona wasn't sure how to react. She almost felt betrayed, although she knew that wasn't rational. A'rlon had told her more than once on Komodoa that he couldn't tell her anything in case Captain T'alak interrogated her. It made sense. If she knew nothing she couldn't implicate him.

Thinking back she realized how obvious it should have been to her that he wasn't a full-blooded Komodoan. The way he didn't object to females looking him in the eyes, how tenderly he treated her, and ultimately risking his life to help her escape.

The lovemaking had been very different and exciting compared to any human man she'd been with, though. She vividly remembered how they had clung to each other afterward, her heart pounding and every nerve ending tingling. Seeing both aliens look curiously at her, she flushed. To cover her embarrassment she gestured to the cups.

"You're very rude not to offer me any, Grreag."

"You really want to go to the brig, don't you?" he said mildly, his voice vibrating through his purr, and pushed his untouched cup toward her.

"Lieutenant Colonel, all I need know for now is how you managed to appear on the *Vallo*. We can debrief the rest later."

Risking Grreag's ire, Catriona pulled her chair up to the desk and sat, sipping the *ealu*. She didn't dare knock it back in case it made her pass out again.

"I have *P'jarra* to thank for that," Haven pointed with his chin to Catriona's pendant. "When I gave it to Beauty here on Komodoa I inserted a clone-actuate transponder into it. Assuming I was on the *L'umina* when she actuated to the *Vallo*, my molecules would automatically leap-frog with her."

"It was not in Catriona's possession when we brought her on board. The Komodoan agent had taken it from her," rumbled Grreag and took a mouthful of *ealu* directly from the bottle, then held it toward Haven.

Haven raised an eyebrow and took the proffered bottle to pour himself another shot.

"I must assume Agent Y'alenon returned to the *Vallo*, in that case?"

"Affirmative. I'll cover that in the debriefing. However, that was back when the *L'umina* caught up with us, several hours ago." His ears flickered inquiringly.

Haven downed his shot and set the cup on Grreag's desk. "I was

148 | *Time Twist*

semi conscious when the clone-actuate engaged. It was pretty much hit or miss where I ended up, but now I understand why I materialized where I did. I am fortunate I did not end up fused with the hull."

"Where did you appear?" asked Catriona curiously. Haven had that endearing bashful look about him that she'd seen before.

"I wasn't certain at first because I must have lost consciousness during the transfer. When I came to I found myself wedged between two narrow walls, everything pitch black." He directed a keen look at Grreag. "Colonel, what use does the Alliance Armada flagship have for smuggling compartments?"

Grreag's purr abruptly stopped and Catriona watched the phenomena of his hackles rising.

"It is of no importance to me," Haven added, "but I thought you should know the freeze-dried food and water casks stockpiled there are open to discovery since I had to break my way out of the compartment."

"Why are you smuggling those, Grreag?" demanded Catriona.

The Leon looked from Haven to Catriona and back again. His hackles had settled and his whiskers flicked in the equivalent of a shrug.

"You'll see when you go down to Earth. Although most major cities are domed and livable, there are places that are not. Many humans go hungry and die needlessly from lack of hydration."

Haven bowed his head to Grreag in admiration. "To care deeply enough to help an alien species against one's own government is commendable, Colonel."

"You helped me, A'rl... Haven," Catriona reminded him.

He rewarded her with a huge smile that made his eyes light up. "Call me Jack."

Despite the ugly cuts and bruises on his face, Catriona was struck at how beautiful he was and she felt absurdly shy again.

"When I make my report to Intelligence, they do not need to know of your private enterprise," Haven assured Grreag. He shifted, reaching with one hand to move his tail to a more comfortable position.

Looking at it Catriona suddenly understood. "Your tail!" she cried, "it's not real, is it?"

"No," he grinned ruefully, "a graft and most uncomfortable. I suppose your Sickbay doesn't run to tail removal, does it?"

"I'm afraid not, Lieutenant Colonel," grunted Grreag, "but they can attend to your wounds. We are finished here for now. Catriona, make yourself useful and escort him to Sickbay." He eyed her white pajamas. "And get dressed!"

"He's what?" demanded Khumalo. Catriona and she sat in the galley, sharing the last of Colonel Grreag's Leontor *ealu*.

"Half-human," repeated Catriona.

"I heard you, but how did that happen?"

Catriona lifted her cup, sloshing the *ealu* inside. "Apparently the Realm used a human woman to test cross-breeding. Never occurred to them once he knew his heritage, he'd change sides." She took another swallow of *ealu* and grinned. "That tail is grafted on. He'll get it removed down on Earth."

Khumalo reached over and ruffled Catriona's hair. "Don't forget to have that vaginal lining put in, y'hear?"

Catriona ducked out of reach. "If you must know, I had that taken care of in Sickbay."

"Yeah, you'll need it with A'rlon around, Haggis."

"Shut up, he's called Jack Haven now. And don't mention haggis ever again or I'll shoot you, do you understand me?"

The engineer laughed. "Are you looking forward to staying on 23rd century Earth?"

"I'm scared shitless. I wish I could stay with you on the *Vallo* while you work on the temporal bubble."

"I know, but you can't. We're rotating shifts and I'll be stationed elsewhere for the next few months." Khumalo lifted the keg of *ealu* and weighed it in her hand. She tilted it and let the last of it drip into her cup. "Are you worried that Leontor Control will find out who you really are? Don't be, the identity I helped Grreag create for you is completely failsafe, girlfriend. You're a fine, upstanding citizen from Ponce de Leon. You'll be fine."

"I hope so."

"You can always contact me if you need moral support. I'll keep you on the straight and narrow."

"What, you? You'd lead me off it in a shot!" Catriona grabbed Khumalo's cup and poured some of the *ealu* into her own. She sighed heavily. "It's going to be so horrible down there with the Earth so dry and dead, and everything so changed."

"At least you'll have Lieutenant Colonel Haven with you; that should help."

"Do you think he turned out to be the Wizard, appearing out of nowhere on board like that to save the day?"

Khumalo laughed. "You never can tell, girl."

Catriona nodded and lifted her cup to drain it. She felt as though she'd been sentenced to purgatory, between worlds. Grreag and Khumalo couldn't predict how long it might take to perfect the temporal bubble, so in the meantime Grreag had arranged for her enrollment in the Alliance Cadet College.

The galley door dilated and Haven stepped inside. Catriona looked up and beamed.

"There's your cue, girlfriend," grinned Khumalo, getting to her feet.

Catriona stood and hugged the engineer tightly. "See you later," she managed, choking back tears.

"Get out of here, Haggis."

Khumalo gave her a friendly push, and Catriona turned and walked over to where Haven waited. Her heart lifted as a smile spread across his beautiful face. Somehow the enforced stay in this century didn't appear quite so arduous, after all.

Part II: Two Years Later

29

Lieutenant Colonel Haven scowled, glancing up from the desk. The air in his office felt heavy and oppressive, as though the oxygen mix wasn't right. He hadn't noticed until his temples began to throb with a nasty headache.

Shaking the mane of shoulder-length black hair away from his face, he inspected the life-support and artificial gravity pods. They registered normal. Wondering what could be causing the fall in pressure, he keyed the desk infomonitor. After a moment, the base's holographic model materialized. He couldn't see any abnormalities and changed the focus to show the star system. Studying the whirling eddy of planets, Haven had no doubt how perfect the placement of this Alliance spy base was on the asteroid. Tucked within the rings of a dying star just outside the Komodoan Realm, the entire asteroid remained invisible to scanners.

Haven sighed, switching off the star chart. He lamented being trapped on this cinder when he could have been with his lovely red-haired lover on Earth. A touch of doubt knifed his heart. He'd managed to persuade Catriona to wait until Chief Khumalo developed the temporal bubble data to a point where a journey back to the 21st century would be controlled and safe. If she returned now she'd have no way back to the future, or to him.

Catriona had agreed to stay the full three-year course at the College, but Haven was away so much he harbored uncertainty that he would return from a mission to find her gone.

He opened his desk drawer and pulled out the oval *P'jarra* icon he carried on every mission. It was the one he had given to Catriona, but she insisted he keep it with him to remind him of her. As though he'd need reminding. His life as a career intelligence officer made intimacy near to impossible, and he treasured what he had found with Catriona.

He placed the icon on the desk and rose to get himself a measure of water. Being in constant recycled air conditioning made him feel dehydrated all the time. His half-Komodoan heritage craved humidity.

A crunching, roaring sound ripped across the base and Haven was catapulted against the wall. It felt like the asteroid had exploded beneath him, the walls buckling around him. The base hull breach alarm, distinctive by its three piercing bleeps, shrilled over and over. Outside his office Haven heard voices raised in fear, as well as crashing and jarring sounds as air rushed from the base, lifting anything in its path that wasn't bolted down.

Struggling to his feet, Haven staggered to the closet to pull out a lifesuit. He ducked, trying to dodge the objects in his office that hurtled and spun past him. He jerked aside to avoid the desk chair as it crashed against the office door. Pinned against the door, he held his breath and struggled into his suit. Just as suddenly as it began, the vacuum ceased. Feeling dizzy from lack of air, Haven swiftly sealed his suit, lowering the transparent helmet over his head. The neck seals hissed as they clicked into place on the suit collar and his air supply came on line. Haven gratefully inhaled as the dizziness passed. That had been close. For a moment, he had difficulty swallowing. Suffocating would be a dreadful way to die.

Getting hold of himself, he dodged the now floating objects and wrenched open the door. The magnetic boots on the suit adhered to

152 | Time Twist

the ferrous sulphate in the floors and kept him thumping solidly on the ground. The base's atmosphere was compromised. His second officer had not been able to get into her lifesuit in time. She floated near her desk, her eyes bloody and bulging. Erratic blinking from her infomonitor caught his eye. He stepped past her bloated corpse to inspect a blurred hologram of the star system. It showed several trajectories, all splaying from a single source close to Komodoan Realm space.

Haven felt something near his face. Adrenaline coursing, he swung round. A suited figure holding a carbine aimed another blast at him. Ducking, Haven rolled clumsily under the desk, his bulky suit and magnetic soles in the zero gravity inhibiting movement.

The intruder blocked the way back to his office and he admonished himself for not bringing his blaster with him. Haven decided to try and get through the analysis room to the armory. He edged along the desk. The figure had moved, stalking him on the other side.

Taking a breath, Haven detached his magnetic soles and launched himself, sailing toward the corridor. The intruder fired and a white beam glanced off his right thigh. Pain scorched through him and Haven balled himself up, diving under the huge analysis table in the center of the room. He wrenched the table out of its anchor onto its side, providing him with slim coverage. His suit's smart-chip had already responded to the damage on the right thigh area. Syntactic foam had hardened around his leg, sealing the breach. He had no way to see how injured he was, but his thigh felt like it was on fire.

A shadow loomed near and Haven ignored the pain, leaping forward to shove the table. It caught the intruder and knocked him to the floor, weapon flying from his grasp and tumbling upward. Haven snatched it mid air and got a bead on his attacker; a Komodoan soldier sprawled, his helmet cracked. Deprived of air, his scaled face and eyes swelled, forked tongue rasping in and out. Haven aimed the carbine right at the soldier's face and sent a beam of white light into him, killing him instantly.

Knowing there had to be more intruders, Haven kept his magnetic soles off the iron-enriched floor and floated from the analysis room to the living quarters. The rest of his three colleagues drifted there, all dead.

His helmet picked up voices over the intercom from the galley. He hesitated. How wise would he be to take on—*P'jarra* knew—how many more armed Komodoans? Yet, what choice did he have? His air wouldn't last more than a couple of hours and he couldn't wait for the Komodoans to leave. He might attempt to escape in the base cruiser, but he'd easily be shot down if a Komodoan Realm warship orbited the asteroid.

For a brief moment, he allowed himself to think of Catriona. He might never see her again. He would never be able to tell her how much he needed her. He admonished himself for thinking like a fool. This indulgence would get him killed.

He listened to the sibilant dialect and caught the words, "Find the epicenter."

"There isn't one, honored Commander," came the reply, "the shock did not originate on the asteroid."

Haven frowned. If the Komodoan Realm had not caused the seismic activity, then what had? He edged closer, risking a look into the galley. Three Komodoans stood around the center table, wearing stolen Alliance suits. A leg in each suit had been stretched so that their long, sinuous tails could be squeezed inside as well. The only way that could have been achieved was to reprogram the suit smart-chip.

"The temporal weapon must have caused it," hissed the Komodoan closest to Haven, "we must leave immediately."

Haven's stomach twisted. After Webster's 'Komodoan Incident,' Leontor Control had confiscated all data and forbidden any further research. Haven considered the veto utter madness. If the Realm had developed the weapon while the Alliance had not, then there'd be little defense against the Realm. The war would end very, very quickly indeed.

His heartbeat went into overdrive as a change in air pressure indicated an actuate bubble close by. Within moments, the Komodoan soldiers had gone, leaving Haven alone. A barrage of fire decimated the walls behind him, forcing him to launch himself away. The Realm warship fired on the base, covering their tracks. Haven's only chance to survive would be to take a surface cruiser and try and hole up in one of the asteroid's underground caverns. He careened through the corridors as fast as he could, bouncing off walls until he reached the cruiser bay. He climbed into one of them, engaged the drive and shot clear. Plotting a course spaceward would be suicide. Instead, he skimmed the asteroid's surface until he found a cluster of underground caverns on the southern hemisphere. Twisting the craft back on itself, he guided it below ground and docked. He could only trust the stars that the Komodoan warship hadn't been fast enough to track him. Sweat poured down his face and he found breathing difficult. He had to get the helmet off before passing out. The air in the cruiser would recirculate as long as the computer stayed on line, but he only had about an hour or so left in his suit. Reaching up, Haven unclipped the helmet seals, pulled it off and took a deep breath.

154 | *Time Twist*

Locating the cruiser medikit, he retrieved painkillers and antibiotic pads. Disengaging the suit smart-chip, he cracked open the syntactic foam around his thigh to reveal sickening blue-gray torn flesh. Through a fog of pain and nausea, he applied both pads. As he sank into a merciful black void, he remembered he'd left Catriona's *P'jarra* icon behind in his office.

30

"WATCH OUT!"

Catriona ducked as an empty keg of Leontor *ealu* hurtled by. It crashed against the wall and shattered, and Catriona retreated into her small bathroom and locked the door. Out in her studio apartment, the noise and destruction continued. She grimaced at her reflection in the mirror. Her unruly mane of hair, normally bound up tightly on the back of her head, had worked loose, escaped strands wilting over her face and neck. Blowing an irritating lock away from her nose, she dampened a towel and cooled her face with it.

It had felt like such a good idea to invite the visiting Leontor students to dinner. Ten young Leons had come to the ACC to take an intensive study course on humanity. As allies and protectors of Earth, they needed to learn about human psyche. Catriona had noticed they kept very much to themselves, resented and shunned by the human students. Catriona suspected the Leons felt as isolated as she. It took her several weeks before plucking up the courage to approach the two females.

Since befriending Colonel Grreag, she had worked hard to learn some of the difficult Leontor language. Although not yet fluent in the guttural tongue, she successfully invited the two females to a meal in her apartment. The males intimidated her, so she hadn't included them. But when her guests arrived, instead of just two, all ten hulking Leons had turned up.

At first Catriona was overwhelmed, but took a deep breath and rose to the occasion. She opened up a second crate of Leontor *ealu*, got out more cups, and for the meal cracked open an extra supply of rations.

Catriona flinched as something heavy crashed against the bathroom door, followed by high-spirited howling. A toxic combination of the *ealu* and some foul-smelling weed they'd brought had encouraged her visitors to behave as they would if socializing on Leontor. Another crash pummeled the door, and Catriona shook her head, forcing the clip holding her hair to break free. As she re-pinned it, she ruefully wondered what Dean Essex would have to say about this. Now, he would have an excuse to throw her out of the college for sure.

Catriona's grades were not what they should be, even though she strove to keep up. The Dean had already given her two warnings for what he termed, 'Second-degree infraction of campus rules.' A third, and she would be expelled. Without graduating, she could never leave the planet. And if she had to stay in this century, Catriona couldn't bear to live on the arid wasteland Earth had become.

Uzi hadn't yet made the temporal bubble safe enough to use, and only the thought of Jack Haven and the prospect of graduating so she could travel in space kept her going.

Catriona smoothed down her hair and took another deep breath. Opening the bathroom door she stepped out into the melee. In the short time she'd left them alone, the Leons had torn up most of the apartment. Catriona gaped in disbelief at her sofa and chairs, cushions shredded by the Leontors' talons. Discarded kegs lay in shatters over the floor, and spatter marks and gouges scored the walls where they had been flung. The treasured Leontor ceremonial dagger Grreag had given to her had been knocked off its place of honor on the wall.

Catriona dodged across the room, trying not to be trampled by her enthusiastic and inebriated guests. She retrieved the dagger and carefully replaced it on the wall. Caressing the delicately woven leather hilt, she wished Grreag had warned her how wild partying Leons could be.

The floor under her feet suddenly shuddered violently and she lost her balance. Startled into silence the Leontor students froze as the walls and floor continued to shimmy and jostle. Catriona's dagger fell off the wall again, plunging point first to embed itself in the floor, inches from Catriona's foot.

"Bloody hell!" she gasped, looking up at the Leons. "What happened?"

The lights flickered and for a moment Catriona feared the atmospheric dome over the city had failed.

Qiterr, the male leader and the one most fluent in English bent to help her to her feet. He didn't know his own strength and pulled her so hard she careened off the floor and knocked into him. He lost his footing and they both toppled to the floor. The Leons yowled with laughter as Catriona spat out a mouthful of fur and disentangled herself.

"Was that an earthquake?" she asked.

"It felt like one," growled Qiterr, soothing down the fur on his hands. He glared at his laughing colleagues, and lunged, tackling the male nearest him.

Catriona didn't need to call Security to quell them; the neighbors beat her to it. Fearing a riot, the campus guards arrived in force, their frantic pounding at Catriona's door almost inaudible above the Leontor din.

Before Catriona could circumnavigate the room to open the door, a stream of black-clad security guards burst in. Qiterr quickly summed up the situation. With impressive alacrity, he quelled the merriment, leading his friends quietly from the apartment. As he passed Catriona, he clapped her on the back, almost knocking her flat on her face.

"Thank you for your excellent hospitality, human!"

Jack Haven arrived on Earth early in the morning. As the passenger ship landed, dawn had just broken, bleeding rose-tipped fingers across the Orlando sky. He appreciated the bright daylight after so many months of darkness. As the ship taxied across the runway, the sun gave Haven's companion's blond hair the look of a halo.

"Thanks for meeting my transport."

"No problem, Lieutenant Colonel," smiled Matthew Gordon. "How's your leg holding up?"

Haven rubbed his injured limb. "It'll be fine. No lasting damage." He studied Matthew's handsome face for a moment, wondering how someone so young could already be a top agent in Alliance Intelligence.

"I'm not sure where Intelligence will take it from here," said Matthew. "The seismic activity last night spread through most of known space. We feared a Komodoan Realm attack. Your information telling us otherwise came as quite a relief."

Haven nodded. "The Realm is running scared, thinking we have perfected Professor Webster's temporal weapon. By the stars I wish we had. Surely they must have realized the Realm would try to create something in retaliation?"

Matthew's eyes narrowed. "Yes," he said slowly, "but they'd need your Catriona Logan's brain patterns in order to make it accurate."

"Ah, yes... Catriona."

"Do you think Captain T'alak will make a try for her again?"

Haven made himself relax. "It's possible. But as long as she's on Earth, she's safe. I have the honor of being the only Komodoan to walk the surface of the Earth."

Matthew raised an eyebrow. "Is that so?"

Haven looked at him sharply. "Half-Komodoan," he amended.

He looked out the window as the ship taxied toward a landing dock and thought about the human who had birthed him. The Realm had captured her, and used her ova to create a Komodoan/human hybrid. Haven had been the first operative planted behind enemy lines on Earth, where he could undermine Leontor influence. To take Earth from beneath Leon protection would change the balance in the war, allowing the Komodoan Realm freedom to conquer.

As though reading his mind, Matthew asked, "How did you come to work for the Alliance, anyway?"

"It's a long story. Let's say I didn't agree with the Realm's methods."

The passenger ship docked and the stabilizing arm connected with a resounding crunch. The sun shone high and blistering above, rendering the air conditioning next to useless. Haven stood, swinging his travelpak over his shoulder. Matthew walked him out and down the steps to the docking bay.

"I'll be in touch." Matthew tipped a hand to his forehead in a laid back salute and moved briskly toward the line of passengers streaming through the exit.

Haven turned toward the capsule station, glad to be off that asteroid base at last. Not that the parched, ruined Earth looked much better. But at least a couple of recreational lakes still graced the planet. Haven longed to immerse his aching body in cool water. It would be worth it, even if it took half a month's salary for the privilege.

His thoughts returned to Catriona and their anticipated reunion. They saw each other as often as possible between his Intelligence missions, their time together passionate and fulfilling as they crammed months' worth into a few weeks. With a warm feeling of anticipation, Haven hefted his travelpak over his shoulder and boarded the capsule to take him to the Alliance cadet campus.

Strapping himself comfortably into a passenger seat, he once again reveled in the absence of his scaly tail, grafted on when he was under cover on Komodoa. He had never grown used to it, finding it awkward and painful. When his hair covered his facial scales, Catriona told him he made an attractive human.

He warmed at the memory of her playful teasing, and his forked tongue flickered out for a moment. He had learned to keep it practically unnoticeable, but occasionally it had a mind of its own. Catriona told him he had an enchanting lisp when it got in the way.

Her campus apartment building took only a short ride from the shuttle docking base. He hadn't had time to warn her of his arrival, but he had a card-key. He relished the thought of burying himself in her soft femininity, for a while forgetting all about Intelligence, Komodoa, and the war. She was the only one he truly trusted enough to share the vulnerable side of his character, the self-doubt he kept hidden deep inside.

Well aware of Catriona's own doubts and insecurity, he wondered how she had fared this quarter at the College. She constantly fretted that Leontor Control might find out she came from the 21st century, or that Captain T'alak might attempt to recapture her.

Haven felt a chill, thinking about T'alak. Sooner or later, his and T'alak's paths would cross again.

Catriona entered Dean Essex's office fifteen minutes after her summons. She stood to attention opposite the impressive mahogany-skinned human, forcing herself not to fidget. Essex finally looked up from his infomonitor, observing her for a few unnerving moments. Stabbing a manicured finger at the keypad, the viewer went dark. He shook his head.

"Cadet Logan, is there no end to your blundering talents?"

Catriona resisted wiping her sweaty palms, remaining ramrod straight.

"I've been more than patient with you," he continued. "I overlooked the time you burnt the chemistry lab down, understanding that on Ponce de Leon you'd had little experience with explosives. I didn't make an official report when you freed all the animal research subjects."

"I should think not!" snapped Catriona. "They shouldn't have been there to start with-" Essex held up a hand, his flashing dark eyes boring into her. "Sorry," she murmured. How could she ever graduate if she couldn't even remember not to interrupt her superior officer?

"We've been through this many times," said Essex, "but there's a limit to what I can overlook." Catriona bit down on the inside of her cheek. *Here it comes.* "It pains me greatly to tell you this, but you are graduated as of today. Congratulations."

"Won't you reconsider, Dean Essex?" pleaded Catriona. "I know I haven't been the best-" She stopped. The Dean wore a resigned expression. "You mean I'm not expelled?"

"You should be, Logan." Essex sat back, folding his arms. "At ease. No, just sit down and listen for once."

Catriona dropped into one of the chairs facing his desk. "I don't understand. I thought for sure that after last night I'd be history here."

"The visiting Leon student program hasn't been effective. They refuse to integrate, and Leontor Control ordered the program terminated. That is, until last night.

"Cadet Qiterr sent a subspace report immediately after returning from your apartment. Apparently we've 'finally assigned a student liaison officer whom they could relate to.'" Essex pursed his lips, steepling his fingers under his chin. "Now, what I'm about to tell you is classified, Logan. It doesn't leave this room, understood?"

"Yes, Sir." Catriona leaned forward, her mind whirling.

"A new spatial rupture caused the earthquake last night. Until we ascertain what caused it, Leontor Control has recalled the students. Having made a breakthrough, we can't drop the momentum. I want you to accompany the students to Leontor until they can return to Earth."

Catriona's jaw dropped. Could she be dreaming? It was too good to be true.

"Are you sure there's not a mistake? I'm hardly qualified."

"Let me be the judge of that. Apparently your ah... friendship with Colonel Grreag proves you to be sympathetic to Leontor culture. You'll be speed-learned in the language and customs, but I'm relying on your instincts to make the rest of the mission successful." Essex unsteepled his fingers, plucking a piece of imaginary lint from his sleeve. "Logan, I think we both know this is your only chance to graduate. Your record has hardly been exemplary." Catriona knew that all too well, but it didn't please her to be reminded. "Stand ready; you'll be briefed when I've made the arrangements." He stood.

Catriona rose also, not sure whether to salute or kick him.

"Oh, and Cadet? Much as this further pains me, no one ranked below a certain status can officially represent us off world." Essex sighed heavily. "No one deserves this less than you, but you are hereby promoted to the rank of Lieutenant Junior Grade, effective immediately. Dismissed."

Haven stood in Catriona's apartment doorway, gazing in bemusement at the mess. Catriona's idea of order left a lot to be desired, but he'd never seen her place in such disarray. Checking the time, he estimated that she should be back in about four hours. Time enough for him to catch up on some sleep, so he'd be fresh and ready to enjoy her company.

Quickly using the spritz, he stretched out naked under the abandoned covers. He smelled her on the sheets, and shrouded by her scent, he swiftly dropped into sleep.

He woke at the sound of the apartment door sliding open. Soft footfalls approached and Haven grinned to himself in anticipation. Face down, he lay still and listened to the alluring rustle of clothing being removed.

Someone kneeled on the bed beside him and he tensed as he felt hands trace the scars on his back from T'alak's flogging two years previously. Then the hands began to massage his neck and shoulders, and he relaxed, already stirring at her touch.

"Ah, Beauty, you know me too well," he murmured into the pillow as her strong knuckles worked out a stubborn knot between his shoulder blades. He groaned in pleasure, somewhere between waking and sleeping, as his lover's hands became balm to his aching body.

SLEEPY STUDENT life had emerged into the new day as Catriona made her way back across the domed campus to her apartment. In her pocket she had a brand new set of stripes to attach to her dress uniform. Her fingers kept slipping inside to touch them. Lieutenant Logan! That sounded so great. And no more Dean Essex or academy. She knew now that remaining in the future had proved the right decision, after all. She abhorred the desert Earth was, but might deal with it as long as she could travel out among the stars.

These stripes ensured that.

Reaching her apartment building, Catriona climbed the stairs, ignoring the elevator. She prided herself on keeping as fit as possible, difficult as it proved in a world where droids performed even the most mundane tasks. Only a tad winded, she made it to the tenth floor to find her door slightly ajar. Of course, the security guards had broken the locks the night before. Fortunately crime was scarcely a problem on campus.

Pushing the door open, her glance went straight to the bed where lay the unmistakable body of her lover, Jack Haven. The breath choked in Catriona's throat to see a naked blond man kneeling over him, sweat slicking his muscular body. His hands caressed Haven's shoulders while he leaned close to feather his lips down Haven's scaled back.

Rage filled Catriona. In one bound she reached the bed, shoving the man off Haven. "You bastards!" she yelled.

The stranger calmly studied Catriona, his blue eyes bright. Sitting up, Haven blinked, looking confusedly from Catriona to the man perched beside him.

"Matthew? What in *P'jarra* is going on?"

Matthew slipped from the bed to put on his clothes.

Catriona controlled her fury. "Just get dressed and get the hell out, Jack! Reptile!" Knowing his Komodoan heritage, that word would insult Haven more than anything.

His face darkened and he rose to retrieve his clothes. Catriona couldn't look at him. She moved away, trying to suppress her shaking. Seeing the Leontor dagger with its blade still piercing the floor, she felt like plunging it into Haven's heart.

Hastily clothed, he approached her. "I think you know me better than this, Beauty," he began.

"Just piss off." If he didn't go she'd break down in tears.

He turned away as Matthew beat a hasty retreat out the door. Haven hesitated, and then strode after him. Catriona slammed the door behind them and with venom engaged the unbroken privacy lock. Had everything about Jack Haven been a lie? How could he do this to her... in the very bed they shared together? She had trusted him, had given up all that was familiar to have him in her life.

His betrayal swept through her, making her feel weak and lifeless. He had been her anchor in the 23rd century, and now he'd gone. And he didn't even know she'd been promoted to lieutenant, she thought sadly, finally giving way to tears.

The college clean-up team with their maintenance droids interrupted, arriving to repair the damage to her apartment. Catriona rescued the dagger from the floor and placed it on the kitchen counter. The droids systematically replaced every piece of furniture, broken or not. With no regret Catriona watched her bed being carted off.

Leaving the crew to its work, she decided to seek out the Leon students to distract herself. She found them camped out in the blistering sunshine under the clear canopy, sitting noticeably apart from the humans. Zerreem, one of the females reached out to pluck one of the flowers nearby. As she popped it in her mouth, Catriona understood why there had been so few blooms this term.

Catriona approached and plopped down on the grass beside Zerreem. All ten stared hard at her.

"What?" she inquired.

"We are being recalled early to Leontor," growled Qiterr. "The ship

Exsequor is on its way."

"And guess who's coming with you!" Purring en masse ensued, and Catriona grinned at the sound of their pleasure. Unbidden, an image of Haven and Matthew swam before her, spoiling the moment. Cheating jerks. Focusing, she saw her new friends staring curiously at her, their purring choked off.

"You are angry, human," growled Qiterr, "do you not wish to visit Leontor?"

"Of course I do," Catriona assured him, "I've just a lot on my mind at the moment."

"Who has done this to you?" asked Zerreem.

"What makes you think someone has done something to me?" countered Catriona, uncomfortable under their intense scrutiny.

"You have a look of the betrayed." Qiterr snarled softly. "Shall I tear him to pieces for you?"

Catriona almost said yes, until she realized him to be in deadly earnest. She shook her head, not trusting herself to speak.

Zerreem's ears flicked forward inquiringly. "You will make *Arrum* before we leave?"

"What's that?" asked Catriona.

The Leon leaned forward intently. "You cannot leave without making *Arrum* or your *rrasma* will be in danger."

Catriona gazed at her, perplexed. *Rrasma* translated loosely as 'soul'.

Qiterr and Zerreem conferred for a moment in their guttural, native tongue, then Zerreem snarled, "He accuses me of overreacting."

"Our beliefs are not applicable to a human," agreed Qiterr, the furry ears on top of his head flicking.

Intrigued, Catriona asked, "How do I make *Arrum*?"

"You offer a gift to appease the... spirits, as you would call them. Something that symbolizes your life. You must ask their permission to forsake your birthplace, and tell them where you go."

Catriona resorted to humor. "You mean leave a forwarding address? Wouldn't spirits already know?"

Qiterr shook his shaggy head and Zerreem touched her arm.

"Do not mock. If you do not make *Arrum*, then you will know nothing but strife in this life and beyond."

Haven slept fitfully in the tourist accommodation he'd booked into, waking up with a start after only a couple of hours. The instincts that made him a born intelligence agent worked, niggling at his subconscious. He considered his job sometimes akin to a jigsaw puzzle, each mission a different picture. Except the pieces rarely came conveniently wrapped up in a box with a photo on the cover. He had to search through the abstract... draw invisible threads together. So far he only had two pieces to this puzzle. A new rupture in space, and that someone wanted Catriona and he separated. How were they connected?

Using a buff cleanser in the spritz to wake himself up, Haven inevitably thought of Catriona. He remembered how she had mistaken his *P'jarra* water shrine for a shower, and he had walked in to find her bathing in it, goosebumps and all. Being the first human he had set eyes on in years, her naked body had stirred long forgotten feelings. Haven had experienced a hair-raising couple of moments as he fought the Komodoan instinct that would have driven him to take her there and then against her will.

Damn it! He slammed the cleanser dispenser closed, stepping out without bothering with the toner. The sooner he got to the bottom of why Matthew had come between Catriona and he the better. Dressing in clean gray pants and white open-necked shirt, he left the tourist accommodation for the cadet quarters.

He had tied his long, dark hair back in a ponytail, making the scales along his forehead more noticeable. Haven noticed the curious glances leveled at him as he strode across the college campus. If he displayed his human heritage as openly on Komodoa, it would be a different story. Tail-less, he would be a social outcast, banished to a life of slavery in the *Uk'n* mines, or euthanized.

The single thing he missed about Komodoa was flowing water in abundance. And perhaps also the music, based on the ebb and flow of the many seas, the relentless timpani of rainfall.

As Haven strode through the perfectly kept ACC gardens, he looked at the manicured flowerbeds and cacti. Quite different to gardens on Komodoa, he thought wryly. There, the most coveted real estate was marshland. The more soggy, the more desirable.

Feeling an overwhelming urge to have cool water caressing his body again, he decided that later he would capsule to one of the recreation lakes and indulge in a lazy swim. It would be worth the expense. Perhaps Catriona would receive him well, and they could go together.

He spotted her then, walking slowly toward her apartment building. She looked weary, her usual ebullience diminished. He followed and watched her enter her building. Climbing the ten flights of stairs a few

164 | *Time Twist*

moments later, he settled himself on the hall window ledge in view of her door. He'd give her a few minutes' grace before knocking.

Catriona felt gratified to see the cleaning crew had done their job well. The beige sofa and chairs had been replaced, facing out toward the window. A new bed stood over by the far wall, already made up with clean bedding.

Catriona turned away from it, going to the kitchenette to find her stash of Glenfiddich whisky, kept only in the case of an emergency.

A green message light blinked on her infomonitor. She pointedly ignored it, pulling the antique bottle out from its hiding place behind the food dispenser. She had not even twisted the cap off when she felt a change in the air pressure around her, indicating an actuate system in operation.

Heart pounding, she ducked into a roll and spun across her living room. If she kept moving, the bubble couldn't lock around her. Catriona cursed that she had no blaster, but remembering the Leon dagger, she grabbed it from the kitchen counter.

A shadow formed within the bubble. Catriona clenched her teeth, holding the weapon in front of her. A moment later she found herself gaping into a pair of very human brown eyes, half obscured by black, beaded braids swinging in front of her face.

"Uzi?"

The newcomer looked the incredulous Catriona up and down, laughing, "Booze *and* fighting, what more could a girl ask for?"

"How's that for priorities?" grinned Catriona, dropping both dagger and bottle to hug her friend. "What the hell are you doing here?"

"Geez, do you ever check your messages?" Khumalo gestured toward the blinking green light. She threw herself down on Catriona's sofa. "The *Vallo's* taking your students to rendezvous with the *Exsequor*. Colonel Grreag pretty much has the old crew on rota again, so here I am."

Getting cups and pouring the whisky, Catriona grinned with delight to see a friendly face. Uzima looked even more beautiful than ever, her deep coffee-colored complexion darker from being stationed planetside under the unforgiving sun.

Uzi's ancestors came from Zimbabwe on the African continent. Catriona had told her many times how regal she thought Uzi looked, and had tried unsuccessfully to get her friend to dress in flowing robes of gold. To her disappointment, Uzima would wear nothing but engineering-green Alliance fatigues, in varying degrees of grubbiness.

This couldn't come at a better time, Catriona thought to herself. She knew Uzi had had to delay work on the temporal bubble, but maybe back on the *Vallo* she might make more progress. She brought the cups over and handed one to Uzi, sitting beside her on the sofa.

Khumalo raised her whisky in a toast. "Congratulations on your promotion, by the way."

Catriona attempted to look diffident, but didn't quite succeed. "Thanks. Pretty amazing, isn't it?"

At least she had *something* to feel good about, even if she got the promotion by default. She fell silent, wondering despite herself where Haven might be. She had expected the message on her machine to be from him. She'd have listened to it when she had been ready... maybe even have called him back, depending on what he had to say.

"Everything okay with you, girl?" asked Khumalo, swishing the golden liquid in her cup. "You're very quiet."

Pushing the hair back from her face, Catriona sighed. "Well, you already know what a mess my two years have been at the ACC. I only got the promotion by default, because no one else can get along with the Leons."

"Oh, come on, Catriona! Lieutenant JG before graduating proper is pretty good for a 21st century immigrant." The engineer gave her a playful punch in the arm. "Besides, your friendship with Grreag is worth more than that," she grinned. "I've made a bundle in cash, thanks to you!"

Catriona laughed, remembering when she'd passed out in Grreag's quarters on the *Vallo*, due to too much Leon *ealu*, and the crew had had bets as to whether she'd actually slept with him or not.

"So, what's up?" persisted Khumalo.

Catriona decided not to tell Uzi about Haven, yet. It would be just too upsetting to go into it.

"I guess I'm just tired. I'll be fine after a good night's sleep."

"Sleep?" Khumalo feigned shock. "You're going to sleep while your friends, whom I might mention, you haven't seen in six months, get ready to leave in a ship they launched specifically so they could see you?"

Catriona tossed a cushion at her. "Don't give me that! I don't believe for one second that Colonel Grreag would even consider launching the *Vallo* just to see me."

"True, but it was worth a try. Come back with me, party pooper." She threw the cushion back. "If you'd listen to your bloody messages once in a while you'd have known we were coming!"

"I'm not in the mood to socialize tonight."

"Now you sound like a Leontor. What's wrong with you, girlfriend? Look, you can either come of your own accord, or I'll knock you senseless and drag you there myself. Your choice."

Through the flippant tone, Catriona heard the concern in her friend's voice. No wonder. Six months ago during main break they had shuttled to where Zimbabwe had been. Once Catriona got used to the unbearable temperature so close to the Equator, she fell in love with it. That part of the African continent held one of the few patches of Earth that had survived the rift. It sported one of the last four remaining waterfalls on the planet. Catriona and Uzi had spent a relaxing couple of weeks acting like fun-seeking teenagers. Now Catriona knew she sounded morose and depressed.

"Well?" demanded Khumalo, unbuttoning and rolling up her fatigues sleeves in mock threat.

Catriona held up a hand in resignation, laughing. "All right, all right! Have it your own way."

With a grin, Khumalo activated her ear communicator. "Mission accomplished," she announced, pulling Catriona up to stand beside her.

A bubble formed around the two women. Moments later, their molecules dispersed and the bubble vanished from Catriona's apartment.

As the air pressure returned to normal, a knock sounded at her door.

Haven stood back in good view of the door monitor. When Catriona did not open up, he could only assume she still felt too angry to see him. How disappointing that she judged him so quickly. He knew how it had looked to her this morning, but surely she could at least give him a chance to explain? He turned from her door. This nonsense had gone on long enough. He resented her assumption of his guilt.

He checked the time. The college offices would still be open. He would see if he could find out Catriona's class schedule for tomorrow, and pin her down first thing in the morning. Veering across campus, he headed for Admin. Locating the bursar, he approached the single clerk, a dour, impossibly skinny young man.

"I need to know the whereabouts of one of your students," Haven informed the clerk. He thought the young man looked like a starving vulture, poised over his infomonitor as though waiting for prey.

"I'm sorry, I can't give out that information," whined the clerk.

"Perhaps I should explain who I am…" Haven pulled out his

holographic Intelligence identification.

The vulture took it, holding the card at arm's length between finger and thumb. Without so much as an acknowledgment, he slapped the card down on the desk.

"Access permitted." He pushed the keypad over and swung the monitor round to face Haven. "Enter the student's last name."

Haven typed 'Logan,' and Catriona's file came on screen. Frowning, he read that she had already graduated and was in active service! How by the stars did that happen so quickly? He attempted to access where she had been assigned, but before he could bypass the security block, he spotted a blond-haired man moving rapidly past the windows behind the clerk.

"Hey!" objected the clerk, as Haven vaulted over both him and the desk.

Haven burst out of the back office fire doors and caught up with Matthew in the gardens. "I'd like a word with you."

Matthew lifted a corner of his mouth in a sneer. "I have nothing to say to you." A sudden slant of sunlight through the skylight lit him up like a spotlight.

Haven narrowed his eyes. The hint of a scar where scales should have been marred Matthew's forehead. Another abstract piece for the puzzle. What had happened to the real Matthew?

Checking that no one observed, Haven disabled him and holding him in a half Nelson, pulled him into privacy behind the shrubbery. A stone bench sat in the shade.

"Take your hands off me, traitor," growled Matthew, attempting to wrench free.

"Sit down."

Haven pushed him onto the bench. He pulled his shirt aside enough for Matthew to see his underarm blaster, and sat beside him.

Matthew laughed softly. "And you thought you were the only one of Komodoan descent walking Earth, *A'rlon.*"

"Care to tell me what you're doing here?"

"You'll find out soon enough, you Alliance lackey."

"What happened to the real Matthew?"

"What usually happens to pretty humans. I'm sure he'll be happy with his new master."

Haven intently watched the impostor's blond-framed face for a moment. "So what was that little game in Catriona's apartment?"

"Just a reminder of what you're missing."

168 | *Time Twist*

"If I wanted reminding, I'd have stayed on Komodoa. Who sent you here?"

Matthew brought his hands together, twisting at the ring on his finger. Lunging at Haven, he thrust a tiny needle into his neck.

Haven saw Matthew's blue eyes flash with triumph as everything went black.

32

REMATERIALIZING IN the *Vallo* actuate chamber brought a smile to Catriona's face. She remembered the first time she had appeared here and came face to face with Colonel Grreag. She looked around eagerly, but an ensign she didn't recognize stood at the control panel.

"Colonel Grreag's waiting for you in the galley," said Khumalo, seeing Catriona's disappointment. "We couldn't have you attacking him again, could we?"

"God, Uzi, you never let me forget anything, do you?"

As they approached the dilating door to the galley, Catriona got a flutter in her stomach. Her friends on the crew would have diligently followed her progress at the College; she felt mortified to think they probably knew of her many stupid mistakes there.

The door dilated to reveal the octagonal galley, crammed full of people.

"Now it's not really for you, we always have a party when the *Vallo* gets launched. But this is the first time Colonel Grreag showed up. You've worked wonders with that Leon."

Catriona spotted the familiar golden face and pushed past a duo of sweaty dancers. The big Leon stood, baring his fangs and breaking out into a loud purr. Catriona grabbed him, giving him a bear hug. She bit hard into his neck, as Leontor custom dictates when greeting a close friend or family member. The degree of pressure depended of the degree of friendship.

Grreag's purring halted and he put her from him, his amber eyes scanning the galley. "Catriona," he growled, ears flattening, "don't do that!"

"God, are you still hung up on what other people think about you? For Christ's sake, lighten up, Grreag. No one's going to lose respect for you, just because you show affection!" She'd forgotten how uptight he was in public. Irritated, she reached up to ruffle his soft, velvety ears. He ducked, grabbing her arm. A warning claw dug into her wrist.

Khumalo caught up with them. "Will you quit? For two people who profess to be friends, you sure have a funny way of showing it!"

Catriona grinned, noticing with pleasure that Uzi had relaxed much more with Grreag.

"It's now a tradition, Uzi. We have to fight whenever we meet."

"Well, beat up on each other later. Show her what we have, Sir."

The Leon released Catriona's wrist, lifting a huge hand to pull out a full-sized ceramic keg from under the table. Catriona groaned inwardly. Leontor *ealu*! And so much of it.

"Slainté, Haggis." Khumalo handed her a steaming cup, raising her own in toast.

"Oh, God, don't talk about haggis or I'll puke."

Khumalo grinned, raising her cup. "Yes, I remember your unfortunate habit of throwing up over people when they mention that revolting Scottish creation. Particularly when the people in question are dying of carbine shot wounds."

"What's this?" demanded Grreag.

"Nothing," snapped Catriona, flushing.

Khumalo threw back her head and laughed. "Nothing? You call that nothing?"

Major Benjamin appeared at their table, his arm around an attractive blonde-haired female. "What's nothing? What did Catriona do this time?"

"Remember when she and I escaped from Captain T'alak on Komodoa? Well, the fucker had half shot my arm off at the shoulder, and the only hope I had was Miz-I-Don't-Like-Blood, over there."

At the mention of T'alak's name, Catriona tensed. "He wanted me for my brain," she said, trying to make light of the memory.

Benjamin's eyebrows raised. "You should have been flattered. Most Komodoans want humans for their bodies, and not necessarily to flay and display on a wall."

"Don't remind me," shuddered Catriona, taking a large gulp of *ealu*.

"Okay," he grinned, "you needn't think you've succeeded in changing the subject. What about this 'nothing' thing?"

Khumalo poured them another round. "Basically, when she strapped my shoulder up, she retched the entire time. I told her she had a nice bedside manner, and called her 'haggis'. Bitch then threw up all over me!"

"Oh, Uzi!" Catriona joined in the laughter.

"I've heard worse than that," said Benjamin. "What about you sabotaging a safety class at the ACC, and they had to shut down the entire dome for the rest of the day?"

Grreag almost choked on his *ealu*. "She did what?"

"Only Catriona could grab a canister of tear gas instead of a fire extinguisher from the college stores," chortled Khumalo. "I wish I'd been there. I can just imagine your tutor's face when she realized your mistake!"

"How do you know it was a mistake?" said Catriona, archly.

Grreag leaned to murmur in her ear, "I sincerely hope it was, for your sake."

"Or what?"

Khumalo, seeing the warning signs of an impending argument, stepped in.

"And what did I hear about you sealing yourself in a model cruiser after a simulated flight lesson? How long before they cut you out?"

Hasty preparations for the Leontor mission had been completed; Catriona's orders were succinct. Accompany the Leon students to their home planet, and meet with their academy director to discuss the possible arrangements for the accommodation and tutoring of ten human students. Lodging had been arranged for her at the Leontor academy.

Catriona both anticipated and dreaded the experience. It sounded as though the Leons ran their training facilities in a barbaric way, if Grreag's teasing remarks were anything to go by.

Catriona massaged her aching temples. She still had a hangover from too much *ealu* at the launch party. She had vague memories of taking exception to something Grreag said and challenging him to a fight to the death. She didn't remember ever before hearing her Leon friend roar so hard with laughter. She then passed out, waking up in Uzi's berth that morning, wishing she'd never heard of Leontor or its *ealu*.

Catriona returned to her apartment to pack for her mission. She hadn't much to pack. Just her dress uniform, a few changes of her fatigues, underwear and socks, and a couple of comfortable sweats to wear when not on duty.

To her disappointment, no messages awaited her. Even though she had thrown Haven out, she had fully expected him to call by now. She had to admit, the longer his silence, the more guilty he appeared. She was relieved to be leaving Earth so promptly for a month on Leontor. Time enough for Haven to cool his heels and think about what he had done to her.

En route to the rendezvous with the *Exsequor*, Catriona speed-learned the Leontor language, a fast and harmless technique. Minuscule computer chips programmed with the desired information were inserted into strategic learning and retention sections of the brain. Leontor Control only sanctioned the use of it in instances such as this, when an agent or representative needed to be fluent on a certain subject in a short space of time. Overuse of the process risked displacement or loss of other memories.

Catriona bunked with Uzi for the two-day trip. She lay on the upper bunk, gathering her thoughts, the rendezvous with the *Exsequor* less than an hour away. It was fitting to Catriona that she travel with her friends to face the second major change in her 23rd century life.

Trouble was, the closer they got to the rendezvous, the more petrified she felt about the upcoming mission. Why her, in God's name? She knew nothing about diplomacy, indeed her very lack of it got her into far too many sticky situations. And she knew even less about the protocol in representing the Alliance. What if she made a fool of herself? Or worse still, did something really awful and broke up the alliance between Leontor and Earth? In the next breath, she chastised herself for her arrogance in thinking that anything she could do would make that much difference.

Once on board the *Exsequor*, she would have a better idea of how to behave. The only Leons she knew on a personal level were Colonel Grreag, Qiterr and Zerreem. Grreag lived amongst humans, and the other two were only teenagers by human standards. What would mature Leons on their own planet be like? Catriona took a couple of deep breaths to calm her fears.

Uzi had filled her in on her slow progress with Webster's temporal bubble. Catriona felt a mixture of emotions ranging from irritation that in two years no significant progression had been made, to downright relief that she didn't yet have to make a definitive decision about returning to the 21st century.

Catriona shifted her focus to what the *Vallo* crew had been up to over the past couple of years. Uzi had told her that activity along the Realm border had increased, alerting the Alliance to possible invasion plans. Catriona had listened intently to the report of skirmishes with Realm spacecraft. To her relief, Captain T'alak's name hadn't been mentioned. After all, when she considered it, why would he bother coming after her when it had been Haven who had betrayed him?

172 | *Time Twist*

Despite the coziness of Uzi's berth, Catriona shivered at the memory of T'alak's unrelenting, black eyes when he spoke of her torture and death. Sometimes she still felt shards of pain along her back where he'd whipped her, even though the scar had long healed. Thank God for Jack Haven. If he hadn't concocted her escape, Catriona's skin would most likely be hanging on T'alak's wall right now.

Sudden tears welled. Catriona slid off the bunk to the floor. She refused to think about Haven. Right now she needed to concentrate on her mission. Locating her black boots on the floor, she placed them by the lower bunk and sat to slip on her discarded fatigues shirt.

The berth door dilated to admit Khumalo, who tossed herself onto the bunk beside Catriona.

"I hate double shift! I've only a few minutes before I report to the control cabin." She looked at Catriona and winked. "Engineering green suits you."

"I hadn't much choice." She laughed. "I'm not authorized to wear command blue, and there's no bloody way I'll be seen dead in the general orange fatigues!"

The only drawback to this particular shade of green was that it looked similar to the color of her old school uniform. She would never be able to wear it without thinking of damp autumn days walking home by the quiet river, kicking her way through piles of golden leaves.

"Ready to go?" Khumalo broke into her thoughts.

"Ready as I'll ever be, I guess."

Catriona studied herself in the closet full-length mirror. Not bad, she thought. Still could lose some weight, but the fatigues flattered her figure, the green setting off her red hair.

Khumalo grinned, her teeth gleaming white against her dark skin. "You're scared to death, aren't you? Don't worry, you'll do just fine."

"I sure hope so." Catriona sat to pull on her boots.

"The first one's always the toughest. Got everything you need?"

"Yeah, I went down to my apartment to pack."

"What does Jack think of your mission?"

"There." Catriona slapped her thighs and stood. "I'm fighting-fit to go." She felt her friend's dark brown eyes bore into her.

"Catriona?"

She sighed heavily. "I don't know what made me think I could hide anything from you. I didn't dare say anything with Grreag about — he'd cut out Jack's heart, for sure."

"What did the bastard do, screw somebody else?" Catriona

hesitated, and then nodded. "I'm not surprised," said Uzi.

"Why do you say that?"

"Remember, he was a double agent. How can you ever trust a guy like that?"

Catriona swallowed. "I guess this proves you can't. Uzi, let's talk about something else. I've had enough of Lieutenant Colonel bloody Haven for one lifetime."

"I know you don't mean that, Haggis."

"I do. I'm finished with him, end of subject." Catriona checked the berth chronometer. "Listen, I have to go. Grreag'll kill me if I'm late."

They embraced, and Catriona moved toward the dilating door. "Take care of yourself and thanks for putting me up here."

"No problem." Khumalo grinned. "Don't screw anything I wouldn't!"

Catriona shot her friend a pained look. "That really doesn't leave much, does it?"

She jumped through the doorway in time to escape the boot thrown at bruising velocity.

✦

Colonel Grreag had already sent eight of the students to the *Exsequor*. Now it was Catriona's turn with the remaining two. He had mixed feelings about seeing her go; he had enjoyed spending time with his only close human friend.

But he'd have enough to keep him busy. Immediately after the *Exsequor* rendezvous, the *Vallo* would investigate the new space rupture phenomena. Grreag, suspecting a Realm plot to lure Alliance Armada ships from the safety of their space lanes, had his mind very much preoccupied with the ship's security measures.

He glowered at the two remaining students. He had hardly spoken to the young Leons. He felt awkward with them even though they reminded him a little of himself when he joined the Leontor Militia Academy. He had been ambitious and determined to succeed. Part of him felt envious of their advantage in visiting ACC during training. Grreag had had no such opportunity.

When he first took command of the *Vallo*, his initial months had been uncomfortable. It took him a long time to find his place. At first, the humans did not respond well to his curt Leontor manner. Grreag felt their more recent acceptance of him was due, a lot, to his friendship with Catriona.

He studied Catriona's face as she prepared to actuate to the

174 | *Time Twist*

Exsequor. She wasn't quite successful in masking her anxiety. Proud of her, he had every confidence she would excel in her new role as liaison for the students. Her outgoing and rebellious ways made her a good choice for this particular assignment.

Growling softly to himself, Grreag realized he had not visited Leontor for over three Terran years. He missed the vast tundra, underground cities unmarring the spread of grass and mountain. He felt regret that he could not accompany Catriona, make her initiation into his society a little easier. But his duty lay with the Alliance. Besides, he reminded himself, Leons did not suffer from homesickness.

He noticed Catriona fought hard to maintain her composure in front of her waiting charges. To Grreag's irritation, the male, whom Grreag recognized as Qiterr studied Catriona with too much interest. Always mindful of his human friend's safety, he hoped all Leon males were as aware of how deadly intimacy with a human female would be for her.

"You!" he snapped, startling both Leons and Catriona.

Qiterr growled, standing to attention in front of Grreag, who towered over him. "Sir?"

"I expect you to see to Lieutenant Logan's welfare both on the *Exsequor* and on Leontor. If any harm should come to her I will hold you responsible."

The teen's golden eyes narrowed in surprise. Perhaps Grreag was mistaken about Qiterr's interest in Catriona, but he felt justified in issuing the warning. As both an elder male and a superior officer, Grreag knew Qiterr would follow his order to the death, as custom dictated.

"Yes, Sir," said Qiterr.

Out of the corner of his eye, Grreag caught Catriona's brief impatient expression. He knew she would resent his inference that she was weak and in need of care. Sometimes her pride equaled that of a Leon.

She moved to his side, her mouth twisting into a wry grin.

"Thank you," she whispered.

Something in her smile told him she knew the reason for his concern. He didn't like that she knew about such an intimate detail as his penile barbs. To his alarm, he also recognized a glint in her eye that foretold of mischief. Before he could move out of range, she grabbed him, pulling him down to her so she could inflict a deep bite to his neck. Grreag was embarrassed in front of the students, and he noticed the *Vallo* actuate operator smother a grin.

"Catriona," he growled in an undertone, "I should tear your jugular out for this."

"Promises, promises," she teased, moving to the actuate dais.

Fighting the urge to laugh, Grreag ordered the operator to engage the system. Only after one of the three bubbles engulfed Catriona did he permit himself a fanged grin.

The figures began to dissolve, then Catriona's bubble buckled.

"Cancel bubble two!" Grreag roared.

The operator's fingers worked furiously at the controls, but the bubble still rippled, in danger of implosion. The other two bubbles vanished. Grreag watched as Catriona's sparked, shimmering out of existence.

"Get it back!" he roared at the operator, and activated his earcomm. "*Vallo* to *Exsequor*," he spat, dropping into his native tongue.

"Go ahead," replied a low growl from the Leontor ship.

"Bubble two malfunctioned. Do you have it?"

Grreag thought he would explode as he waited for the reply.

"Negative, *Vallo*. Bubble two has disbanded."

"I've got it!" yelled the operator.

Grreag strode to the dais. The bubble began to shimmer into view. But empty. Catriona's molecules had been scattered in space.

He paged Chief Khumalo in the control cabin. "Sweep the area," he insisted, "locate any disturbances within range."

There might still be time to pull Catriona's molecules back into a bubble, he thought. Hadn't she come onto the *Vallo* that way in the first place?

After a moment or two, Khumalo reported. "No disturbances, Colonel. Nothing within range but the *Exsequor* and an unpopulated asteroid." Her voice sounded thick with emotion.

Grreag shouldered the actuate operator out of the way and continued attempts to find Catriona. After several abortive scans, the horror dawned on him. His only human friend in the Alliance had gone.

A dishonorable death where she would never know peace.

33

CATRIONA PREPARED herself to arrive on the Leontor ship as the actuate bubble engulfed her. A moment later she rematerialized on an alien ship, but not the *Exsequor*.

Eyes quickly adjusting to the new surroundings, Catriona's heart almost stopped. A green-hued mist swirled around her, and she smelled a musty, mossy scent. A Komodoan ship.

The actuate operator stepped from the shadows. There was no mistaking his race... the long, supple tail swinging behind him, and the arch of scales on the forehead. For a second Catriona hoped it might be Haven's idea of a practical joke, but he would never do a thing like this.

Two Komodoan guards converged on her and held her between them. Footsteps rang on the metal floor as someone marched toward them. Catriona twisted, struggling against the guards' hold.

As the footsteps grew closer, she doubled her efforts to free herself. One of the guards struck her across the face and she slumped forward. Her lip stung and she tasted the hot iron of blood. Blinking the dizziness away, she concentrated on the floor as a pair of black boots came to rest in front of her. She took a sharp breath, letting her eyes travel up. Long legs encased in thigh-high, military black boots, a glimpse of his exultantly arched tail, a muscular chest straining against its long, padded gray tunic. T'alak, captain of the *L'umina*, flagship of the Komodoan Realm.

T'alak smiled at her recognition, his dark eyes glittering in triumph. "So, earthworm! We meet again."

Catriona swallowed hard and kept her gaze averted. He looked as intimidating as she remembered him. He nodded and her captors released her arms. She resisted rubbing them to get the circulation back. To show weakness in front of T'alak might escalate his brutality.

As he studied her, Catriona sensed the suppressed excitement emanating from him. She vividly recalled the last time he'd studied her like that, but then Haven had stopped him from harming her.

T'alak raised a hand and Catriona tensed, but he only lifted a finger to smear the blood from the corner of her mouth. She shuddered at his touch, her stomach churning as he licked the finger with his long, forked tongue.

"Bring her!" he commanded, turning on his heel and stalking out.

Catriona shivered on the floor of the pitch black cell, hugging herself to keep warm. The walls and floor were sheer metal; she hadn't been able to touch the invisible ceiling. She'd lost track of how long she'd been there. Probably no more than a couple of hours, but it felt like days.

Catriona shifted her weight on the hard floor, her legs feeling cold and beginning to grow numb. She berated herself for letting this happen: she should have gone back to her own time, despite the rupture, and not let Haven talk her into staying. She should have known she'd never be free of T'alak while she remained in this century.

Angrily, she blamed Haven. He'd been away with Intelligence more than he'd been with her, and she'd spent most of the past two years isolated and lonely. And now alone she had to face Captain T'alak.

As though her thoughts conjured him, the door slid open and T'alak stood silhouetted, light flooding into the cell around him. Heart pounding, Catriona scrambled to her feet, leaning against the wall to support her shaking legs. A humid, mossy scent wafted through the open door.

"Are you ready to talk?" he asked in an uncharacteristically mild tone.

Catriona swallowed, trying to relieve her parched throat. "About what?" She could see T'alak's tail flicking to and fro behind him.

He took a step inside the cell and folded his arms across his chest. "About your lifemate," he said softly, his dark eyes gleaming in the light from the corridor. "Tell me about Colonel Haven."

Catriona bit her lip, forcing herself not to shrink from him. "He... we're no longer together," she faltered.

"My report says otherwise. Tell me, earthworm, are human males not enough for you?"

She met his look. "Jack Haven is half-human."

He backhanded her, knocking her hard against the wall. Head ringing, Catriona shrank as he leaned in close, his hands on either side of her face.

Revulsion and terror lent Catriona strength. With a strangled scream, she shoved him back and struck him on the larynx. He staggered, gasping, and she ran from the cell.

The blow might have incapacitated a human, but it only caused a hesitation in T'alak. He gave chase, snatching at her long hair and tripping her. She toppled to the floor and he dropped to one knee beside her, his tail stretched out behind him. His hand rested on her shoulder, and then he slid it along the curve of her waist and hip. Catriona jack-knifed away.

"You don't know when to give in, do you?" he asked.

"I'll never give in," she whispered.

Footsteps approached. T'alak rose to his feet and looked at the soldier.

"Honored Captain, we've been recalled to Komodoa."

T'alak's tail twitched. "Put the human back in the cell and don't feed

178 | *Time Twist*

her," he ordered as he strode away. "It'll make her hide easier to remove."

⤙

"Of course I'm sure!" insisted Haven for the third time. He stood in Alliance Intelligence headquarters, facing the Leontor Brigadier General Xorrog across her desk. "How do you think I ended up in the rose bushes, unconscious?"

The Brigadier observed him through keen, yellow-gold eyes, her ears flicking restlessly on top of her head.

"Lieutenant Colonel, Logan died in an actuate accident mere hours ago. Colonel Grreag verified it himself."

Haven checked himself, attempting to sound more reasonable. He would get nowhere challenging Leontor authority. Unclenching his fists, he purposefully lowered his voice.

"Brigadier, I can see how the facts appear indisputable. But I know T'alak. Catriona is alive. He has taken her; he's engineered the whole thing. I must go to Komodoa and bring her back."

Xorrog's ears flattened. "Lieutenant Colonel, we have no evidence that T'alak has done this. And as for Matthew Gordon, there is no record of him in Intelligence."

Haven sat on the luxurious leather chair in front of the Brigadier's desk. He knew he couldn't push the issue because Xorrog mustn't learn of Catriona's significance as a time traveler. But he had to try, without giving her away.

"Regardless, Ma'am, I must leave for Komodoa at once."

Xorrog studied him with her piercing, ochroid eyes. "Request denied."

Haven surged to his feet. "Brigadier, if you won't accommodate me, then I have no choice but to resign my commission with the Alliance."

Xorrog rose to face him across the desk, her ears drawn far back. "Lieutenant Colonel Haven, it's obvious you're distraught. Both the last mission and the loss of your friend have taken their toll. I'm going to recommend you take a few weeks off on Ponce de Leon before accepting your resignation. By the Great Fang, make sure it's what you want, for we won't take you back once you've gone."

Haven met her molten gaze. "All right, Ma'am," he said agreeably. "I'll go one better. I hereby request all accumulated leave. Which adds up to several months, I believe."

He saw Xorrog relax imperceptibly. That reassured him she didn't want to lose him.

"Very well," she growled. "Granted. But if I hear of you even going within a parsec of Komodoan Realm space, you'll be under penalty of death for treason."

"You won't hear about it, Brigadier General," he assured her, masking his smile.

✦

"You've gone too far, Captain T'alak!"

T'alak smarted under General B'alarg's reproach. He stood in the General's office, having been summoned there as soon as he docked. He remained still, concentrating on the sound of the water sculpture cascading down the walls. He would not allow B'alarg to goad him. Honor had obliged him to recapture the human female; his right by the Law of Exactment. He had lost face by her previous escape, and he had thought of little else but that for the last two years.

The elderly council member spoke for the first time. "Don't be too hard on him, my friend."

T'alak slid his gaze to study Governor C'huln, his wizened body clothed in a long, civilian robe. The cloth shone richly with turquoise and silver threads, reflecting the ever-moving liquid on the walls.

"As this alien comes from the 21st century, I think Captain T'alak has provided us with an excellent study project." C'huln's tongue flickered in and out as he spoke. "There will perhaps be many things about humanity we can learn from it."

B'alarg stopped pacing, coming to stand beside the ancient globe of Earth by his stone desk. Fingering the painted planet, he glared at T'alak.

"It is well for you that the Governor is gracious, Captain. You are a tail's-breadth from execution."

T'alak's tail flicked in reflex. After waiting so long to take back Catriona Logan, would he lose her to research so soon? He bowed to C'huln. "I shall deliver the human to you without delay, Governor."

The elderly man held up a hand. "I have pressing matters to deal with in the Capital first. Incarcerate her until I am ready for study."

A shiver of anticipation rippled through T'alak's tail. He bowed again. "Yes, honored one."

C'huln nodded to B'alarg and left. B'alarg approached T'alak. Lifting his tail he thumped him hard across the back of his knees, making him stumble. T'alak's expression didn't waver, but his skin flushed olive. B'alarg shoved his squat-featured face close.

"The Realm has no use for rogue captains," he hissed. "This is your

180 | *Time Twist*

final warning. Step out of line one more time and I'll see your entrails hung from the spire for all to see, even if you are from an Imperial House. Do you understand me, T'alak?"

The two officers glared at each other.

"Perfectly, General," answered T'alak, deliberately leaving out the required 'honored'.

B'alarg hissed and retreated to his desk. Lifting an infopad, he flicked it on, handing it to T'alak. "Here are your orders concerning the space rupture. After you take care of the human, proceed immediately."

Outside B'alarg's office, T'alak's tail arched and slammed against the floor in rage. B'alarg had no right to address him so, let alone strike him. Superior officer or not, B'alarg still remained the son of a peasant, not worthy to look T'alak in the eye.

As he made his way back to the *L'umina*, he wondered where by the stars he would keep Catriona until C'huln sent for her. He decided the safest place would be at his house. Not his quarters on base, but the remote estate on the other side of the planet. It lay empty, periodically maintained by a couple of servants. Too many memories for T'alak to be comfortable there anymore, but it would be an ideal prison for the human. Completely isolated, the estate sat at the center of a vast marshland. One had to either travel by yacht or actuate directly there. T'alak's great-grandfather, in his time a Realm admiral, valued privacy so much he had built the mansion on the northern hemisphere far from civilization.

Once T'alak had loved the house, frequenting it to see his new bride on shore leaves. But now… He wrenched his thoughts away. His mate, T'alak-ra, had been dead for many years. The house had been cold, dry, and bleak since then. A perfect prison.

34

CATRIONA HAD been limbering up for about an hour in the frigid darkness. It stopped her dwelling on Haven and her regret at not going back to the 21st century. Besides, it was better than sitting scared, imagining Captain T'alak decorating the wall in his quarters with her skin. This time she stood ready when the cell door slammed open. "Come out!" ordered T'alak.

She edged toward the doorway, squinting at the light. He gripped her upper arm, propelling her along beside him to the carrier. His tail hung stiffly, hardly swaying at all as he walked. The pleasure of her capture had extinguished. She realized something had changed, and wondered what.

Emerging on a landing pad, T'alak marched her to a silver star-yacht. It looked like the same type he had before, which with Haven and Uzi's help, she had stolen to make good her escape from him two years ago. He shoved her inside its open hatchway.

"Where are you taking me?" Remembering his remark about removing her hide she searched for any sign of a knife.

"Be silent."

He pushed her into the co-pilot's seat so hard she almost fell through the large tail gap in back. He took the pilot seat beside her and briskly engaged the drive. He looked preoccupied, Catriona no longer the focus of his attention.

The yacht eased off the landing pad and soared from the *L'umina's* belly. Catriona watched the hexagram above become a pinprick, then clouds obscured it. The planet stretched out below them, richly mauve from its many oceans. Catriona felt giddy from lack of food and drink. She wondered if she'd at least have a chance for a proper wash before T'alak killed her. It had been so long since she felt really clean, the dryness of Earth still gritty in her throat.

T'alak ignored her, staring out of the viewscreen. His forked tongue flicked over his dry lips. Covertly, Catriona studied his holster. If she could snatch his carbine and subdue him, she had no doubt the space-worthy yacht could take them back to Alliance space. At this point, she had nothing to lose.

She waited until T'alak's ramrod back relaxed a fraction, then surged from her seat. Slamming a fist into the side of his head, she yanked the carbine from his belt. The yacht dipped as T'alak lost control for a second. Catriona caught her balance, aiming the weapon at him.

"Plot a course for Alliance space," she ordered.

He met her gaze, eyes sparking like black flints. Raising a skeptical eyebrow, he returned his attention to the flight console.

"Don't try anything, you piece of shit." She waved the carbine in his face and he sneered. Rage consumed her and she fought against the desire to blast him into a million atoms; she might need him as hostage to clear Realm space. She watched him program the coordinates and satisfied, stepped back. "Now get up. Slowly."

The Captain unfolded himself from the pilot seat. His solid frame

182 | *Time Twist*

filled the yacht's interior, and Catriona felt intimidated, despite holding the weapon on him. T'alak's eyes glinted, his tail raised and curled to the side.

Recognizing the tail's body language of attack, Catriona ordered, "Lie on the floor, face down. He eased to a crouching position and rested there, watching her. "All the way down, bastard."

He did not move. She leveled the weapon between his eyes. One squeeze on the trigger, and his mocking sneer would be gone forever. Her hand shook.

T'alak's lip curled. "You don't have the courage."

She lowered the carbine to his crotch and fired. T'alak's hissing laugh rang in her ears as she realized he'd duped her. The carbine had no power.

"Good try, earthworm," sneered T'alak, "you've learned a few things since we last met."

Catriona spun the carbine round in her hand, slamming the butt at his skull. His arm flew up, parrying the blow. The weapon bounced from her hand. Lunging to his feet, T'alak punched her in the face. Catriona rocketed backwards against the flight console and rolled out of the way, just escaping his fist. The yacht lurched, out of control.

They both clung to the ceiling, rendered useless by gravity as the yacht plunged planetside. Catriona managed to wedge herself into the corner, but the craft slammed into something, dislodging her. She catapulted forward, then was flung back again.

The yacht shuddered to a halt and Catriona opened her eyes. She blinked, disoriented. Above her flames crackled from the console, smoke mushrooming through the cabin. They had crash-landed, upside down. By some miracle she hadn't been severely injured, but her entire body pulsated with pain.

T'alak lay in a crumpled heap nearby. The fire began to eat its way through the cabin and the smoke choked Catriona, making her cough.

She crab-walked along until she located the emergency hatchway in the ceiling at the stern of the vessel. Wheezing with the effort, she used both legs to shift the release lever. The hatch blew off, letting in a blessed rush of clean air. Peering out, she drew a sharp breath. They had crashed into a forest. A massive big-limbed tree had broken the fall, suspending the craft about fifteen feet above the ground.

Heat licked at her legs. The fresh oxygen had further fed the fire and flames reached out toward the hatchway. Catriona readied to jump out when she saw T'alak move. She froze, tempted to leave him. But reason prevailed; she might need him to survive in the alien forest below.

"Come on, you shit!" she yelled, kicking at him.

T'alak stared dully at her. Through the smoke Catriona saw dark green blood spurt from an ugly gash on his left temple. The scales on his forehead had protected him from worse damage. With the flames moving nearer, she struggled to drag T'alak's heavy bulk to the hatchway. Finally he understood, pulling himself to the opening. Heat lashed Catriona's back.

"Jesus, get a move on!" she screamed in his ear.

In desperation, she pushed him with all her might and he fell through the hatchway. She scrambled to follow, but caught sight of an emergency kit by the hatchway. Grabbing it, she leapt as a scorching roar thundered at her back.

Landing beside T'alak on the damp, swampy forest floor, she saw the yacht shift, about to plunge down on both of them. Tossing the emergency kit aside, she grabbed T'alak under his armpits and hauled him from under the hanging inferno.

She got clear and managed to drag him behind the trunk of a massive tree as the yacht crashed to the ground. Catriona covered her ears, collapsing against the tree. The roar and crackle of fire soon diminished to a sullen hiss, the marshy forest floor sapping its strength. She didn't know how long she lay, slipping in and out of consciousness. Something warm and wet trickled on her arm. Yelping, she sat up. T'alak's blood, oozing green, dripped steadily.

Catriona rubbed her eyes and focused. T'alak would be no use to her if he bled to death. She eased round the tree trunk and groped among the damp fauna for the emergency kit. For a moment she exalted in the breathing in of real air, the coolness on her skin. It had been a long time since she'd walked 'naked,' as Earth dubbed those who could survive on the pockets of the planet without the domes.

Bringing the kit back, she saw T'alak's eyes were open, but glazed. She tore open the kit. Rummaging through it she found a disinfectant pad, and began to clean his head wound. It stung him lucid.

"Don't touch me," he hissed, attempting to sit up. His head injury must have been worse than he thought, for he fell back, face strained.

Catriona dabbed at his forehead again and T'alak pushed her hand away. "Don't be such a baby!" she snapped.

His black eyes widened in disbelief. Scarcely believing herself, she resumed her work, all the time aware of his eyes on her. Digging around in the kit, she pulled out three different colored, sealed pads. Applied

184 | *Time Twist*

to flesh, the pads would infuse medicine directly into the bloodstream. She held them up.

"Which of these prevents infection?"

T'alak pointed with his chin to one and Catriona unwrapped it, pressing it to his temple.

"And which is the painkiller?" He didn't react. "You are no use to me if you can't concentrate, Captain. Which one?"

After a long moment he gestured to one of them and she applied it to his neck. A moment or two later he visibly relaxed, letting out a long hissing breath.

Catriona investigated her own injuries. She had been lucky, just a few scrapes and bruises. But her jaw was badly swollen and every move she made jarred her with pain. She applied a painkiller pad to her own neck, allowing T'alak the satisfaction of knowing his punch hit home. Then she cleaned up the worst of the cuts, aware that T'alak studied her every move.

She found a packet of ration wafers and a canister of water in the kit. With the immediate danger over, she remembered how hungry and thirsty she was. Ripping open the packet, she ate two wafers and drank from the canister. The wafers had no taste and felt greasy in her stomach. Fighting nausea she rewrapped the package. Glancing at T'alak she held it out to him. He shook his head and she dropped it back in the emergency kit. She took another sip of water and offered that to him. He drank a couple of mouthfuls and handed it back.

"Why did you save me?" He sounded unsure of himself.

Catriona curled her lip into a sneer and looked him right in the eyes. "Maybe I've been studying Leontor culture too much, but there'd be no *honor* in letting you die like that."

She saw his eyes harden, but inexplicably, he no longer terrified her. The crash had evened the odds.

Catriona dropped the water canister into the emergency kit and stood, looking about her. The gloomy forest's tall trees obscured the daylight. It resembled a Terran forest, but the swampy floor encouraged more reed-like plants to grow. The tallest of these had dark blue, spiky blooms. Catriona wondered if they were marsh-peonies. She could sure use some of their soothing gel right now.

T'alak pulled himself to a standing position, flexing his muscles. Catriona saw that his tail hung limply behind him, and spotted the scar she'd given him two years ago. He lifted the emergency kit and moved toward the smoldering yacht, his movements slow and stiff.

She followed, not wanting to be alone in the forest's darkening gloom. She watched as he sifted through the wreckage and pulled a large corner of the hull free.

"We wait for rescue in here," he announced, placing it so the torn gap pointed away from the ground.

Catriona looked inside the piece of hull. There was only enough space for them to lie down side by side.

"Why wait in there?" she asked, baffled.

"The *Letum*. It's almost nightfall. We cannot be on the ground when they are active."

He extracted a silver cigar shape from the emergency kit. With a flick of his wrist it unraveled. Catriona recognized an emergency blanket. She remembered an aluminum-sprayed version in her father's old camping gear.

Shivering, she looked about her. Why couldn't they climb a damn tree? But she saw why. There were no branches within reach under the canopy of foliage. The gloom of the forest grew more oppressive, the silence menacing. A sharp squeal rent the air.

"Get in if you want to live, earthworm!" snapped T'alak.

Catriona scrambled onto the hull fragment and dropped into the coffin-like interior.

"What the hell was that?" she whispered as T'alak followed.

The metal hull shuddered around them as he affixed the emergency blanket across the entrance.

"The first *Letum* call," came his disembodied voice in the dark as he settled down beside her.

Catriona hated having to lie beside him. She edged as far away as possible, pointedly turning her back. The hull still felt warm from the fire; Catriona's aching muscles relaxed as she stretched out. T'alak quickly fell asleep, his breathing becoming deep and even.

Catriona dared not sleep, afraid she'd wake up to find T'alak removing her skin as an extra layer of warmth against the night. Lying in the blackness, she wondered what might be happening on the *Vallo*. They thought she was dead, and life would go on as though she'd never been alive. No one would come looking for her, not even Haven.

Her throat burned as she thought of the last angry words she had said to him. She had been too quick to judge him. He'd tried to talk to her after she found him with Matthew, had seemed as shocked as she to find Matthew there. Oh God, why hadn't she given him a chance to explain? She'd been too angry to think clearly when it happened.

A tear slipped out of her eye and ran down her nose. She'd give anything to have the chance to tell him she forgave him.

35

CATRIONA WOKE with a shock. Overhead she saw the emergency blanket had come away, allowing a lessening of the gloom above. The hull had long since cooled. She shivered with cold, scarcely feeling her hands or feet. The painkiller had worn off and her jaw throbbed.

In the darkness she spied a large, undefined shape at the hull opening, intent on coming in.

"Captain!" Catriona shook him awake.

"Take your hands off me," he hissed.

"It's one of those *Letum*!"

T'alak got to his knees. In one swift motion he extracted a knife concealed in his boot and executed a clean swipe. The creature squealed and fell away from the opening.

"Should discourage other curious *Letum*," he said, lying back down and wiping his hands on his tunic. "What's that noise?"

"M-my teeth chattering. It's freezing." Catriona gasped as his hand snaked out to grab her arm and felt her fingers.

"You won't be any use to C'huln on ice," he said.

"Who's C'huln?"

He didn't answer, reaching up to unfasten his tunic. Catriona squirmed back as far as she could, setting her back against the hull. He opened the tunic and forcibly pulled her to him. Catriona strained away, kicking hard.

She saw his eyes flash with anger, and he spoke through gritted teeth. "Human, this will make us even for the life I owe you." He cocooned them both in the thermal fabric, one arm under her head, the other around her.

She lay rigid, face against his bare chest, sick to her stomach with the forced intimacy. To her relief his breathing slowed as he fell back asleep, and Catriona made herself relax, grateful for his warmth.

She stretched out under the crisp linen sheets, back in Stonehaven,

Scotland. The Highland spring air brought a fresh ocean scent through the open window. Haven held her close. Catriona luxuriated in the feel of his strong arms around her. She uncrossed her arms from her chest and reached a hand round to gently run her fingers down his scaly back. When he didn't respond, she freed a leg, draping it over his to draw him to her while she moved provocatively against him. Feeling him grow hard, she grinned, raising her face to seek his lips.

An alarm sounded in her head. Struggling from the dream, she opened her eyes. Her stomach lurched. This was no Scottish morning. She lay in the eternal gloom of a Komodoan forest, intimately entwined with her hated enemy, Captain T'alak.

He met her gaze, his dark eyes glittering, and raised himself up on an elbow. She braced her arm to keep him at bay but he just watched her. She realized his hand cupped the back of her head, and a thumb moved slowly down the side of her neck.

"I'm sorry," she gasped, shocked, "I dreamed you were Jack."

It worked. At the mention of Haven's name, T'alak recoiled. He pulled away, letting her head drop with a thud and he clambered out of the piece of hull. Catriona stiffly sat up and rubbed her head. Surely T'alak couldn't possibly have thought she'd wanted him? The touch of his thumb had felt like a caress, and she shuddered. Moving slowly, every sinew in her body ached as she climbed out of the hull.

T'alak had disappeared. Catriona shivered in the purple dawn filtering through the thick branches. She stepped over a green, putrid mess by the hull, the remains of the *Letum*. It looked like a giant slug, big enough to engorge a human whole.

She tensed as the air pressure about her changed. Three Komodoan soldiers shimmered into existence before her, tails lashing expectantly. A grim, granite-jawed officer wearing a similar rank clip to T'alak stood in the middle, flanked by two subordinates. He had lighter-colored eyes than she'd seen on a Komodoan before, and a wide mouth that surprised her by curving into a friendly smile. He held out a hand and helped her to her feet.

"Where is Captain T'alak, human?" he inquired, tipping her chin so she looked into his unusual eyes. Catriona found the admiration in his gaze compelling and couldn't look away.

"M'arlaak, you old chameleon!"

T'alak stepped from the darkness of the trees, the yacht emergency kit in his hands. M'arlaak turned from Catriona to greet him. Catriona had never heard such warmth in T'alak's voice before. Nor had she witnessed Komodoans interacting like this. As T'alak and M'arlaak approached each other, they hissed softly, their two tail-tips curling around each other. She saw that M'arlaak looked a few years younger than T'alak, but older than Jack.

"Forgive the long delay in finding you, T'alak." M'arlaak uncurled his tail first.

"You came quickly, considering the location."

M'arlaak moved to inspect the wreckage. "What caused the crash?"

"Malfunction," grunted T'alak.

Catriona almost laughed. He didn't want to lose face by admitting she had overpowered him.

M'arlaak turned his sparkling smile on her and she resisted the urge to return it.

"If the human were cleaned up, she-"

"Not this one, my friend," interrupted T'alak, taking a pad from the emergency kit. "The council has plans for her."

"Public execution?"

"First we wait for C'huln."

"A pity."

Catriona's skin tightened at the grim expression on M'arlaak's face. Alarmed, she looked at Captain T'alak. "Who is this C'huln?"

"Be silent!" he ordered.

"But I have a right to know."

"You have no rights, earthworm," snarled T'alak, slapping the pad on Catriona's neck.

In a moment, her world wavered and went black.

Catriona woke to a soft voice calling her name. She opened her eyes to a blinding pain. Lifting a hand to her face, she felt her swollen lip and jaw. Her fingers found the sedative patch T'alak had attached on her neck and she peeled it off. She'd been lying on a hard, stone floor. A waterfall roared from somewhere beyond the tiny arched window. The sound made her realize how dehydrated she felt.

"Catriona Logan?"

She twisted round to see a Komodoan woman about her own age standing in the open doorway. She wore a short blue robe, similar to what Catriona had worn on her last sojourn in the Komodoan Realm.

"Where am I?" Her voice sounded thick and cracked.

The Komodoan shook her head, her long, black braid swinging from side to side. She took a step into the room. Catriona saw she held what looked like a collar and leash in her hands.

"This put on," she said in English with a strong accent, tossing the restraints at Catriona's feet.

"No way." Catriona sat up, resting back on her hands.

"You put." The woman pulled a Realm military hand-carbine from her belt and fired it within a couple of inches of Catriona's hand. A scorch-mark seared the stone floor.

Catriona realized there was no point in arguing. Picking up the restraints she found they were designed for wrists, not her neck. She stood up and slipped on the cuffs. The woman advanced, snapping the locks in place and taking hold of the leash. As she turned back for the door, Catriona noticed her tail looked narrower than the male Komodoan tail. This was the first Komodoan female, apart from Agent Y'alenon, that Catriona had met. From what she knew of the males, she had expected the females to be very submissive, but this woman showed no sign of it.

"Where am I?" she demanded.

The Komodoan met her gaze with eyes as dark as T'alak's. "You come."

"Not until you answer my question."

She tugged hard on the leash and dragged Catriona a few feet across the floor. "You come."

Catriona bit down on her throbbing lip, and let the woman lead her through the door to a flight of stone steps circling down, a little like those found in Norman castles on Earth. They curved down to an octagonal landing, where a large water-shrine flowed in the center. Catriona longed to taste that cold, clear water, but knew better than to touch the shrine. Several arched, wooden doors stood in a semi-circle around the landing. The Komodoan led her past these, down a wide, opulent, stone staircase to the main floor. Carved snake-like creatures formed each banister, twining round each other in Medusan frenzy. The main hallway looked impressive, adorned with water sculptures in flux down the two walls on either side of the staircase. A large arched window above the massive, wooden front doors let in an abundance of light to play in the flow of the sculptures. The effect appeared much like sunlight prisms through crystal.

Catriona stopped, dazzled at the unexpected beauty. The Komodoan liked her appreciation. Tail twirling, she allowed Catriona to pause and admire her surroundings. More doors led off the hallway, but the woman took Catriona down yet another narrower flight of stairs to the basement.

190 | *Time Twist*

"I suppose there's no point in my asking where you're taking me?" asked Catriona.

The woman shot her a pinched look. "Smell bad," she announced. "Human bathe."

Catriona had to admit the Komodoan spoke the truth. A night spent in a swampy forest did not leave her smelling like a rose and the thought of a proper wash in real water sounded great. The huge bathroom stretched over most of the basement floor, its opulence reminding Catriona of the Roman baths at Bath, England. Steaming, aquamarine water bubbled in a large pool, about twenty-foot square with four elegant pillars in each corner, the tiled walls and floor a deep shade of terracotta. Catriona held out her wrists to be uncuffed. That water looked wonderful; she could hardly wait to sink into it.

The Komodoan unwrapped the short, blue robe she wore to reveal her nakedness underneath. Catriona's jaw dropped. The woman had no breasts! Not even a nipple marred the flat smoothness of her torso, and she had no umbilical evidence or pubic hair. Haven had nipples and hair, but then he was half-human. She knew he did not need to shave regularly, but hadn't realized why until now.

The woman approached Catriona. "Turn."

Catriona reluctantly obeyed, keeping an eye on the Komodoan. Looking over her shoulder, she caught sight of webs between the woman's toes as she deftly tied Catriona's leash to the pillar. Catriona stiffened at a swishing sound. Cold metal touched the back of her neck, then she felt her fatigues shirt and trousers being sliced neatly down the back. Her bra pinged, releasing her breasts, and then the knife cut through her panties. The woman knelt behind her, lifting each of her feet to remove her boots and socks. Catriona gritted her teeth, trying to stop herself from shivering. The fact that a female removed her clothing didn't guarantee her safe from rape. The Komodoan untied her from the pillar and stepped back, letting the leash drop to the floor. Catriona breathed a little easier, turning to face her.

"What's your name?" she asked as she stepped out of the remains of her clothing. "I usually like to know who's undressing me," she added with a brittle laugh.

"Name L'ticia," said the woman, handing Catriona a soap-filled sponge.

L'ticia looked as disconcerted at Catriona's ample breasts as she had been at the Komodoan's lack of them. Her dark eyes kept darting to them in unease, as though Catriona bore a horrible deformity. She showed Catriona how to soap herself down, including her hair, rinsing them both off with a spray of sweet-smelling water. The water drained away through grates in the stone floor. Catriona moved her head to catch some of the spray in her mouth. L'ticia smiled, aiming so Catriona could drink her fill. Then she lifted the leash and drew Catriona into the pool. The water smelled rich in minerals, with a scent similar to jasmine. L'ticia unhooked the leash and uncuffed her, and Catriona sank into the healing warmth.

"Take." The voice jerked her awake. Catriona opened her eyes to see L'ticia offering her a ceramic cup from the side of the pool. She felt so damn tired, she could scarcely focus. Stumbling over, she pulled herself out to sit on the edge. She reached both hands to take the cup from L'ticia. Seeing the skin on her hands had turned prune-like she wondered how long she'd been asleep floating on her back.

"What is this?" Catriona peered into the cup. A thick, dark green liquid steamed inside.

"Heal. Is herb."

The liquid tasted sharp, like pomegranate juice. She finished it and it took effect almost immediately. Drowsy, her head became too heavy to hold up. She heard L'ticia say, "Human sleep, now? No try escape."

Yes, agreed Catriona. No try escape. For now.

36

"Rupture dead ahead, Colonel," reported Lieutenant Larrar from TactOps.

Something resembling a giant mouth appeared on the viewer. Behind the ghostly lips stretched a void so black, it appeared to reach into infinity against the backdrop of stars.

"No wonder that thing blasted clear across Alliance space," exclaimed Khumalo from NavOps. "It's vast."

Grreag nodded agreement, his ears flattening. "Are we alone?"

Khumalo checked her console. "Affirmative, Colonel."

"Launch a probe."

Larrar sent a miniature bell-shaped projectile hurtling into the giant mouth, and they waited for data to be relayed back to the *Vallo*.

Grreag stared at the screen. He found it hard to accept that Catriona had died such a pointless death. Yet space travel has risk, and Catriona knew that. The Leon glanced over at Khumalo. She had put together a memorial service, insisting on having a party afterwards. Grreag had thought it a lack of respect, but Khumalo asserted it to be a Celtic custom and Catriona would expect no less. Grreag was confused when he found himself amused at the stories told about some of Catriona's gaffs at the ACC. It felt so crude to find humor at a funeral.

The operations panel bleeped, spewing data. Khumalo's slim fingers sped over the controls, deciphering the codes.

"Report," ordered Grreag. "What happened?"

"The probe's disappeared into the rupture, Colonel. We've lost trace of it." Khumalo swiveled her chair round so she faced him. "Sir, if the rupture originated from the past, we should at least have been able to partially track the probe after it entered."

"You have a theory?"

"If Webster's temporal bubble had been perfected by the Komodoans, the probe could have been sealed off in time, impenetrable to our scans."

"You think they have the temporal weapon after all?"

She gave a shrug. A twist of black hair had escaped its braid, straggling over her forehead. "It's possible. They've had two full years to develop it since we duped them into thinking we had it."

Grreag felt a growl vibrating in his throat. He controlled it, remembering Professor Webster's short sojourn on the *Vallo*. He ground his teeth at what a close call it had been when Captain T'alak had possession of both Catriona and Webster's data.

Larrar's console bleeped. "Colonel," she reported, "the rupture is becoming unstable. I recommend we withdraw to a safe distance for observation."

"Agreed. Move us to safety, Chief. Put up full armor plating, Lieutenant."

Another warning bleep sounded from TactOps. "Sir," growled Larrar, "a Komodoan Realm warship has entered the sector."

Grreag snarled. He should have known the *Vallo* would not be alone for long. But he hadn't expected the Realm to enter Alliance space openly like this. On the viewer a massive hexagram spun across the stars, slowing its rotation as it approached the rupture.

Khumalo breathed in sharply. "That's the fucking *L'umina!*"

Grreag's fur rippled but he didn't reprimand her. He well understood Khumalo's reaction to the Realm flagship, the very one she had been taken captive on two years ago.

Khumalo cleared her throat. "Sorry, Colonel. Shall I ping them?"

"Yes." Grreag shifted in his command chair, watching the enemy ship turning effortlessly before him. It was likely that T'alak still captained the *L'umina*, and Grreag knew his intentions could not be benign.

"*L'umina*!" he boomed. "You have invaded Alliance territory. I demand an explanation!"

Tension mounted in the control cabin as the seconds ticked by with no response. It appeared T'alak was quite prepared to wait them out for as long as it took. Grreag felt the hackles rise all along his back and turned to Khumalo.

"Go ahead with what we are here for. Prepare another probe for launch; keep its velocity at minimum."

"Aye, Colonel."

He watched as the probe slipped from the *Vallo*, on a direct course for the rupture.

"Colonel," growled Larrar, "the *L'umina* is powering up her carbines." Her voice increased in volume, like a revving motorcycle.

The probe shrank to a pinprick as it moved toward the rupture. A stream of phosphorous-white fire sliced through space from the *L'umina*, exploding the probe in a ball of white light.

"Ping them again, Chief," he rumbled. As Khumalo opened the channel, Grreag puffed himself up. His bristled fur made him look twice his size. "*L'umina*," he intoned. "You have initiated an act of war. Prepare for battle."

Captain T'alak's image replaced the hexagram ship on the viewer. Grreag heard Khumalo gasp.

"Colonel Grreag." T'alak's forked tongue slid across his lips. "I knew our paths would cross again."

"Let's not play games, T'alak. You know exactly why we both are here."

"Why, Colonel," the Komodoan leaned closer to the screen, his dark eyes drilling into Grreag's, "I had hoped we could... pool our resources in this scientific investigation."

Grreag levelly met his gaze, although every hackle shimmied with rage. "Oh?"

"If you would care to actuate to the *L'umina* I would be glad to share our knowledge on the rupture."

"I must decline," growled Grreag.

"Very well," nodded T'alak with a smirk.

The communication terminated, the Komodoan's face vanishing from the screen. A volley of white fire bounced off the *Vallo's* armor, causing it to rock violently.

194 | *Time Twist*

"Colonel," announced Larrar, "the *L'umina* is registering a power surge off the scale."

Grreag frowned, "What's causing it?"

It became very clear as two bolts of amber fire lashed out from the *L'umina's* carbines. The *Vallo* rocked again, almost unseating Khumalo.

"What by the Fang was that?" demanded Grreag.

"Ionizer bolt," reported Khumalo shakily. "They've doubled their weapons fire capacity since our last encounter."

Grreag watched the screen with horror as the rupture swelled open like an infected sore. A dazzling stream of light reached out from the void like a luminescent arm to surround the *L'umina*. In moments, the Realm ship hurtled from her position and was sucked into the rupture.

"Get us out of range!" roared Grreag.

As they backed to a position of safety, Grreag demanded, "What happened?"

Khumalo swallowed hard. "Like the probe, the *L'umina's* disappeared without trace."

The tantalizing aroma of cooking food woke Catriona. She stirred, causing the gel-bed to ripple around her. It made her feel buoyant and safe, and she found it difficult to rouse into action. At length she undid the harness holding her head and dragged herself from the ooze, ignoring the unattractive sucking sounds the gel made as she crawled out. Dizzy for a moment, Catriona crouched beside the bed, taking in her surroundings... a windowless chamber with a large, unlit fireplace, and a couple of fur rugs spread over the stone floor. Looking closely at the rugs, Catriona grimaced. Leontor pelts. She found it utterly revolting that Komodoans had such little regard for life.

Apart from the bed, the somber chamber held only a cabinet, small table and backless chair, and one lamp by the bed. She saw a kimono-type robe like the one L'ticia wore draped over the chair.

By this time the gel had vanished from her body, leaving a musky scent. Catriona slipped on the lavender-colored robe, fastening the wide belt around her waist, and padded to the door barefoot. Pulling open the heavy, wooden door, a hissing stopped her in her tracks. A yellow lizard the size of a Labrador retriever guarded the sunlit, stone corridor. Swaying its tail from side to side, it thumped on the floor with chunky front legs.

L'ticia appeared in the corridor. "Is Tukki," she stroked his scaly back. "Go now." With its tail held high, the lizard obediently trotted off down the corridor.

"Human well?" The Komodoan woman studied her charge.

"Human hungry," retorted Catriona.

L'ticia nodded. "You eat soon. First, I show. Come." She gestured for Catriona to follow her.

The corridor led into the kitchen. A huge room, the walls filled with pots and pans, clay jars, and mysterious looking accouterments that could have been torture devices. The oven resembled a massive Aga stove from 21st century Earth, and a large kidney-shaped wooden table with backless chairs stood by a curved window.

"Look after eat," said L'ticia, pulling Catriona by the arm.

They went through an archway leading directly into the great room. Catriona's breath caught in her throat. She had not expected such splendor. Opposite, the north wall was almost entirely made of arched windows, allowing light to stream in across a tile floor that looked like pressed crystal. A huge unlit fireplace stood in the east wall, its design reminding Catriona of an enormous ormolu clock frame. Stone serpents entwined elaborately around each other above the fireplace, two lean dragons guarding each side. Padded chairs low to the ground with spaces cut into the back for tail comfort clustered around the fireplace, with several large floor cushions and pillows scattered around. Catriona scowled at the sight of Leontor pelts over the floor.

Between the kitchen doorway and the great area, a rectangular dark-wood table of massive proportions stretched the length of the room, separated from the fireplace area by six pillars like the ones in the bathroom. Beyond, a double door to the west led out to the water-sculptured hallway.

L'ticia walked past the table to an ornate wooden cabinet. She touched a panel beside it, and the wood slid back to reveal a viewscreen. Activating it, the Komodoan pulled up a diagram of the structure they were in.

"You here, Catriona Logan." L'ticia pointed to the screen. The diagram spread to display that a high wall enclosed the grounds. "Here safe." Then the screen expanded further to show the estate in relation to the surrounding area.

Catriona's mind boggled at how isolated they were. Beyond the walls began the edge of a massive forest that stretched in all directions for hundreds of miles. Beyond that the ocean appeared to reach into infinity. A city showed on the east edge of the map, but it had be at least a hundred miles away.

"Not safe." L'ticia encompassed the forest area. "Human escape walls, human die. Understand?"

Catriona understood all too well. One encounter with a **Letum** had been more than enough. Heaven knew what else lived in that forest. Morosely, she nodded.

"What is this place?"

L'ticia switched off the screen. "Is House of T'alak. You prison here."

"Where is Captain T'alak?"

"Not here. You good, I no lock. But you bad, I lock in spire."

"Are you Captain T'alak's wife?"

A smile spread over L'ticia's narrow face, the tip of her tongue flickering. "Servant of house."

Catriona wondered if she might possibly find an ally in this woman? At least she had a sense of humor. She nodded. "Okay. You don't need to lock me in the spire. I'll be good." At least until she could find a way out of here.

L'ticia covered over the screen and gestured to the kitchen. "Now we break fast."

Catriona's stomach growled loudly. It had been a long time since she had gagged down those emergency wafers. After she'd eaten a decent meal, she would think about how to escape. There had to be some kind of communications system she could access, and as they were so far from civilization, L'ticia must have transport. If luck were with her, it may even be another of T'alak's space-faring yachts.

37

HAVEN LAY on his stomach, watching the medic peel off the protective hand wear. "How does it look?" he asked.

The medic shot him a grin over his shoulder. "Beautiful, Lieutenant Colonel. Absolutely beautiful. You'll be the envy of Komodoan males."

"Huh."

"You'll find this one a lot more comfortable than the last. It's been modified so it weighs less and you'll be able to move it fairly naturally when the local anesthetic wears off."

Twisting to the side, Haven looked behind him at the long, scaly tail sprouting from his coccyx. "Heavy, isn't it?"

"You'll get used to it. Now, do we need nipple removal, too?"

"I don't intend to get that close to anyone." He shifted himself off the gurney and stood facing the medic.

"Take it easy, Lieutenant Colonel. Don't sit for twenty-four hours, and be careful going to the bathroom."

"Thank you," answered Haven dryly. "I have been through this before."

"Oh, and Lieutenant Colonel?" said the medic. "My nurse will take care of the fee."

"Naturally," grunted Haven.

It was after hours, the office deserted but for the pretty Asian nurse behind the reception desk. "That'll be twelve thousand notes, sweetheart," she grinned.

"Gone up a bit, hasn't it?"

"Oh, the tail graft cost only five thousand. The rest is for the secrecy."

"Figures." Haven handed her his note card. He squinted at his reflection in the mirror behind the desk, smoothing his newly cut bangs down to cover his scales.

As the nurse slipped his card through the deduction machine, she gave him a sly grin. "So, wanna show me how useful that tail can be?"

Haven arched an eyebrow. "Not in the way you're thinking."

"And what am I thinking, sweetheart?" Coquettishly, she leaned on the desk, holding his card up for him to take.

Haven mirrored her, leaning on both elbows, inches from her attractive oval-shaped face. "This tail can choke the breath from a man in five seconds flat, after I've twisted it around his neck." Plucking the card from her fingers, he grinned innocently at her shocked expression, and strode from the office.

Although he wore a long cloak that adequately covered the new tail, he kept to the back streets, moving rapidly through Orlando's shadows beneath the gigantic dome. Loud music and raucous laughter told him he approached his quarry. Emerging from an alleyway, he stopped across the street from an old converted warehouse. Above the narrow entrance door blazed a large red neon sign that gaudily informed the world that *Morelli's Bar* lay within. Morelli had actually been dead since he fell foul of a Leontor dealer he had tried to cheat. But Haven knew he'd find what he sought amongst Morelli's faithful clientele.

Slipping across the deserted street, he thrust his way into the dingy building. An overweight, greasy-haired bouncer with the name 'Rodney' sewn on his shirt gave him the once over, then nodded. Haven moved

198 | *Time Twist*

past him into the throng of rowdy drinkers, where an acrid stench of sweat and tobacco assaulted him. The Alliance's anti-smoking laws meant little in here.

The decor replicated a 1950's Hollywood bar. Haven remembered bringing Catriona here once, curious to find out how accurate Morelli's furnishings were. She had laughed, then said the bar made her sad. The old autographed pictures were phonies, some not even resembling the movie stars they professed to be. The chrome and formica furnishings looked gaudy, and nothing matched. They had never gone back.

Haven considered slipping into one of the booths to observe the patrons in the darkened bar, but a twinge of pain reminded him of the newly grafted tail and the medic's warning. Not being able to sit for a number of hours would be tiring.

"You gonna order something, or you just gonna stand there all night?" demanded a petulant female voice. A petite waitress with a shaved head and a myriad of dragon tattoos in place of her hair glared up at him.

"Ale."

"We have the usual piss-water; which one?"

He smiled. "Anything more interesting than the usual?"

She stood back to look him up and down. "It'll cost ya."

"That's not a problem." Haven waved his note card at her.

A smile finally slid across her petulant face. "Gold, huh? Right color, gorgeous. Follow me."

She sashayed through the crowd to the far side of the bar. Haven followed close behind, careful to keep his tail hidden by the cloak. It started to hurt like hell as the anesthetic wore off. No one took any notice as the waitress led Haven to a closed door across the room. Knocking twice, she winked at him as the door opened.

"Enjoy yourself, stud. And don't forget me when you pay your bill."

"I won't," he assured her, slipping through the door. It clicked shut behind him. A serious group of four men threw him a glance, then returned to their card game. He walked past their table to the small bar against the far wall. Unlike the main bar, the lights were bright and uncompromising. Haven hoped his hair adequately covered his facial scales. A short, balding man emerged through a curtain at the side of the bar.

"What'll it be, buddy?" he demanded, fixing Haven with a stern look.

"Leontor ale." Haven placed his note card on the bar.

"Sure you can handle that?"

"I wouldn't ask if I couldn't."

The bartender nodded, running the card through his machine before serving the steaming *ealu* brew. Haven raised his tankard in salute, and downed half in one gulp. As the initially innocuous taste turned to blaster fire in his throat, he thought of Catriona again. She had introduced him to the ale two years earlier.

His chest tightened as he imagined what T'alak might have done to her. *If* she were still alive, he reminded himself. But knowing T'alak, he would enjoy tormenting his new human acquisition, like a cat playing with a mouse before the death blow.

That picture stirred him to action. Without looking at the bartender, he said, "Now, I wonder how a guy could find a freelance pilot and deep space ship around this town."

The bartender wiped down the counter in front of Haven. "Refill?"

"I'll buy a keg. But keep it here for me."

The bartender ran the couple of thousand notes through Haven's card. "Check your receipt, buddy." He pushed his card across the counter. "See you in a while, crocodile," he added, deadpan.

Haven eyed him, not sure if the bartender had rumbled his Komodoan heritage. He pocketed his card. "Make sure 'tattoo-girl' gets a taste of that ale," he said in parting.

Outside in the street, he inspected his card. A man's name and a private docking bay address had been scrawled in erasable ink on it. Pleased with his night's work, Haven memorized it and wiped the card clean. He then made his way to the tourist accommodation he had rented several blocks away.

"Not worth it, mate."

Haven had expected such a response from the pilot. It wasn't even dawn, yet. He'd snatched what sleep he could before the anesthetic wore off. The base of his spine felt like carbine fire on his nerve endings, and the tail felt heavy and unnatural. But the medic had been right about more mobility. Once the pain dulled completely, the tail would prove almost as flexible as a full-blooded Komodoan's.

He leaned against the battered craft the pilot proudly referred to as *Dream Lover*. "What would make it worth it?"

"Nothin'. I ain't riskin' life and limb to go near them reptiles."

"Very well." Moving on to the next stage of the negotiation, Haven thumbed dismissively at the ship. "How much for the rust-bucket?"

The wiry pilot's face darkened. "Don't you be callin' my *Dream*

200 | *Time Twist*

Lover names, sunshine. She's seen me through more scrapes than you've had hot dinners."

Haven smiled dryly. "I doubt that. How much?"

"I'd never sell my *Dream Lover*. Why, she-"

"Shall we say a hundred and fifty thousand notes?"

The pilot's face gleamed with avarice. Haven knew the man would be lucky to get seventy-five for her.

"Done!" he beamed, holding out his callused hand.

Every man has his price, thought Haven ruefully, his purchase completed. *Dream Lover* would win no beauty contest, but she was sound and fast, installed with a black market Leontor hyperdrive, plus a pirate listening device that could tap into other ship's communications. She was the ideal vessel for his mission, customized for low profile operations that might require a fast getaway.

"Well, *Dream*, I hope we'll be happy together." He patted her grimy hull.

He arranged to buy the contents of her hold, pushing the cost up significantly, but if he wanted to make his cover as a smuggler believable, he needed booty. A few bolts of real cotton cloth, so rare nowadays, Terran spices and incense, pure Leon silver, and many kegs of Leon *ealu*, should help lubricate his way into the Komodoan Realm.

Haven made his way to the nearest shopping mall. He needed to buy one last important item. When he returned to the docking bay, he carried an adjustable stool under one arm. A little minor tailoring and it would take the place of *Dream Lover's* command chair, made for a human. Now Haven could sit at the helm, draping his tail down the back of the stool. He didn't even want to think about how he would manage in the head, also designed for humans. Oh well, he would cope.

A couple of hundred notes took care of his take-off from Earth. He shook his head as he got permission to launch. It had been too easy. The Leontor governors did not expect subterfuge from their human protégés, and smugglers had been taking advantage for years. The Alliance had turned too much of their attention spaceward, neglecting affairs on the planet.

Dream Lover's take-off proved powerful. She surged upward, soaring gracefully through the cloudless, blue morning to the hazy rim where baby blue became jet black. Haven felt himself relax. To be in action once more, hurtling through star-studded space on a mission sent a thrill of adrenaline through him. It felt so good to be out in the field again; he'd been stuck too long on that asteroid base.

Slipping past the moon, he whimsically saluted the 'man' on its face in the Apennine Mountains before putting *Dream Lover* into hyperdrive. He set a course for Komodoan Realm space, settling back for the long journey.

38

GRREAG LOOKED up from his office desk on the *Vallo* and gazed at the picture of Earth. He wondered why the humans were so intent on re-terraforming their scarred planet. Leontor colony ships could easily relocate them somewhere more habitable, close to *Ferrla*, or Ponce de Leon, as they'd named the new colony planet. He bared a fang in amusement. After all these years the humans still believed that Leontor Control didn't know of their private joke in choosing the planet's name.

His job had certainly become easier, of late. He remembered the difficulty he had experienced getting along with his human crew before Catriona Logan came along to help bridge the gap.

Not wanting to think any further about his lost friend he checked his chronometer. Chief Engineer Uzima Khumalo would be here to meet with him any moment. Of all his crew members, he respected her the most. She had proved to be a dedicated worker, although her abruptness and sometimes apparent disrespect constantly caught him off guard.

Khumalo entered the office thirty seconds early.

"Chief," greeted Grreag, his ears pricked forward in expectation. "I need your hypothesis on the cause of this spatial rupture." He gestured that she take a chair.

The ebony engineer did so, letting out a sigh. It would have been inaudible to a human, but Grreag's sensitive ears picked it up.

"I found something interesting about the location of the new rupture, Sir," she said. "According to my calculations, it's at the exact location where we fought the *L'umina* two years ago. If you remember, that's where Professor Webster created the temporal bubble that took him and his assistant off the *Vallo*." Grreag's ears flicked.

"Colonel, I think that because this spatial rupture originates from two years in the past, we're seeing the after effects of that temporal

202 | *Time Twist*

bubble. As far as I know he hadn't tested it before initiating it, so we had no way of knowing what consequences there'd be by plunging a temporal bubble out of this time continuum without balancing it from this end."

Grreag scowled, rising to pace the office. "And we don't know if Webster created a corresponding temporal bubble at his destination before jumping, do we?"

"No, Sir, there's no way of telling. If he did, it's right outside this ship where that rupture is. If he didn't, then the rupture must be nature's way of closing the gap between time frames." Khumalo paused and Grreag flicked an encouraging ear at her. "The other interesting discovery, Sir," she continued, "is that there's an odd lattice of energy flows emitting from the rupture. Before it disappeared the probe reported that the energy is in the form of coherent tachyons of very low mass. The significance of that is as yet unknown."

"Is there any way to determine if Webster created a corresponding temporal bubble?"

Khumalo shifted in her seat. "Only if someone enters the rupture in a cruiser. Then we could get an accurate reading. How that someone gets back again is another matter altogether."

Grreag growled low in his throat. "Too risky. We don't know what's inside that rupture."

"The only way we're going to find out is by taking that risk, Colonel! Do we really want a Komodoan Realm ship two years in the past?"

Grreag nodded slowly. If he followed Leontor Control standard procedure, he'd be forbidden any possible contact with something like this—that threatened the space and time continuum. But in his opinion it would be more criminal not to take action.

He'd have to pilot the cruiser himself; he couldn't expect his crew to do something so against Control's policy. Major Sam Benjamin was capable of captaining the *Vallo* in his absence. He felt a lurch at the thought of not being on board to supervise, and a thread of doubt slipped into his mind. But Sam had been at his side since he took command. He had to trust him, or trust no one.

"If your hypothesis is correct, we've got to act fast before Captain T'alak realizes where he is and corrupts the time line."

Khumalo nodded. "I'd like to volunteer to take the cruiser in with you, Sir."

The Leon's ears flickered in surprise. That he hadn't expected, but her technological expertise would be invaluable. In fact, he hadn't even given thought to how he would engineer the bubble by himself. "So be it, Chief." His expression softened. "But be careful, I don't want to lose you."

The engineer smiled, the lines of tiredness on her dark face falling away. "Thank you, Colonel. Maybe I'll make an officer, yet."

Grreag bared both fangs in a rare smile. "If we make it back from this one, I promise you will."

Within the hour, the human engineer and the Leon Colonel were aboard one of the cruisers, Khumalo piloting as Grreag set the cruiser recorder in motion. As they slipped toward the rupture, she could see a maelstrom of colors and patterns swirling within.

"I am now picking up data the probe couldn't relay," announced Grreag. "There is a discernible point the tachyon emissions originate from. Dispatching coordinates now." His fingers sped over the controls as he fed the data to the *Vallo's* main computer.

Khumalo took a deep breath as the cruiser edged into the opening of the rupture. The craft jostled about as the twisted rainbow enveloped them, and the heat in the cabin shot beyond comfort.

"Shit!" cried Khumalo, gripping her console. It felt like the cruiser was being microwaved.

A large hand reached across the cabin, closing over hers.

"Be calm, Chief," said Grreag.

Khumalo gave his fingers a grateful squeeze, again marveling at how Catriona's friendship with the Leon had changed him.

The cruiser's hull creaked under the increasing pressure. Both Khumalo and Grreag covered their eyes as a blinding light encompassed them.

"Well, that wasn't so bad." Khumalo blinked, leaning forward to check the cruiser's instruments.

The rupture streamed behind them; they had traveled through to the other side. She felt more confident now the craft was no longer in threat of buckling or being melted around them.

"We have lost contact with the *Vallo*," growled Grreag.

"Not unexpected. The question now is, where in hell are we?"

"Or when." He scanned the rupture. "Interesting. The readings are different from this side."

Khumalo scrambled to look over his shoulder. "How so?"

"The coordinates don't exactly mirror those back where the *Vallo* is, they're several meters off. Also, the rupture itself does not appear to have the same substance as on the other side."

She studied his screen. "It's weaker here by twenty-five percent." She sat back down and checked their coordinates. It might allow them more time on this side to find out how to mend the rupture. "We're exactly where we were on the other side," she announced, relieved. "And probably just over two Terran years in the past." She swallowed hard. All her work on Webster's temporal bubbles hadn't been this successful. A thrill went through her at the possibilities this offered.

She studied her console. "According to these readings, there are no ships within range, but there's a faint tachyon trail leading from the rupture. It might lead us to T'alak."

"The trail is weak, but leads to a planet about sixty spatials from here," rumbled Grreag. "That's where we'll find him."

39

CROUCHED IN front of the baking hot oven, Catriona heard the main door open. Just in time, she thought. L'ticia had taken the house skiff off to do errands in town and had been gone for hours.

"In here!" she called. Footsteps rapidly approached. "I need help, this is heavy." She opened the oven door and used a two-pronged fork to prod at a large joint of dark roasted meat.

A hand grabbed her by her long hair, and she froze at the cold touch of a knife under her chin.

"Who are you?" demanded a heavily-accented male voice in English, pressing the blade against her throat.

Catriona raised the fork and jabbed it backward into her attacker's leg. He yelled, dropping the knife. Catriona twisted, extricating her hair from his grasp.

"T'alak-zan!" said L'ticia from the doorway. "Honored Sir, how good to see you back home again."

Catriona pushed the hair back off her face to see a younger version of T'alak wrench the embedded fork from his thigh.

"What is this human doing here?" he demanded.

"She is your father's prisoner," answered L'ticia. "He ordered her kept here until Governor C'huln sends for her."

Catriona got the gist of what L'ticia said. She'd tried to learn as much Komodoan as she could. *T'alak's son*, she thought. She might have known. He'd be as violent as his father.

"Why is she roaming free? Are you not under orders to guard her?"

L'ticia kept her eyes on the floor at T'alak-zan's feet. "Sir, where would she go? She'd die if she left the grounds."

"Don't contradict me!" He lifted an arm and backhanded her across the face. Catriona gasped, but L'ticia didn't react.

"The reason I am here," he continued, "is to arrest you with treason, servant." L'ticia paled. T'alak-zan circled her, his tail pendulating. "I saw you in the Third Quadrant with a known smuggler and traitor to the Realm. N'elak has evaded capture for a long time. Now I know where he gets his information from-"

"That's not so," said L'ticia.

"Be silent!" He grabbed her by the throat. "It's my duty to take you to the capital city for punishment, but first I will discipline you for betraying our House."

T'alak-zan's long tongue flickered out and slithered over L'ticia's face, reminding Catriona of how T'alak had so assaulted her. She understood enough of what had been said and felt sick as she imagined what T'alak-zan might have in store for L'ticia. And also for her, once L'ticia's protection ended.

T'alak-zan's gaze fell on Catriona. "Lock the human up," he snarled.

L'ticia obeyed, pressing Catriona toward the hall and up the stairs. T'alak-zan followed close behind as they climbed up the winding, stone steps to the small spire room.

Before they locked her up Catriona knew she had to act. She'd never escape if T'alak-zan took L'ticia away. Whirling, she slammed a punch to his face, then jarred her foot into his kneecap. With a roar of fury, he lost his footing and tumbled down the spiral steps. Running down after him, Catriona saw the young Komodoan lying at an impossible angle, his neck obviously broken. A wave of nausea swept through her. She clung to the wall to stop from falling.

L'ticia grimly bent to inspect T'alak's son, then straightened with a shake of her head, her tail tensed.

"My God," whispered Catriona. "I didn't mean for him to die."

L'ticia swiftly propelled her back up the stairs and closed Catriona in the little room, locking the door behind her.

206 | *Time Twist*

"L'ticia!" yelled Catriona through the solid door. "Don't leave me in here, damn you!" Her voice reverberated around the empty chamber. When L'ticia didn't return Catriona slumped down by the small window, forcing herself not to panic. She never thought she'd ever have to kill anyone. She kept reliving the moment she had attacked T'alak-zan, and seeing his broken body at the bottom of the stairs. If she had only just hit him and not kicked his legs from under him, he might be alive, now. And then a part of her rationalized his death; she'd had to stop him from hurting L'ticia so she could survive.

She couldn't understand why L'ticia had locked her up. Could she have run away and left Catriona to starve to death? Panic rising again, she forced her thoughts elsewhere, noticing her knuckles torn and bleeding. In the adrenaline of the moment she had forgotten all the attack fight moves Grreag had shown her.

Tears welled as she remembered her first lesson with Grreag when he asked her why she wasn't afraid of him like other humans were. She'd give anything to see him break down that door and rescue her. But he didn't know she was on Komodoa and wouldn't be turning up to save the day. The thought that she'd never see him again had tears pouring down her face.

Dusk had fallen, the light fading. As she crouched in the empty spire room, the darkness crept through the window, reaching over her like a smothering dark hand.

She must have fallen asleep. When she opened her tear-swollen eyes, black night filled the room. Struggling to her feet Catriona headed for the door. She cursed when her shin connected with something hard and unyielding.

"What the...?" The room had been empty when L'ticia had put her in here. Bending down, she reached out and her fingers fumbled across a smooth surface and touched... a lamp? She snapped it on, then sat back on the floor in amazement. How could she have slept through all this being brought in? Besides the low table she had bruised her shin on, the room had a desk with a computer, a shelf lined with data disks, and a low, futon-type bed. No swampy Komodoan bed for her anymore, she thought. L'ticia must mean to keep her locked up until T'alak's return.

Straightening, she looked at the length of the crimson rug covering the stone floor. Thank God it wasn't a Leon pelt. Then her jaw dropped. She might have slept through furniture being brought into the room, but never through construction! Beyond the rug, an open door revealed a tiny bathroom, complete with a water shower unit just like back on

21st century Earth.

What the hell had happened? Dashing across the room, she tried the door leading to the stone steps. Still locked. She lifted both fists and pummeled heavily.

"L'ticia! Goddamn you, let me out!" She strained in the silence for a moment. "Jesus Christ, L'ticia! If you don't come and open this door right now, I'll smash everything in this room!"

A light came on in the hall downstairs; Catriona saw it dimly under her door. She took a deep breath as footsteps approached. When the door opened, Catriona almost passed out. Captain T'alak stood there, wearing a jade-green brocaded gown. She backed away, lowering her gaze. He must have returned as soon as he learned she had murdered his son.

He came into the room. To her shock, his face creased into a smile. "What's wrong, Catriona? Did you have another bad dream?"

Her mind whirled. T'alak would never speak to her like that. Thunderstruck, she couldn't move when he drew near to her.

"T'alak-zan…" she stammered.

He cocked his head, gazing down at her in puzzlement. "Look at me." She did so. "What about my son?" he asked.

She held his gaze, not detecting any deception from him. "I, em… dreamed he'd died."

T'alak hissed a laugh. "I'm honored by your concern, dear human. But I assure you he is perfectly well, I received a message from him this evening, in fact."

Catriona swayed. What could be happening? She gasped as T'alak enveloped her in his arms.

"The bad dreams will pass," he assured her, his lips on her hair. "It cannot be easy, finding yourself thrust into an alien world."

Her head forced against his chest, Catriona listened to the slow beat of his heart. She decided she must either have gone insane or she had been given a hallucinogenic drug. In any case, this could not be T'alak. Except for Haven, she hadn't known any Komodoan to embrace like humans, and T'alak had only ever touched her in violence.

"You have been a great help to us, you know that?" he hissed softly. She swallowed. "In what way?"

The Victory could not have succeeded without you."

What the hell was he talking about… had she been asleep for years instead of hours?

"Try and sleep, sweet alien. It will be a busy day tomorrow." His tongue gently caressed her forehead, then he released her, striding for the door.

Catriona spoke quickly. "Captain?"

He gave her an interrogative look. "Why do you call me that?"

"Oh. My dream."

"I understand. What is it?"

"Must you lock me in?"

A look of regret passed over his dark features. "It's for your own safety. Sleep well." He closed the door.

Hearing the lock being thrust back in place, Catriona knew there to be no other way out of the room. Disgusted, she wiped his saliva from her forehead and slumped onto the futon with a heavy sigh. Sleep was an excellent idea, she agreed. Perhaps by morning this might make sense. She lay down and enforced the mental relaxation exercises she'd learned at the ACC. The futon felt firm and supporting under her. Soon, she fell fast asleep, dreaming of a whirling rainbow.

40

"CHIEF" GROWLED Grreag. "The *L'umina* is orbiting the planet."

"Have they detected us?"

The Leon shook his shaggy head. "We just picked up their trace as they went to the far side, they won't detect us for another twenty Earth minutes."

"Shall I take us into orbit, Colonel?"

"Negative. Take us to the dark side of the third moon."

"Yes, Sir. I'll do that while you ensure we're ready for combat." She ignored the incredulous look the Leon shot her. She knew their measly little weapons systems on the cruiser would be as effective as a mosquito bite to the colossal *L'umina*, but it made her feel better to think they had some protection.

The tiny craft slipped up to hide in the shelter of the luminous third moon from the planet.

"Is this planet charted?" wondered Khumalo, pulling up the stellar cartography files from the computer. "Colonel," she called, "look at this."

The Leon extricated himself from his seat and joined her at the screen. "Interesting," he rumbled, "and too much to be a coincidence."

"Yes," breathed Khumalo. "The Alliance marked this planet as a possible new colony until two years ago, when seismic activity became too unstable for settlement." She gave a triumphant grin. "How much do you bet we'll find some important answers down there?"

"We need to actuate down without detection," rumbled Grreag.

Khumalo leapt from her chair, moving to the engineering console. "I think I can rig an actuate relay system between the three moons and the planet. If we time it right, we can activate it when the *L'umina* is out of range again behind the planet."

"Can you ensure our safe return to the cruiser?"

"Not a problem. I'll program the onboard computer to actuate us out of there after a specified time." She lifted the cover off the console. "Colonel, could you hand me that splicer, please?"

Almost three hours later they stood ready to actuate down. Grreag checked the coordinates one last time.

"Scanners indicate life-signs here," he said, indicating the holographic planet map circling before them. "Recommend we actuate a short distance away and move in quietly on foot."

"Agreed. For all we know, the life-signs may be the *L'umina's* crew."

"Here." The Leon handed her a powered-up blaster.

She tucked it into her belt, smiling as Grreag checked his own weaponry. Aside from the blaster, he had a variety of knives and dartguns tucked into unexpected places under his Alliance fatigues.

"Man, remind me not to get too close to you." She grinned, indicating a sharp, stiletto-type blade protruding from his sleeve.

Tucking it in, the Leon tersely replied, "I do not think that will be a problem."

Khumalo snorted. "Which, getting stabbed or getting close to you?"

Grreag looked sharply at her, understood her to be jocular rather than offensive, and permitted himself a fanged smile.

"Okay." The engineer returned to her task. "Let's get this show on the road."

Activating the actuate system, a bubble encircled them. Khumalo forced herself to breathe easily. She had prepared herself for the long process as the relay system bounced their molecules between the three moons, then down to the planet, but it felt like forever.

"Good choice," she complimented Grreag as they rematerialized.

They had arrived in a shady glen, with plenty of cover from the trees and bushes. Grreag activated his tracker.

"This way," he growled, taking point.

210 | *Time Twist*

Khumalo followed, happy to let him do so. If they were going to walk into a bad situation, she wanted the huge Leon in front where he could run interference.

The planet looked beautiful, like an unspoiled Earth. Bees buzzed close by and multicolored birds chirped above them in the trees as they quietly made their way along a natural forest path. No wonder the Alliance had earmarked it for colonization. If she had a choice, she'd rather live somewhere like this, than on the planet Catriona had dubbed, 'Dustbowl'.

Grreag suddenly went into a crouch, waving his hand to her to do the same. She eased down, sidling over to him. He pointed through the bushes.

Khumalo almost swore aloud to see Captain T'alak. He sat comfortably in the sunshine in front of a large, wooden structure, talking to a man with his back to them.

"I can't hear," she whispered in frustration.

The Leon adjusted his tracker so they could make out the conversation through the long-range microphone.

"*The Victory* has been set in motion," said T'alak. "I shall return through the rupture as soon as I have established a base on this planet." His expression was triumphant.

"Captain, you can't leave anyone in this time; you'll pervert the space and time continuum."

Khumalo frowned. That voice, it sounded familiar. She stared intently at the back of the man's curly, brown head. Who the hell was he?

"A little late for that, don't you think?" sneered T'alak. "But if it will salve your puny human conscience, Komodoan troops are already on their way. Personnel indigenous to this time frame. But," he continued, "either my crew stays here or they will be eliminated. I cannot allow anyone who holds this knowledge return to the future."

"But you are returning."

"Your objections tire me, Professor."

Khumalo's jaw dropped as she met Grreag's thunderous look. Professor Webster! So he hadn't died when he disappeared from the *Vallo*. And now because of him, the outcome of the war was in serious jeopardy.

As though to confirm her fears, T'alak continued. "When I return, the Realm will be the supreme power, the Alliance annihilated two years ago. Thanks to your technology, I contacted myself in this time frame. We arranged to intercept you and your weapon before you even got on the *Vallo*. Our ascension to power is due to your experiment!"

"I'm going to dismember Webster," snarled Grreag in Khumalo's ear.

She laid a restraining hand on his big arm. "Don't. We need him to try and fix this mess."

"You will find a way to mend the spatial rupture, immediately," T'alak ordered Webster. "Once I go back through, we do not want to risk an Alliance sympathizer trying to emulate what we have achieved here. Guards!"

Two soldiers emerged from the wooden structure, tails lashing. Moving to either side of Webster, they jerked him to his feet. "Make sure the professor is comfortable in his laboratory."

They dragged Webster into the building, his futile struggle sending up a small dust cloud. Captain T'alak made a hacking sound. Reaching to activate his wrist communicator, he pinged the *L'umina*.

"Bring me up. This planet is too dry." He disappeared in an actuate bubble.

"Oh, shit!" said Khumalo through gritted teeth.

"What?" demanded Grreag.

"The actuate bubble! I only created it to encompass two. When we get Webster one of us is going to have to wait on the planet while the other creates a new bubble."

The Leon pondered. "Chief, once we acquire Webster, you and he actuate. I will wait."

"So, how do we get dickhead?"

"What?"

"Professor Webster, the dickhead," she said, "without whom none of this would be possible. All right, all right," seeing his look, she held up her hands. "I am taking this seriously, Sir, just my way of dealing with it."

"I understand," he nodded, "you and Catriona are alike."

"I'll take that as a compliment."

A Leon fang showed. "Let's go get *dickhead*," he offered.

Khumalo beamed.

They kept to the trees, moving under their cover to the right of the structure. They studied the building, looking for a way in. Standing about three stories high, it had been fashioned from logs, laid horizontally on top of each other. Essentially wedge-shaped, the building had what appeared to be solar panels at an angle on the roof.

Khumalo checked her chronometer. "We only have thirty minutes to get back to the actuate bubble, Sir. If we don't make it…"

The Leon nodded. Then he pointed up to a second-floor open window. Khumalo saw their opportunity. A tall tree stood right beside

212 | *Time Twist*

the building. Assuming they could climb the tree, they would have their entrance.

41

WAKING UP at first light, Catriona bounded out of bed and into the tiny bathroom. A real water shower at last! She reveled in the warm, flowing liquid for as long as she dared as her mind ticked over what could have happened during the night. She could think of no plausible explanation for the changes that had occurred, but she'd get to the bottom of it today.

She dressed in one of the jewel-colored robes that had mysteriously appeared in her closet during the night. Unlike the light shifts she and L'ticia had previously worn, these dresses were woven from rich, heavy cloth, and beautifully made. She chose a teal-blue gown with a long, full skirt. As ever, the front crushed her breasts and the back bulged to accommodate her non-existent tail. Turning sideways to look in the mirror, Catriona decided it gave the costume a bustle effect, reminiscent of Victorian Earth.

Remembering how L'ticia wore her hair in a long braid down the back, Catriona did the same with hers, fastening it with a shell-like clasp she found in the bathroom. She slipped on a pair of shoes that matched the fabric. They felt a little wide around the toes, but it felt good to have footwear again. Then she sat down to wait. Fiddling idly with the computer, she discovered the compact disks to be social studies on Komodoan society. They covered everything from language, history, and geography, to politics and science. Catriona decided to memorize every subject. This inside information would prove valuable information indeed for the Alliance.

She stood to attention at the sound of the door being unlocked. T'alak entered, now dressed in a long, quilted robe of gold cloth. The bulky tunic made him appear larger than ever. He wore a black insignia sash over one shoulder and Catriona wondered if he had left the military to become some kind of ambassador.

He smiled approvingly at her. "How Komodoan you look! Are you feeling better this morning?"

She swallowed. Well, if he insisted on playing this game, she could play it too. And better. "Thank you, yes." She crossed to him to give him a peck on the cheek.

He hissed softly, reaching a hand to touch where she had kissed. "Come." He turned to go down the spiral steps.

She followed, suppressing a shudder at the memory of T'alak-zan's broken body at the foot of them. She wondered if T'alak could be exacting revenge by playing games with her mind.

The first landing surprised her. All the doors leading from it lay open, revealing large suites being attended to by a fleet of female servants. Catriona had had the impression the chambers were empty except for the suite reserved for T'alak, but the house looked fully occupied. Continuing down to the hall, Catriona hesitated on the stairs at the sound of voices.

T'alak glanced back at her, so she caught up. Obviously he expected her to know what was going on.

"You look distracted, human."

Catriona noted an edge to his voice, reminiscent of how he usually addressed her. So, something was still rotten in the House of T'alak.

"I am a little nervous."

He watched her in silence for a moment. "Of course. But only the *L'umina* officers are here at the moment. You are already familiar with them."

Steadying herself, she allowed T'alak to steer her into the great room, his hand in the small of her back. Five officers in military uniform turned as one. Catriona's heart almost stopped. Jack Haven stood before her. He had come to the rescue, after all! Or *A'rlon*, as he would be known on Komodoa. It took all her self control not to run to him, but as he was here under the guise of a tailed Realm officer, she would blow his cover. Her heart soared. She should never have lost faith in him; of course he would come for her.

All the officers ignored her completely, as did T'alak. As far as she could tell, her role here appeared to be merely ornamental. A tame human to show off.

"Captain A'rlon," hissed T'alak in pleasure, curling his tail around A'rlon's. "How are you treating my lady?"

A'rlon bowed. "The *L'umina* misses her true master, Governor T'alak."

A thought struck Catriona, almost knocking the breath from her. Something was very, very wrong. A'rlon could not possibly have taken captaincy of T'alak's ship. When he had rescued her from T'alak, he had exposed himself as a Terran agent, consequently a traitor to the

214 | *Time Twist*

Komodoan Realm. He could never walk freely here again. She stared boldly at him until he made eye contact with her. Seeing no flicker of recognition in those dark eyes she gave an involuntary shiver. A frown crossed his face before he returned his attention to T'alak.

Catriona edged away, moving to one of the tall windows to look outside. None of this could have happened overnight. Something fundamental had occurred, something that had altered events in some way. But what? Bright beams of light criss-crossed into the room from the two morning suns, illuminating the pressed crystal floor into rainbow shards. Catriona stared at the floor, studying the dancing rainbows at her feet. A touch on her arm made her jump.

"Catriona," T'alak loomed over her, "you are neglecting my guests; come back from whatever dimension your head is in." He propelled her toward the tray of silver cups on the table.

Trance-like, Catriona lifted the tray, noting the cups were already filled with the rich Komodoan liqueur, *picht*. As she held out the tray to each officer, something began to worm itself into her mind. Yes! That had to be it. When she had left Earth, a spatial rupture had just occurred. Could it be possible it had somehow affected time?

With a start, she came to, realizing she stood in front of A'rlon, staring blindly at him. He gave her a stern look, she presumed for making eye contact with him, and reached for the last cup on her tray. She had to engineer a way to talk to him alone. Even if this were another dimension and he didn't know her, she knew all about him and could convince him of the truth. Jerking her arm, she spilled the thick, purple liquid over the front of his tunic.

"I'm so sorry!" Dropping the tray with a clatter, she turned to T'alak. "Forgive me, Governor. I will make amends immediately." He nodded, his black eyes glittering with anger.

Catriona drew close to A'rlon. "Captain, I apologize for my clumsiness. Please come with me so I can clean this before it stains."

A'rlon stood quietly through her apology, shaking his head. "It is not necessary, human," he announced, in perfect English, "the stain is of no importance."

Damn him! Even in this dimension where he didn't know her, he protected her from T'alak's temper. No, bless him, she amended, her heart melting.

She leaned closer. "I believe it's absolutely necessary, *Haven*."

Without another word, he followed her into the kitchen and through to the small utility chamber beyond. Catriona flinched as he grabbed her, twisting her arm behind her back.

"Who are you?" he demanded curtly. "Who sent you?"

"Let me go and I'll tell you." He did so and she turned to face him. "This is going to take a certain amount of faith on your part." She looked up into those much-loved, but stranger's eyes.

"Get on with it."

"I think there's been a perversion of the space and time continuum. A short while ago, you and I were..." she swallowed hard, "having a quarrel on Earth. You left the Realm two years ago when you rescued me and Professor Webster's temporal bubble data from Captain T'alak. That's how I know who you are. You're a half-human product of Komodoan Realm genetic experimentation, your tail has been grafted on."

He stared at her in obvious cynicism. She had told him nothing she couldn't have learned through Alliance Intelligence. What else could she say?

"In your cabin on the *L'umina*," she continued desperately, "you kept an old wooden box from Earth. Inside was a silver *P'jarra* pendant, which held a long-range communication chip. You told me it was your last link with the Alliance!" Now she had him. His face contorted in astonishment.

"All right," he said slowly, "if this is true, why are you the only one aware of this change in the continuum?"

"I don't know. I only worked it out myself just now. I'm willing to bet T'alak knows, though."

A grin broke across his face, looking more like the Haven she knew. "You say we were quarreling in this other time?"

"Yes."

"A lovers' quarrel?"

"You could say that," she nodded, discomfited. She froze at the sound of T'alak shouting for her, his footsteps approaching. "I haven't cleaned your tunic!" she gasped.

"Forgive me," whispered A'rlon, and promptly smacked her across the mouth. As she staggered back, he flipped her round, bending her over the sink. "If we're already lovers this won't be too offensive." Pushing up her skirt, he adjusted his tunic and positioned himself behind her as though engaged in intercourse. "I'm sorry," he whispered.

Through her tears, Catriona understood. Even now he protected her from T'alak. The door to the utility chamber slammed open.

"Captain!" hissed T'alak, "stand away from my human."

A'rlon did so, letting his tunic drop back into place. "I felt it

216 | *Time Twist*

necessary to punish her, Governor."

Catriona straightened up from the sink, smoothing her skirt down. She could taste blood from her cut lip.

"I thank you," answered T'alak formally, his tail swishing angrily back and forth. "*I* will ensure she is punished adequately."

Catriona stared at T'alak. Did he know what was going on? More importantly, did he realize she knew something to be amiss?

"I will actuate to my ship and procure a clean uniform," said A'rlon, bowing to T'alak before marching out.

T'alak approached Catriona. "Are you hurt?"

"Just my lip." She fingered it delicately.

"The rape did not harm you?"

Catriona cringed. "He had hardly begun."

T'alak's tongue flickered out and he leaned close to lick a trace of blood from her mouth. Catriona forced herself to endure it.

"I have restrained myself from taking you for I believed the experience would harm you."

She frowned. Why would he even care? In the other time line he had tried to rape her repeatedly, enjoying the opportunity to violate a human. But then she remembered the caress of his thumb on her neck that morning, when they had taken refuge in the hull of his crashed yacht.

"We are of a different species," she muttered.

"True, but our ancestry is similar, we only evolved in different ways."

Oh, God, how revolting. Forcing her now would not be enough; he wanted her to participate willingly. She shuddered at the thought of it.

T'alak regarded her. "Did A'rlon's touch please you?" he inquired softly.

Catriona's stomach lurched. He knows, she thought. He *knows* A'rlon and she were lovers in that other time. Somehow, T'alak was responsible for all these changes, for how else could he know? She needed more time. Long enough to find a way to reverse the changes.

"No, I wished it had been you," she almost choked on the words.

T'alak raised her face and carefully cleaned the remainder of the blood from her cut lip with his tongue. Catriona suppressed her revulsion.

"I will remedy your wish," he hissed in Komodoan pleasure, "after the conference."

⇟

In his cabin on the *L'umina*, A'rlon accessed all available data on Professor Webster and the Komodoan Realm procurement of his experimental weapon. He hadn't given much thought as to where

T'alak had obtained his human; it wasn't unusual for those who could afford it to have exotic alien slaves. Logan's name was not mentioned in any log entry. She had not been on the crew or passenger roster of any captured alien vessel. So where had she come from?

To A'rlon's memory, T'alak had had her since the remarkable coup he had pulled, capturing Webster before the Alliance could access his research.

Once the temporal bubble theory had been put into practice, it had been a simple matter for the Realm to enclose Alliance planets in bubbles, retarding enemy strongholds. The entire operation became known in history as *'The Victory.'* In a mere two years, the Komodoan Realm had dominated all charted space. And T'alak had been lauded as a Realm hero.

There had since been many changes for the Komodoan people. Richer lifestyles, more leisure. Pickings had been good from the conquered worlds, and slaves there were in plenty. Not so many Leontor, however. They had shown such resistance to *The Victory* that they had all but committed genocide. The leonine race had never been as popular an adornment for Komodoan homes as humans, who were more similar in appearance to Komodoans, therefore more attractive to the eye. And elsewhere, thought A'rlon dryly, counting mentally how many of his acquaintances owned human slaves.

With an impatient hiss, A'rlon snapped off the computer. He would learn nothing from these files. He would have to engage Logan again, interrogate her more thoroughly. She said they were lovers in the other timeline. Somehow it did not surprise him. Reaching round behind the computer, he pulled out the wooden box she had told him about. Only he and his original contact in the Alliance knew about the communication chip. And he had made sure that contact had been eliminated in *The Victory*. It was a disquieting feeling, suspecting that the life he felt so secure in, may not be so after all.

Straightening his clean tunic, he returned to the House of T'alak for the upcoming conference. He needed to be there, as captain of the Realm flagship. Discussions were in effect about changing the structure of the fleet. *The Victory* had made a need for a conquering army all but obsolete. Governor T'alak, hero of the Realm, had been awarded the honor of hosting the conference at his home, a great accolade indeed.

A'rlon would ensure to arrange another private meeting with Logan before the conference finished.

42

"Colonel Grreag!" hissed Khumalo from the bottom of the tree.

From several feet up, the Leon peered down at her. "Come up!" He gestured impatiently for her to follow him.

"It's too high," she objected. "The branches are too far apart for me to get a hand hold."

Grreag growled low in his throat. They'd be spotted before they achieved anything at this rate. "Wait there!" Effortlessly, he dropped the twelve feet to the ground, landing on bent legs.

"Wow," Khumalo breathed in admiration. "That was neat."

"Quickly," he turned his back to her, "hold on tight."

"Piggy-back?"

"Leon-back," corrected Grreag. "Hurry."

She clambered onto his back, holding on round his neck. As though she weighed nothing, the Leon swung up into the tree, moving from branch to branch until they were even with the open window.

"Colonel," announced Khumalo, a little breathless, "remind me to come get you the next time I need to clamber around my engines. You'd make my job easier by half."

"I am at your disposal," he rasped, setting her down gently on the branch beside him. "Providing we return to the ship."

"We will," Khumalo said grimly. "We have to."

Grreag flashed a look that showed his pessimism and indicated the window. "Shall we?"

At her nod they moved in. Grreag slipped in first, ducking down against the inner wall to cover her entrance. Eyes adjusting to the darker interior, Khumalo looked about her. The room looked tastefully decorated in a simplistic style.

"The entire structure is wooden," warned Grreag. "Our progress will easily be overheard."

They eased past a large bed with a wooden frame that dominated the room. Grreag slid back the paper-paned door to reveal a roomy corridor. Operating his tracker, he gestured for Khumalo to follow. They edged along the wall until they reached the top of a large staircase. Through the banisters she spotted Webster and his two Komodoan guards below and over to the right.

Grreag pocketed the tracker, and Khumalo extracted her blaster.

Time ticked by relentlessly while they waited. Finally, one of the guards moved within range of the staircase. With a leap, Grreag soared over the banister and floored the Komodoan. Simultaneously, Khumalo aimed her blaster at the other guard and picked him off. A sharp crack followed by a bumping sound told her Grreag had been equally successful.

"Clear!" he called.

Khumalo scurried down the stairs and ran toward Webster. The thin scientist had his hands held up in surrender until Khumalo got close enough for him to recognize her.

"Chief Khumalo!" He dropped his arms, taking a step toward her. "Are you the Chief from this time or the future?"

Grreag loomed behind Khumalo. "Get whatever you need to mend that rupture and come with us immediately!"

"I can't," stammered Webster.

"You have no choice," Grreag informed him.

"Grreag," said Khumalo, gesturing to a covered body laid out on a table by the fireplace.

The Leon nodded to her and she drew back the cover. It was Pauline Morrison.

Webster looked stricken. "T'alak shot her."

"We only have a few minutes to get to our actuate point," urged Grreag. "We need to go now, Professor."

"I can't leave her!"

Khumalo drew close and laid a hand on his shoulder. "Professor, she's gone. She wouldn't want you to stay and help T'alak — she'd want you to put everything right again."

Webster nodded, and with a last look at Morrison's body he turned away. "All right." He lifted a metal case and a foot-long silver cylinder from the nearby desk. "I'm ready."

They hastened out the front door, heading at a run across the sunny lawn where T'alak and Webster had been conversing earlier. Khumalo noticed Webster had difficulty keeping up and reached out to take the cylinder from him. It felt heavier than it looked.

"Be careful with that," gasped Webster.

They skidded to a stop at the rendezvous point, both Khumalo and Webster breathing heavily. Only Grreag looked unscathed by the exertion. The Leon consulted his tracker.

"Eight Komodoan guards have come down. They're heading this way."

"How long have we got?" asked Khumalo.

"Not long enough," snarled Grreag. "Take Webster, I will head for

220 | *Time Twist*

cover. Make sure to maintain radio silence. Send a bubble down in…" he consulted his timer, "exactly ten Earth minutes. That should give me long enough to dispatch the reptiles." He headed off for the shelter of the trees.

The air pressure changing indicated the arrival of the actuate bubble. "Here, Professor," Khumalo grabbed his sleeve. "Stand close."

Within seconds they were on the cruiser. Khumalo set to work, creating a new actuate relay timer to pick up Grreag.

"Okay," she sat back, allowing some tension to ebb from her. "Now we wait."

Webster settled into one of the pilot seats. "Chief, can't the *L'umina* detect us?"

"Not right now," she replied, "but it won't take them long to search the moons."

She studied the professor. He looked more angular than two years ago, but his eyes remained a piercing blue. Khumalo remembered Catriona's reference to him as the 'Scarecrow' from *Wizard of Oz*. That was even more apt now. His brown and gray speckled hair had grown long, bunching out in wild clumps from his head. He shivered, either from fear or cold, and Khumalo thought the goosebumps on his white arms looked like chicken skin.

"I assume you followed T'alak through the rupture," he said, shifting in discomfort under her scrutiny. "I've been working on finding a way to close it. I'm almost there."

"What caused it?"

Webster paused, studying the floor. "An oversight on my part. When I formed the temporal bubble on the *Vallo* two years ago, it didn't have set coordinates for a corresponding bubble. It left a temporal imbalance, which has manifested itself by forming a rupture."

Khumalo opened her mouth to deliver a tirade. He held up a hand. "Chief, I had no idea of the repercussions. Believe me, if I'd even suspected, I would never have done it." He sighed. "I've paid dearly for my oversight, *dearly*."

Khumalo looked at his haggard face and believed him. "Why did T'alak kill Dr. Morrison?" she asked, one eye on the timer. Grreag would be due in a couple of minutes.

"She tried to defend me," he answered dully. "He shot her at point blank range."

"He considered her a traitor to the Realm," said Khumalo. "Dying that way would be a lot preferable to the way they normally deal with traitors."

"You're right." Webster made an effort to recover. "Time caught up with us, now we have to put it right. We were fools to think we could escape."

The actuate system suddenly fizzled, but Grreag did not appear.

"Shit!" Khumalo hurried to check the readings. She ran a scan of the planet. She wasn't getting any humanoid life-signs at all. An insistent buzzing issued from the console, indicating an incoming transmission. Khumalo clenched her teeth as a message piped through, flashing the viewer to life.

"Alliance vessel," announced Captain T'alak from the screen. "We are aware of your presence. Your Leontor commander is aboard my ship. We are prepared to offer him in exchange for Professor Webster. Reply immediately, or he dies."

<hr>

The conference had gone on for almost two days, with few breaks. T'alak ordered Catriona to stay out of the way, particularly after the evening banquet on the second night had been served. She knew why. Komodoan males needed to mate after feeding, and they weren't particular with whom.

After dark most of the dignitaries had retired for the night. Catriona felt relieved that in the humdrum of the banquet, no one had remembered to lock her in the spire room. She desperately wanted to talk with Captain A'rlon again. Keeping to the kitchen, she had one ear always cocked for his voice in the great room. She knew he would find a way to contact her soon; their last conversation had been too startling for him to leave it there.

L'ticia had no time for her. Catriona had been unable to talk to her about T'alak-zan, so busy had the servant been overseeing the preparation and serving of the banquet. She had plenty of staff on hand to serve; some of them had stayed in the great room with the guests afterwards. Catriona had so wanted to witness what went on at a Komodoan feeding frenzy, but L'ticia had lifted a hand to slap her when she tried to peek into the great room.

Now in the early hours of the morning, the ground floor looked deserted. Catriona crept out from her hiding place in the utility chamber to the darkened kitchen. The pet lizard, Tukki, had kept her company. He scurried away down the back corridor, after nocturnal pursuits Catriona could only guess at. She had been surprised earlier when he skittered rapidly across the floor to rub his head affectionately against her legs.

222 | *Time Twist*

Catriona heard someone groan softly in the great room. She slipped across the kitchen and listening intently, she ducked down, keeping out of sight. On the other side of the long table stood L'ticia, with T'alak behind, holding her close against him.

From her crouched position, Catriona saw that T'alak had pushed L'ticia's robe up around her waist with his tail snaked up between her legs. The tip of the tail vibrated against where Catriona had to assume was the Komodoan equivalent of a human clitoris. The two species were similarly placed, but Komodoan females' sexual organs sat a little further back.

Catriona knew she should leave them their privacy, but the alien love-making mesmerized her. L'ticia's tail whipped round behind her, feathering over T'alak. He eased her robe off as his long, forked tongue slipped in and out, dancing over L'ticia's neck and shoulders, his hands stroking her breastless torso, keeping rhythm with the pulsating of his tail.

Catriona swallowed. She had not known T'alak to be capable of such gentleness. She felt her muscles contract as she watched L'ticia's shudders increase, her tail kneading him more forcefully. T'alak bent her over the table, not entering her yet, instead using a hand to tantalize her further. Just when Catriona could hardly stop herself from calling out in empathy with L'ticia, T'alak shrugged off his own robe. Positioning himself, he hitched L'ticia's tail aside and plunged into her. He moved slowly and sensually, his tail still working for L'ticia's pleasure.

Catriona watched in fascination, her body throbbing with longing. L'ticia arched her back, letting out a long, shuddering sigh as she climaxed and Catriona gasped involuntarily.

T'alak looked right at her, locking her with glittering eyes. Her heart racing, Catriona scrambled to her feet and ran for the door to the hallway.

A hand reached out of the darkness and clamped over her mouth. "It's me," hissed A'rlon. "Where can we talk in private?"

Catriona quivered against him. After what she had just witnessed, the familiar touch and scent of the man she loved was almost too much to bear.

Fighting for control, she rasped, "L'ticia's chamber. She's... occupied right now." She led him to the servant's room just off the back corridor.

"I need more information," said A'rlon as Catriona lit the lamp. "For instance, if the timeline has changed as you claim, how is it only you're aware of it?"

Catriona shook her head, "I think maybe it has something to do with the fact that I'm from another time."

"You are?" A'rlon's voice dripped with sarcasm.

"Yes, I came here from the 21st century as a result of one of Professor Webster's experiments."

"What do you know about Webster's work?"

Catriona gestured impatiently. "Look, we're wasting time. This isn't like you, Jack. We should be finding a way to put things right, not pussy-footing around!"

A'rlon raised a single sardonic eyebrow. "You must truly believe what you are saying, human, or you would not dare address a Komodoan male so."

"A *half*-Komodoan male," she reminded him. She didn't like this A'rlon very much. "And that's another thing," she said. "If T'alak has engineered this time change somehow, then he knows you're a potential double-agent."

He studied her. Catriona met his gaze, despite it not being acceptable to look a male in the eye. Her desire had quickly waned. He wasn't much different from T'alak.

"Very well," he said at last. "I discovered enough discrepancies in the *L'umina's* logs to give credence to what you claim."

Catriona nodded in relief. "So, how do we proceed from here?"

"I will look further into the situation as opportunity permits during the conference. For now is keep T'alak under surveillance. If he is responsible for these alleged changes, knowing him as I do, he'll make a mistake. When he does, I want to know about it."

This was more like her Haven. "How will I contact you?"

"I will be in touch." His manner softened a little. "Your audacity in approaching me lends more credence to your story than anything else. You are courageous for a human."

"If you could hear yourself, Jack! I had no idea you were this arrogant."

He gripped her wrist. "Take care not to call me by that name again. If T'alak were to overhear-"

"Let go of me! You have no right to touch me in this timeline, none at all."

With a smile he released her. "I can see life would not be boring in this other dimension. Do you give my doppelganger as hard a time?"

"I don't need to," she countered, "he knows how to behave."

43

"HE'S DESPERATE," said Khumalo in response to T'alak's transmission. "He needs you, Professor. We might yet be able to salvage this situation."

"I'm perfectly prepared to accept the exchange for Colonel Grreag, Chief."

"Don't be absurd! You're our ace in the hole. If we give you back, how can we fix the temporal imbalance?"

"Well, as I see it," answered Webster slowly, "first and foremost, we need to get T'alak out of this timeline, back into his own."

Khumalo slammed a fist down on the console. "Yes, but he's already *changed* his own timeline! We need to reverse what he's done here before sending him back and sealing up the rupture."

"Chief, think this through." Webster lifted up the case he'd brought from the planet and unsealed it. "This is a copy of the updated temporal bubble research that T'alak sent to his counterpart in this time. If we can go back a few hours, then we could possibly prevent him from imparting this information to his people, get him back to where he entered this time to start with, and send him back to the future!"

Khumalo cast incredulous eyes upwards. "Man, have you any idea how much you sound like a mad scientist in the movies? How do you propose we do this?"

"Simple. I'll set up a new temporal bubble pair and actuate us to a time before the *L'umina* came through the rupture. Then we can collect Pauline before T'alak kills her. I'll dismantle the bubbles, we'll move back through the rupture, and the Alliance can set up a guard while I work on eliminating the rupture behind us."

"Sounds too good to be true, Professor." Khumalo tapped her nails on the console. "And where does Colonel Grreag come into all this?"

"If we go back in time far enough, he won't even have left the *Vallo* when we get back."

"How can you be sure it'll work out that way?"

Webster sighed. "There are no guarantees, but I don't see what other options we have."

Khumalo got to her feet, pacing the small cabin. He was right. They were out of options. Heaven only knew what kind of life waited for them back in their own time if they didn't try something. A Komodoan-dominated galaxy did not appeal to her at all.

"All right, get started on the new bubbles; I'll stall T'alak."

She prepared a message for the *L'umina* and broadcast it, careful to bounce the signal around so it couldn't easily be traced to their location behind the moon.

"Captain T'alak," she announced in a commanding tone, "we are considering your ultimatum. Stand by." There. Her imperious manner would have done Colonel Grreag proud.

She watched Webster pull out a variety of disks, and download them to the cruiser's onboard computer.

"Professor, what will you do about preventing the Komodoan Realm from stealing this from you in the future? Now they've had a taste of what it can offer, they won't stand for the Alliance having it."

Webster replied without hesitation. "I'm going to destroy everything as soon as the rupture is mended. This has gone on long enough. I had my concerns about the project before the Alliance got involved. The temporal bubble has done more harm than good, don't you agree?"

"Yes, I do." She touched him on the shoulder. "I know you created it for a better purpose, but humanoid nature being what it is, I guess we're just not ready for such power."

He smiled for the first time, making him look much younger. "This is going to take a while."

"I'll leave you to it."

Khumalo sat down to think through Webster's proposed plan. It sounded simple enough to work, if they could execute it. If they did get back to their own time and the *Vallo*, how would Grreag take the news that he had been captured? She marveled at his arrogance, thinking he could single-handedly take on eight armed Komodoan guards. His pride would be his downfall. Would already have been, she amended, if this didn't succeed.

Catriona waited in her room in the spire. She knew T'alak would appear soon. She heard footsteps on the stairs and stood, bracing herself. At least he would be unlikely to want to mate with her after his exertion with L'ticia.

T'alak strode in. His eyes looked heavy-lidded, as though drugged. Kicking the door shut behind him, he said, "Have you any idea what your fate might have been if it had been one of my guests you spied on?"

Catriona blinked in surprise at how tired and aged he looked. The

226 | *Time Twist*

skin on his face dragged in folds. Did having sex take that much out of him? He leaned a hand on her desk, looking as though he were about to collapse. What could be the matter with him?

"Governor, are you ill?"

"It is merely time for the morph. No doubt you will find it distasteful, so as your punishment, you will assist me with the ritual."

"What's the morph?"

"A seasonal shedding of the outer skin. Hurry." He moved toward the small bathroom.

Catriona followed reluctantly. "Surely a Komodoan would be a better choice than me?"

"The timing is inconvenient. I do not want my guests to witness my indisposal, and with the servants entertaining, there is no one suitable to assist." He began to remove his clothing. "Don't just stand there, assist me! You are acting worse now than the first time I taught you to bathe me."

Catriona hid her astounded look as she bent to help pull off his boots. *Bathe* him? She couldn't envision herself ever willingly doing a personal thing like that for him. Haven was not the only changed person in this timeline, she thought, a lump forming in her throat.

As T'alak slipped out of his robe and ceremonial sash, Catriona saw how advanced the puckering on his torso appeared. The flesh around the scales on his back looked putrid and sore.

"How long will this take?" she asked, averting her eyes as he turned to face her.

"A few hours. I will stay in here for the duration; it is less disorderly." He doubled over in pain and slumped into the shower, his tail curled up in a tight twist.

Catriona tried to ignore his alien penis which, even shriveled in his pain, appeared very large. "What should I do?" she asked.

His hands, heavy with loose skin, indicated where his torso flesh had split down the left side. Reaching into the shower, Catriona took hold of the clammy membrane and gently eased it away from his body. It came away stickily, reminding her of the cleansing cucumber face-mask she had used back in her time. Remembering how much easier it came off when she soaked her face in warm water, she reached up, running a soft trickle of water over him.

It lasted four hours. Drenched to the skin, her hair plastered flat to her head, Catriona finally pulled the last piece from him. She had remained by him the entire time, but they had spoken little. He looked exhausted, lying helpless under the trickling shower, his new skin as red as a fresh-peeled prawn. No wonder he didn't want his guests and dignitaries to see him like this, she thought. He would have lost face before them, and possibly undermined his position of power in the conference.

"Come on," she said briskly, turning off the water. He allowed her to pull him forward and pat his smooth, new skin dry with a soft towel. Using her as a crutch, he straightened, moving from the bathroom into the bedchamber. With a hiss, he sagged onto the futon. Lying on his side, he watched Catriona through hooded eyes.

She felt drained. Her neck and shoulders ached from the constant attention she had been forced to give him. She hid her revulsion as she returned to the bathroom to peel off her sopping clothes. That had to be the most obscene thing she'd ever seen. As his flesh had shed, it came away green and slimy in her hand. And it smelled horrible. Catriona had fought nausea until she felt too tired to care. Drying herself off, she pulled on a clean robe. She used the wet towel to shove T'alak's shed skin under the sink. It smelled so foul, she couldn't bring herself to touch it. Once it dried out a little, she could dispose of it.

How ridiculous! she thought, catching sight of her tired reflection in the mirror. Sometimes life proved just too strange to believe. She had just helped her reptoid captor shed his skin, now he lay helpless as a babe on her bed. If she wanted to repay him for all the pain he'd caused her, this would be her chance. And God knew he deserved to suffer; he had brought her nothing but grief in both timelines.

Moving back into the bedchamber, she looked at him, curled up fetus-like on her futon. No matter what he had done, she knew she couldn't bring herself to hurt someone as vulnerable as he was. She'd be no better than T'alak if she stooped to his level.

With a start, she realized he'd been watching her. Clearing her throat, she inquired, "Are you feeling better?"

"Bring me some water."

Catriona got him a cup of cold water from the bathroom. Moving to the futon, she knelt beside him, handing him the cup. He drank deeply, his dark eyes glittering over the rim as he studied her.

"Tell me your thoughts, human."

Catriona sat back on her heels. "Your morph made me think of an old folktale my mother used to tell me as a child."

"Go on." He placed the cup on the floor between them.

Catriona took a deep breath. "There's an ocean animal on Earth, called a seal. It's said there are enchanted seals that are half-human.

228 | *Time Twist*

The Celts call them *Sealkies*-"

"Celts?" frowned T'alak.

"What I am. My heritage."

He nodded. "Continue."

"When *Sealkies* take human form, they are so beautiful they can enchant any human, but if you find and capture its skin, you'll force them to stay with you forever. There are many myths of lonely fishermen finding *Sealkie* women and bringing them home as their wives. But if she finds her skin, she's irresistibly drawn back to the sea, lost to her husband forever."

"You have my skin, human. Do you wish to bind me to you forever?"

Catriona dropped her gaze. She could think of nothing worse. T'alak sensed her rejection.

"Bring my robe!" he ordered, rising from the futon. Slipping it on, he winced, the cloth obviously harsh against his new skin. "You will remain in the spire for the duration of the conference," he announced, shuffling toward the door.

How could she keep in contact with A'rlon if she were locked up? Thinking quickly, she ran ahead and kneeled in front of him.

"Honored Governor, forgive my lack of tact. I just could not believe that someone like you would deign to be bound to a mere human slave. You do me too much honor."

It had been exactly the right thing to say. T'alak gently tipped her face up to look into her eyes.

"Your guilelessness is hard to resist," he said, indicating she should rise. He leaned close and caressed her face with his tongue. "After the conference I shall bestow on you the same favor I showed the servant, L'ticia."

44

"Chief Chief!"

Uzi's elbow slipped off the console as she jerked awake. "Man, how long was I out?" she demanded, astounded she could sleep at all.

"Just a couple of hours. The new temporal bubbles are in place; we can go through."

She cleared her dry throat. "Let me get something to drink, first. You want anything?" She moved to crack open the box of supplies.

"No, alcohol wouldn't be advisable before time travel."

"Professor, is my reputation that bad? I meant a measure of water."

Webster gave her a self-deprecating grin. "Sorry. Yes, a measure would be great."

They downed the precious liquid.

"Okay, the sooner we do this, the better," said Khumalo.

"Agreed." Webster sat at the computer console and strapped himself in. "I'd advise you to do the same. This is going to be a bumpy ride."

Khumalo took a seat at the navigational console so she could record their progress for posterity. Just in case they got lost forever in some distant dimension. "I'm ready."

Webster's fingers sped over his keypad. In moments the cruiser's interior looked like it had been submerged under water. Everything slewed out of focus, and the craft shimmied. Looking across at the professor, Khumalo noticed the distortion made him look like a twisted reflection in a fairground hall of mirrors. She felt nauseous; her head throbbing like it would explode. The grating sound around them grew to such a peak she expected the cruiser to blow apart at any moment. Then suddenly, all became still.

Consulting her instruments, Khumalo gave a brittle laugh. "We're by the first moon, now! How'd you manage that?"

"Good. That was the configuration a few hours ago. The moons orbit each other. What date do you have?"

"I don't know. Looks like our jaunt flabbergasted the computer. The chronometer is dead." She rapped at the offending instrument.

"Never mind, we'll just have to trust my calculations were accurate."

"But it means only one of us can actuate down to the planet, Professor. The timer's shot; I wouldn't risk attempting to program a delayed bubble pick-up."

"I'll go. I'll be as quick as I can."

"Make sure you are. I don't even know why I'm permitting you to go get Dr. Morrison in the first place."

"Because you have no choice," he said. "Look, I know there's no love lost between you and Pauline-"

"It's pretty fucking hard to forget what she did two years ago. But she and I can discuss it later." She moved to the actuate console. "I'll put you down in front of your dwelling. I'll give you three minutes, and then I'll send a bubble every thirty seconds. Hurry it up."

230 | *Time Twist*

"Understood."

In a moment he had gone. Khumalo sat moodily waiting for the three minutes to be up. This was insanity. Why an intelligent man like Webster would bother with that Komodoan spy was unfathomable.

The three minutes were quickly up. Uzi activated the bubble and was surprised when both Webster and Dr. Morrison appeared. Professor Webster lifted the cylinder he'd brought on board and placed it into Morrison's arms. She clutched it protectively.

Khumalo looked hard at her. The woman still had her facial scales, but no tail. "You," she snapped, "sit down over there, and shut up."

The erstwhile spy ducked her head and obeyed, making sure the cylinder was secure on her lap. Khumalo felt almost disappointed, realizing she'd been anticipating a confrontation. They had a lot of unfinished business between them. "You just can't stay dead, girl, can you?" she added, unable to resist.

"What do you mean?" demanded Morrison.

Webster stepped between them. "This is neither the time nor place. Please, let's just head through the rupture as soon as possible."

Khumalo turned on him. "What about the decay in this time from the temporal imbalance? I thought you needed to take care of it from this end?"

"Calm down, Chief. I did it while you were sleeping. Look, you can check it yourself." He swiveled the screen to show her. "It will desist the moment I dismantle the one in your time. The same goes for the new ones that brought us here. Once we enter the rupture, they'll disband completely."

Khumalo's nostrils flared. Her personal feelings were interfering with the job at hand. "All right. Get strapped in."

She dropped into the pilot's seat and engaged the drive. The cruiser shifted position and shot toward the rupture.

"Hang on!" she yelled, as the dazzling rainbow reached out to envelop them.

"This is what I've got so far."

Catriona opened her eyes to see A'rlon pulling the desk stool over to sit near her. Flabbergasted, she checked to make certain that the quilt covered her. "How did you manage to get in here without my hearing you?"

"Obtained the coordinates and programmed an actuate bubble to take me here. Now, as far as our little problem goes, I believe I've uncovered the truth."

"It's the space rupture, isn't it?"

"Yes. There is a whole different report to be found on *The Victory* when one knows where to dig." He imparted how he had been able to confirm her claim of a different timeline, and how the *L'umina* had gone back in time by two years and changed it. "And T'alak arranged to have one of our actuate systems pick up your molecules instead of the *Vallo* when you first arrived from the past."

Catriona sat up. "You mean I've been living like this for two years? How come I only remember the original timeline where you and I met?"

"Probably because you're from a different time frame altogether. Possibly too far removed to be affected. It wouldn't surprise me if over a period of time you began to forget it and this would be your reality."

Catriona reached out and grabbed his arm. "We've got to fix the timeline before that happens!"

The quilt slipped down. Seeing A'rlon's gaze drop to her exposed breasts, she tugged it over her again.

"Don't do that." He pulled it away. "It's been many years since I've seen a human woman. May I?" His hand hovered near her.

Dumbfounded, Catriona gaped at him. Taking her silence for acquiescence, he gently cupped a breast, running a thumb over her quickly hardening nipple. Catriona looked into his eyes, so like Haven's. "We need to discuss how we're going to put the timeline right," she said weakly.

"Later," he murmured, flipping the quilt completely off and slipping from the stool to kneel beside her.

"A'rlon!" she gasped. "You are not Jack."

He leaned over her, pressing her back against the pillow. "But I am." He bent his head and captured her lips with his.

Catriona found herself responding and her arms slid round him, holding him to her. He moved his head down, exploring her breasts with his lips and tongue. Catriona sighed, closing her eyes and running her fingers through his black hair. With a smile he sat up and unfastened his tunic belt. Shivering, Catriona helped, pushing the bulky garment back from his shoulders. He shifted, sitting back to remove his military thigh boots, then shrugged the tunic completely off.

Catriona recoiled. His smooth torso without nipples bluntly reminded her of what he was. He stretched over her, his long tongue continuing its exploration of her quivering body. This was not Haven, yet her body betrayed her into responding to him.

232 | *Time Twist*

"A'rlon, I can't do this."

His dark eyes flickered, but he didn't reply. Shocked, Catriona realized he wasn't going to stop. He positioned himself and eased into her. As he thrust into her over and over, her outrage quickly evaporated. His touch and scent were so familiar, the line between A'rlon and Haven became blurred. She closed her eyes and held him tightly against her.

He finished quickly and caressed her cheek, looking down into her eyes. "I hope I didn't hurt you."

"The man I know wouldn't have continued after I'd objected," she snapped. "You had no right to do that."

He rolled off and lay beside her. "You would be correct if we were in your society. But here, this *was* my right. My double in your time may know how to be human, but I do not." He fell silent for a long moment. "But you have given me much to think about. I... apologize for insisting."

Catriona turned her head and looked at him, surprised. That was quite a concession for a Komodoan.

"It's all right," she murmured. She had felt more disillusioned with the sex than violated; only he had been satisfied in the encounter. "Forget it."

She got up and lifted her robe. "Let's talk about reversing the timeline. I've been more than patient, A'rlon. We need to act now." She looked down at him, lying on his side because the hard futon would hurt his tail if he lay on his back.

"As I see it," he said slowly, sliding off the futon and standing, "our only option is to access Webster's temporal bubble data and go back to where we can prevent Captain T'alak from entering the rupture."

"And you're willing to do this?"

He paused and studied her face intently. "Yes."

"You don't sound very sure." Naked, he looked so alien, she wondered how she could have fooled herself into imagining him to be her Haven. "How can I trust you? You have everything in this timeline. Prestige, power... why would you want to change it?"

"You are perceptive, human. But with such rewards the challenge diminishes. The very talks downstairs are about taming the military. I've been bred to serve as a soldier; peace does not suit my nature."

"Your life is nothing but challenges in my timeline. In fact, many times you've told me how burned out you've been getting."

He hissed a laugh. "That sounds preferable to this political dance we perform. Besides, I think I like the thought of knowing you as an equal in that other world. Here, you are nothing but an alien slave, and T'alak's property at that. I took a risk coming here tonight. I may never have access to you again."

"Probably just as well. You need to learn a little more about pleasing a woman before I'd consider granting you access again." She tried to infuse a bantering tone into her voice, but it came across sounding resentful.

He looked closely at her. She couldn't define what expression flickered across his face. "I *can* do better," he murmured, moving toward her. "Let me make it up to you."

Catriona stepped back as he reached to untie her robe. "No. I *mean* it, this time."

"Are you sure?" He smiled, his hand on her robe tie.

Hesitating, Catriona swallowed hard. A'rlon pulled the tie and her robe fell open. Without another word, Catriona allowed him to ease her back toward the bed. Kneeling over her, he used his long, forked tongue in ways that sent her spiraling until she gladly welcomed him into her again.

Even though she found the second encounter more satisfying, Catriona felt uneasy that he had still persisted when she had told him to stop. She wondered about the Haven in her timeline. How much of this domineering Komodoan side did he keep hidden from her?

Daylight began to filter through the windows.

"It's time for me to return to the ship before I'm missed," said A'rlon, getting up to dress in his discarded uniform.

"How can you actuate up and down without your crew knowing?"

"Captain's privilege. There's a private Actuation in my quarters. I expect that's how T'alak caught your molecules without having to make an official report."

"Let me come with you." This way she could escape before T'alak was ready to 'bestow his favor' on her.

"I'll consider it." Activating a wrist control, he had gone, leaving her alone to greet Komodoa's two rising suns.

Arrogant bastard! Guilt gnawed at her, coupled with resentment. Unable to sleep, she fiddled with the computer, pulling up the Komodoan language tutorial. Catriona found it difficult to follow as the instructions were in Komodoan. She noticed an icon on the screen that symbolized a headpiece. Finding such a device in the desk drawer, she slipped it over her ears, and clicked on the icon.

Searing pain lanced through her. Crying out, she grabbed at the headpiece, managing to rip it off before she toppled from the seat.

45

"Colonel Grreag," announced Chief Khumalo. "A vessel is emerging from the rupture."

"Put it on the viewer. Can you identify it?" He studied the silver pinprick winding its fragile way from the gaping maw of the rupture.

Chief Khumalo spun round in her seat to look at him. "Sir, according to these readings, it's one of *our* cruisers."

"Impossible," objected Major Benjamin. "All *Vallo* cruisers are accounted for." His panel at Command Center bleeped. "They're pinging us, Colonel."

"Well, don't keep them waiting," growled Grreag, settling himself into his chair, forcing his hackles down.

He started in surprise at the sight that greeted him. But of the *Vallo* control cabin crew, none could be more astonished than Uzima Khumalo. She stared in disbelief at the image of herself on the screen.

Her double turned to someone out of sight of the viewer and said, "Thanks for the warning, man!"

"Chief Khumalo!" boomed Grreag.

Both Chiefs looked at him, then the Khumalo on the *Vallo* turned her attention back to her counterpart on the viewer. She watched a myriad of thoughts flicker across the well-known face, recognizing the thought behind each and every expression. She decided she'd take the beads out of her hair; it looked unprofessional and messy. She grinned in spite of herself. How many people got to check their hairstyle appropriateness as accurately as this?

"Colonel Grreag," said the other Khumalo. "T'alak's on his way in the *L'umina*. On no account let him near the rupture, and for Christ's sake don't fire on them or act in such a way they'll fire their new ionizer weapon on you."

"She's correct," interjected Larrar. "A Komodoan Realm warship just entered the sector."

"Chief Khumalo, who do you have on board with you?" demanded Grreag.

Professor Webster stepped into view. "Hello, Colonel."

"Great Fang, you!"

"Yes, well, you see-" He broke off as the Khumalo beside him interrupted.

"Sir, it's imperative we stop that warship from firing. Don't have time to explain. Can you actuate Professor Webster to the *Vallo*?"

Grreag turned to the Khumalo beside him. "Chief? Use the main actuate chamber."

On her way, Khumalo wondered what might happen if she met her double in person. There were all sorts of theories about meeting yourself from another time. Common thought hypothesized that if they physically touched, they'd cancel each other out. So far no one had experimented, and Uzima didn't want to be the one to make that particular history.

In the control cabin, Grreag asked Lieutenant Larrar, "How close is the Realm ship?"

"Three minutes away, Sir."

"Chief," he addressed the viewer, "take the cruiser round behind us so the Komodoans can't pick you up on their scanners."

"Aye, Sir. Stand by." The ghostly lips of the rupture replaced Khumalo's image.

Grreag suppressed a growl. When were the repercussions to Professor Webster's work ever going to end?

"Colonel," came the indigenous Khumalo's voice. "The rupture is becoming unstable. I recommend we move both the *Vallo* and cruiser to a safe distance."

"Agreed."

A warning bleep sounded from Larrar's panel. "Colonel," she said. "We're out of time. The Realm ship is within range."

"Chief, hold your position!" ordered Grreag.

"Armor, Colonel?" asked Larrar.

"Wait for my order. Put the ship on the main viewer."

The massive hexagram spun across the stars, slowing its rotation as it approached the rupture.

The *L'umina*. Grreag growled low under his breath, then ordered, "Ping them, Lieutenant."

Captain T'alak replaced the hexagram ship on the viewer. "Colonel Grreag," he sneered. "I knew our paths would cross again."

Grreag wondered how to defuse the situation, if they were to avoid fire and prevent the *L'umina* from entering the rupture. He bared a fang, forcing warmth into his tone.

"Captain! It's an honor to meet such a worthy opponent again." It went against everything in his being to address T'alak so, but he forced himself to continue. "As you are here to inspect the rupture, I will

236 | *Time Twist*

overlook your incursion into Alliance space. I would be happy to share any information we have on the phenomena."

The Komodoan captain paused for a beat. "What an unexpected pleasure, Colonel," he said, his tongue flickering. "If you agree to actuate to my ship, I will be willing to also share our knowledge."

I'll bet you would, thought Grreag. *And I'd find myself under trial on Komodoa before I could say 'crocodile.'*

An interruption from Larrar saved him from replying. "Colonel, I'm detecting a large buildup in temporal displacement."

"Get us out of range of the rupture, Lieutenant."

"It's not originating from there."

Sudden thunder like a sonic boom reverberated through the *Vallo*, and a blinding flash dazzled them for a second. When Grreag's eyes recovered, he saw a second *L'umina* had appeared beside the first.

"Holy Fang!" he growled. "Lieutenant, ping *this L'umina.* Split the screen."

A very Komodoan-looking Haven filled half the viewer. He gave Grreag a cynical grin, his eyes hard. On the other half of the screen Captain T'alak's expression turned apoplectic.

Grreag's ears perked with interest. "I'm assuming you're not Lieutenant Colonel Haven of Alliance Intelligence?"

"Ah, so you are familiar with this paragon of virtue, also. No, you are addressing Captain A'rlon of the Komodoan Realm. But not captain for much longer, I wager."

"*Captain* A'rlon?" spat T'alak. "What by *B'llumni* are you talking about?"

"Simple." A'rlon raised a sardonic eyebrow. "I came from the future to prevent you from entering that rupture. I don't much care for the way you changed the timeline. And neither will you, it lacks... challenge."

"You cursed Alliance traitor!"

"Gentlemen," Grreag stepped in, bringing all his diplomatic Alliance training to bear. "I'm sure we can discuss this in a civilized manner. Shall we retreat from the rupture to-"

"Be silent, Leon!" the two Komodoan captains said as one.

Grreag resisted a sudden, inexplicable urge to laugh. Instead, he leveled both Komodoans with a homicidal glare.

"A'rlon," hissed T'alak, "you deprived me of revenge two years ago, but not this time!"

Two bolts of amber fire lashed out from T'alak's ship's ionizer destroyers. Larrar changed the viewer focus to show the two *L'uminas* in front of the rupture. A'rlon's ship rocked from the impact.

Grreag watched in horror as the rupture suddenly swelled open like an infected sore. A dazzling stream of light like a luminescent arm soared out from the void to surround T'alak's *L'umina*. In moments, it snatched the Realm warship from her position and sucked her into the rupture. That's what the chief had tried to warn them about, Grreag realized.

"Chief Khumalo," he pinged.

"Aye, Sir?" they responded in stereo.

"I mean on the cruiser," he added. "I'm going to ask Captain A'rlon to meet with us on your craft. Stand ready." He ordered Lieutenant Larrar to ping A'rlon's *L'umina*.

"I am making preparations to take a temporal bubble further back, Colonel," A'rlon told him.

"He can't do that," interjected Khumalo, listening in from the cruiser. "Professor Webster warns there are already more temporal wakes than this timeline can handle. Any more and we'll irreparably tear the fabric of time."

"Is Webster still with you?"

"Yes, he hadn't time to actuate to the *Vallo* before the warship arrived."

"Captain A'rlon, are you willing to join us on the cruiser?"

"Of course." His dark eyes showed no expression.

"Chief, bring the cruiser round to starboard and transmit coordinates to the *L'umina*."

When Grreag arrived on the small craft, Khumalo stood face to face with A'rlon.

"And not only are you a two-timing bastard, you are a fucking shit-for-brains liar. What do you have to say about that?"

A'rlon smiled. "I'm relieved to hear Haven isn't the god I heard he was."

Grreag narrowed his amber eyes, ears pricking forward. From whom would he have heard of the Haven in their time?

"Ah, Colonel," Ar'lon greeted him. "To business. If we are unable to create any more temporal bubbles, I suggest we follow T'alak in and destroy him."

"I think we have another option," said Webster. Everyone turned to him. "I don't believe a *stationary* temporal bubble would be detrimental."

"Explain," demanded Grreag.

238 | *Time Twist*

"Let me think." Webster attempted to pace the cabin, but with so many crowded into the small space, he gave up and sat down at the computer console. "We have a couple of options: one could be used as a backup if necessary."

"For God's sake, Professor, get on with it!" Khumalo looked like she wanted to strangle him.

Dr. Morrison, who had sat like Shakespeare's Banquo at the feast, suddenly spoke. "You should address him with more respect! I can understand your despicable behavior toward me, but don't extend it to Scott."

As Khumalo scowled, an incredulous expression appeared on A'rlon's scaled face. "You! Agent Y'alenon! How do you fit into all this? No," he held up a hand, uttering a short laugh. "I'd rather not know. In my world you are a heroine."

"That doesn't surprise me," muttered Khumalo.

"You are the agent who brought Webster to us. Then you donated your half-breed dead bastard for science."

Pauline went white, her arms tightening around the cylinder she still clutched. "Our half-breed bastard, as you so eloquently put it, is most definitely here and *alive*."

All eyes went to the cylinder. It was far too small to hold a two year-old humanoid child.

Webster moved to Pauline's side. "It was a difficult birth. We've placed him in stasis until we find an expert on hybrid humanoids."

Khumalo swallowed, too sympathetic to continue hating a woman whose baby had to be carried around like a frozen turkey.

A'rlon raised an eyebrow. "Odd how those gene-covering drugs made you compatible enough with humans to breed. I am genetically half-human, yet I cannot father offspring with either species."

"I'm sure this is all very fascinating!" roared Grreag, his patience pushed to the limit. "Can we get back to the matter at hand? Professor Webster, continue."

"It's all right, the, ah... discussion gave me a moment to collect my thoughts. Now, we can both go in after T'alak and enclose him in a time bubble, holding the entire ship in time for a selected period. Between us, we should be able to tow him back out in a traherence stream, and keep him there until I repair the rupture. And in case we are not successful at catching him, we could enclose one of our two ships in time for a while so that it would be immune to the alternative timeline that T'alak would create. Then, after he returns through the rupture, we can re-emerge and go through to reverse the timeline again."

Khumalo leaned forward. "What if T'alak forces Webster from that other time to mend the rupture before the enclosed ship emerges?"

"Good point, which is why the first option would be optimal, Chief."

Grreag turned to Captain A'rlon. "We need to act fast. Are you in agreement?" The spy still hadn't given his reasons for coming through time to stop T'alak, but no matter, it suited their purpose to have the sister *L'umina* aid them.

"Absolutely. I recommend we implement Webster's plan as soon as possible," said A'rlon.

Grreag nodded. "Very well. Chief, I want you and Webster to stand by on this side. We'll send a probe through if we need your help."

As he vanished in the bubble, he understood the somber look in the chief engineer's eyes. What would happen to the woman if she got trapped in this time, along with her doppelganger?

46

CATRIONA OPENED her eyes and immediately screwed them shut again. The blinding sunlight crucified her. Squinting through her eyelashes, she saw the discarded headpiece lying a few feet away, a high-pitched whine emanating from it. Slowly sitting up, she tentatively felt her head. No harm done, as far as she could tell. Just the worst headache she'd ever had.

She kicked at the headpiece and slammed off the computer. That would be the last time she'd try anything new with that device. How long had she been out?

Catching sight of her rumpled futon, she remembered what had transpired on it only a few hours ago. Butterflies coursed through her stomach. Damn that man, he was irresistible in any timeline!

Yet she didn't feel happy about waiting for him to take action on her behalf. What if he decided not to bring her with him when he went back in time to stop T'alak? Going to the futon, she opened a drawer in the small cabinet beside it. She lifted out her most treasured possession, the gold locket her mother had given her for her eighteenth birthday. Flipping it open, she slipped a fingernail underneath the picture of her parents. A glimpse of silver confirmed the copy of Professor Webster's

240 | *Time Twist*

data disk was still safely hidden. No one but Uzima Khumalo knew she had it. Just before Leontor Control confiscated Webster's research, she had given the illicit copy into Catriona's keeping, 'just in case'. The disk had some kind of quantum shielding, making it undetectable in scanning. The catch on the locket looked loose. She'd better be careful not to lose it. Slipping the locket over her head, Catriona sighed. What use would the disk be to her? She had no idea how to replicate Webster's temporal bubble experiment. Hell, even if she could, she had no idea how to even access the files.

Washing and dressing, she avoided the vile slime under the bathroom sink. Thank God A'rlon didn't shed like that. Or maybe he did and had kept it from her. She never wanted to go through that again.

The suns were well up by the time someone came to the door. She yanked it open as soon as she heard the lock pulled back.

"About time," she snapped. L'ticia stood outside, holding a tray. "My head's killing me." Catriona stepped back to allow the woman to pass. Her tongue felt too thick for her mouth, and to her surprise, she drooled a little as she spoke. She saw L'ticia gaping at her. "What?"

"Are you aware you're speaking fluent Komodoan?"

"No, I'm not!"

"I assure you, you are. And like it's your native tongue."

"I couldn't be!"

"Then tell me how come you understand everything I'm saying?" L'ticia placed the tray on the desk. "Do you understand this?" She spoke a couple of phrases that sounded like gibberish to Catriona. "That was Terran English, human. Did you access the fast-learn program?"

Catriona stooped to retrieve the headpiece. "Yes, I did."

"You're more of a fool than I thought! I warned you it hadn't been calibrated for you. You're fortunate to be cognitive at all."

L'ticia may have warned her in this timeline, thought Catriona, but she only remembered the original one. That must be why her tongue felt strange. Not used to forming the alien words. "So it's replaced one language with another?" Her voice rose.

"Obviously. But it's a lucky side-effect; you don't need your ugly language anymore."

Catriona hid her glare. There was no substitute for her own language. In her opinion, no poet could write like Wordsworth or Shakespeare. Or Sylvia Plath, for that matter. She could always fast-learn English the safe way after she escaped this place. It would only be a temporary setback, she assured herself.

Lticia placed the tray she'd brought on Catriona's desk. "Thank *P'jarra* the neural input didn't kill you."

"Yes, indeed," agreed Catriona, tossing the headpiece onto the desk. She wiped another dribble away from the corner of her mouth. This would take some getting used to, Komodoan being such a sibilant language.

"It will make my job a little easier, being able to explain to you what I'm doing." Lticia lifted the cover from the tray.

Catriona's eyebrows rose. Instead of food, a variety of odd-shaped instruments and jars littered the tray.

"Where's breakfast? I'm starving!"

"No food for you until the feast of *O'tium*, human. Governor T'alak has informed me of his intention to favor you at the festival, so we have four days to prepare."

"Now, wait just a minute! Humans need to eat every day. I know you Komodoans go three or more days between meals, but I cannot." Then the rest of Lticia's statement sank in. "What do you mean, prepare me?"

Lticia smiled, her tail swirling enthusiastically. "I think you will enjoy it. First I must remove all your body hair, then massage a combination of holy oils and herbs into your skin. This we must do twice daily until the feast. The Governor tells me that in previous encounters with human females, they are damaged because they do not have adequate capacity to accommodate him. So," she lifted a phallic object from the tray, "we need to take care of that."

Catriona boggled. "You've got to be kidding. I am not having any part of this, Lticia. T'alak can go to hell, for I won't be allowing him to 'favor' me now, or at any bloody feast!"

Replacing the object on the tray, Lticia said quietly, "I don't believe you have a choice in the matter, Catriona Logan. T'alak is master here, and you are an alien slave."

Catriona took a deep breath. "I think it's time you and I had a talk." The fluent Komodoan would prove itself invaluable. "I do have a choice. I'm getting the hell out of here, and you're going to help me."

Lticia scowled. "Human, don't make me-"

"Don't make *me* tell T'alak about N'elak and the Third Quadrant!"

The Komodoan woman hissed, almost staggering. "How in the name of *P'jarra* do you know about that?"

"It's a long story; one I'm not prepared to go into right now." Catriona felt power surging through her as she took control. It was as though she'd woken up from a bad dream. How she could have lived as

242 | *Time Twist*

a captive slave for the past two years she couldn't fathom.

L'ticia's tail whipped from side to side in distress.

"Don't worry," Catriona assured her, "I have nothing to gain from telling T'alak about N'elak. Just help me before this *O'tium* feast and your secret is safe."

The Komodoan's tail drooped. "What do you want?"

"Two things to start with: get me access to T'alak's space faring yacht, and find a way to get Captain A'rlon up here to talk with me, without T'alak knowing."

"You don't ask for much," muttered L'ticia. "Why don't you have the Captain offer to buy you from T'alak, if that's what you want?"

"That's not what I want," grinned Catriona wryly. "But thanks for the idea. If all else fails, I may consider it."

"I don't understand. The House of T'alak is the most respected noble caste in the Realm. Where is better than here?"

"Oh, L'ticia, if you only knew. Just trust me when I tell you that this world is not what it should be."

"And just how should it be, human?" Both women jumped at T'alak's voice. "How interesting that you suddenly speak fluent Komodoan."

A wave of nausea slewed through Catriona. How long had he been there?

T'alak watched her for a moment, then turned to L'ticia. "Get out."

The servant shot Catriona a frightened look, and obeyed. T'alak regarded Catriona.

"It's always been A'rlon, hasn't it?"

Her headache reached explosive proportions. "What do you mean?"

"You know about the altered timeline, don't you?" T'alak grabbed her by her hair and pushed her onto her knees. "I don't know how, but you do. And you still want Commander A'rlon, Terran cunt!"

He threw her to the floor. Catriona heard a swishing sound, and saw T'alak take off his belt. She tried to roll away as he bent toward her, but he jammed a foot into the back of her neck and ripped her dress open. Catriona tensed as she heard the belt snap through the air. Then T'alak's weight lifted, and she saw A'rlon wrestle the belt from his grip.

The pain became too much, and everything went hazy as she blacked out.

In the other timeline, after Captain A'rlon met with Colonel Grreag on the cruiser, he glanced around the skeleton crew loyal to him on the

L'umina. Over the years he had cultivated friendship and allegiance from a select few: each qualified to run a battleship with little support, if need be. Interesting what a promotion here, a gift of land there, will do for a man's loyalty, he mused. Each and every one agreed with his decision to follow T'alak back to the point where he changed the timeline and correct it. Like himself, none had families, no one to mourn should they never return.

His counterpart in the original timeline had a better deal than him. He had a challenging career as an undercover operative, plus the love of a human like Catriona Logan.

He frowned. "Get me Colonel Grreag again," he ordered.

When the Leontor appeared on the viewscreen, he curtly advised him to delay pursuit into the rupture. He would alert them when ready. Without further explanation, he cut the communication and made his way to his quarters.

How fascinating to be dealing with the Alliance again. So xenophobic was the Komodoan Realm, he hadn't had direct contact with aliens for over ten years. He found it stimulating. Particularly having the opportunity to be intimate with Catriona. Because of his tail's lack of dexterity and human-sized penis, he had been reluctant to be intimate with Komodoan females. Remembering Catriona's compelling scent and silken skin, he hoped the human surgeon on Earth to whom he had brought her could bring her out of the coma.

He had been about to actuate to the *L'umina* when the servant L'ticia intercepted him. She scarcely made sense, babbling about Governor T'alak and the spire room. Fearing Catriona might be in trouble, he took the steps up to the spire three at a time. Rage consumed him to see T'alak brutalizing the helpless human. Before he knew it, he had tackled the Governor, ripping the leather belt from his hand.

"You filthy reptile!" he bellowed, raising the belt and striking T'alak with it. They glowered into each other's eyes, mere inches apart.

"So, A'rlon. You show your true nature at last."

"As do you. Only a coward treats a defenseless captive like this." He hurled the belt across the room.

"She's my slave, A'rlon. There is no cowardice in disciplining her."

"She's not your slave! She shouldn't even be here. None of this should!" A'rlon stretched his arms in emphasis. "You have perverted our world with your interference. The Realm should rise to power in its own time, not because you cheated. Nothing good can come of this."

T'alak's eyes grew hard, his tail lashing. "You understand that this knowledge means I cannot let you live? I had hoped this life would give you a second chance to pledge allegiance to the Realm. Our brotherhood meant something to you once, or so I thought. I'm a fool to think a half-human abomination would have honor. I see nothing I do to help you will make any difference." He stepped back, his tail raising to the side. "Prepare to die, traitor."

Before A'rlon could react, he heard a loud crack, and T'alak slumped heavily to the floor. L'ticia stood behind him, a heavy kitchen utensil in her hand.

"He'll only be out for a while," she cautioned. "Take the human and get out. Please, before he finds out who hit him!"

A'rlon nodded his thanks. "I will make sure this action is rewarded." He checked Catriona for a pulse. Finding a faint flutter under his fingertips, he pulled her into his arms and activated the automatic actuate signal to his quarters on the *L'umina*.

Nothing he did revived her. Scanning revealed severe neural trauma compounded with a fractured skull. If he wanted her to recover, he had only one option. Take her to a human specialist, and those could only be found on Earth where good medical care was encouraged for the alien slaves. Their physical well-being meant better service for the Realm.

So, he had left all nonessential crew on Komodoa, and taken the *L'umina* without delay to the Komodoan-dominated Earth. Once Catriona had been safely ensconced in a hospital, he took the ship out of range of Earth, and had his science officer activate a temporal bubble to bring him here, beside the *Vallo*, to where it all began.

He had one last thing he deemed important to do before he entered that rupture. Accessing the computer, he created a message and sent it through the subspace communications system so it would be delivered to a certain person within the hour. When he had finished, a feeling of contentment washed over him.

Now he felt ready for battle.

47

COLONEL GRREAG pinged Webster on the cruiser. "Professor, how close are you to finding a repair for the temporal imbalance?"

"Almost there, Colonel. Just a bit of quantum mechanics and we should be home free."

Looking at the scientist's image on the screen, Grreag thought he'd never seen a frailer human. "I'm having our Chief Khumalo position a quantum-shielded buoy in these coordinates when we leave. Will you please ensure all black box data pertaining to the repair is piped to it?"

"Understood, Colonel. I'm sure Chief Uzima will take care of that."

"You can be sure of it, Sir," she said.

Grreag nodded. If all went as planned, the two would not be here when they emerged from the rupture. But that repair data had to be available so they could prevent T'alak from entering it again. Grreag had also added his own logs to the buoy should they need to access the information.

The *Vallo* pirouetted and approached the rupture.

"Chief?" inquired Grreag. "Do you want to say anything to your counterpart?"

Khumalo shook her head. "No thanks, Colonel. The girl sent me her log on the mission already; there's nothing to add."

Grreag took his command chair. He wondered how he might have reacted to seeing his doppelganger appear on the viewer. The ebony human appeared to have taken it well, but she was inclined to put a brave front on most things. Like him, she let very few see her vulnerable side.

"Major Benjamin, monitor the *L'umina* during our entrance."

His First Mate nodded, eyes intent on Command Central. Best to keep constant tabs on Captain A'rlon. Grreag didn't trust him. Never had, not even in this timeline, despite Catriona's unfortunate association with him.

They slipped inevitably closer to the swirling rainbow. Something stirred in the pit of his stomach, a sensation he hadn't experienced in a while: the thrill of danger.

"Brace yourselves," he warned as the ship shimmied around them.

They emerged from the rupture on the other side, disoriented by the time travel.

No sooner had the shuddering and grinding stopped, when a bolt of ionizer fire blasted the *Vallo*. T'alak had been waiting.

The discharge kept coming, slamming against the armor. Grreag cursed under his breath. He should have anticipated this.

"Chief, head straight into the *L'umina*, evasive maneuver before impact," he ordered. "Larrar, see if you can incapacitate their weapons array."

246 | *Time Twist*

With Major Benjamin monitoring from Command Central, the *Vallo* zoomed toward the hexagram. The silver ship grew larger at their approach. It looked like a Terran celebration firework, spinning while it spewed out streams of fire. Khumalo called T'alak's bluff.

Just as it appeared the *Vallo* would ram the *L'umina*, the alien ship flipped horizontally at the last minute, avoiding impact.

"Excellent," said Grreag. "Take us in back of them, Chief, then pass control to Lieutenant Larrar. Get in position for implementation of the temporal bubble." He watched the chief smoothly swoop the ship into position, then slip from her seat to join Benjamin at Command Central. Larrar took Khumalo's place, transferring control of both Ops there.

"Lieutenant, calculate the optimum fire position," directed Grreag.

Benjamin stepped back to allow Khumalo to work at the console, her fingers tapping over the keys. "What's keeping A'rlon?" he demanded.

"He has just emerged from the rupture," announced Larrar.

On the viewer Grreag watched the second *L'umina* position herself on the opposite side of T'alak. "How long do they need to be in position for the bubble, Chief?"

"Just a couple of minutes. If they're not fired on."

Grreag looked over his shoulder at Larrar. "Lieutenant, take out T'alak's destroyers."

"Aye, Sir." Having been given free range, the young Leon demonstrated where her talents lay. A burst of staccato torpedo shots ricocheted into the *L'umina's* four destroyers. A series of ionizer bolts followed, and the *Vallo's* viewer was lit a satisfactory red as two of the *L'umina's* destroyers were ruined. T'alak attempted to evade, but Larrar had foreseen that. Her exact calculations had his *L'umina* turning into the barrage.

Grreag bestowed a fanged smile on the Lieutenant. "Good work, Larrar."

"Captain A'rlon is ready for the bubble," announced Khumalo, "and he compliments you on your strategy, Colonel Grreag."

Grreag growled softly. A compliment from a Komodoan was not one he appreciated. "Snare our prey, if you please."

"You got it," she grinned, rapidly typing on the keypad. "Implementing temporal bubble — *now*."

✦

T'alak hissed with satisfaction as his yacht shot away from the *L'umina*, moments before the ship was swallowed by the temporal bubble. He suspected Grreag and A'rlon might try something like that.

Leaving during the shooting had bought him enough time to get round the planet's far side. The rigged quantum shielding hiding the yacht only lasted mere minutes. If *B'llumni* were on his side he would avoid detection. Colonel Grreag and the temporal bubble had duped him once; never twice. The fact that A'rlon had appeared captaining the *L'umina*, proved this strategy had worked once before. Now all he need do was contact himself in this time once more and reset things in motion. He would instruct himself to pick up Webster from the research facility on Suzerain Base, Earth, before Colonel Grreag received the orders to accommodate his experiments.

Ah, and he'd be sure to intercept Catriona Logan's stray molecules ahead of the *Vallo*. The delight he felt at the thought of having something that A'rlon wanted grew intense. Governor C'huln or General B'alarg would not learn of her existence in the altered future. T'alak would win the human's trust, then train and mold her to obey only him. Even though A'rlon would never know her as he did in the original timeline, he would still want her. But as T'alak's property, he would never have her.

He plunged the yacht planetside, homing in on the two humanoid life forms detected on his scanner. In moments he would have Professor Webster, and *The Victory* for Komodoan Realm world domination would be set.

But this time no *L'umina* would return with him.

This time he would leave no margin for error.

Haven's tail felt more like it belonged there. The pain had diminished to a dull throb, and he'd snatched several hours' sleep en route to the Komodoan Realm border. He plotted a meandering course through Realm space that made his route look random. If nothing too much had changed since he had left two years ago, he knew where he could bring *Dream Lover* in to dock on the planet without inviting interest from the military. Haven prayed luck would be in his stars.

He maintained radio silence up to the border, not wanting to alert the Alliance of his intent. Offering a prayer to *P'jarra* he hoped Catriona had avoided being tortured by T'alak. He couldn't bear to think of her being hurt. She wouldn't be in this peril if he hadn't begged her to stay in the 23rd century. He'd been selfish, only thinking of himself. He should have let her go back to her own time. She could have escaped danger when the rift would strike in 2001. She had knowledge of where the safe areas would be and she could have settled there, taken

248 | *Time Twist*

precautions to survive the disaster.

He had never questioned that expecting her to wait around faithfully while he absented himself on Intelligence missions, might perhaps be cruel. He had prevented Catriona from making other attachments in this century, and had contributed to her isolation at the ACC.

Haven hadn't realized how much he had come to depend on her until her absence. She deserved so much more than he had given her, and by *P'jarra*, he'd make damn sure to make it up to her.

As he slipped *Dream Lover* across the Komodoan border, he switched the subspace radio back on. It would look odd to the Realm authorities if he didn't; they'd suspect he had more to hide than contraband alcohol and luxuries.

A series of bleeps startled him, shattering the velvet serenity of space. Incoming message? Impossible! No one knew of his location. With unease, he downloaded it.

"Greetings, Lieutenant Colonel Haven," said an image of himself, but harder looking, with short hair. "If this message reaches you instead of being piped back to me, then I will have been successful in my attempt to restore the timeline corrupted by T'alak. And if you are half the man I am, you are on your way to rescue your human mate, Catriona Logan. She is being held in the House of T'alak, in the Third Province." The image raised one eyebrow. "She deserves better than a life of slavery. May the stars aid you. A'rlon out."

Haven sat back in complete surprise. Although he shouldn't have been so taken unawares; he would do exactly the same in his counterpart's place. His spirits soared at the confirmation that Catriona hadn't been killed in the actuate accident, but then plummeted at the thought of her imprisoned in T'alak's estate. By the stars, he would destroy T'alak if he had harmed Catriona.

A distorted timeline, his counterpart had said. He thought carefully. If the other A'rlon knew Haven to be Catriona's lover, then he must have heard it from her. Somehow she must not have been affected by the distortion. He shook his head. Too many unanswered questions. He wished the message had contained more information than it had, but trust himself to be so cryptic.

48

THE APPLAUSE was deafening. For a moment Catriona had no idea what the sudden rush of noise was, but years of training and discipline brought her up sharply. She moved forward just as she felt the hand on the small of her back, pushing her into action.

With a brilliant smile, she moved to the front of the stage in front of the footlights, where she could glimpse the first couple of rows beyond. On its feet, the audience stamped and clapped their ovation. Dazed, Catriona lifted her crinoline gown and dropped into a deep curtsy. The applause increased, punctuated with whistles and calls. Catriona's head felt like it would split in two with the worst headache she had ever had. When she bowed, pain shot across her temples. She winced, almost stumbling but for the supporting hand under her elbow. She glanced sideways and her heart leapt to see Grreag beside her.

The actors behind her joined them, fanning out in a long line across the stage. She bowed as one with them, once, twice, a third time. Then the curtain came down and she could relax.

But only for a moment. She most certainly was back in her London Fringe production of *Beauty and the Beast*, but when? Her heart raced. How did she get back on Earth? When was the temporal and spatial rift going to hit?

The stage emptied quickly as her colleagues dashed to change out of their sweaty costumes. She reached for Grreag, then drew back when she saw him remove his mask. Jason, who played the part, winked at her and trotted off into the wings.

Catriona tried to calm her racing heart and stood watching as one by one, everyone trickled away, leaving her alone. The stage dimmed to the dullness of work lights as the crew got the set ready for tomorrow's performance. But which tomorrow?

She felt an overwhelming sense of loss. If she had ever doubted her decision to stay in the 23rd century, she had no doubt now. The very thought of being back here filled her with despair and her head hurt all the more. It was imperative she find out the date. She tried not to imagine what she'd do if she'd missed Professor Webster's first experimental time bubble.

Suddenly it all came back. Being captured again by Captain T'alak, the alternative timeline, the A'rlon who wasn't Haven. Jesus, she must

250 | *Time Twist*

have been brought back to Earth, but didn't remember it. Had the timeline been distorted beyond repair? If Webster didn't arrive when he was supposed to, then she would be forced to stay on Earth and flee to where she could survive the coming devastation of the planet. Then the Leontor would arrive and make first contact with Earth.

She wondered how Leontor Control would react, finding a human fluent in Komodoan, but not her own language? She was in as much danger here as on Komodoa.

Stung into action, she marched across the stage, almost tripping on her period costume gown.

"Coming for a drink, Cat?" yelled Bill, one of the stage crew.

She stopped, looking up at him as he swung a piece of scenery into place. His speech sounded garbled. How could she get by if she only knew an alien language?

"Hey, you owe me a beer! See you in the *Elephant and Castle*?"

Catriona recognized the words. "*The Elephant and Castle*?" she repeated, testing them.

Bill swung down one of the ropes to land neatly on the stage. "Hurry up or you'll be late."

To her relief she understood him. "What date?" she stumbled.

Bill looked at her askance. "What's the matter with your voice?"

She coughed apologetically, patting her throat. "Today date," she said more emphatically. The more he talked the more her ear retuned itself.

"Saving your voice, are you? Thought you sounded a bit rough tonight. You're not coming down with a cold, are you?"

"Date?"

"June 21st, you dork!" He pretended to knock on the side of her head. "Hello, anyone home?" He chortled with childish glee as he skipped off to finish his work.

So, tomorrow would be the 22nd when Professor Webster had come. *Would* come. But that meant she had to do one more performance as Beauty!

The realization hit her. Tomorrow, the rupture would ruin Earth. Panic flooded through her. She should warn someone…

Forcing herself under control, she tried to think rationally. Who would she warn? Who would listen? Scenarios from dozens of science fiction movies ran through her head. No one would believe her. She'd be wasting her time, trying to warn anyone.

Her heart actually hurt, felt swollen under her ribcage. She choked back a sob. She had to choose. Go to Heathrow Airport tonight and try and get a flight to the African continent, where the rupture was least destructive, or wait it out until tomorrow night when Professor Webster was scheduled to test his temporal bubble.

Taking a breath, she managed to calm herself. There really wasn't any choice, she realized. She could never live in peace unless she attempted to get back to the 23rd century, and the new life she'd made for herself there.

Having decided, she concentrated on the problem of getting through another performance of *Beauty and the Beast*. If her command of English didn't return pronto, she could fake laryngitis. Besides, she didn't know if she could remember the lines of the show, let alone sing them. It had been too long, over two years.

She made her way to the dressing room she shared with the other female cast members. They had already changed into their street clothes.

"Jesus, Cat—get a move on!" said Maggie, who played one of her sisters in the show.

Catriona stared. Yesterday Maggie had been dead centuries ago, now here she stood, pinning back her light blonde hair from her face.

"Mags!" Catriona moved to embrace her.

The girl laughed, returning her hug. "You're acting really weird, you know that? Come on, you need a drink."

Catriona nodded with a grin, hurrying to change out of her gown. 'Drink' was a word she well understood. She rummaged around in the dressing room first aid kit and found some aspirin for her headache.

Alone, she slathered her face with cold cream and washed off the greasy stage makeup. The heavy, powdered wig she wore on stage had made her hair flat and lanky-looking, so she fluffed it up and sprayed it with gel. She found her blue jeans, ivory tank and black leather jacket she'd worn to the theater. How rough and constricting the garments felt compared to the Komodoan robes she'd become accustomed to wearing. She hadn't worn footwear for so long, she almost left the dressing room in her bare feet. Pulling on white socks and sneakers, she grabbed her purse and followed her colleagues to the nearby *Elephant and Castle*.

The smell of London's evening air assaulted her with choking car fumes and an overall aroma of staleness. *Poor Earth*, lamented Catriona, thinking of the bracing freshness of northern Komodoa. She stopped in confusion, to the annoyance of a man walking behind her.

"Bloody tourists!" he snapped, diverting round her.

Surely she couldn't miss Komodoa! Had she lost her mind? Oh God, let Webster arrive as planned tomorrow, she prayed.

252 | *Time Twist*

Arriving at the pub, Catriona hesitated on the pavement. She knew exactly how it looked inside. Beyond the glass doors lay the faded, marble hallway where the temporal bubble had caught her. Beyond that the noisy, smoky interior of the bar. Threadbare red velvet stools and carpet, dark wood bar and wall-panels, a plethora of brass and leather paraphernalia adorning the walls. It would be crammed with patrons: tourists and locals, all talking, drinking and smoking.

Catriona shuddered. She couldn't face it. If she wanted to go through tomorrow's performance of *Beauty and the Beast,* she'd need to go home and study the libretto and listen to the tape a few times. Relief flooded her as she turned away.

Moving to cross the road, she jumped out of the way of a speeding black London taxicab. The cacophony of the traffic sounded unbearably loud as Catriona made her way toward the *Elephant and Castle* underground station.

She took a short cut down a deserted side street. Halfway to the station, a couple of youths stepped in front of her.

"All right, bitch, hand us yer bag," demanded one of them in a course Cockney accent.

She hesitated, eyeing them. They looked scrawny, not too fit, by the looks of them. Probably stealing for their next fix, she thought. What had her world become?

"Come on, bitch, give it here and you won't get hurt."

"Piss off, you wee bastards!" shouted Catriona in her best Glaswegian accent.

The youths looked taken aback, obviously not used to resistance. "Scottish whore!" spat one, reaching for her purse.

Catriona hoisted the purse up and slammed him under the chin. He staggered back and she spun round, smashing the heel of her hand into the other youth's nose. Without a beat, she kicked her leg back and caught the first youth in the balls.

Bolting for the brightly lit station ahead, she glanced back to see the downed youth being helped up by the other, his hand pasted to his broken nose. She sent a prayer of thanks for the karate lessons at the ACC.

Once in the comparative safety of the Underground, she dug around in her purse for her railcard. The half hour ride to her bedsit in Brent Cross passed uneventfully, but she found riding the train unpleasant. The carriage was filthy. Litter clogged the passageways, and every time the doors opened at a station, a smell of rotting garbage wafted in.

At last the train rumbled and hissed into Brent Cross. Catriona stepped onto the deserted, dirty platform. She paused to watch the train rumble off without her. In its wake, a whirlwind of litter and flattened paper coffee cups danced on the track. This world felt so grubby and despondent. Catriona climbed the many stone steps from the platform and emerged into the street.

All the shops except Mr. Aziz's were closed. She gave him a cheery wave as she always did when passing. He looked lonely and depressed huddled at his counter, but he flashed a white-toothed grin in return.

The rest of the street lay quiet as she walked the hundred yards to where she lived. Catriona shuddered with distaste as the house came into view. How pleased she had been with it when she first found it. She rented the upstairs front bed-sitting room, and shared kitchen and bathroom with the other three tenants.

A strong scent of decaying roses assaulted her as she turned into the front yard. She'd always loved this odor, but tonight it smelled cloying, sickly. The landlord, who lived in the lower half of the house also dealt in junk, so the path to the front door had an obstacle course of decrepit, rusting fridges and ovens. How ugly it looked. Catriona fervently prayed to God that Professor Webster would show up tomorrow. She could not live like this; she'd even take T'alak's spire room!

She unlocked the door and clambered up the creaky stairs to her room. The hall smelled of leaking natural gas and cat piss. She switched on the light in her bedsit, pushing the door closed behind her. Lord. How come she hadn't noticed how disgusting that wallpaper looked before? It all looked so dingy and primitive. Sinking down onto the bed, Catriona burst into tears. She curled up and cried until her head hurt so much she had to force herself to stop.

All her doubts about staying in the 23rd century had vanished. She missed Haven, Grreag, and Uzi so much it physically hurt. Rousing herself, she searched for tissues to blow her nose, but had to settle for toilet paper. Crying would get her nowhere. After all, she only had to stay here for one night, and then she'd be far, far away.

49

CATRIONA SLEPT fitfully. The mattress felt lumpy and unsupportive under her. Every time she rolled over, the covers twisted

254 | *Time Twist*

around her in a most constricting manner. Her sore joints ached for the supple pliancy of a gel-bed's warm cocoon.

The early morning trains at the nearby station jerked her awake. She lay for a moment, unsure of her surroundings. At five thirty, the dawn had just started to creep over the rooftops. From her window Catriona saw a pink half-moon silhouetted in the tentative sunrise between red brick chimneys.

She felt too apprehensive about the day ahead to go back to sleep, so she got up to shower and dress. The four people who shared the bathroom and kitchen with her were not yet awake. Just as well. What could she possibly say to them?

By the time she headed out the door toward the underground, she had decided where she'd go. About forty minutes later she emerged from Westminster station. The train had been crowded even that early in the morning, but the throng of regular commuters hadn't yet barged into the day.

The early sun shone brighter as Catriona walked along the embankment by the river Thames toward Westminster Bridge. The picturesque Elizabethan Houses of Parliament sat on the opposite side, perfectly reflected in the still, sunlit water. Big Ben's thunderous boom announced that seven o'clock had struck. On the other side of the bridge the London Eye was still, rising high above the Thames in a giant, glittering white ring.

Catriona walked halfway across Westminster Bridge, then stopped to gaze out over the Thames. She had wanted to do this ever since she had read William Wordsworth's sonnet *Composed Upon Westminster Bridge*, but never made the time to go. Looking about at the sleek, high-tech buildings mingled with the elegance of the treasured ancient ones, Catriona mused how different it would have been back in 1802, when the sonnet had been written.

This City now doth, like a garment wear
The beauty of the morning; silent, bare...

Catriona smiled ruefully. Silent and bare? She could hardly hear herself think above the continuous roar of the morning traffic on the bridge behind her, and the clackity-clack as trains crossed the river. She wished she could feel, even for one moment, the silent majesty of the city back then. Shocked, she regretted the thought. Tomorrow after the rupture struck, this city would be silent.

Focusing on her task ahead, she felt grateful she had been put back a day early in time. It had given her an opportunity to say good-bye to this world, something denied her last time. She realized she could even make *Arrum,* as her Leontor colleagues had demanded she do. Not that she believed it would make any difference to her fate or the Earth's, but it couldn't hurt.

At her dinner party, so long ago, yet so far in the future, Qiterr and Zerreem had told her she must make a gift to appease the spirits, asking their permission to leave her birthplace. What had she to make a gift of? She fingered her locket, feeling physical pain at the thought of losing it. Her glance fell on the watch she'd retrieved from her jewelry box. It was more ornate than the one she'd worn the first time she'd been taken to the 23rd century — a replica of one of the Duchess of Windsor's pieces. Fashioned as a bracelet, the watch face lay hidden under a diamanté lid. Its faux stones glittered brashly in the morning sun, and Catriona decided it would be a perfect gift. Not only would this be a symbol of her complicated, fake-feeling life in the 21st century, it was also the very representation of time itself. Unclipping it from her wrist, she removed Webster's disk from her locket and slipped it under the watch's lid. She couldn't bring Webster's data back to the future. There must be no chance of the Komodoan Realm ever getting hold of it again. She held the watch over the stone railing of the bridge.

"Please, *please* spare the Earth from the rupture," she whispered before letting the watch drop. "And please let me go back to my life in the future."

Catriona stood in the wings, wanting to throw up from nerves. She'd spent all day in the theater, practicing her songs and lines. She found the words came back to her very quickly. She almost didn't need to know their meaning as long as they phonetically fell into place. She felt fairly confident she'd get through the performance okay.

During the day, she'd decided to inform Professor Webster exactly what effects his temporal bubble would wreak in the future. She wrote a long, detailed letter, describing how the Komodoan Realm would stop at nothing to get the invention, including posing a genetically altered agent as Webster's assistant, Pauline Morrison.

Now made up, corseted and dressed like a peasant girl, Catriona stood ready for her opening number as Beauty. When the overture struck up, she realized this would be the very last professional performance she'd make as an actress, whether she got off this doomed planet or not.

256 | *Time Twist*

Before she knew it, the show had almost finished. As Catriona watched the Queen of Roses transform the Beast into a prince, she felt a stab of pain, knowing these to be the last moments of her acting career, and perhaps of her life. But what a wonderful way to end it, she comforted herself.

She almost missed her cue, moving forward just in time to embrace the prince. Then they had the last chorus, and she took her final bow. She stayed just a little too long at the footlights to soak up the applause, much to the irritation of the rest of the cast.

Finally, the curtain came down and she made her way to the dressing room, peeling off her sweat-soaked gown.

"Coming to the anniversary party, Cat?" asked Maggie.

"You bet!" Catriona looped her arm through her friend's as they left the theater together.

The cast flooded into the *Elephant and Castle*, their rambunctiousness almost clearing the bar. The bartender produced several bottles of inexpensive champagne and everyone lifted their glasses in toast: "One more year!"

Catriona looked around with a heavy heart at the enthusiastic and happy faces. Thanks to the rupture, in a couple of hours all this would cease to exist.

She dragged over a stool and squeezed amongst the crowd at a table where she could easily survey the entire bar area. She nursed her champagne until it became flat and warm.

What if Webster didn't come?

The dissonance of chatter and clinking glasses around her made it hard to concentrate. Her head ached worse than ever, and she fought against nausea. She needed to visit the loo, but didn't dare leave her vantage point in case she missed the professor.

Watching her colleagues, Catriona felt a little in awe of the inflexibility of time. She went over in her mind the last time she'd sat here, two hundred and sixty years ago. Or a few moments ago, depending on how she looked at it. She could remember word for word the conversation they had about one of the pages forgetting his lines during the show.

Catriona kept an anxious eye on the door. She couldn't remember exactly the moment when Professor Webster appeared; only that he had collided with her on her way out.

An hour passed, and Catriona still nursed the champagne. She needed the loo even worse now. Where could he be? What if he didn't come at all?

"You all right, Cat?" demanded Bill. "Here!" he called to the bartender. "This girl's having serious alcohol withdrawals. Send us over a Glenfiddich!"

Catriona laughed, déja vu making her feel giddy. "That sounds exactly what the doctor ordered," she agreed.

The shot of golden whisky appeared before her. Catriona lifted it up and downed the fiery liquid in one swallow.

A movement at the bar caught her eye. Through the fast-growing crowd she watched the bartender spill a glass of beer, leaping aside. Then she saw him, half-obscured in the shadows to the right of the bar. Professor Webster at last. Relief flooded her.

Her heart lurching, she stood. Looking down at her colleagues, she rapped the table. "I have to leave now," she announced, fighting the threatening tears. "You guys take care."

They didn't hear her over the noise they made. She met Bill's eye and he winked, then took over her stool. Swallowing the painful lump in her throat, Catriona turned and approached the man at the bar, huddled in his raincoat. He half-twisted away when he realized she made a beeline for him.

"Professor Webster." She touched his arm.

The man's jaw dropped, his blue eyes widening in disbelief. "Who are you?"

"It's a long story. I must return with you when you reactivate the temporal bubble. It'll all make sense later."

"But who are you?"

"No one important. But I got caught in your bubble the last time we were here, and in order for things to work out the way they're supposed to, I need to get caught in it again."

"Now, wait a minute." Catriona watched Webster's panicked face reflect the many thoughts careening through his head. "We're in some form of Möebius twist if this is happening for the second time. If you weren't supposed to be in my bubble the first time, then in order to right events, you mustn't be in it the second."

"Professor," hissed Catriona, grabbing hold of his arm hard enough to dig her nails into him. "I've invested over two years of my life at the Alliance Cadet College, and I'm a lieutenant, for Christ's sake! Not to mention I have a relationship with an Intelligence officer that needs mending. And there's something you need to know about what happens to our solar system tonight."

258 | *Time Twist*

Relaxing her grip, she told him as briefly as she could about the rupture that would strike the Earth at any moment.

His blue eyes grew wide with horror. "Dear God in heaven! Lieutenant, surely you must realize it's your presence in the bubble that causes the rupture?"

Catriona stared at him, her soul sickened to its very core. Her thoughts tumbled in confusion. If her presence caused the rupture, she had to stay here. But if she didn't jump tonight, without her T'alak would capture Webster and the disk, and the Realm would make the temporal bubble weapon anyway. And she wouldn't meet Grreag and help him relax with humans, and Jack... Without her, Jack Haven would never leave the Komodoan Military and would be cold-hearted A'rlon for the rest of his life.

Bringing all her Alliance combat training to bear, Catriona manhandled Webster toward the door. "Let's get out of here where we can hear ourselves think." She let go of him in the shabby marble hallway, and spoke urgently. "Listen to me; you must tell Colonel Grreag on the *Vallo* exactly what's happened here. Tell him to trust Uzima Khumalo implicitly. You must also tell him to find a way to contact a Commander A'rlon in the Komodoan Realm Military... Oh, God," she choked, realizing how useless this was. Her breath came in ragged gasps.

"Hold on, Lieutenant. We can't calculate how you not going will affect the future you remember." He pulled out his device, his fingers speeding over the keys.

"What are you doing?" she demanded. He ignored her. "Professor, tell me what the hell you're doing!" She knew her panicked voice sounded pathetically high and thin.

"Wait, Lieutenant. I'm just..." With a flurry he finished and grinned lopsidedly. "I think I have a way to do this without causing the rupture. I've recalculated the bubble for both of us. To balance the change, we'll be put back earlier than we left — by how much I'm not entirely certain. I will return to the lab, but I'm afraid your molecules cannot, as the original bubble is singular."

Catriona stared, her heart racing in relief and hope. "Don't worry about me; I'll get picked up by someone," she assured him. She prayed to God, the Great Fang, or *P'jarra* that she would.

"It will still impact the continuum, because only a single entity arrived here, but I assure you it won't cause a rupture, just a hiccup."

Catriona's throat felt bone dry. "You're absolutely positive?"

"Ninety-eight percent sure, and those are good enough odds for me. There are no accidents in science, you know."

"No?" Catriona felt like beating him senseless. "Here," she fished out the letter she'd written and thrust it into his hand. "Make sure you read this thoroughly when you get back to your lab. It's vital you do."

Thoughtfully, he took the folded paper and slipped it into a coat pocket. He checked his timepiece. "I will, I give you my word. Get ready, it's time."

Catriona held her breath, offering a prayer as a light surrounded them, whipping them away from the hallway of the *Elephant and Castle*.

50

COLONEL GRREAG strode into the control cabin. It had been an uneventful run since Catriona Logan's memorial service, he thought, moving across the cabin.

Benjamin looked up from Central Command. "Rupture dead ahead, Colonel," he reported.

"Don't get too close," ordered Grreag. "All stop."

He took his command chair and studied the rupture on the main viewer.

"No wonder that thing blasted clear across Alliance space," exclaimed Khumalo from NavOps. "It's vast."

Grreag nodded agreement, his ears flattening. "Are we alone?"

She checked her console. "Affirmative, Colonel."

"Launch a probe."

Larrar sent a miniature bell-shaped projectile hurtling into the giant mouth, and they waited for data to be relayed back to the *Vallo*.

"It's certainly impressive looking," said Benjamin, watching from Central Command.

"Most deadly things are," observed Grreag.

TactOps bleeped, spewing data. Larrar's golden-furred fingers sped over the controls, deciphering the codes.

"Report," ordered Grreag, trying to locate the probe on the viewer. "What happened?"

"The probe's disappeared into the rupture," said Benjamin.

Khumalo swiveled her chair round to face Colonel Grreag. "Sir, if this rupture was caused by Realm temporal experimentation, the probe

260 | *Time Twist*

could have been sealed off in time, impenetrable to our scans." Her console emitted a second warning bleep. "The rupture is shrinking in on itself," she reported.

"A Komodoan warship has entered the sector," announced Lieutenant Larrar.

On the viewer a massive hexagram spun across the stars, slowing its rotation as it approached the rupture.

Khumalo breathed in sharply. "That's the fucking *L'umina!*"

Grreag's fur rippled. He looked at Benjamin and said, "You're relieved, Chief. The Major will take over."

"No, Sir, please." Khumalo kept her voice even. "I'm fine. I need to be here for this."

Grreag nodded. "Very well."

"Thank you, Colonel. Shall I ping them?"

"Yes." Grreag studied the enemy ship turning effortlessly before him. It was likely that T'alak still captained the *L'umina*, and Grreag knew his intentions could not be benign.

"*L'umina!*" he said. "You have invaded Alliance territory. I demand an explanation!"

The *L'umina* didn't respond.

"I don't believe it." Benjamin pointed at the screen. "The idiot's heading into the rupture!"

"The rift has shrunk too much to allow an object the size of a ship through," reported Khumalo.

Grreag leaned forward in his seat. "Ping the *L'umina* again," he ordered. "What by the Fang are you doing, Captain T'alak? Your ship will be crushed!"

T'alak appeared on the viewer. "Don't try to trick me, Leontor," he snarled. "You can't keep me from my destiny."

He snapped off his screen, leaving Grreag watching the *L'umina* spin into the rupture.

"His destiny?" Benjamin shot Grreag a puzzled look.

Grreag shrugged, one ear flicking forward.

On the viewer, the *L'umina* had reached the rupture's maw. The hexagram-shape flipped horizontal, and began entry into the swirling rainbow within.

"He's not going to make it!" gloated Khumalo.

The *L'umina* got halfway into the rupture when the ghostly lips closed around it. Spectacular lightning bolts of varying shades spurted out from the ship.

Grreag began to shake his head, the gesture following through his hackles and body until he found himself on his feet. Much as he thought the universe would be better off without T'alak, he couldn't stand by and watch his ship and crew disintegrate.

"Chief, bring us closer. Lieutenant Larrar, lock traherence on the *L'umina* and tow her out of there." He ignored the dubious look Khumalo shot him. "Make it quick, she hasn't much time left."

He felt the *Vallo* jolt under him as the invisible stream latched onto the Komodoan ship. The edge of the rupture billowed in and out as the *L'umina* struggled to escape its grip.

The ship tremored around them as power increased the stream. The shaking had reached a peak of bone-shattering intensity when the *L'umina* slipped free.

Larrar ran a scan over both ships. "The middle section of the *L'umina* is warped. No one could have survived on those decks."

Grreag stared at the viewer in disbelief. The *L'umina* had crinkled at the center, bending up on either side. Behind her, the rupture had become nothing but a ghostly trail of interstellar dust.

"Ping T'alak again," ordered Grreag.

T'alak appeared on the screen, his face waxen. "How dare you interfere, Leontor filth!" he hissed.

"Do you need assistance, Captain?" asked Grreag.

"No!" Once again he disconnected.

Grreag met Benjamin's grin. "You're welcome," he growled, his ears relaxed.

The *L'umina* began a halting spin, testing her engines. Grreag wondered that the ship could be functional at all. The Komodoan vessel spun unevenly away.

"Doesn't that take the cake?" snorted Benjamin. "He'd be dead, and his crew with him if we hadn't intervened. And by the looks of those spinners, it'll take him a while to get home."

Grreag bared a full-fanged smile. "Maybe it'll give him time to think about his witlessness, attempting to enter a closing spatial rupture." He paused for a moment. "What did he think could be in there that made it so imperative he go after it?"

"I suppose that's something we may never know," answered Benjamin.

"Colonel?" Khumalo frowned at her console, "I'm picking up an Alliance security transmission: apparently there's a quantumly shielded buoy nearby..."

51

AFTER WEBSTER'S temporal bubble snatched her from the *Elephant and Castle*, Catriona found herself back in T'alak's estate on Komodoa. It looked like everything had gone to plan, although how much earlier she was in time she couldn't be certain. And what of the Earth? Had Webster's adjustments to the temporal bubble successfully deflected the rupture?

She needed to effect an escape from Komodoa without delay. She did not reveal to L'ticia that she now spoke fluent Komodoan, allowing her jailer to speak in broken English when addressing her.

Standing in the open doorway of T'alak's house, Catriona watched as L'ticia flew over the walls in the house skiff and disappeared from view. She turned from the door and made straight for the kitchen utility chamber. Secreted under the sink at the back of the cupboard, she had stashed a bundle of rope and a small ax, honed to razor sharpness.

In the kitchen, Catriona packed herself up a supply of cold meat, bread, and a container of water. She glanced around the kitchen for a moment before going into the hall. She hoped L'ticia would not get in trouble, but Catriona had to get away. If she waited around any longer, T'alak would be back to deliver her to the scientist, Governor C'huln.

Guilt gnawed at her. She had tricked L'ticia into providing the means for her escape. The Komodoan had taken Catriona along to forage for some roots outside the walls. When they entered the edge of the forest, L'ticia had referred to a small disc in her palm. Although there appeared to be more than four directions on the compass, Catriona learned which symbol pointed toward the town, a hundred miles away to the east, where L'ticia bought her supplies.

After they returned, Catriona noted L'ticia left the compass on the windowsill in the kitchen. It remained there a couple of days later, and Catriona moved it out of sight. When it hadn't been disturbed for another day, she took it and kept it with her constantly, fingering it as a talisman of hope.

Out in the hallway she chose a heavy cloak hanging on the wall, and wrapped it around herself. Made from a black, silky pelt, it smelled of brine. Stepping outside, she made sure she closed the door. She avoided the locked gate, heading around the side of the house where the wall had crumbled enough for her to scale.

Moments later she stood on the other side, moving down toward the nearby lake. The air felt moist and cold, the mauve sky threatening, but Catriona's heart lifted. With the ax to hew hand and footholds in the tree trunks to avoid the *Letum* at night, she should make it to the town in a few days. The black pelt had a hood she could put up once she got there, and hopefully make her look less conspicuous. In the town she'd have more chance of finding a communicator, no matter what she had to do to gain access to it.

The forest closed in around her with smothering gloom. The mossy green mist grew thicker, and Catriona pulled out the compass and held it in her palm. The pointer swung to the north, and she headed off accordingly.

The trunks and branches became dense, reminding Catriona of a scene from the animated Disney *Snow White*, where the princess ran panicked through the forest. Avoiding scratches and cuts from the thick branches proved impossible. Dismayed, Catriona pulled out her ax and hewed her way through. Blisters began to form, slowing her down. It would take her a week at this rate, and her food and water wouldn't last more than a couple of days.

She kept going, trying to ignore the painful sores on her palms and fingers. The sudden, chilling yowl of a *Letum* made her realize she'd lost track of time. Quickly, she scrambled up onto the lower branches, and hauled herself high enough without using the ax. Settling herself precariously on a branch, she pulled the cloak tight about her, and ate a little cold meat and drank some water. She could hear the sickening squelching as *Letum* congregated in the darkness below. Disgusting, filthy creatures. She shuddered and hugged the cloak tighter.

Lights slashed through the blackness. Catriona tightened her numb fingers around the trunk to steady herself. L'ticia's skiff lowered through a gap in the trees and hovered several feet away from Catriona. Her heart pounded. How had L'ticia found her so quickly?

The side hatch slid open. A metal rung ladder protruded downward and L'ticia appeared in the open hatch. In the light from the beams, the Komodoan's eyes looked like dark pewter, glinting with fury.

"Jump here!" she shrieked over the engine thrum.

"How did you find me?" yelled Catriona.

"You only alien in province, stupid. Jump or I feed you to *Letum*!"

Numb and rigid with fear, Catriona couldn't get her limbs to move. She'd never make it to the ladder. "I can't!"

L'ticia lifted a carbine and aimed. Catriona knew from experience

264 | *Time Twist*

that the Komodoan wasn't bluffing. She raised herself to a crouching position on the branch and lunged. She grabbed hold of the hatchway, almost losing her grip. L'ticia reached down to grab her wrist and yanked her into the skiff.

With the hatch closed against the hostile forest, L'ticia pushed her into the passenger seat and piloted the skiff back to T'alak's estate.

"L'ticia, I'm sorry," began Catriona.

"Be silent!"

During the tense and swift ride back, Catriona's mood swung between despair and anger. Wasn't it every prisoner's obligation to try and escape? Wouldn't L'ticia do the same if their roles were reversed?

Once docked, L'ticia dragged Catriona from the skiff into the house. She took her straight down the stairs to the baths.

"You know I must punish," she said.

Catriona didn't struggle as L'ticia hauled her to one of the pillars and tied her to it. The rope cut into her flesh, and her damp clothes didn't help. Captain T'alak had flogged her back only once, but the memory of the slicing pain stayed vivid with Catriona. She gritted her teeth, hoping it would soon be over.

The lash came as a shock, nonetheless. Cutting through both clothing and skin, Catriona cried out. She sagged against her restraints as L'ticia struck twice more. Then the whipping ceased and Catriona slumped against the pillar, her back flaring in pain. L'ticia moved close behind her.

"Oh, *P'jarra*! Human skin thin. I not know."

She took off the restraints and Catriona felt the torn clothing gently being removed. Taking Catriona by the hand L'ticia led her to the side of the bath, where she had her sit, legs dangling in the water. Gently, she washed the human down, and patted her dry.

Exhausted, Catriona allowed L'ticia to care for her. It felt very good to be so comforted as though she were a child. L'ticia smoothed a cool substance over her back, and Catriona recognized the sparking instant relief of marsh-peony gel.

Then L'ticia led Catriona to her own chamber, where she gave her a cup of something herbal to drink. Like before it affected her immediately. Catriona's muscles loosened as all the tension and pain ebbed from her.

Head supported in a harness, she lay in the gel-bed. The soft warmth of the liquid surrounded her, keeping her as safe as though she were in the womb. Someone moved behind her and held her close. Catriona sighed in pleasure, relaxing against the firm, strong body.

Hands caressed and soothed Catriona's breasts, softly tempting her nipples to arousal. A pressure eased up between her legs, searching for the part of her that ached the most with desire. Catriona gasped and shivered as the pressure found just the right place. Her world became a myriad of sensations, soft and beautiful, achingly sensuous. The pressure increased slowly, swirling and pressing, vibrating and teasing, until Catriona thrashed in complete erotic abandon. She climaxed, shuddering over and over as spasms of satisfaction ebbed from her. Then she slept, dreamlessly and deeply.

Catriona opened lazy eyes to the diffused morning light. Her body felt airborne, relaxed, and at peace. Then she moved and pain registered down her back. She tried to look round but the gel-bed harness restrained her head. Unsnapping it, she twisted round to find herself sleeping with L'ticia, head-to-toe in the gel-bed. The Komodoan's tail was curled around her ankle. Had *L'ticia* brought her to orgasm? Confused and a bit panicked, Catriona thrashed out of the gel-bed. L'ticia, woken by the tidal wave, eased out of the bed.

"You well, Catriona? Pain better?"

Catriona allowed the gel to dry on her body. "Ah, much, thanks." She paused, watching L'ticia slip on her robe. "Em... did we... you know."

"We pleasure? Oh yes."

Catriona felt her face flush with embarrassment.

"What is matter?" asked L'ticia. "You not like?"

Catriona barked a laugh. "I did like; that's the problem."

"Why?"

Catriona paused, considering her answer. "I don't know how to explain. I've never been with a woman before. Well, a Komodoan woman. Or any woman."

"Is normal for Komodoan please each other. Honor goddess *P'jarra*."

"I see." Catriona didn't know what else to say. "Thank you."

52

CATRIONA STOOD back to admire her handiwork. A myriad of glowing, colored lights hung throughout the hallway and the great

266 | *Time Twist*

room. Coupled with the ever-flowing dance of the water sculpture, the effect resembled a glittering mass of rainbow light, flickering like luminescent fireflies. *Perfect*, thought Catriona. L'ticia and her goddess would be happy. She paused mid-thought, frowning. It had been dark for at least an hour, and L'ticia had still not returned from her weekly visit to town for supplies.

Catriona had found the decorations moldering in the storeroom. Asking L'ticia about them, she learned it was the custom to adorn Komodoan homes for the *O'tium* festival, rather like holiday decorations back on Earth. Looking for something to pass the time while L'ticia was away, she decided she'd string up the lights as a surprise.

Since Catriona's abortive escape attempt had brought them closer, she made sure to warn L'ticia of T'alak-zan's interest in her visits with N'elak in the Third Quadrant. L'ticia, dumbfounded at her human prisoner's sudden and very fluent knowledge of the language, had no reason to doubt her. As a result, she stayed home on the day T'alak's son would have spotted her, so he never came to the house, and Catriona did not kill him. She never told L'ticia that in the other timeline, the servant had engaged in sexual relations with T'alak. Some things were just better not shared, she decided.

L'ticia had chosen to coach Catriona in Realm culture, in response to a remark Catriona made about T'alak treating her like a savage. Learning how to be a female servant in a Komodoan household could scarcely be considered obtaining vital Realm military secrets, but Catriona clung to the fact that anything she could learn would be valuable to the Alliance, if... *when* she escaped.

Outside, this part of Komodoa lay blanketed in a brittle, frosty rose-hued snow. Along with the colored lights, the sight reminded Catriona of Christmas time on Earth. Padding from the hallway to the great room, Catriona looked in pleasure at the *O'tium* lights, strewn gaily across the room to surround the pillars. The fireplace flickered with a flame more red than it would be on Earth, bathing the room in a rich scarlet glow. It looked lovely. In a short time, the over-heated, alien stone house had become strangely familiar. She gave a bitter laugh, the sound reverberating in the lonely mansion. No one could wish for a more luxurious and peaceful prison, she thought. But the peace couldn't last.

A log in the fireplace sputtered, sending a spark out near the floor cushions. Catriona moved to put the fireguard back in place. Kneeling down, she gazed into the flames, watching them reach upward to escape the confines of the grate.

A sudden wash of bright light slashed across the windows. L'ticia had returned at last. Catriona ran to the hall to greet her and struck a pose.

"What do you think?" she asked, holding out her arms with a flourish. The smile froze on her face. Captain T'alak stood in the open doorway, his dark eyes hooded in the shadows.

He stepped inside, slamming the door behind him. Catriona quickly recovered. Taking a deep breath, she lowered her eyes.

"This female apologizes and welcomes the honored Captain home." She just couldn't address him as *master*.

She felt T'alak's eyes boring into her. "Where is L'ticia?"

"The honorable servant is in town getting supplies," she answered, continuing the formal address L'ticia had drilled into her. From under her lashes, she watched him look around the sparkling hallway, his tail twitching in disbelief.

"I will bathe," he announced. "Then you may serve break fast." He stalked past her down the steps to the bathroom.

Catriona hesitated. She knew a servant should soap T'alak down and rinse him before he entered the pool. And if she had to serve his food... What kind of people were they that the males would expect to mate with almost anyone after he'd eaten a meal?

Controlling her nerves, she followed T'alak down the stairs. He had unfastened his tunic, his tail hanging tiredly behind him. Catriona soaked a sponge and filled it with soap. Eyes on the floor, she approached in dread.

He turned. With a hiss, he plucked the sponge from her. "Bring me a house robe."

Catriona bowed and hurried back up the stairs in relief. She hadn't relished the prospect of seeing him naked again; witnessing the morph in the other timeline had been more than enough.

In the hallway, she stopped, her heart pounding. Oh, why hadn't she tried again to escape? Now she'd left it too late.

Then she remembered that T'alak had probably arrived in his yacht. And she knew exactly how to get into it. Running upstairs to the upper floor storage, she found a long, red tunic of soft quilting. When she returned to the basement, T'alak floated peacefully on his back in the pool. Keeping an eye on him, Catriona draped the robe over the stone seat by the pool, and lifted his uniform tunic.

Back up in the hallway, she rummaged through the hidden pockets of the uniform. Finding the yacht card key, she ran from the house, taking care not to let the front doors slam. She slithered over the

268 | *Time Twist*

crystalline snow to where the craft had docked. It looked similar to the one she had crashed in the forest; most likely it would be space worthy.

Blinding light sliced through the darkness. The approaching craft aimed right for her. Ducking, Catriona slipped and skidded to her knees. The skiff screeched to a halt and L'ticia jumped from the craft.

"You stupid tail-less fool!" she hissed. "Look!" She lifted a handful of snow, tossing it against T'alak's yacht. On impact, the entire vessel crackled as an electrical security shield lit up around it. Catriona stared at the yacht in dismay. "Only T'alak's DNA can deactivate the shield," said L'ticia. "He got tired of you stealing his craft, I think. Come on." She turned back toward her skiff, which looked clumsy beside the sleek yacht. "Hopefully, he is not aware you took his card." She began to unload her purchases into Catriona's arms.

"He's in the bath," said Catriona. She trailed L'ticia into the warmth of the house where L'ticia lifted T'alak's uniform from the floor and took it with her into the kitchen.

"Put the card back where you found it," she advised.

Catriona did so, slumping down at the table. "What happens, now?"

L'ticia laid T'alak's tunic over the washstand, as though ready to clean. She then busied herself unpacking her purchases. "Hopefully nothing bad if you behave."

"It's a bit late for that, isn't it? Now he's back, I'll be sent to Governor C'huln."

"Maybe not." L'ticia stopped unpacking, turning to look at Catriona. "If you can remember all I've taught you about our ways, the Captain may consider you worth keeping here."

Catriona snorted. "So I can be a slave for the rest of my life?"

"Friend, it's up to you. I've done all I can." She smiled. "I saw the *O'tium* lights from miles away. Thank you."

"It's a pity *he* had to come and spoil it."

"A pity indeed."

Both Catriona and L'ticia started. T'alak stood in the doorway, looking hard at Catriona.

She bowed her head. "This female apologizes, honored Captain. She spoke out of turn."

"Servant, prepare me some food," he ordered L'ticia, moving into the great room. As an afterthought, he addressed Catriona. "Come in here, human."

Catriona slid a frightened glance at L'ticia, and followed him, watching as he gazed round at her *O'tium* decorations. She wondered if he remembered anything about the alternate timeline, and longed to ask him what had happened at the spatial rupture, if he'd encountered the *Vallo*.

"You have been busy, human. Learning our ways, our language." He settled himself onto the floor cushions in front of the fire. "Serve me some wine."

This was more like T'alak's milder behavior in the other timeline, thought Catriona, moving to the cabinet to fetch the *picht*. She felt his dark gaze on her as she brought the silver ceremonial flask and cup on a tray and placed them on the low table beside him. The scrutiny made her nervous. With unsteady hands she uncorked the flask and poured the mauve wine in the traditional Komodoan manner, measuring it out in three stages, twisting the flask clockwise each time. Lifting the cup, she held it out to him, waiting while he tasted it. He nodded, reclining back against the cushions. With relief she turned to leave.

"Sit."

She froze at the order, at last raising her eyes to meet his. His expression looked more perplexed than angry. Stomach fluttering, she lowered herself onto a floor cushion.

"Did L'ticia instruct you?" he asked.

"She is a good teacher, honorable Captain," she evaded.

He drained his cup, holding up a hand as Catriona moved to refill it. She watched him pour his own wine, the liquid sparkling like garnets in the light from the fire. "What else have you been doing?"

"A lot of thinking," she answered after a moment. She found it difficult to maintain the formal mode of speech. She hoped he wouldn't be angry if she dropped it. Should she dare question him about the *Vallo*?

"Such as?"

"Well, as I couldn't escape, I could either make the living pleasant or unpleasant. I opted for pleasant." She waited to see where the conversation led. If an opportunity arose, she'd ask then.

He took another drink, studying her over the rim of the cup. She knew her transformation had confused him.

"How did you learn our language so quickly?"

Catriona licked her dry lips and began to talk. She lied about how Komodoan sentence structure was similar to the French language on Earth, which made it easy to grasp. She had just launched into a monologue about the differences in Komodoan and Terran cuisine when she noticed T'alak had dozed off. She caught his cup just before it dropped from his hand.

Sitting back and finishing the wine herself, she studied her captor. Asleep he looked years younger, the lines of his cruel mouth softened. She wondered what drove him, what made him so brutal and hate-filled. Right now he didn't intimidate her at all; just an exhausted soldier, too worn out to stay awake for his dinner. Unknown to him, she had already seen him at his most vulnerable, during the morph. What would his arrogant pride say about that if he knew?

53

HAVEN CONGRATULATED himself as he approached Realm space, having met no resistance on the way. The beauty of the Realm never failed to move him. Smoky mauve and green clouds of the nebula hung like a giant guardian dragon against the blackness of space. Wafts of what resembled wings, claws and a large tail billowed out to greet him. Legend said the dragon was the spirit of *B'llumni*, holding Komodoa in His mighty claw.

As he drew nearer to the planet, he began to encounter other ships. The smaller ones he ignored, concentrating on scanning for military vessels. As he approached orbit, a fleet of five ships in a zigzag snake formation emerged from the atmosphere, spinning past him at high speed. They had no time for a small-time smuggler like him in a rusty old boat like *Dream Lover,* but he needed to make his contact before Military Control challenged his presence.

He fed a contact number into his communication system, and waited. In a few seconds, his commscreen sprang to life, showing the image of a cantankerous-looking elderly Komodoan man. A grin spread across his scaled face at the sight of Haven.

"You snake, A'rlon," he hissed in delight. "Never thought I'd see your tail again. Business can't be so hot for you, if you're piloting a junk-heap like that F2."

"D'elag, you still baby-sitting N'elak? Thought a seasoned warrior like you would find a better calling."

"Get down here, before someone blasts that disgusting excuse for a ship out of existence! Transmitting coordinates now."

As Haven approached planet-fall, the cabalistic mauve of Komodoa took shape, the piercing peninsulas and islands clear as sparkling moonstones in the unpolluted atmosphere.

N'elak's operation was located in the city of *H'berna*, on the less inhabited northern hemisphere of Komodoa. Haven steered *Dream Lover* over the outskirts of a forest, across an ocean, and slowed down as he approached *H'berna*. He remembered Catriona's description of the cities from above; she said they looked like a huge, white Earthen birthday cake, the many spires of the dwellings resembling party candles. *H'berna* stood on a narrow peninsula and the city had grown upward rather than outward. Haven found the sight breathtaking, the elegant spires towering against the mauve sky.

D'elag waited on the dock as Haven brought *Dream Lover* to rest in the bay. Shutting down her systems, he popped the hatch and climbed out. D'elag approached, hissing softly. The older man's tail reached out for Haven's. With an effort, Haven concentrated on his coccyx. A stab of pain shot through him, but he was pleased to find this tail a lot more controllable than his last. He hadn't yet mastered it, and his tail jerked as it met D'elag's.

"N'elak's waiting." D'elag led him toward the huge warehouse adjacent to the bay, his tail curled arthritically behind him.

The air smelled deliciously moist and cool, an almost transparent green morning mist shrouding the courtyard.

"Business been good?" inquired Haven, matching the man's slow gait.

"Better than ever," grinned D'elag with a hiss of laughter. "Hope you've got some good pickings on board that boat?"

"Plenty, old friend. Especially for a thirsty warrior."

They walked through the warehouse, past boxes and crates piled high, until they came to an antechamber where N'elak greeted him. "Welcome, my brother!"

Warmth flooded through Haven at the sight of his old comrade and friend. They had seen many battles together during his years with the Realm. Their tails twisted together, Haven masking the pain it caused him.

"Good to see you, N'elak. You still fencing for every bit-smuggler on the planet?"

N'elak raised a dark eyebrow. "Of course. But I've dipped a few more scales than that in the brine. I have many more, shall we say, *interests*, than when we last met. So, what brings you back?"

"Some export... along the lines of living produce."

N'elak cocked an eyebrow, his tail swishing appreciatively. "I see. A little live cargo you need smuggled out of the Realm? Sounds expensive."

Haven studied his friend. He moved closer, his face hardening. "Expensive enough to cover one or two occasions when I prevented your name from appearing on General B'alarg's execution list."

His friend's tongue flickered in and out. "And then we shall be even?"

"I will consider your debt paid in full."

"Excellent." N'elak placed a proprietary hand on Haven's shoulder. "Come, let us discuss it over a cup of *picht*."

T'alak groggily opened his eyes to the lavender glare of a snow-laden afternoon. He stretched, arching his tail to get a kink out of it. A covered tray of cold meats and fruit sat on the table beside him and he picked up a *dinar* apple. L'ticia had not disturbed him, instead keeping the fire going and leaving the tray for when he woke. As he finished the apple, he studied the pattern of the colored *O'tium* lights.

His mission had been a complete failure. He had ruined his much-awaited chance to engage Grreag in the *Vallo* and the space rupture had rapidly closed in on itself before he could enter it. Even so, he desperately needed to try. An urgent message, apparently from himself in a different time, had been downloaded to the *L'umina*, telling him to enter the rupture at any cost; the reason why would become obvious on the other side. But he had failed. He longed to learn what had been on that other side. Another timeline, from where the message had possibly originated?

T'alak's hands curled into fists as he remembered the shame of his ship becoming trapped in the rupture. And the ignominy of the *Vallo* rescuing him! It had been all he could do to head back for the Realm as fast as possible. Only his standing as head of an Imperial House prevented him from execution. But the humiliation felt untenable. General B'alarg ordered him to take leave from active duty to reflect on his failure. T'alak suspected his career was on a fast downward spiral.

Throughout the journey back, he had fortified himself with how he would be entertained by Catriona upon his return. Governor C'huln had been assassinated, so she was finally T'alak's to do with as he wished. The change in her had astonished him. If she kept this behavior up, he hesitated to torture her, for it would feel like tormenting a pet lizard. No honor in that, and no satisfaction.

Catching movement outside the window, he turned and saw the human climb onto the estate wall. She stood immobile, raising her face to the sullen sky before dropping out of view on the other side.

"L'ticia!" he shouted.

She came from the kitchen, her face drawn and pinched with strain.

"Is the human supervised at all?"

"Most of the time, honored master."

"Then tell me why she just climbed the wall and left the estate." He watched a smile flit over his servant's face. Apparently some of the human's annoying habits had rubbed off.

"She walks down by the lake every day."

"Unsupervised?"

"Honored master, this servant has come to trust her. I consider her to be a friend."

T'alak moved close to her, staring down at her bent head. "I find it difficult to believe that the daughter of a trusted officer would befriend a human. This isolation has affected your judgment, woman." He reached out, gripping her chin so she looked at him. Her skin felt smooth and supple under his fingers. As she met his gaze, he felt a stirring. But it would be dishonorable to take advantage of a subordinate's daughter. He dropped his hand.

"You will return to your father's house for *O'tium* at once. I will reassess your position in this house whilst you are gone."

As she turned away she shot him an angry look, which she obviously thought he couldn't see. The human had infected her; a couple of days with her family would snap her out of it.

Glancing out of the window again, T'alak strode to the hallway to find a cloak and a pair of boots. He left the house, pulling the warm pelt about him. Approaching the high, ornate gates, he activated the lock. They strained open with difficulty, rarely operated when it was so simple a matter to clear the wall in a yacht.

Between the barren tree trunks, T'alak glimpsed the lake, but no sign of the human. The freezing air stung his lungs, making him cough. No Komodoan in his right mind would venture out in this temperature! As he drew nearer to the lake, he saw Catriona, crouching down at the base of an angular tree. Hearing his approaching footsteps crunching through the snow, she twisted round, standing to face him.

He was struck at how white her alien skin appeared, reflected against the snow. The sight of his mate's clothing draped over the alien's body filled him with rage.

"Who told you you could wear those boots and cloak?" he hissed. Before she could answer, he ripped the cloak off her back.

274 | *Time Twist*

Her blue eyes flashed, but she controlled herself, dropping her gaze. He had been hoping she would revert to her former nature and retaliate. He would know how to treat her, then.

"This female apologizes, honored Captain," she murmured.

Leaning back against the tree trunk, she bent down and removed the boots, one at a time. He caught a glimpse of her white thighs. Inadequate looking, without a tail to balance them.

With her eyes still lowered, she held the boots out to him. At a loss, he took them. He hadn't actually intended to make her stand barefoot in the snow. It did not give him pleasure to see her webless toes already turning blue.

"Put them back on." He thrust the boots back. "What were you doing here?"

"Sometimes there are *quato* roots beneath these trees. They taste a lot like sweet potatoes on Earth." She huffed with the effort of pulling up the long boots. "But it looks like I've already dug them all up."

He tossed the cloak at her, turning to go back to the house. Just then, the house skiff cleared the wall, streaking off above the trees. Catriona stopped in her tracks, staring after it. T'alak relished the dismayed expression on her face.

"L'ticia has gone home for *O'tium*. It will give you an opportunity to impress me with your new-found Komodoan skills."

In the hall, he handed her his cloak. "Warm some wine," he ordered, pulling off his boots and padding barefoot across the heated floor to the great room.

By the time Catriona brought him a generous tankard of heated *picht*, a blizzard had started up. T'alak watched the human light the lamps in the darkening room. Settling back into the cushions in front of the fire, he drank deeply, enjoying the warmth after the iciness outside. He tried to ignore Catriona, who hovered nearby.

"What is it?" he finally hissed.

She dropped to the floor in front of him, looking right into his face. "Captain, did you see the *Vallo* when you were away?"

Enraged at her audacity, T'alak raised a hand to cuff her, but she blocked him, gripping his hand. To his shock she held onto it, running the tips of her fingers over his knuckles.

"Such long, sensitive fingers shouldn't be used in violence," she murmured.

As though hypnotized he said, "A long time ago they were artist's hands." She stared into his face, alien-blue eyes widened, pupils large.

Unnerved, he pulled his hand free. "Leave me!"

She scrambled to her feet and ran from the room. T'alak stared into the fire in confusion. His defeat at the rupture must have affected him more than he realized.

54

CATRIONA RETREATED to L'ticia's chamber, not daring to venture out until nightfall. What had come over her, engaging T'alak like that? She was horrified at her stupidity. Her impulsive behavior might have cost her her life.

She heard a skittering sound at the door and rose to let in the pet lizard, Tukki. "I suppose you're hungry, aren't you?" She stroked his scaly back. The lizard hissed in pleasure, his tongue flickering out at her leg. "Come on, let's find you something."

The creature scuttled after her into the kitchen, his claws clicking loudly on the stone floors. Opening up the larder store, she found some leftover meat but Tukki turned up his scaly nose at it. "Oh, you picky reptile!" Catriona got down on all fours, trying to entice him. "I'm sorry, but I just can't bring myself to give you something still alive. Please take it." Tukki tongued the meat, finally accepting it. He gobbled it up as she scratched his head.

"I, too, am hungry," came T'alak's voice from the great room doorway. "However, I trust you can provide something more substantial than that."

Catriona scrambled to her feet and bowed. "Of course, Captain."

He nodded, retreating from the kitchen. She knew he would still be hungry. The food L'ticia had left him earlier had hardly been adequate to break his fast. She could only hope that he would have no sexual interest in her afterward. Perhaps if she poured him enough wine, she could get him too drunk to think about it.

L'ticia had kept the larder well stocked, and had instructed Catriona how to prepare a standard break fast. She piled a huge silver platter with *volator* meat, a black-fleshed fowl, surrounding it with rolls of whiter meat from the *sk'ndo* boar, then spread out to the edge of the platter a combination of raw fruits, vegetables, and grain-filled pastries. It looked enough to feed four Sumo wrestlers and Catriona would be

276 | *Time Twist*

amazed if T'alak managed all of it at one sitting. She hefted the heavy platter up in both hands and bore it into the great room. T'alak waited by the fire, drinking heavily, by the looks of it. Catriona approached and slid the platter onto the low table beside him.

"Where's the napery?" he asked.

Gritting her teeth, she ran back to the kitchen and lifted a wad of crisp, white napkins from the larder. She put them on the table by T'alak and retreated.

From the kitchen she heard a most peculiar sound and sneaked a look around the arched doorway. She'd never seen anyone eat like T'alak before. He stuffed the food into his mouth as fast as he could swallow. Disgusted, she crept away. L'ticia also used her fingers, but ate a great deal more genteelly than him.

Catriona had a small meal of *sk'ndo* and vegetables, chewing thoughtfully on the sweet, pale meat while she considered her next move. Somehow she had to use T'alak's DNA to disarm the security shield around his yacht. She had overpowered him once; she supposed she could do it again. That yacht was her only hope of getting out of here.

Catriona heard the door into the hallway slam and T'alak's heavy footsteps heading up the stairs. She went to fetch the platter. T'alak had left food debris all over the Leontor rug. Revolted, Catriona crouched down and wiped up the mess with his used napkins, transferring everything back to the platter. How could any living thing eat that much at one sitting?

"Leave it!" T'alak strode back into the room.

Catriona's stomach lurched, furious with herself for not waiting longer. T'alak laid a large pile of canvases on the table. Standing back, he motioned for her to look. Mating appeared to be the last thing on his mind, so she obeyed.

"You did these?" she asked.

He nodded. Lifting the first one, she found the texture of the canvass different than she expected. Hard and resilient, it felt like skin stretched over a drum. Studying the painting, Catriona was transported to a golden sea in a storm, almost hearing the wind as it whipped the waves into their frothy tango with the cliffs.

"You really were an artist," she murmured.

She studied the next few canvases, two of this house and several of different Komodoan landscapes. Then she lifted a portrait of a Komodoan woman. Catriona thought her stunning, despite her alienness. The woman's almond shaped dark eyes sparkled merrily from beneath her sprinkling of scales. Entranced, Catriona studied the careful brush strokes. Every detail shimmered with life; T'alak had obviously cared a great deal for her.

"Who is this?" she asked.

"My lifemate."

The rest of the canvasses showed the Komodoan woman in various moods and settings. Catriona carefully piled the paintings back the way they were, aware of T'alak studying her every move.

"T'alak-ra died a long time ago," he said. "Then I joined the military."

"And have been dead yourself ever since," murmured Catriona, turning to face him.

"The Alliance murdered her!"

She met his angry eyes. "So that's it. How?"

"A cowardly attack staged to look like an accident."

Catriona frowned. "I have never heard of the Alliance ever *initiating* an attack on the Realm. When did it happen?"

"Twenty years ago. T'alak-ra was on her way home from a visit to her family on the moon, *S'ola*. All three hundred civilians murdered."

"Captain, I can't believe for one moment the Alliance would deliberately do such a thing."

"Of course you can't; you're one of them!"

"Regardless, it's not their way. Look, I could find out exactly what happened. Let me contact them."

"Do you take me for a fool? Is this what your false concern is about—a petty trick to alert your precious Alliance of your position?" He backed her against the table. "You almost had me fooled, earthworm."

Catriona's heart beat fast. "Listen to me. I'm not trying to fool you. I'm sincerely telling you that I do not believe the Alliance would do such a thing."

She saw he believed her and watched the anger seep out of him. He stepped back, moving to fill his wine cup again.

"Clear the platter now."

Catriona did so, tossing it into the dishscrub in the kitchen. The door to the hall slammed and she heard T'alak going back up the stairs. After banking the fire she decided to take a bath before going to bed. Moving into the dark hall, she heard a sound she had been straining to hear for weeks. The bleep of a communications device, barely discernible above the rush of the water sculptures.

Creeping up the stairs, she held her breath as she approached the first landing. At the top of the staircase she halted in her tracks. A door gaped in the paneling where a door most certainly had not been before. Edging to peer in, her heart leapt to see the elusive communicator. She knew there had to have been one. Catriona scanned the landing, but saw no sign of T'alak. She hesitated on the threshold of the hidden chamber. If she tried to access the communicator now and failed, she would never have another chance. Yet still she hesitated. With a shaky sob, she turned to go back down the stairs and into the baths. She shook with a mixture of hope and fear, and not even the buoyant water could relax her. Images of the communicator kept invading her thoughts. Between locating that and the presence of T'alak's yacht, her chances of escape had doubled.

"I have friends planted in all the Imperial Houses." N'elak poured Haven another *picht*. He filled the goblet, dispensing with the complicated rituals. "Leave the traditions to the women, that's what I say." He laughed.

"And you have someone in the House of T'alak?"

"Happily so, my friend. But not for much longer."

"Indeed?"

"I've finally decided to bond, and L'ticia has agreed."

Haven gave a human bark of laughter. "You? I never thought I'd see the day you'd settle for one woman, N'elak."

N'elak swished the wine round his mouth for a moment before swallowing. "Growing older changes a man's perspective, A'rlon."

"You are only a year or so older than me," objected Haven.

"Yes, but you already have a mate. One for whom you are willing to risk your life."

Haven raised an eyebrow. N'elak confirmed what he had already been thinking. He would offer formal bonding to Catriona when he brought her home to Earth. He should have done it two years ago and hoped he wasn't too late.

N'elak broke into his thoughts. "When do you wish to visit the House of T'alak?"

"As soon as possible." The stars above knew what Catriona had suffered at T'alak's hands.

"Let me contact L'ticia and learn the human's status." N'elak put down his cup and keyed his infomonitor.

Haven saw the *picht* bottle had run dry, so went out to *Dream Lover* to procure another from her hold. He returned to find a grave-faced N'elak waiting for him. "Bad news?" he inquired.

"L'ticia informed me Captain T'alak sent her home for *O'tium*. Your human is alone with T'alak."

CATRIONA SAT in the kitchen, thinking hard. She couldn't let this opportunity pass. There'd never be a better chance to attempt escape. T'alak would be sated after a huge meal, full of wine, and most likely off guard. But now she knew the communicator's hiding place, plus the yacht stood outside. She had to engineer a way to get T'alak's DNA to disarm the security field. Her stomach had flutters; her palms clammy.

Controlling her nerves, Catriona put on a clean robe and prepared a tray with two ceramic cups and a generous decanter of *picht*. A few moments later she climbed the stairs. The hidden communications chamber had been sealed again, so she moved to T'alak's bedchamber door and knocked gently. After a second he threw open the door. "What is it?"

Catriona almost dropped the tray when she saw he was naked. She bowed her head, averting her gaze, although she'd been confronted by his alien nudity before.

"Honored Captain, I thought you might like a cup of wine before going to sleep. To help relax."

She kept her eyes lowered, praying he'd agree. Out of the corner of her eye, she spotted his carbine and belt on a side table. She looked at his tail to get an idea of his thoughts. It swished to and fro, not quite decided.

"As you've brought two cups, you intend to join me?" He took a step back and closed the door as she passed.

"If that is acceptable," she murmured. "L'ticia and I usually have a nightcap together. It's a human ritual, and... I'm missing her."

"Indeed?"

God, she realized this had been a really stupid idea. Of course he would suspect her motive.

"I need someone to talk to," she said, biting her lower lip and looking up at him for the first time. He had fallen for her ruse of liking him in the other timeline, why not this one? Her heart lifted to see his

280 | *Time Twist*

eyes flicker with interest.

"Pour the wine." He moved to retrieve his robe from the floor and slipped it back on.

Catriona knelt near the roaring fire on the pillows and did as he told her. He joined her and sat opposite, the crystal decanter of wine on the floor between them.

Catriona studied the chamber. Both the floor and ceiling were made of the same crystalline tile in the great room below, and the walls a smooth lapis lazuli paneled finish. An oval gel-bed dominated the center of the chamber, two narrow pillars on either side at the head reaching up to the ceiling. The fireplace looked similar to the one downstairs, although less ornate. Above the crackle of the fire, Catriona heard something else. Straining her ears, she followed the sound and discovered that the pillars by the bed were clear, with running water spiraling down inside.

"What do you and my servant talk about over your *nightcap*?" inquired T'alak.

She kept her gaze on the rug at her feet, trying to ignore that it was a Leontor pelt. "Anything we feel like, I guess."

"Very well, let's talk about the Alliance Cadet College."

Catriona stiffened and glanced briefly at him. "I'd rather not." Trust him to try and press the advantage.

He leaned back on the cushions. "I don't have to remind you I can use a brain scanner at any time if you refuse to cooperate."

"There's nothing to tell you!" Catriona threw up her hands in frustration. "I'm a rotten student, that's about it."

"Yet somehow you managed to become a commissioned officer. What other information have you concealed?"

Catriona didn't know whether to confess she knew about the alternate timeline. But then, she couldn't be sure that T'alak had any memory of it.

"Tell me about the cadet college, Catriona," he hissed softly.

Catriona smiled to herself that he thought he'd win her trust by using her first name. She decided to tell him something that might satisfy him without giving anything important away.

"You must already know quite a lot about the College through your sources planted there," she fished.

He smiled without warmth, the glow from the fire flickering over his saturnine face. "I want to hear about the visiting Leontor students."

"I'll be happy to tell you about them," Catriona stretched out her legs, forcing herself to look relaxed, "if you'll answer a couple of questions for me."

His tail lashed. "You are in no position to bargain."

"The information I'm seeking is not of an official nature."

He studied her for a moment. "Proceed."

Catriona took a deep breath. "The *Vallo*. Did you meet up with her while you were studying the rupture?"

T'alak's eyes flashed. "How did you know the *L'umina* went to the rupture?"

"A calculated assumption. Are they all right? Was Grreag... did you engage them in battle?"

"That's two questions."

"Are they all right, Captain?"

His tail twitched. "We had no battle. The *Vallo* was intact when I last saw her."

"Did you see Colonel Grreag?"

"My turn."

Catriona took a sip of wine. "The project is an experiment in giving Leon cadets insight into Terran officer training. Please, did you see Grreag?"

T'alak shifted, his expression hardening. "Yes," he hissed, "I saw the filth."

"Don't call him that!"

"What is the alien slime to you?"

"Is that an official question?"

"Answer me, earthworm."

She sighed. "He's my friend."

T'alak hissed in derision. "A Leontor with a *human* for a friend?"

"It's not impossible!" snapped Catriona.

He clasped his cup and took a long draught. Catriona lifted the decanter to refill it, but T'alak took it from her and poured it himself. "Why were you traveling to Leontor?"

"To see about setting up a similar program there for human students. Did they inquire after me?"

Her question caught T'alak off guard, but he recovered quickly. "No."

Catriona's chest tightened. "I don't believe you. They'd never give up looking for me."

"They believe you to be dead, human. They have gone on with their lives." A lump formed in Catriona's throat. T'alak emptied another cup of wine. "They did share some information with me, which I believe you

282 | *Time Twist*

should hear." Catriona leaned forward. "The traitor, A'rlon, is dead."

The chamber suddenly swam. Fighting for composure, Catriona swallowed hard. "I don't believe you."

T'alak poured himself another refill. "Apparently, the *Vallo* crew held a touching memorial service for you both."

Catriona found trouble breathing. She felt hot, her vision blurred. Haven dead? Her love, her anchor, the only man she'd ever really loved, gone? Tears pricked her eyes, her throat constricting.

"How many Leon students have visited Earth?" demanded T'alak.

"Ten." What was the point of anything now?

"What aspects of training did they experience?"

"Why have you not killed me?" demanded Catriona.

He frowned. "I don't understand."

"What's the point in keeping me here? It's obvious this C'huln person isn't coming for me, so why am I still alive?" She couldn't see any reason to live, with Haven dead. She had nothing to lose; nothing to escape for.

"You are becoming tiresome."

Catriona grabbed her cup, wanting to pitch it in his cruel face. Haven was dead, and she blamed T'alak.

"What training did the students receive?" he asked as though nothing had happened.

"Shut the fuck up!" Catriona shouted.

The ceramic cup shattered between her hands, blending with her blood to splatter onto the Leon pelt. T'alak stared at her, his expression a mixture of shock and anger. Didn't he understand that she had loved Haven more than life itself? Losing all control, rage surged her forward, closing her hands around his throat. "You fucking bastard!"

He caught her wrists, and Catriona tensed, waiting for the blow that would surely take her life. Startled, she found herself enveloped in his arms, just like in the alternate timeline. She trembled against him, hating him yet finding comfort in the embrace, and sobbed until she exhausted herself.

Finally T'alak spoke. "It is the *O'tium* Festival, human. A time to forget grievances and grudges. If you wish to die I will oblige, but if you want to live, I offer you the protection of my House." Catriona felt too drained and weak to answer. He withdrew his arms, laying her gently on the cushions. "Stay here, if you wish."

Confused, Catriona feigned sleep, watching him beneath her damp eyelashes. He stood over her for a few moments, his face hooded and contemplative. Then he gathered up his weapons belt and left the chamber. Curling into a fetal position, Catriona wished she could go to sleep and never wake up.

A SUDDEN crackle from the dying fire started Catriona awake. Her palms throbbed sharply. Looking at them in the firelight, the smears of dried blood sharply reminded her of what had happened.

T'alak stood at the window, gazing out into the night. Catriona sat up, her heart hammering. "Captain?" He didn't react, lost in thought. "Captain T'alak?" she said more clearly.

He turned, his tail whipping from side to side. "Do you still wish to die, human?"

Haven's dark, beautiful face swam before her. Even though he had gone, he would not want her to give up. "No," she whispered.

He nodded. "I have received word from Headquarters. General B'alarg is paying a visit, today. He intends to reassess your status."

The hair on the back of Catriona's neck rose. "What does that mean?"

"Execution or relocation in a research facility. As you have accepted the protection of my House, I will take measures to prevent B'alarg from taking you."

"What kind of measures?"

"You forget yourself! Do not question me."

Catriona angrily dropped her gaze. One day she would find a way to repay him for the humiliation he continued to subject her to. But for now, she needed to survive.

"Go and prepare for the General," ordered T'alak. "I will expect you to demonstrate your so-called civilization to him. He will not accept it if he does not witness the transformation for himself."

Catriona got to her feet, swaying a little. She felt wretched and drained as she headed for L'ticia's chamber to clean up and change. Daylight just began to show itself, making a pale ghostly halo above the trees outside.

The Komodoan suns still rose, despite Haven's death. And no doubt the sun also rose somewhere over Earth, too.

284 | *Time Twist*

T'alak stood in front of the great room fireplace to await General B'alarg. The thought of the peasant invading the sanctity of his home infuriated him. One of these days B'alarg would push him too far. But with T'alak's recent disgrace, he dared not deny him access.

What by *B'llumni* had possessed him to offer the human prisoner the sanctuary of his House? Once that protection had been offered and accepted, honor dictated he stand by it. But for an alien slave? She had bewitched him, or he had lost his mind.

He reached down and straightened the hem of his uniform tunic, donned for the occasion. What a pity B'alarg had not met with some unfortunate accident before this. When the rupture incident had died down, perhaps the time had come when T'alak might call in a couple of favors to take care of him.

The air about him hummed, indicating the imminent appearance of an actuate bubble. Smoothing his face to a neutral expression, T'alak stepped forward and saluted as B'alarg arrived.

"I am honored by your visit, General," he hissed, "please be welcome."

B'alarg nodded, his tail lightly tapping T'alak's in as brief a touch as permissible without insult. T'alak noticed B'alarg's protuberant eyes run over the room and widen. The House of T'alak would be a lot more opulent than B'alarg would expect, only having seen T'alak's sparse quarters at the base.

"Will you break your fast with me, honored General?"

"Thank you, no. I must actuate back to my ship as soon as possible."

"Are you back in the field?" asked T'alak in surprise. A humiliating demotion, if so.

"Fleet inspection," hissed B'alarg.

So, he had been demoted, thought T'alak with relish. B'alarg in his turn had taken disgrace for T'alak's failed rupture mission.

"May I offer you some *picht*?" he asked, gesturing for B'alarg to be seated by the fire.

B'alarg nodded, sitting down on a couch. T'alak touched the panel by the fireplace to summon Catriona.

"I am surprised to hear the human still lives, Captain."

T'alak watched Catriona enter the room, carrying a decanter and cups on a tray.

"It entertained me to keep her around," he said.

He would lose face if she reacted negatively in front of B'alarg. He watched as she placed the tray on the table beside the General and uncorked the decanter. Then she knelt at B'alarg's side, balancing the tray on one palm while holding the decanter in the other. So far she performed the ritual perfectly and he found it amusing that B'alarg remained oblivious.

The General turned his head to watch his wine poured, and T'alak hid his enjoyment as B'alarg looked up at Catriona, startled. The General took the human's proffered cup in astonishment, his tail curling in and out.

As Catriona repeated the ritual with T'alak, B'alarg spluttered, "You've trained her well, T'alak! I can scarcely believe my eyes."

"It's gratifying how civilizing a little discipline can be," answered T'alak.

B'alarg studied Catriona. "Perhaps I shall break my fast with you, after all, Captain."

"Forgive me, honored General, but do you not have to leave without delay for your... inspection?" T'alak enveloped the last word in sarcasm.

"You are correct. I shall take the human with me."

Catriona lost her grip on the tray and dropped it with a clatter, her eyes blazing. T'alak glared at her, willing her to stay quiet.

"I'm afraid that isn't possible, General," he said quietly. "I've taken her as my consort."

B'alarg rose to his feet, a hiss of disbelief escaping him. "Have you lost all reason, T'alak? You cannot take an alien as a consort!"

T'alak looked at Catriona, who stood gaping at him as though he had five tails. "You may leave," he ordered her in irritation. "Wait in my chambers," he added. Catriona shot him a look of apprehension before obeying.

"I presume my insisting that you hand her over is useless?" inquired B'alarg.

"Yes, General. There is nothing in our laws that say I cannot take an alien consort if I choose. And I don't have to remind you that as my consort, she is my sole property."

"I'm well aware of the law," hissed B'alarg. "I'm sure I don't have to remind you that there are those higher up who will be displeased. Having an alien as consort will not be taken lightly."

T'alak gazed levelly at his superior officer. "Nor would the knowledge that a certain general in the Realm Military had his superior officer murdered for a promotion."

He stood firm as B'alarg blundered toward him, his tail lashing from side to side. "You have no proof, T'alak! And if I do go down, I'll take you with me."

"I do not have as much to lose as you, General."

T'alak waited while B'alarg's face became stoic again.

"I will take my leave of you," B'alarg grunted. "For now."

"You are always welcome," replied T'alak, as B'alarg signaled his ship and disappeared in an actuate bubble. He would have to doubly watch his back now, but he shouldn't hear any more about Catriona from B'alarg. And his family name and reputation remained intact as long as B'alarg kept quiet.

Striding up the stairs to his chambers, he found Catriona had lit the fire, perching on a cushion in front of it.

"What does being your consort mean?" she demanded.

Under the circumstances, he let her bad manners go. "You're protected. No one can touch you."

"Except you?"

He raised an eyebrow. "If I wanted to."

"Do you?" She watched his face.

T'alak couldn't speak for a moment. To cover his confusion he moved to look out the window at the sullen, snow-laden morning. When Catriona had been nothing more than an enemy prisoner-of-war, he had wanted her very much, but for different reasons. If he felt attracted to her now, he'd be nothing more than a perverted savage, rejecting the purity of the Komodoan race.

He felt her eyes on him and turned to look at her. With only the fire to light the gloomy morning, her pale, human skin glowed with an amber hue, her red hair reflecting the flickering flames. With a jolt he realized she was beautiful by human standards, but her frank, blue-eyed gaze disconcerted him and made him angry. She pretended Komodoan ways but didn't truly know how to behave, staring at him like that.

The tumult of conflicting emotions battled within him. He spun away from her gaze. Overwhelmed, he leaned against the sill.

"Are you all right, Captain?" he heard her ask.

He gripped the sill hard, wishing her out of this chamber and far away from him.

"Is it the morph?" She had come to stand beside him and he flinched as she laid a hand on his arm. "No, it can't be, you just had it."

The statement shot through his confusion, focusing him. His head snapped up and he stared at her. How in the name of *B'llumni* could she possibly know about that?

Catriona realized her blunder too late. She had gotten her timelines mixed up. By the tight, suspicious expression on T'alak's face she knew she couldn't backtrack.

"How do you know about my recent morph?" he demanded, his voice low and dangerous.

Catriona cleared her throat, her mind racing. What harm would there be in telling him what she remembered? He couldn't change it now. If the Professor had followed her advice, his data would all have been erased, and the temporal bubble weapon destroyed. T'alak could never go back and pervert the timeline again.

"Tell me, earthworm," insisted T'alak, tense and watchful.

"You'd better get comfortable," she acceded, moving to sit on a cushion by the fire. "It's a long story."

She poured some wine from the crystal decanter into his empty cup, and he settled himself on the cushions opposite.

Catriona related how his interference had made the Komodoan Realm dominant in the galaxy. She answered his questions, but left out where she and the A'rlon of that time collaborated on returning the continuum to normal. She couldn't bear to speak about Haven, yet. Besides, T'alak hated him so, his uncertain temper might explode at the thought of them still attracted to each other, even in another timeline. She wondered if Haven's death had been caused by something A'rlon did to fix the rupture.

When she had finished, T'alak stared in silence into the fire. Catriona's throat ached from talking for so long and she stared at his half-full cup of wine and wished she hadn't broken her cup.

"So, I treated you well in this other timeline?" he asked.

"Mostly. I suspect I was no threat to you there."

"You're no threat here."

Catriona made a very Komodoan hissing sound of impatience, much to both of their surprise. T'alak hissed a laugh, then fell silent, studying the depths of his cup. She looked at the dwindling *picht* in the decanter and realized he'd drunk a great deal. His expression grew morose, and she watched him battle between his pride and the obvious need to talk.

When he spoke, his voice was so low she had to lean close to hear the words. "T'alak-ra was everything I was not. When I told her I wanted to be an artist rather than follow my father's military career,

288 | *Time Twist*

she encouraged me.

"She believed she could change the world. And I have no doubt she would have, if she'd lived." He paused for so long Catriona thought he had finished, but then he half-smiled, looking into her eyes. "She had quite a temper, rather like you-"

"I haven't got a temper!" she retorted.

They looked at each other for a beat before bursting into laughter. Catriona ended up coughing and T'alak handed her his cup. Slaking her thirst, she poured a refill from the decanter.

"Captain, accidents do happen, however strange their circumstances." She watched the muscles moving in his face as he clenched and unclenched his jaw.

"We had a serious disagreement and talked in anger of terminating our bonding," he continued. "She visited her family on *S'ola* so she could think. She had made her decision and was on her way home when the Alliance ship killed her."

Aghast, Catriona stared at him. "And you never resolved the disagreement?"

He shook his head and gazed unseeing into the fire. Catriona could empathize a little, remembering the last angry words she had said to Haven. With a jolt she remembered that Haven no longer lived to remember those words, and a sickening pain of loss shot through her. She shouldn't be sitting here with T'alak, who had tortured Haven, who had wanted his internal organs displayed in the capital of Komodoa!

Struggling for a moment, she reconsidered. Who better? Haven had considered T'alak a friend. It hadn't been easy for him to betray T'alak and leave the Realm without an explanation.

"We both have lost those we loved," she said.

T'alak stared at her, his dark eyes reflecting the fire's flicker. He leaned toward her, and Catriona didn't draw back. He plucked the cup from her hand, turning her so he could lift the long hair away from her neck. As his tongue feathered the back of her neck and around her ears, goosebumps rose on her body and shivers ran through her. T'alak leaned over her, using his weight to press her down under him until she lay on her stomach. His tongue continued to caress her neck as his hands eased her robe from her shoulders. Suddenly he stopped.

"What happened here?" he demanded. Catriona had forgotten about the healing wounds on her back. L'ticia had never told him Catriona had tried to escape. "No matter." His tongue gently caressed the scars and moved down her spine.

The sensation felt both soothing yet exciting. Catriona twisted round, maneuvering so she lay on her back, under him. The raw desire on his face acted like aphrodisiac. She reached up and clutched the back of his head, her fingers gripping his hair. Pulling him down to her, she clamped her mouth against his in a ravenous kiss. His hand moved clumsily to her breast, roughly squeezing and twisting the nipple. His erection became very evident, and abruptly, Catriona felt disgusted with herself. Letting T'alak ravage her body would be no remedy to her pain.

He shifted position so he could enter her and Catriona twisted away, preventing him. She tried to push him off, but any strand of tenderness had gone; T'alak was lost in his desire.

Her hand fell on something cold and sharp. A shard from her shattered cup. She grabbed it. With panic for impetus, she thrust the shard upward, plunging it through his robe and catching him in the side. Green blood spurted over her. She squirmed from under him as T'alak gasped, clutching the wound. Grabbing the heavy crystal decanter, she lifted it high over her head and knocked T'alak cold.

The door burst open. Catriona's jaw dropped to see A'rlon and another Komodoan standing there, with blasters trained on her.

57

HAVEN TOOK in the scene before him and holstered the blaster, folding his arms over his chest. "Doesn't look like she needed us after all, N'elak."

He couldn't be certain exactly what he'd busted in on. Half naked, Catriona stood astride the unconscious T'alak. She stared at the newcomers, speechless, her normally clear blue eyes hooded and dark in the dimly lit chamber.

"Well?" he demanded, "do you need our help or not?"

"What are *you* doing here?" snapped Catriona in Komodoan.

Startled by her tone and command of the language, Haven frowned. He wondered if this might be a Catriona from an alternate timeline. She marched over to him. Expecting an embrace, he was startled when she yanked the front of his tunic apart. He moved to hide the secret there, but realized what she sought. Dropping his arms he let Catriona inspect the very human nipples on his chest. To his relief the harsh

290 | *Time Twist*

lines of her face softened, restoring the girl he knew and loved. A smile spread across her face and he pulled her into his arms.

"Jack, T'alak told me you were dead!"

"I've never been more alive." He reached to pull her robe up to cover her shoulders. She tensed, shifting away. "Exactly what did we interrupt here?" He moved to inspect the prone T'alak.

"My attempt to persuade him to let me go," murmured Catriona, not meeting his eyes.

Haven looked at her sharply. There was more to this than she said. "You weren't successful."

"No."

"Where is L'ticia's chamber?" inquired N'elak.

Catriona looked at him, puzzled.

"He needs to collect her belongings—she will not be returning here," Haven explained. "N'elak and she are to be bonded."

Catriona gave directions and N'elak disappeared. As soon as he'd gone out of earshot, Haven confronted Catriona. "What really happened here?"

She evaded the question. "Did you know about T'alak's wife?" To his nod, she continued, "No wonder he's the way he is."

"It's senseless of him to blame the Alliance for one accident, Catriona."

"If we could prove it had been an accident and not an attack like he believes, maybe we could change his mind. He's not such a bad person, really."

Haven reached out and tilted her chin up so she looked at him. "Why do you say that?" Ice formed around his heart at the thought that T'alak might have seduced her.

She pulled free. "There's been a perversion in the space and time continuum-"

"Yes, I know," he interrupted.

"Well, for whatever reason, I've kept my memories of the alternate timeline. T'alak was a different person there, as were you."

"I see." The thought did not bring him comfort.

"How do you know of the timeline, Jack?"

"My counterpart sent me a transmission, telling me where to find you. He was—taken with you."

Catriona looked away. "I'm glad he succeeded in restoring the timeline." Tension suddenly flowed from her. "Life on Komodoa is not much fun for an alien slave."

"You appear to have things under control. What do you want to do with T'alak now?"

She gave a half-hearted grin. "Maybe I should take him home to Earth and keep him as a slave. See how he likes it."

"If the Alliance approved of slavery, I'd be the first to applaud that. But—"

"I know. But we can't leave him here like this; he needs medical attention."

Haven stooped to examine T'alak more closely and rolled him onto his side. "It's just a flesh wound. He'll be fine." His eyes narrowed. "What did he do to make you do this to him?"

"He did nothing," she murmured, with lowered eyes.

Lucky for T'alak, thought Haven. Otherwise they'd be leaving a dead body behind. "All right, we'll talk about it later. Come, we must leave. At the moment I'm covered as an *H'berna* smuggler, but if I'm detected in this province, it could get risky."

"We can't just leave Captain T'alak like this!"

"Yes, we can."

"But you say L'ticia won't be coming back. What if he needs help?"

Haven fought the rage rising in him. "Catriona, what do you care if he does need help? If there's any justice, he'll bleed to death."

N'elak reappeared in the doorway, his tail twitching. "We need to get going," he advised. Gazing at T'alak's prone form, he stepped inside. "Why don't we take him along? He's got to be worth a couple of my men in exchange."

"It's your call," answered A'rlon. "If you can carry him, you can have him."

N'elak hauled T'alak up and over his shoulder, and led the way to the skiff. Inside, he bound T'alak tightly, securing him to the back passenger seat before taking the helm. Haven placed a sedative pad onto T'alak's neck to ensure the Captain did not revive before they'd reached *H'berna*. If they intended to use him as an exchange for some of N'elak's people, they couldn't allow him to see where he'd been taken.

Haven sat beside Catriona as the skiff took off. He glanced at her, slumping down in her seat. He wanted to broach the subject of Matthew, but how to start? After a while, Haven realized she'd fallen asleep. He eased her onto her side so that her head lay in his lap.

"You need to stay planetside for a couple more days, my friend," said N'elak. "If you leave so soon it'll look suspicious. My deals take an average of three days."

Haven nodded, working out the tangles in Catriona's long hair. "I'll

292 | *Time Twist*

do some trading, perhaps for some ***picht***." He paused. "Maybe a few bottles of that will help Catriona come to her senses," he added with a wry grin.

Catriona woke up and found herself cradled in Haven's arms. For a moment she enjoyed the close contact with him, but then unease replaced the feeling of comfort. If she had given in to temptation with T'alak, Haven would have walked in to see them rutting like a couple of animals on the floor. She felt ashamed.

The skiff began its descent to ***H'berna*** and slowed as they reached the city's outskirts. Catriona glimpsed tailed Komodoans walking in the streets, even at this late hour. Their vessel slipped into a bay alongside the ugliest old ship she'd ever seen. She sat up to get a better look, easing out of Haven's arms.

"How are you feeling?" he asked.

"Fine, thanks." She didn't meet his gaze. She didn't know how she truly felt, only that she didn't want to talk about it.

Haven draped a cloak over her shoulders. "Put the hood up."

They climbed from the skiff onto the dock. A figure emerged from the shadowy warehouse to meet them and Catriona smiled when she recognized L'ticia.

"Hello, friend." L'ticia swished the end of her tail in greeting. "So we both are free from T'alak at last!"

N'elak laughed. "Not yet, my hatchling! We have a package in the skiff that needs attention."

L'ticia peered into the craft. "Where are you going to put him?"

"The basement of the guest quarters is a suitable place, don't you think?" He gave the order and a couple of his men carted T'alak away.

Catriona followed the others into a tall building left of the warehouse and up a long, stone spiral staircase. Her thighs ached by the time they reached a carved, wooden door at the top.

Inside, the dark chamber glowed with an eerie lavender hue from the city lights outside. Catriona shivered as N'elak lit a lamp, revealing the chamber to be a high-ceilinged room with a fireplace and small adjacent bathroom.

"I trust you'll be comfortable here," he said.

"I'm sure we will." Haven thanked him. "Been a long time since I slept in a gel-bed."

Catriona she moved to look out the window. "Is this the capital?"

"No," said L'ticia, moving to light a fire to warm the damp chamber. "That is on the other side of the planet."

Catriona gazed down on the alien street. What a dismal place it looked at night from up here, so murky she couldn't see the ground. She leaned further out to get a better look.

Haven touched her arm. "Catriona, keep out of sight of the window!"

Catriona moved away from him and went to help L'ticia with the fire. "Is this where T'alak-zan would have spotted you?" she asked.

"Yes, but thanks to you, he didn't." She brushed soot from her hands and gave Catriona a brief embrace. "Now, we will leave you and A'rlon alone. I'm sure you have much to talk about." She moved toward the door, her tail curling around N'elak's as they left together.

"We do have much to talk about." Haven advanced on Catriona. "You're not yourself. What's the matter?"

Catriona felt trapped. "I don't want to talk about it. I'm too tired."

"Tired or not, I'm going to find out why you flinch from me."

"I told you, I'm just tired-"

"I can explain about Matthew."

"You don't need to."

"Catriona." Haven gripped her shoulders. "Did T'alak rape you?"

"No, he didn't."

Haven picked up on her inflection. "*He* didn't? Who did, then?"

"No one! Look, can't we just drop this?" She tried to break free.

"No. I cannot allow this to go on any longer."

Catriona's eyes darkened as rage coursed through her. "Can't you understand? I've had it with being told what I can and cannot do! If I don't want to talk about it, I bloody well don't have to, A'rlon."

"*A'rlon*? My counterpart did something to you, didn't he?"

Catriona twisted her head away. She wished he would just leave her alone; she felt confused enough. "He did nothing to me. He... you still protected me from T'alak there. Please, drop it, Jack." His proximity was having its usual effect on her, giving her stomach butterflies and confusing her.

He dropped his hands from her shoulders. "Catriona, were we intimate in the other time?" She nodded miserably. "May I know how it happened?"

"What do you mean, how?"

"Did he force you?"

Catriona looked up at him. "No. He just didn't stop when I asked him to."

He fell silent for a long moment. "You were right when you said I was a different person there. I'm not sure I like the sound of myself."

"You had never returned to the Alliance in that time, Jack. You were totally Komodoan. But you did admit you were wrong for not stopping."

"Well, that's a relief," he snorted.

"The thing is, I was willing enough to do it twice." Her voice cracked. "I'm sorry, everything felt so much the same I kidded myself he was you." She couldn't bring herself to tell Haven about L'ticia. She didn't know if he could cope with that on top of everything else.

"I think I understand," he said. "Look, he and I really are the same. It's all right."

"And then when T'alak..." Her voice shook.

Haven's face hardened. "He will pay for touching you."

Chills ran up Catriona's spine at his tone. There did appear to be more of the Komodoan side to him than she had known until meeting his counterpart. "Let it go, Jack. I understand why T'alak is the way he is."

"I fail to see why you defend him!" snapped Haven. "Are you sure you didn't fuck him, too?"

Catriona felt like he'd slapped her across the face. She turned away. "I guess I deserved that."

Haven reached out a hand. "No, you didn't. I'm sorry."

She took it, holding it to her cheek. "No, I'm sorry. Look, I-" She broke off. What could she say? The fact that his double had insisted on sleeping with her had made her cautious of Haven? It would sound ridiculous.

He embraced her briefly. "Catriona, we're both exhausted. Why don't we just get some sleep?" He disengaged and turned away to undress.

Catriona felt a hollowness inside her, and wondered if it could ever be filled again.

58

T'ALAK STRAINED his ears in the blackness, trying to discern his surroundings. He had come to a while ago, finding himself bound and trussed like a *volator*, his arms tied together behind his back and his tail strapped to his bound legs.

By the feel and scent of the humid air he knew he wasn't in his own house. Had the human found access to his yacht and taken him captive? She must have had help, but from whom? Shifting position to try and get the circulation going in his arms, a pain in his side reminded him that Catriona had stabbed him. She had to be the most irrational being he'd ever encountered. One day a savage, the next civilized. One moment giving him mating signals, the next repulsing his advances as though *he* were the savage. She had been the only human he had ever wanted to mate with, instead of using sex as a tool for humiliation and control. Not to mention he had offered her the highest honor a slave could hope for, to be his consort. Her rejection was inconceivable.

He passed some time, imagining his revenge. He had been misguided to treat her with any respect at all; she had proved she had no concept of honor by immobilizing and imprisoning him like this.

He froze at the sound of a bolt being thrown. Light flooded in through an open door, blinding him. He attempted to sit up and be less vulnerable, but the ropes binding his tail to his legs made it impossible. He twisted his head round to see a hooded figure step inside, carrying a heavy bag and an oil lamp. Dropping the bag, the figure reached a pale hand to push back the hood of the cloak. Catriona. Behind her he saw silhouetted a Komodoan male armed with a carbine. He watched her set the lamp down and come closer. Seeing him awake, she turned and closed the door.

"Have you come to gloat, human?" He wondered whom had she found to help her.

"Not at all, Captain." She knelt beside him. "I came to check on you because they didn't want you to see them. I had no idea they'd left you like this." She tested the ropes, making a face at their tightness.

"Who are *they*?"

"I can't tell you. Is there anything you need?"

T'alak glared at her. If he did, he had no intention of showing weakness in front of her.

He stiffened as she leaned over him, pulling his robe aside. "Let me check your wound," she murmured. T'alak could do nothing but submit. He frowned at her sharp intake of breath. "This looks infected." She dragged over the bag she had brought with her and pulled out a medikit. "I brought this just in case."

T'alak waited while she cleaned the stab wound and covered it with a dressing. He decided to ask one thing of her. "I cannot sit up like this, human. Will you unbind my tail?" If he had that free then at least he would have leverage to break the rest of his bonds.

296 | *Time Twist*

Her eyes glittered. "I will, but if you hurt me or try to escape, you will be killed. Do you understand?"

"Perfectly." He smiled grimly. "There would be little point in my harming you. But my time will come."

"That may be so," she murmured, "but it isn't here yet." She rolled him over and began to work at the rope around his tail.

With his face in the dirt, T'alak vowed that he would destroy Catriona once and for all at his earliest opportunity. She had been nothing but a crook in his tail since he encountered her. Finally the pressure on his tail lifted and he stretched it out, whirling it around to get it moving again. He resisted the temptation to wrap it around Catriona's neck and throttle the life from her. She may be the nearest thing to an ally he had in this place. He eased himself to a sitting position, using his tail to balance.

"I'm sorry I cut you," she said.

Curious in spite of himself, he asked, "Why did you?"

"I guess I panicked." Her expression suddenly darkened. "You told me Haven had been killed, Captain. Why did you lie?"

"Ah, so he's behind this. Your precious A'rlon. Who's helping him?"

"Why did you lie?" she insisted.

"I don't have to answer to you."

She reached out and grabbed his face between her hands. "In case you hadn't noticed, T'alak, you're the one who's a prisoner now. And I'm the only thing standing between you and death!"

"How touching," he said, and snaked his tongue out to lick at her face.

With a noise of disgust, she dropped her hands and belted him hard across the face. He lost his precarious balance and toppled to the side. Catriona used her weight to thrust him over onto his back, and he stifled a yowl of pain as his tail got pinned under him. He struggled, but Catriona pushed down harder.

"This *is* most exhilarating," she breathed, her face over his. "Now I see why you enjoy torture so much. What would you do next, if our positions were reversed? You'd rape, wouldn't you?"

T'alak stared at her in disbelief. Catriona shifted so she straddled him, right where the most pressure crushed his tail. He felt like it would snap off.

"My tail," he said, through gritted teeth. If he tried to dislodge her, he would dislocate it.

"Do you want me to stop?" Catriona circled her hips, grinding all her weight into him. "Beg, T'alak. Beg me to stop."

T'alak's mouth closed into a thin line. He'd rather die than beg a human for mercy. He would never have believed this from Catriona. Yet even as he thought it, he realized *he* was responsible for it.

As he watched through a fog of pain, her blue eyes cleared and widened. She slipped off him, relieving the fierce pressure on his tail. He breathed easier, but still couldn't raise himself up.

"I'm sorry," she murmured, rolling him onto his side. "I'm no better than you, to act like that. Is your tail all right?"

He tested it. It felt like he'd torn a ligament. "It's fine."

Catriona sat back on her heels, head bowed. After a moment she leaned across him and T'alak steeled himself, but she merely untied the rest of his bonds. *At last,* he thought. He'd kill her with his bare hands.

The bonds loose, he snatched hold of her by the throat. Twisting her round, he slammed her onto the floor. She made a *whoomp* sound as he knocked the breath from her.

"You have no tail to crush," he hissed, "but I can break you in other ways." She didn't fight, just lay under him. "Have you nothing to say, human?" he demanded.

She shook her head. "I can't believe I'd stoop so low as to brutalize a helpless captive."

Her words hit him like a slosh of icy water. He stumbled to his feet, stretching his aching limbs. To his consternation, Catriona remained spread-eagled on the floor, staring into space. Leaning down, he pulled her to her feet.

"Human, if anything, this raises my estimation of you."

She came to life. "I don't give a shit what you think of me."

"I believe we are even, now."

She gave a bitter laugh. "Not even close. You've cost me far more than you'll ever know. You'll be happy to know that my 'precious' Haven isn't mine anymore. Thanks to you screwing up the timelines, too much has happened for things to ever be the same again. Oh, what's the use, why should you care?" She moved to where she'd left the bag. "Here's some water and food. And a receptacle if you need to, well…" She curled her lip and slammed out of the room.

As the bolt slid back into place, T'alak felt a great sadness overwhelm him.

59

CATRIONA RAN up the many stairs to the guest quarters. Out of breath, she collapsed onto the floor. Haven and N'elak waited for her in the warehouse, but she couldn't face them just yet. She had never felt more confused or miserable in her whole life. The wash of violence that had surged through her frightened her. In that moment where she'd had T'alak helpless beneath her, she had been thrilled by the power.

She wondered if she might be losing her mind. She had untied T'alak, knowing he'd want to retaliate. She'd *wanted* him to kill her.

She knew she'd have to pull herself together and report to the warehouse or Haven would come looking for her. Running a comb through her hair and wiping a smear of dirt from her face, she climbed back down the stairs and slipped into the warehouse.

"How is our guest?" inquired N'elak.

"Fine," she muttered, avoiding Haven's penetrating stare.

"Not for long," said N'elak. "He's to be executed."

"I thought you were going to use him in exchange for prisoners?" Catriona asked.

"Realm Military won't discuss it. General B'alarg was more open to setting our people free if T'alak were to disappear."

Catriona looked at Haven, who gazed at her from implacable dark eyes. "But you know General B'alarg hates T'alak. This is the opportunity to get rid of him that he's been waiting for."

"B'alarg insisted T'alak is more valuable dead than alive," replied Haven.

"And you believed him?" Catriona heard N'elak's intake of breath at her scathing tone. Komodoan females never addressed their mates so. Haven's face looked drawn and dark, making him appear more like his counterpart, A'rlon.

"Stay out of what you don't understand, Catriona," he said. "It will serve us to have T'alak eliminated and you won't have to fear him coming after you again."

He didn't understand that even though the whole mess had been T'alak's fault, he had saved her from B'alarg by claiming her as his consort. How could she stand by and let T'alak be killed, now?

Haven returned his attention to an infomonitor on N'elak's desk. Catriona wandered round the chamber, looking at the various little 'treasures' N'elak had stored there. Boxes of spices gave the air a pleasant, earthy odor, the swathes of brightly colored cloth in startling contrast to the gray walls and floor. It resembled the curtain-laden interior of a sultan's seraglio.

She took a deep breath and announced, "*I* want to execute T'alak."

"Impossible!" snapped Haven.

"Why? Haven't I more right to take his life than anyone?" Her voice shook. "He's destroyed mine."

N'elak nodded. "I believe this to be an admirable solution. If we leave evidence that your feisty little human executed him, then our organization will escape repercussions."

Haven studied Catriona. "Are you sure this is what you want?"

"It's my right by Komodoan law, is it not?"

With a sigh, Haven unholstered his blaster and pushed it across the desk toward her. "Then be thorough."

Catriona took the weapon, feeling the weight in her hand. She gazed into Haven's cold eyes, usually so filled with warmth and love for her. Swallowing back tears, she turned to leave, heading back to the guest quarters. The skiff they'd traveled in from T'alak's house sat beside the old ship called *Dream Lover*. Catriona slipped into the skiff for a moment before going down to the basement.

Drawing her weapon, she unbolted the door and slipped inside. The oil lamp she'd brought still burned, but wasn't adequate to light the cell properly. A shape loomed out of the shadows.

"Back so soon?" came T'alak's voice.

Judging by the state of his hands, he'd been attempting to dig up the dirt floor.

"Captain, I just heard the Military won't barter for you, so you're to be executed."

He saw the blaster in her hand. "No doubt you've been waiting for this moment a long time."

"I believe that by Komodoan law, once I claim the right of execution, I can administer a mercy clause. I'm doing that now." She slipped the weapon back into her belt.

"You disgrace me, human. You have no claim on me."

"I don't want a claim. All I want is you out of my life for good."

"The clause means I will be indebted to you by law. I refuse to live with the dishonor of being obligated to a human!"

"Oh, don't be ridiculous! Just staying away from me for the rest of my life will cancel your debt nicely."

300 | *Time Twist*

"Does A'rlon know of this?"

Catriona flushed. "I must blindfold you, T'alak. I can't let you see where you are. There's a skiff just outside that can take you out of here."

"How do you suggest I pilot a course blindfolded?"

"I'll plot it."

T'alak stared at her, his alien face a picture of bewilderment. "I don't understand. After all that's passed, why would you help me escape?"

"I can't let you be killed when you saved me from B'alarg. But I don't want to have to look over my shoulder for you any more, T'alak. I won't live in captivity, I'd rather die."

"You have made that abundantly clear." He took a step toward her. "Is a life as my consort so unacceptable to you?"

"It wouldn't work out, T'alak."

He nodded. "Very well. In that case I discharge you."

"Thank you." Catriona stepped back. "Let's get going, then."

"We will meet again, human."

"I hope not. Unless it's to discuss a peace treaty between the Realm and the Alliance."

He hissed a laugh. "They should make you an ambassador. You are tenacious enough."

Catriona paused. "If I were, would you consider peace negotiations?"

"Ask me again if you become one."

She moved toward the door, wondering if he were serious. As head of the highest Imperial House, his opinion would have weight with the Realm. She stopped.

"Wait. Blindfold."

She ripped a strip out of her cloak, reaching up to place it around T'alak's head. As she tied it securely, T'alak bent his head, found her mouth and kissed her. Catriona drew back and studied his blindfolded face.

"Why did you do that?"

"Remember that, not the rest."

Disquieted, Catriona took his arm, guiding him toward the door. Opening it, they stepped outside. She started at the sound of Haven's voice.

"What the hell do you think you're doing?"

He came down the stairs toward them. She felt T'alak stiffen under her hand and he reached up to yank off the blindfold. Catriona drew herself up.

"I've administered the mercy clause, Jack. I'm letting him go."

"Give me my blaster," he demanded.

T'alak made a swift movement, pulling the weapon from Catriona's belt before she could stop him.

"Commander A'rlon," he hissed, "I have long waited to have you on the receiving end of a blaster."

Haven snorted, "Preferably one that is charged, T'alak! You don't think I'd send a female out with a loaded weapon, do you?"

"What?" Catriona snatched the blaster out of T'alak's hand. "You didn't think I could handle it? What sort of imbecile do you think I am?"

"Imbecile enough to defy me."

"Let us pass. I'm sorry you can't understand why I have to do this. T'alak saved my life-"

"Your obligation has been fulfilled, Catriona. You didn't execute him. Now, leave us."

Catriona glared at the man she loved. He looked as alien as T'alak, violent and rage-filled. She knew if she left he'd kill T'alak. She couldn't let that happen.

Dropping her gaze she moved between them, heading for the stairs. Just as she passed Haven, she whirled, smacking him over the back of the head with the butt of the blaster. The weapon discharged, narrowly missing him as it sent a bolt of fire into the ground. Aghast, Catriona caught him as he crumpled into her arms. He had trusted her with the blaster after all! His ruse had worked well. Too well, he'd almost died for it. She eased him down to a sitting position on the stairs.

"I cannot trust my scales," said T'alak. "You knocked your lover cold!" He convulsed in hissing laughter.

"Shut the fuck up," snarled Catriona, leaving the blaster with Haven and moving to replace T'alak's blindfold. She couldn't believe she'd done it, either. Haven would never forgive her, but she couldn't live with T'alak's death on her hands.

Pulling T'alak at a run, she led him to the docked skiff, and popped the hatch. She felt like she had left part of herself lying back on those stairs. She pushed T'alak into a passenger seat.

"Get settled and fasten your seat belt," she ordered, reaching for the pad she'd hidden in her sleeve. She kept a wary eye on T'alak, just in case he had ideas about piloting the skiff himself with her inside. But the Captain sat and fastened himself in. Catriona marveled that he trusted her, but then, why wouldn't he? She had just hurt Haven to help him.

"So, it is over for you and Komodoa, human?" he asked.

Catriona looked at him. Something told her it was not. She unsealed the sedative pad and moved to lean over him.

"It's not over until the fat lady sings," she murmured.

Impulsively, she bent down and kissed him on the lips as she pressed the pad to his neck. He jerked with surprise and his mouth grew slack against hers as the sedative took effect.

Moving to the helm, Catriona engaged the drive. Pulling up the autopilot scanner, she plotted a course that would take T'alak a couple of hours east of *H'berna*. He should be flying two hundred feet above the Forest of *Tre'kar* when he came to. Then he could safely get himself home. She set a detailed take-off program on delay start, then scrambled out of the skiff, slamming the hatch sealed behind her. Backing toward the guest quarters building, she ducked as the craft eased out of the bay, floated upwards and then shot off at great speed. Catriona hoped that would be the last she'd ever see of Captain T'alak.

HAVEN STILL lay where Catriona had felled him. Crouching down, she gently tapped his face to bring him round. Her heart pounded, she knew he'd be furious.

"Jack, please. Wake up!"

He began to come round, his eyelids fluttering until finally they opened fully. Catriona brushed a wayward strand of long, black hair off his face. He looked so beautiful. For a second she saw a glimmer of warmth in his dark eyes, but as he remembered what had happened, they hardened to black flints.

He shrugged off her touch. "Did you let T'alak go?"

"Yes, I sedated him and sent him off in the skiff. Please try to understand, by Komodoan law I had the right-"

"You are altogether too fond of quoting Komodoan law to me, Catriona! I think it is time you bore the brunt of that law yourself." He rose to his feet, winced, and put a hand to the back of his head where she'd hit him with the blaster. "Come with me." He moved up the stairs to their guest chamber.

She followed. "I'm really sorry, Jack. I know you're angry, and you have a right to be. But surely you can see-"

"Be silent! If you want to use Komodoan rules, then you will have to use them all. Females do not speak unless invited to do so." They had reached the top landing, and Haven opened the bedchamber door, thrusting her inside.

"Don't be ridiculous, Jack! I am not Komodoan, and you're only half."

He hissed a short laugh. "That hasn't stopped you from quoting Komodoan law to suit you whenever convenient." He slammed the door behind him and advanced on her. "You've gone too far this time. Whatever made you think it acceptable to disobey me and knock me unconscious?"

"I'm sorry! I really am." Catriona bit her lip, fighting tears.

He pulled a stool from against the wall and sat on it, facing her. "Come over here," he ordered. She did so, hoping he would relent, but gazing into his hard eyes she saw no forgiveness in them. "You're completely out of control, Catriona. I should never have let it get this far. You need disciplining, and as your mate, the duty falls to me." Reaching up he yanked her down over his lap.

"No, Jack! I'm not a child to be spanked! Let me go, you *bastard*!" she yelled as his hand came down hard on her buttocks. She couldn't believe it. Furious beyond reason, she twisted and kicked, but he managed to hold onto her, smacking her all the harder for her efforts. Tears of mortification flowed down her face.

"How could you?" she sobbed, the fight gone from her.

"How could *you*? I trusted you, Catriona. I disobeyed direct orders from Intelligence to come to Komodoa to rescue you only to find you romping in T'alak's bedchamber. And then you admit you slept with my counterpart from the other timeline." He gave her a sound smack for good measure, and pushed her so she slipped to the floor.

Catriona looked up at him through red-rimmed eyes. "Have you forgotten that I walked in on you and Matthew together in my bed? Don't go being judge and jury to me when you're guilty of the same thing!"

"If you remember, he was merely massaging my back. You never gave me a chance to explain. I thought he was you. He turned out to be a Komodoan spy."

Catriona blinked, realizing how much in the wrong she was. She choked back a sob. "Jack, I'm sorry. My judgment is not always sound, I know that. But if I can't resist you in this time, what makes you think I could in any other?" She buried her head in her hands.

"What about Captain T'alak?" asked Haven after a moment. "Did you also sleep with him?"

304 | *Time Twist*

Her head snapped up. "I wanted to. He told me you were dead and I wanted to use him to forget the pain of losing you, but I couldn't. He put the honor of his House on the line to stop General B'alarg from raping and killing me, and I couldn't stand by and let him be executed in turn. I had hoped you would understand."

"Why didn't you tell me he saved your life?"

"I did! You wouldn't listen." She noticed Haven slumping forward as though light-headed. "What's the matter?"

He put a hand to touch the back of his head. It came away with a bloody green smear across his palm. "A testament to your strength," he murmured.

"Oh, Jack!" She hesitated, torn between wanting to storm from the chamber and wanting to tend to him.

She went to the small bathroom to dampen a cloth. Moving behind him, she cleaned the painful-looking cut where a sharp angle of the weapon had connected. Not able to help herself, she held his head gently between her palms and leaned down to feather his wound with her lips.

"I'm sorry," she whispered.

He reached up and grasped her forearm, pulling her round in front of him. The anger had gone from his eyes, replaced by the liquid warmth that always put her stomach in flutters. He drew her down, Catriona sinking to her knees in front of him. He held her close, gently covering her mouth with his. She clung to him, all her desire and love for him flooding back.

When at last he let her go, he said, "We've stayed here long enough, my Beauty. We need to go home, where we can put this behind us. I'm going to prep *Dream Lover* so we can get the hell out of here."

Catriona did a double take. "Why call it *Dream Lover*?"

His mouth quirked. "I just named her after you."

Catriona lifted a hand to give him a playful thump, then hesitated. "Do you feel well enough to pilot her?"

"You didn't hit me that hard. But it serves me right for showing you where to hit a man to knock him cold."

"You showed me a lot more than that, if you remember." Catriona's heart lifted. Perhaps everything might be all right, after all.

"So I did." He smiled. "We'll have to recap on our return journey to Earth. Make sure you remember *everything* I showed you."

Jerking to consciousness, T'alak tried to sit bolt upright, but the strap across his chest restrained him. The skiff flew with no one at the helm! Ripping the safety belt free, he vaulted to the controls. Autopilot. At least he hadn't been in danger of crashing. He switched to manual control and slowed the skiff.

Fragments of a dream flashed into his head. Probably inspired by Catriona kissing him as she administered the sedative. He pulled the pad from his neck, fingering it thoughtfully. Part of the legend leading up to the Festival of *O'tium* was that *P'jarra*, the Goddess of Water, betrayed *B'llumni*, once the God of Peace, with a kiss as she tried to drown him in a fit of jealous rage. In retaliation, he transformed into a God of War and the two deities only came together in peace once a year. Somehow the legend had become mixed up in his dream, where he had been involved in *k'vet*, a ritual sword fight. Although his foe had been unseen, as the fight progressed, it became obvious his opponent was female. The encounter grew more and more erotic as her form became like liquid, flowing over him. He had been encompassed with a warm, sensual caressing, to which he had totally succumbed. He had a vague impression that the mellifluous lover bore Catriona's face.

The skiff's control panel showed that he flew over the Forest of *Tre'kar*, several thousand kilometers northwest of the Third Province. He smiled grimly. The human had learned a lot since he had first taken her captive. She had surprised him with her ingenuity. He wondered if she had thought everything through, and pulled up the flight program. Sure enough, the entire flight path was there on record; he could easily backtrack and find out where he'd been held. He slowed the skiff further until he hovered above the forest, then pulled up a holomap so he could check the point of origin.

The scanner emitted a series of short beeps. Frowning, T'alak concentrated it on the source. He couldn't believe the readout. A craft of non-Komodoan origin hovered just above the camouflaging canopy of trees beneath. What by *B'llumni* could it be doing down there? Altering course, he took the skiff lower, zeroing in on the alien craft. As he grew closer it became apparent by its structure to be a Leontor-made vessel. The Alliance, infiltrating the Realm? Perhaps he had better withdraw and report his findings to the Military before investigating alone. Before he could adjust the coordinates, General B'alarg appeared on the viewscreen.

"Captain T'alak, stop engines and prepare for an actuate bubble." He terminated the communication before T'alak could respond.

306 | *Time Twist*

T'alak's tail twisted in consternation. How was it his superior officer should be here and unconcerned at the presence of an enemy spacecraft? A quick glance at his instruments told him why. With no other ship within range, B'alarg had to be *on* the spacecraft. He killed the engine and set the auto-anchor. A moment later he stood face to face with his superior officer on the flight deck of the alien craft.

B'alarg wore a frown of unease. "The last I heard you were being held hostage by the Underground. How did you find the restricted zone?"

"What zone? I have full security clearance, yet I know nothing of this."

"Answer my question!" B'alarg approached, his tail lashing from side to side.

T'alak noted the group of four soldiers standing ready.

"I effected an escape." He refused to confess that Catriona Logan had administered the mercy clause; that would be too shameful.

B'alarg raised his tail and slammed T'alak around the knees, making him buckle over.

"You tire me, Captain. You have for a long time. I thought I'd seen the last of you, but I might have known you'd show your Imperial tail in my business again. People of your caste should not be in the Military, you are nothing but a liability." He gestured to the soldiers and two of them moved to either side of T'alak. "Have a seat, *noble* Captain," said B'alarg. The soldiers took T'alak's arms and pushed him into the command chair. "Leave us." B'alarg fingered the carbine in his belt as the soldiers exited the control cabin. T'alak's tail had been tromped on in the scuffle, further injuring the already torn ligament, and the alien seat hadn't been designed to accommodate a tail. Shifting his weight, T'alak watched B'alarg through narrowed eyes.

"I am not the only one weary of your kind, T'alak." The General paced the control cabin, his tail curling and uncurling with triumph. "There are several key high-ranking officers who resent as I do, the influence the Imperial Houses continue to have with those in power. For some years now, we have been building an underground of our own, within the Military."

"And what do you hope to achieve; overthrow of our government?"

B'alarg hissed. "Nothing so crude, Captain. Our Cadre will infiltrate and influence the government, eventually phasing out your kind."

T'alak stared. "May I know how long your Cadre has been in existence?"

"Since before the alien formation of the Alliance. The Realm has been due for a rebirth, Captain. It is time we dispensed with the nobility and let the people take power."

"A revolution?" scoffed T'alak. "You'll never succeed."

A cold smile slid across B'alarg's face. "There's something I've wanted to tell you for years." He moved closer, looming over T'alak. "You have blamed the Alliance for the spacecraft collision that killed your mate." T'alak grew very still. "But your hatred has been misguided. Did you ever see the passenger list? The proconsul elect traveled on that ship. When our Cadre sabotaged it and its engines blew, an Alliance ship answered their distress call. We sent a detachment to intervene. Once we had terminated the alien crew, we used their ship to stage the accident." He pushed his face closer to T'alak's. "Effective ploy, don't you think? Many like you pledged to destroy the Alliance for that. While you Imperial heroes were off trying to gain supreme Realm dominance over the galaxy, we were making sure the right kind of power would be wielded." He bowed. "Thank you, T'alak. Your alien extermination has been invaluable to the Cadre."

T'alak choked in disbelief. T'alak-ra, murdered by her own kind? By *B'alarg*? Deadly cold rage crept within him. Before he could grip B'alarg by the throat and tear the life from him, the General had extracted his carbine, holding it against T'alak's head.

"One move, Captain, and you may join your mate. But I'd prefer it if you restrain yourself. The ship we are now in, is scheduled to 'attack' the *Gr'avitas*, a visiting dignitary ship as it returns from *S'ola*. Exclusive as your castes are, the group consists of representatives from seven Imperial Houses. They will be wiped out in the collision. And as you are already reported as having been kidnapped by the Underground, your charred remains found aboard will be evidence enough to incriminate the rebels. Once again, T'alak, you are invaluable."

61

COLONEL GRREAG felt someone at his back and spun round. He scowled into the startled brown eyes of Uzima Khumalo. "You should not creep up on me like that, Chief."

"I didn't," objected the human. "You were lost in thought."

He growled. Indeed he had felt many light years from the *Vallo*, gazing at stars from its observation room. He chided himself for having

308 | *Time Twist*

been so remiss as to not hear her approach.

"You miss Catriona, huh?" she asked.

Grreag looked sharply at her. Was he that obvious?

"I do, too," she sighed, leaning her forehead against the pane as she looked out. "I just can't believe she's really dead."

"Neither can I," rumbled Grreag. That was just what he had been pondering: dying in an actuate bubble, to have one's molecules scattered for all time. It had not been an honorable death for his friend. He knew Catriona had not made *Arrum*, and although not her custom, the thought that her soul might be wandering the far reaches of space without rest felt unbearable.

"What did you make of the whole spatial rupture saga?" asked the Chief, studying him in the reflection of the window.

"I would not have believed it possible, if the quantum-shielded buoy had not been retrieved," he admitted.

"The buoy was a piece of brilliance by you in the other timeline. Otherwise we would never have known what had happened. I found it fascinating to hear our conversations recorded there, yet to have no memory of them."

"Has the timeline been fully restored, Chief?"

The engineer spread her hands in a gesture Grreag recognized well. She wasn't certain. "It all appears to be. According to the buoy data, Professor Webster changed his route of escape three years ago, when he and Dr. Morrison..." She hesitated for a beat. Grreag knew she loathed Webster's assistant-turned-spy. "When he and Morrison first jumped by temporal bubble out of there. This time he fixed it so the imbalance left couldn't threaten the fabric of time. But it means he can never come back."

Grreag frowned, turning to face Khumalo. "If that is so, why did a partial rupture remain, which Captain T'alak attempted to enter?" None of this made any sense to him.

"I can only guess because that was the point of entrance and exit of so many temporal bubbles over time. Excuse the pun." She grinned. "This confuses even me, and I'm supposed to be the engineering expert."

Grreag showed his fangs briefly. Khumalo reminded him very much of Catriona. "It is difficult to believe that T'alak entered the rupture three times, the first foiled by you and I, the second a combined effort between the half-Komodoan A'rlon and the *Vallo*, and third —the one we actually remember—when T'alak's ship got caught in the mouth of the rift."

"I'll bet he was livid when we towed him out!" Khumalo laughed, slapping her thigh, then sobered. "Pity with all this time travel that we couldn't have gone back and retrieved Catriona before the actuate accident. After all, Webster made sure he got Morrison."

Grreag had thought that, too. But he knew the answer. "Catriona should never have existed in our time, Uzima," he reminded her, uncharacteristically using her first name.

"Yes, I know." The ebony human sighed. "I suppose we should be glad for her; she's at rest at last. I don't think she was very happy in this century. And that Haven didn't help."

Grreag's body hair bristled. "What do you mean?"

"He hurt her, Sir. I guess I can tell you about it, now she's gone. She found the bastard in bed with someone in her apartment."

Grreag's hackles flared. "I knew that Komodoan slime couldn't be trusted!"

He knew it pointless to be angry now, but he had never liked that double agent. He would have to have a little talk with the reptile when next their paths crossed.

Khumalo gave a short laugh. "S'funny, 'cos on the tape, even the A'rlon from the other timeline said that Catriona's Haven had sounded too good to be true. He would have known himself, better than anyone."

Grreag stemmed the ripples of anger surging through him. His ears pricked forward. "How could the other A'rlon have heard what Haven was like?"

He watched the human's eyes as comprehension flooded into their chestnut depths. "You don't think-"

"We may be reaching for hay, Uzima," he warned her. To his consternation, she burst into laughter. Too surprised to growl, he asked, "What is so funny?"

"You mean, 'grasping at straws'!"

He stiffened, then relaxed. It felt good to hear someone laugh again. "Come, let us investigate." He bestowed a full-fanged smile on his engineer.

Major Benjamin's voice came through the computer wall monitor. "Colonel Grreag to the control cabin."

"What is it?"

"We're picking up what I think is a distress call from a civilian Leontor craft, Sir," replied Benjamin. "It's right on the border of Komodoan Realm space and we need your clearance to decipher the code."

Grreag glanced at Khumalo. "With me, Chief." He led the way

310 | *Time Twist*

to the control cabin. What by his ancestors could a civilian Leontor vessel be doing out by the border?

The viewer displayed the craft, a sleek arrow-shaped deep space shuttle. Grreag strode to operations and Lieutenant Larrar vacated her seat for him. He ran a rapid scan over the Leontor vessel.

"The distress is general," he rumbled. "The Komodoan Realm will have received it also."

Sam Benjamin shook his head. "What kind of idiot is piloting that craft?"

"Either someone with a death wish, or it's a trap," answered Grreag. Having identified the code, he let Larrar take back her seat.

As the *Vallo* drew closer, the scans showed more detailed results. "There are four Leontor life signs aboard, Sir," advised Larrar.

"Weaponry?"

"Nothing beyond standard defense blasters. Not detecting anything suspicious." She growled. "We're within pinging range now, Colonel."

Within moments the viewer showed the images of two anxious-looking Leons, their whiskers stiff. "Ah, the *Vallo*," said one in relief. "We hoped it would be you."

"Identify yourselves!" snarled Grreag.

Two more Leons stepped into view of the monitor and Grreag's ears flicked in surprise. He recognized them as two of the students who had accompanied Catriona from Earth.

"Colonel Grreag, I am Qiterr."

"I know you. What are you doing out here?"

"You ordered me to see to Lieutenant Logan's welfare," growled Qiterr, "but I failed you. However, perhaps I may make reparation. I am not satisfied that she died in the actuate incident as we first believed.

"Even though traces of her DNA were found in the collapsed bubble, in later analysis Zerreem found key components to be missing. It appeared to be a copy of her trace patterns, not her original."

Zerreem nudged Qiterr aside. "I know she is not dead, Colonel. She had not made *Arrum*, and the spirits will not allow her rest until she does—"

"Shut up!" growled Qiterr.

"What the heck are they talking about?" inquired a perplexed Benjamin.

"You have documented evidence that the DNA in the bubble was copied?" asked Grreag.

"Correct. We also found an irregularity in the hyperdrive wakes. The volume showed more than could have been caused by the rendezvous between the *Exsequor* and the *Vallo*."

"Another ship?"

Qiterr bared a fang. "We believe a Komodoan vessel was secreted behind a nearby asteroid. We came to investigate, but our ship has developed a fault. None of us is knowledgeable in engineering."

"I take it you are here without the consent of the Leontor Militia?" inquired Grreag.

"We are here on our own reconnaissance."

"A pity he hadn't thought to bring an engineer along," muttered Benjamin. "Bloody students."

Grreag suppressed the urge to laugh. Being so long with these humans had affected him; he gave in to amusement far more than healthy for a Leontor. "Cadet Qiterr, we will bring your ship on board; prepare for traherence. Then we'll have a little talk about your DNA findings."

<hr/>

T'alak paced the small cell in the brig where B'alarg had incarcerated him. One wall looked open, but a reverse-traherence stream locked it.

Once the truth about his mate's death had set in, a cold fury gripped him. He had spent the most part of his life avenging her murder. To discover his hatred had been misplaced was devastating. His loathing for the Alliance had been born with T'alak-ra's death, and fueled as his bitterness increased. Over the years he had tortured, raped and killed more Terrans and Leontor than he could count, and enjoyed his quest of terror.

Until recently, he didn't know that humans were very much like Komodoans, with equal intelligence, passions, and fears. He had considered any non-Komodoan race savages; infestations that spoiled the planets and worlds they inhabited. How could he have thought he had provided valuable service for the Realm by eliminating as many as possible? An unbearable pain grew inside him at the thought of how many lives he'd ruined. And all for nothing. T'alak-ra's real murderers roamed free, benefiting from his vendetta with the Alliance.

And now he had been imprisoned on an Alliance ship, to be used as a pawn in another one of B'alarg's attacks. History was to be repeated; they were en route to intercept the *Gr'avitas* on its way back from *S'ola*. General B'alarg had divulged that T'alak would be alone on board while the ship would be remotely guided into its collision course.

To further wound him, B'alarg informed him he had planted several Cadre sympathizers in T'alak's crew on the *L'umina*. Assigned to escort the *Gr'avitas*, the Cadre infiltrators aboard would sabotage the engines to prevent the *L'umina* from intervening when the Alliance ship 'attacked.'

T'alak stopped pacing as footsteps approached. B'alarg stood on the other side of the traherence stream.

"I've come to take my leave of you, Captain. You'll be in command of a vessel for the last time. How fitting it should be an enemy ship."

"I wish extermination for you and your sons, B'alarg! You dishonor the Realm by this treachery."

A long hiss escaped through B'alarg's teeth. "It is nothing more or less than you have done for what you believed in, T'alak."

"What I did, I did for the good of the Realm. You plot to overthrow the very essence of our society."

"Spoken like a true noble. Your time is finished, T'alak. Your House will fall with the rest of them-"

"My son-"

"Sublieutenant T'alak-zan will follow the new order or die! There will be no House for him to inherit, no noble lines to uphold. It is over for your kind!"

T'alak's mouth curved to a sneer. "As a human once told me: 'It's not over until the fat lady sings.'"

62

"**Good-bye, N'elak.** Thank you for everything." Haven bowed to his friend, and then held out his hand, Terran fashion.

N'elak took it. "I forget your mixed blood sometimes, my friend. I wish you would stay here with us. We could use someone of your experience."

Haven grinned. "Perhaps one day, you old reptile."

N'elak glanced behind him at L'ticia. "You wish to bid your human friend farewell, N'elak-ra?"

She moved forward, taking Catriona in a full human embrace. "*P'jarra* be with you, friend."

"And with you."

Catriona lightly kissed L'ticia on the cheek and withdrew. She found it discomforting that L'ticia had to wait for permission from N'elak to speak; she had traded one form of servitude for another. At least with Captain T'alak, L'ticia earned a wage, and had a position in a noble house. But, Catriona reminded herself, L'ticia's choice wasn't her concern.

"Better leave quickly, A'rlon," advised N'elak. "Perhaps Captain T'alak…" he shot Catriona a dark look, "is already searching for you."

Catriona resisted the temptation to intone the mercy clause to N'elak; she'd already been in enough trouble with Haven for quoting Komodoan law. Her face burned at the memory of his 'discipline'. Haven threw a casual arm around her shoulders as they turned toward *Dream Lover*. Her heart warmed, knowing his gesture to be silent support in the face of N'elak's disapproval.

Dream Lover looked as bad inside as she did on the outside. Her metal interior had not seen care in many years. Dark splotches of oily residue adorned most surfaces, making the cabin dingy. Catriona settled into a seat to the rear of Haven's pilot stool. Watching his tail draped down the back of the stool, she'd be glad when he had the revolting thing removed. She suppressed a shudder. It reminded her too much of T'alak.

As *Dream Lover* rattled into action and began her ascent above *H'berna*, Catriona anxiously scanned the skies for any sign of T'alak. He would have long since emerged from the sedative she'd given him. With luck, his honor would make him accept the terms of her mercy clause and never come looking for her again.

"Once I get us clear of the planet, I'm going to grab forty winks," Haven said. "Think you can keep an eye on the ship?"

She nodded. "You believe we're going to get away without trouble?"

"We should. Though we need to run by *S'ola* on our way out of Realm space. *H'berna* traders make the most profits in the black market there. It would raise unwanted questions if we didn't stop by." He caught her look. "It won't take long, you can hide out and take a nap while we're there."

Catriona chewed on her lip. She didn't like keeping what happened with L'ticia from him. If they were to repair the damage to their relationship she'd have to be honest with him.

"Jack," she said, then hesitated.

Hearing the strain in her voice he looked at her. "What is it, Beauty?"

"I need to tell you one more thing." His expression grew tight and

314 | *Time Twist*

she saw the trepidation in his eyes. "It's about L'ticia," she continued. "We became... close at T'alak's house. Just one time."

Haven frowned. "How close?" Catriona picked at a hangnail on her thumb. "Catriona, I know you immersed yourself in Komodoan society when L'ticia guarded you. There's a phrase for it if an agent does it—'going native'. If you mean close in the way I think you do, I cannot blame you. That is a common thing between Komodoan females."

"That's what L'ticia said. You're sure?"

Relief flooded his face. "I just wish I'd been there to join in." He smiled tentatively, and Catriona loved him all the more for trying to make light of it.

He turned back to *Dream Lover's* control panel and Catriona watched the city below with all its spires shrink to a pincushion, the planet plunging rapidly away. The violet sky soon tinged burnt orange, darkening to the inky black of space.

Haven's fingers sped over the controls, and then he shifted from the pilot's stool to stretch out over a couple of seats in back. "She's on autopilot to take us within range of *S'ola* in just over an hour. Don't touch anything."

Catriona got up and leaned over to kiss him. He squeezed her hand and she stroked his forehead before moving away to sit on the pilot's stool. She remembered the last time she sat at the helm of a ship, making an escape from Komodoa. Once again, it had been Haven who had helped her get away, and she thought he'd been killed in the process. Watching her sleeping lover, she admitted things could never be the same between them again. She had changed from that frightened, helpless civilian he rescued two years ago.

A soft bleeping from the pilot console distracted her. Straightening her slumped shoulders, she turned to inspect the source of the noise. According to *Dream Lover's* instruments it looked like another ship approached them. Catriona activated a scan over the other craft as they moved into its sector. When the readout flipped onto the screen, Catriona's jaw dropped.

"It couldn't be," she murmured. But another scan confirmed it: an Alliance ship approached, all the way out here in the heart of Realm space.

Excited, Catriona jumped up to shake Haven awake. "You're not going to believe this. Take a look at the tracking screen."

"I thought I told you not to touch anything."

"Just look, will you!"

Sluggishly, he moved to the console to do as she bid. "Impossible," he announced, initiating a more detailed scan from the ship's computer.

"Looks like they've spotted us," observed Catriona, watching the ship change course. "I wonder if it's a rescue ship sent for us?"

Haven shook his head. "Not likely. I don't feel good about this. Let's see what their communications reveal."

He initiated *Dream Lover's* pirate listener. Its high-frequency signal tapped into nearby ships' communications and deciphered all possible scrambler codes. Thanks to N'elak, Haven had added the latest Komodoan Realm descrambler.

A wall of horrified silence fell between Catriona and Haven at what they heard. B'alarg's plot to overthrow Realm government became very clear.

Haven put together an encoded message and sent it through subspace on an Alliance secured frequency. "Let's hope someone picks that up in time," he murmured. "Now, I think we should…"

His words disappeared in the volley of fire that erupted from the approaching ship. Bright orange flashes lit up around them as *Dream Lover* took a direct hit. Thrown to the floor, Catriona covered her ears to block out the screeching alarm klaxon.

The cabin became an inferno, deadly heat roaring around them.

"Catriona! Come on, wake up."

She stirred, jarring into awakeness when inhaling made her cough. She lay on a hard floor, dazzled by a bright light.

"What happened?" she managed between coughs.

Haven knelt beside her, supporting her as she sat up. "*Dream Lover's* been blown to smithereens. We're on the Alliance ship."

Catriona succumbed to another fit of coughing.

"This might help."

A plasticup of water appeared on the floor beside her. Catriona looked up sharply at the familiar voice.

Captain T'alak regarded her as she spluttered, "Why, you lying, filthy, shit-faced son of a-"

"Catriona." Haven laid his hand on her arm. "Captain T'alak did not abduct us. Not this time, anyway." He shot T'alak a look. "He's a prisoner here, too."

Catriona looked from Haven to T'alak and back again.

"General B'alarg?" To Haven's nod, she slumped, lifting the cup and finishing the water. "Is there any way out of here?" she inquired when the cool liquid had eased her throat.

"We're still working on it," replied Haven, checking her pulse.

"I'm fine." she shrugged his hand away and scrambled to her feet.

Haven's face appeared blackened, otherwise unharmed. Catriona grinned at his sooty appearance.

"You're not so pristine, yourself. We both got somewhat 'well done' when *Dream Lover* went up." He reached over and wiped at a smudge on her cheek.

"Very touching," commented T'alak. "As we've ascertained we're all alive, can we concentrate on how to stay that way?"

Haven hissed a brief laugh. "You're right, *sekke*. Let's have another try at the access panel."

As he moved toward the traherence stream, Catriona blinked. *Sekke*? He'd used a Komodoan term of affection between blood brothers. Evidently the two men had been talking over their differences. She didn't know how to take it, her lover and erstwhile captor friends again.

"Not enough evidence," Colonel Grreag said.

There was nothing he wanted more than to plunge into Realm space and search for his friend, butchering any Komodoan he met on the way. But he couldn't risk the Alliance's outcome of the war on such flimsy data.

"It is nothing more than wishful thinking," agreed Benjamin. "A decayed DNA trace in a temporal bubble, some Leontor superstition. Sorry," he added, catching Grreag's glower.

"What about the extra wake signature the Leon students detected?" demanded Khumalo.

"Inconclusive."

Khumalo slammed a fist down on Grreag's desk. "Fuck it, Colonel! Don't be so small-minded!"

Grreag's ears flattened. "Chief, may I remind you that you're addressing your superior officer, and a Leontor. This conversation is over. You're dismissed."

"Like hell I am! What more proof do you need?"

Lieutenant Larrar's voice intruded over the communications net. "Sir, we've a transmission coming in from Komodoan Realm space: emergency priority."

Lieutenant Colonel Haven's voice piped through, informing the Alliance of B'alarg's treacherous plan to shoot down the dignitary ship. In closing, Haven added that he had Catriona Logan with him, alive and well at the time of transmission.

Grreag's purr swelled within him and he met Khumalo's look. She folded her arms across her chest and struck an attitude.

"Proof enough, Sir?"

63

HAVEN SHOVED himself back from the traherence stream access panel in frustration. "I can't trip it! It's designed so if tampered with, it sends a new signal to loop into the original."

Catriona watched Captain T'alak join A'rlon at the panel. "Can you decrease the frequency?" he asked.

"Yes, though the stream will still be powerful enough to dismember."

"But not enough to kill?"

"No."

Catriona saw the look that passed between them. A surge of panic swept through her, bringing her to her feet.

"No!" she yelled, too late. Haven bent over the panel as T'alak stepped into the stream. Lesions of light sparked in all directions, and his dark face contorted in agony.

Haven whirled. "Come on, Catriona, follow me!" He stepped through the gap in the stream, Catriona right behind. T'alak stumbled after them, collapsing on the floor. Catriona rushed to help him.

He had managed to keep his head and most of his tail free, but his back and shoulders looked horribly burned. Catriona felt sickened at the seared flesh.

"I can't believe you did that." She took his arm to help him up, keeping her eyes averted from the seething burns.

"I'll find the control cabin," said Haven. "Try to get the ship off the collision course."

T'alak gasped, "No. Program irreversible. Only chance…" He convulsed, then whispered, "only chance, escape pods."

Catriona met Haven's eyes. She could see he trusted T'alak's word. The Realm must have used this kind of program before.

"All right." Haven took T'alak's other arm. "Hurry."

They made their way through the ship as quickly as they could, half-carrying T'alak between them.

318 | *Time Twist*

At the escape pod bay, Haven left Catriona to support T'alak while he investigated the three pods docked there.

"We'll get you some medical attention as soon as possible," she assured T'alak, who sank to a kneeling position while they waited.

Crouching in front of him, she used her sleeve to wipe the sweat from his face. "Thank you for getting us out of there."

"It was... necessary," he managed. "I owe you, Catriona Logan."

She looked at him, annoyed. "I thought we'd already sorted that out. You don't owe me a thing from the mercy clause-"

He held up a hand. "No. I learned that my hatred of the Alliance has been misguided."

Haven returned, preventing Catriona from asking what he had learned. His expression looked grim.

"What is it?" she asked.

He shook his head. "Only one pod is functional. And there's only room for two in it."

T'alak roused himself. "The choice is clear, *sekke*. You and Catriona must go."

"Surely we can find another way..." began Catriona.

"I will not tolerate argument," he insisted.

Catriona recognized that tone. Short of bashing him over the head and dragging him off, he would not be swayed. She glanced over her shoulder at Haven, who nodded to T'alak and stepped forward. With concentration, he brought his grafted tail around to meet T'alak's.

"Captain, I rejoice we came to an understanding. May your sacrifice bring honor in the Celestial Home," he said formally.

"*B'llumni* aid you," hissed T'alak from his kneeling position. "Live the life you both were meant to. Now go! We waste time."

Catriona stared at T'alak. Things were happening too fast for her to get a grasp on them.

"Come on, Catriona; we have to leave," urged Haven.

She reached over, cupping T'alak's face between her hands. "Thank you," she whispered, leaning forward to kiss him on the lips.

He took her hand briefly in his. "Go," he said.

Blinded with tears, Catriona got to her feet and allowed Haven to propel her toward the pod. Once they were strapped in, Haven activated the escape sequence and they were thrust at unimaginable velocity from the ship.

Aboard the *L'umina*, General B'alarg dominated the flight deck. He oversaw their progress as they joined the *Gr'avitas'* side, and the official escort to Komodoan commenced. Suppressing his excitement, he greeted the dignitaries' courier, exchanging pleasantries, then continuing toward the planet. Any moment soon, the *L'umina's* engines would fail and they'd drop behind the *Gr'avitas*.

Keeping his face neutral, B'alarg slid a glance at the *L'umina's* new captain. A capable man, but dispensable. False situations had been woven so that the blame for the sabotage would fall on his shoulders. A link to N'elak's underworld had been created; more than enough evidence to have the man eliminated without trial.

B'alarg permitted himself a smile. What an honor that he should live to see the extermination of the Komodoan noble castes.

He felt a small lurch beneath him, and the *Gr'avitas* shot ahead on the viewscreen as the *L'umina* slowed to a halt. B'alarg assumed a concerned expression.

"Report!" he demanded. With satisfaction, he watched as the enemy ship came into range, heading straight for the *Gr'avitas*.

"General, an Alliance vessel is approaching the dignitary ship," reported the tactics officer.

"Get our engines on line without delay!" hissed B'alarg.

On the screen, the *Gr'avitas* slowed, attempting to turn and rejoin the *L'umina*. Purely a civilian craft, she needed to rely on the *L'umina* for defense.

B'alarg shouted orders for weapons ready, and feigned angry disbelief when he learned they were unavailable. His flight crew watched helplessly as the *Gr'avitas* attempted to defend herself.

"I'm going to puke!" Catriona's stomach lurched as the escape pod spun out of control.

"Please don't." Haven reached out squeezed her hand. "It'll soon stop, Beauty. Hang on."

With the other hand, he worked at the controls. The pod swung violently like a fairground ride, smoothing out to a bearable undulation.

"Can you see anything?" inquired Catriona, her eyes closed.

Haven glanced at her. She really did sound like she might be ill, which would be disastrous in the tiny capsule with no gravity.

"The *L'umina* has been disabled as B'alarg threatened. She's immobile."

320 | *Time Twist*

"Where is the Alliance ship?" Catriona recovered enough to peer out of the tiny portholes, but she could see nothing.

"Try not to move; you're upsetting the instruments." He studied the miniature viewer. "The ship is closing in on the *Gr'avitas*."

"T'alak," she whispered.

He looked at her, thinking back to the cell where all three of them had been held. While Catriona lay unconscious, the two erstwhile friends had had quite an enlightening talk. A much humbled T'alak had told him what B'alarg had revealed: the Cadre, created to oust the noble castes from the Realm, and how his lifemate had been killed so many years ago. T'alak confessed his dismay at learning his hatred for the Alliance had been misguided. Haven knew that T'alak's decision to remain behind while he and Catriona escaped was an attempt to make restitution for the harm he'd caused.

"What's that bleeping, Jack?"

Catriona's words brought him out of his reverie. Checking the instruments, he discovered another ship soaring into the sector at top velocity.

"What *is* it?" Catriona almost set the pod rocking again as she strained to see. "Damn you, Jack, tell me!"

"Catriona, will you ever learn to be patient?" he snapped. His next words were lost as a bright light filled the escape pod and an actuate bubble surrounded him.

"Let me out! I'm going to vomit!" Catriona unstrapped herself and pushed frantically at the hatchway.

They'd been transferred out of space and inside a ship. Which one wasn't yet apparent. Catriona didn't care, her mind on more urgent matters. Haven reached up and unsealed the hatch.

Catriona hauled herself out of the pod and emptied the sparse contents of her stomach on the actuate chamber floor. Anxiously, Haven pulled himself out after her.

"You have some explaining to do, reptile!" thundered a familiar voice.

Haven was relieved to see Catriona's Leontor friend, Colonel Grreag, standing with his arms folded across his ample chest. The Leon had done it again, rushing into Realm space to their defense.

"Colonel, it's good to see you. We need to stop that Alliance ship from colliding with the *Gr'avitas*." He followed the Leon's concerned amber eyes to where Catriona crouched, still heaving. "Zero G nausea," he explained, moving to her side. "All right, Beauty?" He massaged the back of her neck.

"Yes," gasped Catriona, taking deep breaths. "Where are we?" He helped her to her feet, turning her round. "Grreag!" Nausea forgotten, she rushed over to embrace him. "Boy, what took you so long, you hairy monster?" She nuzzled against his furry cheek.

"It is good to see you, Catriona," rumbled the Leon through his purring, a gleam in his eye. "But I do not understand Komodoan."

"Oh, I forgot. Is this better?" She grinned, translating.

"Much. We believed you to be dead; I am glad we were wrong."

"It's a long story."

"Yes, it is," interrupted Haven. "One for later. Now we need to get to the control cabin and take action against the Cadre's stolen Alliance ship."

Catriona stiffened, grabbing Grreag's arm. "There's still someone left on that ship. Can you actuate him off?"

"Who remains on board?"

"A friend. Please, Grreag, get him off before it's too late!"

"There is no time."

"Well, make time!" She looked to Haven for support.

He shook his head. "It was T'alak's choice to stay, Catriona. Let him go with dignity."

Grreag growled deeply. "You want me to actuate *Captain T'alak* onto the *Vallo*?" He shook his craggy head. "I wouldn't help that reptile if we had all the time in the universe. Come."

They hurried through the ship, Haven filling Grreag in on B'alarg's tactics. Catriona lagged behind. So intent on the exchange of information, neither of them noticed when she stopped and doubled back.

When General B'alarg saw the *Vallo* soar into the sector, his face mottled gray with rage. Somehow, that traitor A'rlon must have contacted them. The *L'umina's* weapons had to be back on line, and now. He pinged engineering.

"Check the thermal conduits, Sublieutenant," he ordered. "Report back immediately."

A moment later, the engines thrummed with life again. Engineering's response came through, "You were right, honored General. A fault so minor, our diagnostic scans overlooked it."

"Full throttle toward the *Vallo*," ordered B'alarg. "We must protect the *Gr'avitas* at any cost."

If he could destroy or disable the *Vallo*, then the remotely guided Alliance craft could still carry out its programming.

He noticed the *L'umina* captain regarding him. No matter. All that need happen was the *Gr'avitas'* destruction, and then B'alarg would be safe. He would become such a powerful force in the Realm that no one would be able to challenge him.

"Tactics," he hissed. "Take us between the *Vallo* and the *Gr'avitas*. When in position, open fire."

"Honored General," said the *L'umina* captain, "I recommend we first fire on the other enemy ship-"

"Follow my orders!" hissed B'alarg.

He obeyed and the *L'umina* spun between the two ships, spewing a volley of white fire over the *Vallo*. A series of satisfying flashes leapt up from her hull with each hit.

"Their armor is down," reported Tactics.

"Destroy them."

A sudden flash of bright light slewed across the flight deck and a bubble appeared, almost on top of B'alarg.

Catriona fought for balance as the bubble dumped her on the *L'umina's* flight deck. She had to act fast before one of the many weapons trained on her fired. B'alarg gaped at her, his flabby face a picture of wrath. Beside him, Catriona recognized T'alak's friend, M'arlaak, and spoke quickly.

"Your Captain T'alak is on that other Alliance ship against his will. You must actuate him off."

Captain M'arlaak's bright eyes glittered, and General B'alarg's arm snaked out, grabbing Catriona by the throat.

"Why should I believe a human slave?" Shoving her at M'arlaak, he hissed, "Kill her, it's a trick."

Catriona clutched M'arlaak's arms and looked right into his eyes. "B'alarg himself imprisoned T'alak there. The ship is being remotely guided by B'alarg's revolution Cadre!"

B'alarg slid a carbine from within his tunic.

"Wait, General," said M'arlaak, stepping between Catriona and B'alarg. "Tactics, run a scan for life signs on board the enemy ship."

"Belay that order!" B'alarg aimed his weapon at M'arlaak. "Why would you listen to a filthy Terran worm?"

Captain M'arlaak smiled. "Because the House of M'arlaak is allied with T'alak's, and I'm certain you know it is the second highest Imperial House in the Realm. Restrain him." He pointed with his chin to a guard behind B'alarg. The carbine flew from B'alarg's grasp as the guard ushered him into the command chair.

"Seventy human life signs; one Komodoan," reported Tactics.

"There's no one but Captain T'alak on board; the others must be faked to mislead you," said Catriona.

M'arlaak nodded. "Actuate the Komodoan here."

In a moment, Captain T'alak knelt on the flight deck floor. He hadn't moved from the position Catriona had left him in and it looked like he'd been interrupted in prayer.

He blinked once, then grinned. "M'arlaak, you old chameleon. Trust you not to give up on me."

"It is this human you have to thank, friend."

T'alak turned his dark eyes to Catriona. "You never give up, do you?" She shook her head, a grin spreading over her face.

Struggling to his feet he concentrated his attention on his crew. "Tactics, destroy the ship I just came from."

Several orange bolts sliced into the ship, lighting the *L'umina* viewscreen with a fiery glow. When it diminished, the ship had vanished.

"Sir!" shouted B'alarg's guard.

They spun round in time to see General B'alarg disappear in an actuate bubble.

64

T'ALAK REFUSED help. With dignity he took his command chair. "Track B'alarg's bubble," he ordered. "Open a channel to the *Vallo*."

The viewscreen filled with the *Vallo* control cabin. Catriona's heart warmed to see Colonel Grreag ensconced in the central chair, Major Benjamin and Haven beside him, with Chief Khumalo to the left and Lieutenant Larrar to the right. Behind Grreag stood a group of young Leontor. With amazement, Catriona recognized her students from ACC. All looked equally startled to see her standing on the enemy flight deck.

"Captain T'alak, why did you fire on us?" demanded Grreag.

"My apologies, Colonel." T'alak bowed his head. "I have only just come on board. Allow your young officer to explain."

Slicking her dry lips with her tongue, Catriona stepped forward and

324 | *Time Twist*

gave a cursory explanation. She avoided the black glare Haven gave her from the screen. She knew he'd be furious with her. Yet again.

Warnings issued from both ships' tactics screens. "Two ships approaching, Captain," hissed the *L'umina's* tactical officer.

"I concur," rumbled Grreag from the screen. "Komodoan configuration."

"B'alarg's Cadre," said Haven.

Catriona watched Grreag rise. "Captain T'alak, if you wish to protect your dignitary ship, may I offer the assistance of the *Vallo*? Two have more chance than one."

T'alak's tail swept back and forth as he studied the Leon. He nodded. "Thank you, Colonel. I accept."

"May I suggest you return my officer first?"

"Of course," hissed T'alak, avoiding Catriona's gaze.

Moments later she found herself in the *Vallo* control cabin next to Uzi, who winked at her. Only now did T'alak meet her eyes from the screen.

"Strap in," advised Grreag as they went to battlestations. "This could get rough. Our armor is weak, so the *L'umina* will take most of the flak while we circle round to fire on B'alarg's ships."

Catriona did so, taking the observation seat next to Haven. She raised a questioning eyebrow. He relented, giving her a resigned smile as he took her hand. Catriona squeezed his fingers, relieved.

Turning her attention to the viewer, she watched B'alarg's two hexagrams spin into view. One flipped sideways and attempted to pass between the *L'umina* and the *Vallo* to get to the *Gr'avitas* behind. The *Vallo* fired, forcing the ship to back off. The *L'umina* moved into position to take the hit as the ship returned fire on the *Vallo*.

Colonel Grreag ordered Larrar to fire on the other ship at the same time. Catriona looked at Grreag in admiration when B'alarg's two ships withdrew as their captains rethought their strategy.

"Chief," demanded Grreag, "how soon before our armor is back on line?"

Khumalo shook her head. "At this rate, not at all. *If* we can avoid being hit, I'll have some form of defense in about ten minutes."

"You have *five!*" bellowed Grreag, as Larrar twisted the *Vallo* out of range of a fusillade from the two attacking ships.

Catriona realized B'alarg's people must know the *Vallo* had limited armor.

"We can't keep this up," growled Grreag, saying aloud what they all thought. "It's only a matter of time before they get a direct hit on us."

Qiterr unstrapped himself and approached Grreag. "Leader, let us use our ship to help. We could draw their fire."

"Negative. You have no weaponry on that civilian craft."

"I can program it to collide with one of B'alarg's ships," countered Haven. "The same tactic they tried to use on the *Gr'avitas*."

Grreag flicked an ear at him. "Accompany Mr. Qiterr to the cargo bay and do so."

Haven jumped up and strode from the cabin, Qiterr right behind him. Catriona twisted her hands in her lap, missing him beside her. Moments later the *Vallo* took a hit that sent the ship into jarring spasms.

"Where the hell's the *L'umina*?" demanded Khumalo, having bumped her head for the umpteenth time on the engineering console.

On the viewer, T'alak's ship put up a noble fight. One of B'alarg's ships fired repeatedly past her at the *Vallo*, the other pummeling the *L'umina*, all the time edging round her toward the *Gr'avitas*.

"The *L'umina's* armor has almost failed," reported Larrar.

Grreag pinged Haven. "What's your progress?"

"Ready now," came the answer. "Keep an eye on the viewer."

A streak shot out from the bowels of the *Vallo* and collided with the ship firing on them. The civilian craft exploded against the ship's underbelly, crippling its weapons systems.

"Good work," praised Grreag.

"Colonel," announced Larrar. "I'm detecting several small craft approaching. Identity undetermined."

"More Cadre troops?" wondered Grreag aloud. "Get a picture as soon as possible, Lieutenant."

Haven and Qiterr returned to the control cabin much to Catriona's relief. Larrar put an image of the small craft on screen.

"Do you recognize these ships, Lieutenant Colonel?" Grreag asked Haven.

"Curse his scales, of course I do!" Haven's face broke into a human grin. "N'elak must have been tracking our progress. He's sent his underworld pirates to help."

"To help whom?" asked Grreag. "How do we know they're not with B'alarg's Cadre?"

Catriona saw the look Haven gave Grreag. He didn't know for sure. She took a breath and swallowed hard. They'd just have to hope N'elak's friendship with Haven proved as strong as Haven thought.

The *Vallo* caught another blow from B'alarg's ship.

"Hull breach!" warned Larrar. Catriona felt a terrifying sucking sensation as the cabin oxygen rushed through the breach. Major

326 | *Time Twist*

Benjamin dashed to the spot, tending emergency repairs.

Catriona's heart fluttered in her throat. The thing she feared most about space travel was losing air and suffocating. She feared it more than drowning.

N'elak's fleet charged onto the scene. About eighty or so small dart-shaped craft zoomed around the attacking ships, their tiny weapons like bee stings on the back of a huge grizzly bear. Just as deadly as a swarm of bees, N'elak's pirates' fire quickly picked off B'alarg's two ships' weaponry.

The two hexagrams spun uselessly, trying to get a lock on just one of their attackers. The tiny craft deftly wove their way around and between. Catriona couldn't understand why none of them collided with each other. Fast, furious, and accurate, the attack succeeded in minutes.

B'alarg recognized his defeat; the two ships turned and spun from the sector.

T'alak came on the viewer to thank Colonel Grreag. Both commanders looked excited and exhilarated.

"Shall we follow them, Captain?" demanded Grreag, almost vibrating from the strength of his purring.

"No. Now they have played their hand, the Realm will seek them out." What T'alak didn't say was more chilling. Catriona could imagine the punishments to be exacted on B'alarg and whomever else in his Cadre. No doubt an extensive Realm 'population control' would ensue over the next few months.

"And what of N'elak?" asked Haven, rising to join Grreag in front of the viewer. "Will his organization still be considered outlaw?"

On screen T'alak's mouth quirked. "There will be many changes in the Realm, *sekke*. Relay my sincerest thanks to N'elak. I shall make sure his deeds today do not go unrewarded." He addressed Grreag. "Colonel, may I offer the assistance of our nearest outpost for repairs to your ship?"

"That is kind of you, Captain," replied the Leon, "but we will impose on you no further. We have safe passage from Realm space?"

"You do." T'alak looked one last time at Catriona and terminated the communication.

Catriona grinned to herself. T'alak just couldn't resist. Thought he had an opportunity at last to study the *Vallo*.

N'elak's fleet disappeared back to Komodoa as quickly as it had arrived. A new military vessel arrived to escort the *Gr'avitas* safely back, and the *L'umina* accompanied the *Vallo* to the border.

After the *Vallo* had been repaired, Colonel Grreag headed the ship straight for Earth, for talks about a possible treaty with the Komodoan Realm. With T'alak's House in power, a resolution to the long war between Komodoa and Leontor was within reach.

Catriona's heart filled with joy when the *Vallo* finally entered Sol. Earth appeared as blue and luminous as she remembered from pictures taken by NASA in the 21st century.

The others were horrified to hear her version of the past, where Webster's first illicit test had inadvertently created the devastating rupture. He had made good his promise to Catriona the second time around; the changes he'd made to the bubble programming had been successful. Time had more or less unfolded the way it should thereafter. The temporal bubble only caused a small rift in 2001, too insignificant to cause disaster. It still brought Earth to the attention of the Leontor, who made first contact. But this time, instead of governing Earth, the Leontor allied herself equally to it, trading technology for the help of those humans willing to tackle space combat. And of those there were plenty. The 21st century had long awaited proof that alien life existed out there, and millions flocked to join the war against the Komodoan Realm.

65

WHEN THEY touched down on the Florida shoreline, beautiful once more, Haven reported to Intelligence, promising to join Catriona as soon as possible.

Catriona returned to her apartment, only to find it reassigned, the remainder of her possessions in storage.

Furious, she stormed to Dean Essex's office, only to be intercepted by two somber-looking men who flashed Alliance Intelligence identification at her.

In trepidation she followed them to offices in a tower block adjacent to the college campus. In plush surroundings overlooking glittering Orlando far below, Brigadier Xorrog informed her why she no longer could be the liaison officer for the Leontor student program.

She left the offices in a daze to find Haven waiting for her in the sunshine. Dashing over, she threw her arms around his neck and laughingly told him what had happened. She scanned his face.

"Do you mind, Jack? I mean, I never thought I'd be working for **Intelligence...**"

He grinned and held her close. "It's not as though you'll be stealing my job from me, Beauty."

Catriona still couldn't take it all in. The Komodoan Realm had requested her to be part of the first Alliance representation for peace negotiations.

"T'alak requested you," Haven told her, flabbergasting her. "But you won't be alone. I've been ordered to accompany you to keep an eye on their military while keeping an eye on you. You know what this means, don't you?" She shook her head. "You'll have to bond with me, now. Make us respectable."

Catriona walked slowly along Westminster Bridge until she reached the center. Once built of stone, it had become a transparent tube stretching across the river. She looked at the rebuilt and remodeled Houses of Parliament. They bore little resemblance to what she remembered from the 21st century. Gone were the Elizabethan casement windows and red bricks. A shimmering metal and glass obscenity sat in its place and Big Ben's timeless clock face had been replaced by a gleaming silver date and time display. As far as Catriona could see, the only improvement appeared to be the quality of the water in the Thames. Once polluted to lethal levels, it now flowed clean and pure, reflecting silver from the buildings lining its ancient shores.

The disk she dropped into the river in 2001 had probably been swept out to sea and lost forever. Professor Webster had taken her warning to heart. No trace of his temporal weapon remained, except perhaps the lost disk. Hopefully its like would never be invented again, but it meant Catriona could never return to the 21st century.

She took out a small silver gift box from her fatigues pocket. *Open only when you've made your decision*, she read on the attached card.

The Thames shimmered brightly in the noontime sun, wending its way like a lustrous serpent into the distance. Another phrase from Wordsworth's sonnet came to mind:

Ne'er saw I, never felt, a calm so deep!

Catriona found herself smiling. She finally did feel a deep calm, looking at the silent majesty of the city.

The decision to never return to her past had already been made. Her answer to Jack would be, "Yes."

Opening up the gift box, she discovered a gleaming silver *P'jarra* icon on a chain. A replacement for the one A'rlon had lost. She smiled and slipped it around her neck.

Catriona turned her back on her past. Leaving the bridge behind she strode toward the crowds at Trafalgar Square, where Haven waited with a cruiser to take them home to Orlando.

When he saw her wearing the *P'jarra* icon, his face broke into a huge grin, and he caught her as she ran into his waiting arms.

About the Author

Lizzy Shannon admits a fascination with stories with themes where people have been thrust completely out of their element, such as the astronauts on the Planet of the Apes futuristic Earth, the lone half-Vulcan Spock in Star Trek, and the English Captain Blackthorne in Shogun, a pilot adrift in ancient feudal Japan.

Thrown out of her own element when she emigrated from Northern Ireland to the United States, Time Twist grew from a facetious what if into a full-blown science fiction/time travel tale.

Lizzy lives in Oregon with her husband and the obligatory multiple-cat household expected of science fiction and fantasy authors.

Visit her website at: www.lizzyshannon.com

Made in the USA